ANITA NAIR is one of India's most acclaimed authors whose oeuvre ranges from literary fiction to noir to poetry to children's literature. Her books have been translated into thirty-two languages around the world and have been adapted for audio, the stage and the screen. She is the recipient of several prizes and honours including the Central Sahitya Akademi Award, the Crossword Prize and the National Film Award.

Founder of the creative writing mentorship programme Anita's Attic which has mentored over 125 writers, Anita Nair is also a High-Profile Supporter of the UNHCR.

Anita Nair's new novel is *Hot Stage*, third in the Borei Gowda noir series.

# HOT STAGE

Anita Nair

A BOREI GOWDA NOVEL

BITTER LEMON PRESS
LONDON

BITTER LEMON PRESS

First published in the United Kingdom in 2024 by
Bitter Lemon Press, 47 Wilmington Square,
London WC1X 0ET

www.bitterlemonpress.com

First published in India in 2023 by HarperCollins Publishers
© Anita Nair, 2023

A CIP record for this book is available from the British Library

ISBN 978–1–913394–96–7
EBook USC ISBN 978–1–913394–97–4
EBook ROW ISBN 978–1–913394–98–1

Typeset by Tetragon, London
Printed and bound in Great Britain by CPI Group (UK) Ltd, Croydon, CR0 4YY

*With gratitude and love for Jayanth Kodkani—friend*
*for almost three decades and first reader of all my*
*writing, and for telling me all those years ago,*
*'Isn't it time you thought of getting your work published?'*

'I may have described it as, "Just sit quietly and look innocent."'

Michael Minerva, defence attorney, Chi Omega Trial
*Conversations with a Killer: The Ted Bundy Tapes*

'I am drunk, Inspector, to-day keep your hand off me.
Inspect me on the day you catch me sober.'

Wafā'I Ahmad Haji, *Baburnama*

# PROLOGUE

## 1

### 27 NOVEMBER 2012, 3 P.M.

A grimy nylon string dangled from a hook in the ceiling that was once the colour of ivory but was now an indeterminate brown. The man standing inside the bar-counter cage grabbed a piece of newspaper from the bunch of squares shoved onto a nail on the wall.

The punter tossed his first cutting of Old Admiral brandy down his throat as he watched the bar attendant hold aloft a boiled egg on a piece of paper and use the string to slice the egg so that it burst into bloom. He marvelled, as he always did, at the artistry. The egg was no longer an egg but a frangipani flower with fat white petals and a yellow heart. He watched the man sprinkle onto it a mixture of pepper and salt from a greasy blue plastic bottle.

Gulping his second cutting, the punter took the paper plate heaped with the sliced egg. He ate it slowly, relishing each bite. The egg-flower followed the Old Admiral into a happy place inside him.

He gestured for a refill. This time a 90 ml, he indicated with his thumb and forefinger. The brandy sloshed against the glass as he walked to the island of tables at the centre of the bar. He plonked himself down in a chair. He had had a good day and had decided to treat himself to an afternoon of pleasure. He looked up, still flushed with a sense of well-being, at the man seated opposite him.

'Namaskara,' the punter said, jumping to his feet and joining his palms together to indicate his total subservience. He gave the man a nervous smile as he took his glass and himself to one of the counters that ran alongside the wall of the dark, dingy bar.

He stared at the brandy in his glass and told himself that he was lucky to have got away without having his nose broken or his teeth on the floor. No one sat at Oil Mill Jaggi's table. Not unless he invited you to.

There was a time when Oil Mill Road was just a road. No one knew it by name. People coming in from the city took it to get to the newly built Jal Vayu Vihar, an apartment complex for naval and air force officers. The army, not to be left out, had set up Sena Vihar across the road, soon turning Kammnahalli into this bustling area with people from different parts of India and foreign countries. It was difficult to walk through this stretch without running into Arabs, Africans, Koreans and God knows who else, the punter thought. Not that it bothered him one bit. He liked crowded places.

But Oil Mill Road was still his territory. He knew most of the shop owners by name and could even squeeze them for a 'temporary loan; return guaranteed'. The punter felt like he belonged there. Usually. But not this afternoon. The presence of Oil Mill Jaggi had unnerved him and made it seem as if he was trespassing in an area he should have steered clear of.

The curtains parted and a man walked in. Even though it was three in the afternoon and the sharp light of the November sun blazed in the street outside, the punter felt a chill down his spine. He recognized the man by face. He wasn't a regular at this bar or at any other. But the punter knew him; knew of him. He was called Military. He didn't speak much but you knew when Military was in a good mood. For he would sponsor a drink for anyone who caught his eye. You also knew when Military was in a bad mood. The punter had seen him smash an argumentative drunk's face into the wall and drag it against the surface, all without a bead of sweat popping up on his brow.

Military walked to Oil Mill Jaggi's table and sat across from him. He gestured to the man in the cage.

'Jaggi,' Military said. 'What are you doing here?'

Oil Mill Jaggi shrugged. 'Do I need to state the obvious?'

'Don't forget... it's a big day—the day after tomorrow. This isn't when you drink yourself into a state where you don't know your elbow from your knee.'

Oil Mill Jaggi narrowed his eyes, and then, as if he had changed his mind, ignored the presence of the glass with some alcohol in it and said blithely, 'Chill, Military. I haven't been drinking. This is where I come to think.'

The man frowned. 'My boss won't like it.'

'Your boss and I go back a long way. Long before you started calling him boss.' Oil Mill Jaggi yawned loudly and stretched. 'Relax and have a drink, Military. Why are you getting so worked up? Or is it that you don't trust me anymore?'

'It's big stakes, Jaggi. I can't relax. I have a lot riding on this,' the man said, pulling out a chair.

'You will be a rich man and so will I,' Oil Mill Jaggi said and pushed the plate of mudde and mutton curry from the next-door Naidu restaurant towards him. 'Or we will be fucked. It can go only two ways, so why stress?'

Military looked at the ragi balls as if they were pieces of dog turd and said, 'I just had lunch. Besides, how can you eat this? It gets stuck in the throat.'

Oil Mill Jaggi flexed his enormous biceps at Military. 'Mudde is what began this and mudde is what keeps it going.' He tore a piece off the purplish brown ball, daubed it in the mutton curry, forked a piece of meat with his fingers and popped all of it into his mouth, almost defiantly. Then he swallowed it with a convulsive movement of his throat.

The punter would have liked the mudde. He looked at it hungrily. And without thinking, he let his gaze wander to Military. For a fleeting moment, their eyes met. His two cuttings dissipated into a thin vapour of fear.

The punter took his glass and moved to the farthest end of the counter. Any further and he would be in the toilet. But it was best to keep his distance from those two, he decided. He didn't want to be accused of listening in. Or get caught in between if the two of them broke into a fight. The punter wondered at their power equation. It was hard to tell who feared whom and who would survive if they got into a fistfight.

He saw Military toss his rum down his throat and leave the bar, squeezing Oil Mill Jaggi's shoulder on his way out. A little later, Oil Mill Jaggi followed. The punter heaved a sigh of relief and finished his drink in one gulp. What a waste of money! He had treated himself to a better brand instead of his usual Silver Cup. It felt like he had drunk one quarter of rasam rather than brandy. 'Thoo, bosadi magane,' he swore, spat into his hand and wiped it on his shirtsleeve. There was something immensely satisfying about calling those two men sons of a whore. It didn't make up for the wasted afternoon but it was some compensation, he told himself.

Then, because it was prudent to do so, the punter drew out a brand-new razorblade still in its sleeve from beneath the multiple red threads wound tight around his right wrist. He took the blade out and popped it into his mouth. It would buy him enough time to escape and flee if either of them decided to pounce on him for being in the bar when they were there.

The punter chewed on the blade as he walked on to Oil Mill Road with the furtive step of a rat on the prowl.

## 2

### 29 NOVEMBER 2012, 2 A.M.

It had been a joke between his wife and him. She called his night wheeze a cat and now he thought of it as just that, except he had chosen to give it a personality: A raggedy, saffron-coloured cat; yellow eyes; a pushy beast; rasping and yowling even as it dragged its claws through his ribcage and tickled his throat with its tail.

All evening the cat had stayed in its place. All evening it had done nothing but purr. And he had thought that there it would stay, without troubling him.

Why did it always choose to stir at two in the morning, he asked himself as a bout of coughing racked him. He turned on his side slowly, hoping it would offer some relief. But the cat and cough persisted.

A ball of viscous phlegm filled his mouth. He tried to swallow, but it was too thick and slimy. He should have accepted his daughter's offer of placing a spittoon near the bed. 'Mary will clean it up in the morning,' she had added.

Instead, he had glowered at her and asked, 'Do I look like a feudal landlord to you?'

It was inevitable that he would have to get up, he thought, as the ball of slime wobbled within his mouth. He kicked the quilt off slowly and turned on the bedside lamp. His glasses were by the pillow. He pushed them onto his nose and sat up carefully. He counted under his breath: one to sixty, as he had been told by his doctor in Dharwad.

Another bout of coughing erupted, and the ball of phlegm escaped his mouth, splattering on the floor. He wondered if he should wipe it clean. It would dry on its own in a bit, he decided. And if it didn't, tough luck. No one expected anything better from eighty-three-year-old men except that they be doddering, clumsy fools.

The bruises on his arm and wrist hurt dreadfully. There was an open wound where the skin had been scraped off on the heel of his palm, and a welt on the side of the palm. He blew on it. Then he touched the scratch on the side of his neck. It stung as well. Somewhere in the bathroom cabinet was a bottle of Nebasulf. If he could summon the energy to get up, he would dust some of it on the scratches.

He reached for the shawl slung on the bedpost. Despite the sweater he wore, he felt the cold deep in his bones. The shawl would help. It had belonged to his wife, Kausalya. Why did she have to die before him? So very selfish of her.

He nudged his slippers towards his feet and slipped his feet into them. He reached for the Vicks bottle at his bedside and popped it into his pyjama shirt pocket. Then he stood up and reached for his walking stick. One step at a time. He inched his way through the corridor to the kitchen, switching on the lights as he walked. The tip-tap sound of the brass cap of the walking stick on the terracotta tiles echoed through the quiet of the November night.

He paused at the bathroom and went in, fumbling with the pyjama fly. He didn't always wear his pyjama bottoms but tonight the chill had seeped through from the floor into his shins. He had pulled them on reluctantly but was now glad for it as a draught from somewhere froze his ankles.

He held his flaccid penis in his hand and aimed it into the bowl. Each time he hoped that by some miracle of mechanics a steady stream of urine would arrive. Each time it dribbled, paused and dribbled. His bladder would never feel empty again, he told himself in disgust. And you really should shave, he admonished the mangy old man staring at him from the mirror on the bathroom cabinet. But the thought of lathering his face and using his old-fashioned razor without nicking himself seemed too much of an effort. He washed his hands. There was grime stuck under his fingernails from the fall. For a moment, he wondered why he was standing there. He remembered the anti-bacterial powder he had intended to use on the scratches. He had almost forgotten about that. He sighed and reached for it.

He had planned for every contingency he could think of. He had put aside money for building the house on the land he had bought on the outskirts of Bangalore many decades ago and for house repairs when the need would arise; his daughter's education and her wedding; and his retirement, hospitalization and funeral. All that was left to do was bequeath his books to the library of the college he had reigned in for several years. First as principal and then as Professor Emeritus. But he hadn't foreseen this. The debilitating of the self with age. Of how, at eighty-three, he would be so incapacitated that what had once been commonplace would somehow turn into a feat.

He washed his hands. The trickle of water from the tap made him want to pee again. He glanced at his watch. It was a quarter past two. He would try peeing again before he went back to bed, he decided.

In the kitchen, he found the electric kettle. His wife had hankered for one after she had discovered a tea-making tray in a hotel they had stayed in while at a conference. When Kausalya was alive, she had never got around to using it, but now it seemed it was all they used: the electric kettle, teabags, coffee sachets and milk powder. So much easier, Appa, his daughter said, as though she was the one who had to make it. What was he paying that flibbertigibbet maid for, he wondered as he plugged it in.

If his daughter really cared about him, she would have moved in here with him and looked after him. Instead, she had asked him to move in with her. He didn't want to be an appendage in that household. Why couldn't she see that? 'Bitch,' he said aloud. And then, because it didn't seem adequate enough as an insult, he muttered, 'Fat, rich, selfish bitch.'

The kettle wouldn't work. The power was off and the house was running on the back-up. He sighed and found a steel vessel. It was big, with an open mouth. It would be ideal for the steam inhalation that he needed to do if he planned to get some sleep tonight. He knew that his daughter would nag him for having used it. Your sambar will smell of Vicks now, she would grumble. 'Fuck off,' he said aloud. It felt good to hear it being said in his speaking voice, which even at eighty-three was loud and strident.

So he said that and a few other expletives he had only read in racy novels while he waited for the vessel to fill. As he struggled to carry the full steel vessel to the stove, he called out for Mary Susheela. When she didn't respond, he called her a few names too. Then he remembered the events of the evening. He wished he hadn't frightened that idiot woman off. It was all his daughter's fault.

It was meant to be a little experiment to validate the paper he was writing, 'The Hegemony of Hearsay in Right-wing Thought'. Besides, it had felt absurdly youthful, uncomfortable as it had been, to crouch on the steps beyond the back terrace, waiting for Mary Susheela to step out. No matter how many times he had told her to put the kitchen waste into the compost pit dug especially for it, she liked to fling everything over the parapet wall onto the slope below. There was a spot she seemed to prefer, he realized, as the stench of rotting food and kitchen waste from the ground hurled up his nostrils. Several sturdy hibiscus bushes grew there. He had found the perfect spot.

As he had expected, she came to the head of the steps to throw out the dinner debris. His heart had beat faster but she hadn't seen him. The wall light barely reached the edge of the cemented terrace and the bulb on the lamppost attached to the wall was flickering. He was well hidden on the fourth step.

As she began to toss the food he had abandoned on his plate, he had reached out and pressed down his late wife's upper denture on her ankle. He hadn't meant to press so hard, but the angle he was crouched at made his feet wobble precariously, and to stop himself from falling at her feet he had put his entire weight on his arm to steady himself. Even then, he should have resisted from pressing the dentures down into her flesh so hard. But the thought of the oversalted, tasteless rasam and the under-sugared, watery coffee she thrust under his nose every day rose to the surface as an acid reflux of desperate fury. Only the old know the helplessness of being too frail to demonstrate anger, he would tell himself several times a day. But in that moment, rage lent iron to his trembling fingers.

Mary Susheela screamed loudly and kicked out to lob away whatever had sunk its teeth into her. Professor Mudgood felt himself totter with the force of the movement. His arm slammed into the rusty iron pipe that was the handrail, and it broke his fall. The hibiscus bushes alongside the handrail rustled as his shoulder crashed into them. They cushioned the impact. He grabbed the handrail to steady himself, even as he felt a bit of the step give way under his feet.

The woman screamed even more loudly as she heard what seemed like rustling and slithering. 'Snake, snake...' she hollered at the top of her voice. His daughter, who was in the work area attached to the kitchen, had dropped the clothes she had been stuffing into the washing machine and rushed towards Mary Susheela. She hurried the distraught woman indoors.

While the women's voices rose, he had examined the dentures. The bloodstained teeth grinned at him. He laughed aloud. A little wheeze of a laugh, for laughter too had gone the way his mobility had. He had hauled himself up with a great deal of difficulty, thrust the denture into his waistcoat pocket and reached for his walking stick slung on the handrail. He shuffled up the steps, holding on to the handrail and hoisting himself up with the walking stick, one step at a time. His arm hurt where he had taken the impact of the handrail, and the skin on the heel of his palm had scraped off. But a wicked chuckle escaped his lips and accompanied him. On to the back terrace and around the house to the front verandah. The giant avocado tree alongside cut the light from the verandah and he stumbled again in the dark, knocking a stack of terracotta pots. Which fool had kept pots on the walking path?

It had been a cold night and he hadn't thought of wrapping his muffler around his throat. He had known even then that the feral saffron cat would keep him awake at night.

His daughter had burst into the verandah a few minutes later. 'Mary has been bitten! I don't know what she is going to need... anti-venom, rabies shots or just a tetanus shot... I can see teeth marks, so I am not taking any chances. I have put a tourniquet above her ankle for now,' she had said.

He had stared at her, trying to get his breath back. He lurched, and as she reached to steady him, he had clutched her forearm.

She had squealed in pain. 'Look what you've done, Appa,' she snapped, peering at the finger marks on her forearm.

'Don't fuss. It will heal in a day or two.' Why on earth was she acting as if he had bitten her?

His daughter had glared at him and said furiously, 'Does nothing matter to you unless it concerns you, Appa? Did you hear what I said? Mary has been bitten!' She repeated it so loudly that their nearest neighbours, the nuns who lived an acre away, would have heard it too.

He had glared back at her. 'I heard you,' he said. 'Look, I have scraped my wrist and scratched my neck. Is there any of that antiseptic powder? Why isn't that idiot Paul Selvam coming anymore? He needs to prune the bushes, and the backyard is a jungle...' He examined his wrist and blew on it. He looked up and added, 'And at my age, I don't give two hoots about anyone. All that is important to me is my life's work.'

His daughter had stared at him with a strange expression. Why did she look so incredulous? She was getting fat, he had thought,

taking in the yellow and green kameez that ballooned around her.
Her rich, real estate developer husband would soon start looking
elsewhere if he hadn't already. She had been a pretty child but
now she reminded him of something else. Then it came to him.
'You are beginning to look like a Dalda tin,' he had said. 'If you
don't look after yourself, your husband will find himself a bit on
the side. Or worse, a slender young bride.'

She had glared at him as if she couldn't believe what she had
heard. Then she had snapped, 'Go to hell!'

She had turned on her heel and slammed the door behind her.
Why was she acting as if he had said something offensive, he had
wondered. People didn't like hearing the truth. They preferred
to believe what they thought was the truth.

His daughter had bustled the moaning Mary Susheela into her
car and driven away with a screech. That had been a few hours
ago. He could already see the rumours shaking themselves off
every parthenium plant on his land: Mary was bitten by a scor-
pion; Mary was bitten by a bandicoot; God knows what bit her.
They say that the land is haunted. Haven't you heard the strange
noises that emerge on new-moon nights? Haven't you heard Mary
had something going on with the old man? It is actually a stab
wound by her angry husband. Professor Mudgood chuckled at
the thought of how hearsay would soon be treated as fact.

The water began to bubble. The lid on the saucepan clanged.
He turned off the stove and waited. The light on the power plug
turned red. The power had come back. He would make a cup of
tea for himself after the steam inhalation. Perhaps he could add
to the notes for the talk he was scheduled to present at the Town
Hall along with a compendium of other speakers, including a
strident student leader from JNU, a movie-star-turned-citizen-
rights advocate, a playwright and a political satirist.

He had titled his talk 'Why I Am Not a Hindu'. It was expected
that he would lambast the Hindutva movement that was gaining

momentum and support by the day. He had already called them
'fascist' at least a few times. His assistant, Gurunath, had left in
a huff that morning. The idiot had taken umbrage at the point
of view of the paper. 'It's one thing that you are playing with fire,
sir,' Gurunath had said. 'But I don't agree with your politics and
I can't work for a man whose politics are diametrically opposite
to mine.'

'Really, and what is your politics? Decimating the minori-
ties? Crony capitalism? Gagging freedom of expression?' he had
retorted.

Once, he may have held back. Not anymore. He was too old
to care and too frail to negotiate sitting on a fence.

His hand hurt when he lifted the saucepan of water. He
placed it on the kitchen table near the wall and found a towel
in the work area where the washed clothes waited to be ironed
and put away. The back door was open, he saw. Mary Susheela
in her consternation had forgotten to latch it. He grimaced as
he pushed the bolt up into the latch.

He sat on the chair and drew the saucepan closer to him. He
opened the Vicks bottle and drew out a blob on the tip of his
index finger. He flicked it into the water carefully before pulling
the towel over his head as he inched his face towards the rising
fragrant steam.

A scurrying noise made him look up. Was it a mouse? What
was that Yeats poem?

> Now strength of body goes;
> Midnight, an old house
> Where nothing stirs but a mouse.

He put his glasses back on. But the lenses were fogged with the
steam. He took them off to wipe them. That's when he saw the
shadow. 'Who is there?' he asked in the loudest voice he could

summon. He put his glasses back on and smiled at his own fancifulness. Next he would start seeing ghosts.

He removed his glasses again and placed them on the table alongside the cauldron. He pulled the towel over his head again. Suddenly, an excruciating pain tore through him as something struck the side of his head. He felt himself slump against the wall.

Several minutes later, Raghava Mudgood stirred. He groaned as he raised his head. What had happened to him? How had he lost consciousness? Did he have a blackout? But the side of his head throbbed. He felt nauseous. He tried to hoist himself up, but he couldn't. His hand hurt and he couldn't put any pressure on it. He whimpered, 'Kausalya,' and tried again to sit up straight.

He felt someone loom behind him, and before he could put his glasses on to see who it was, his head was being pushed into the cauldron of hot water. The heat cut through the pain and he tried to drag his face away from the vessel, when something or someone—man, beast or ghost—pushed his face into the saucepan of scalding water.

He struggled, but the hand held him down. His hands groped for anything he could find. He heard his glasses shatter on the floor. Water entered his nostrils and mouth and burnt the skin on his face. He clawed at whatever it was he could reach to escape the grip. The table, an arm, life itself.

After a few minutes, he stopped struggling. It was 2.45 a.m., 29 November 2012.

# 30 NOVEMBER 2012, FRIDAY

## 1

Their seats were together but separated by an aisle. 'That way it won't look as if we are travelling together,' Gowda had said, not quite meeting Urmila's furious gaze.

She had shaken her head ever so little, a wry tilt and the raise of an eyebrow to show what she thought of his forever pussy-footing. 'Whatever suits you, Borei,' Urmila said with an affected breeziness.

Gowda swallowed down the dread he felt. He could see she was annoyed, hurt even. He had tried to make up by being extra attentive. He insisted on stowing her bag in the overhead locker. He bought her a tin of salted almonds and juice when the stewardess came pushing her trolley down the aisle. Urmila had accepted them without a word or a smile and buried her nose in her book. Gowda watched her work her way through the nuts without even offering him a nibble.

When Urmila had said she was taking him away for a short trip, he had protested. 'Why do we need to go anywhere?' he had asked.

'Precisely because we don't go anywhere. It's always your home or mine. I want to do things with you. Like normal couples do.'

He had flinched at the word 'couple'. Or was it the word 'normal'?

'I want to go to bed with you, wake up in the morning with you there, have breakfast, lunch and dinner with you, without you looking over my shoulder or at your watch or mobile once. I want to go to a movie with you. Go for a walk, share a cab with you...'

'Things most people would call mundane,' Gowda had interrupted softly.

'Except for us it isn't, Borei,' she had said. And then she stared at him, as if demanding, is it?

The perversity of human nature—or was it destiny—struck Borei Gowda like a shard of ice. What Urmila wanted was what Mamtha, his wife, had, and to whom it meant nothing at all. And perhaps Mamtha wanted what Urmila had. What about himself? What did he want? And as was customary for Gowda to do, he parked the query in a remote corner of his mind.

He had pulled himself together, and, summoning what seemed like a fair proximation of enthusiasm, smiled at her as he asked, 'Where shall we go?'

'Is that a yes?' Urmila's eyes had lit up.

She had planned it all. The flights, the hotel, the houseboat cruise, the stroll through the streets of Fort Kochi and his birthday dinner. They had come back from a day of exploring the Alleppey backwaters in a houseboat and were sitting in the balcony of their posh hotel and watching distant boats bob on the water when the doorbell had rung. A steward had come in holding a cake aloft. Behind him was another steward pushing a trolley with covered dishes and a bottle of champagne in an ice bucket. Gowda had flushed with pleasure and embarrassment. No one had made such a production of his birthday ever.

He had thought she wouldn't remember it was his birthday. 'Why do you think I insisted on us going away?' she had said from across the table, on top of which sat the ornately iced, square-shaped cake lit up with fifty-one candles.

Gowda had reached out to take her hand. What does she see in me? he had thought, looking at the stately Urmila with her

clear, light skin, chiselled features and long, straight hair; all grace
and graciousness, and a full, fruity voluptuous perfume.

She had intertwined her fingers with those of the tall, broad
man whose once striking features had blurred into a mostly
harried-looking expression. She often teased him that he must
be the only policeman without a moustache. Men with a cleft
in their chin make me go weak at the knees, so I am willing to
overlook your lack of a moustache, she would add, and he would
grab her and press her to him with a mock growl.

As Urmila nuzzled into his chest, he had felt the slight curve
of her paunch sink into his more defined one, and known an
indefinable happiness that he never had when their bodies had
been svelte and their minds hungry. The thing about middle-aged
love, Gowda had thought, was that you grew less conscious of how
you looked or how the other person did and instead sought to
please each other in ways you wouldn't have imagined in youth.

With the tips of her fingers, she had traced the tattoo on his
arm. A wheel with wings. 'Maybe I should get one too,' she had
said.

Gowda had grunted.

She had hoisted herself on her elbow and peered into his face.
'Shall I get one on my belly? A flower around my belly button?'

He had stared, unable to decide if she was serious or joking.
'It's very painful U...' he had said. 'You would be better off getting
a Ganesha sketch or a little butterfly on your forearm.'

The perfection of that evening had wrapped them in a cloud of
happily together forever. Except, as it is with perfection and all
other unnatural states of being, it didn't last, and here they were,
sitting together on a flight but separated by an aisle. It felt like the
ocean and not seventeen to nineteen inches of carpeted space.

Gowda looked at her from the corner of his eye.

She was engrossed in her book. And as if that wasn't enough,
she had her headphones on. Gowda sighed. He closed his eyes

and tried to sleep. But his mind wandered to what awaited him at Neelgubbi Police Station.

A body had been found in one of the eucalyptus groves beyond Doddagubbi Lake, Head Constable Gajendra had messaged him last morning.

A shepherd had found the dead man and notified someone who had called the police. Gajendra had sent him a photograph. A muscular young man with scars on his face. He had been found wearing a half-sleeved shirt and jeans. His feet were bare. There were no stab wounds. His lip was split and nose broken. Blood had crusted around the bridge of his nose. Even with the shirt on, Gowda could see the man's shoulder jutted at an awkward angle as if it had been dislocated. He looked like he had been in a fight which didn't go his way.

Gowda looked at the photo on his phone again. Something bothered him. Then he realized that the light-blue shirt the man wore was spotless. There wasn't any blood, or even a dirt smear on it. Something wasn't kosher, as Urmila liked to say.

The body had been sent for postmortem. No Missing Person complaint has been registered for him yet at the station, Gajendra had added in his brief message. And neither did the deceased match the description of any missing male anywhere in the city limits.

Four months ago, another body had been found in one of the abandoned quarries. A burly young man. Just as the latest body, he had been wearing almost-new clothes that weren't smeared with dirt or blood. He had been barefoot as well, and Gowda had noticed his blackened soles and dirt-encrusted toenails. In his late twenties, Dr Khan had told him. The young man had several concussion spots and two sets of fractures—the fingers of the right hand and his shin—but what had killed him was a brain haemorrhage, the forensics surgeon had continued. 'And

Gowda, what is puzzling is I don't see any blunt-force trauma on his skull. If someone hit him with a wooden club or even a metal object, there would be a skull fracture. But this is curious... almost like someone bundled him into a sack and beat him to death.'

Gowda had stared at Dr Khan, who was washing his hands again. For a moment Gowda saw Lady Macbeth instead of Dr Khan. In high school, they had performed the play, and Gowda, much to his chagrin, had been chosen to play the part of one of the witches. He had been forced to wear a bra padded with rags, a black caftan and a straggly wig. None of the boys in his class were thrown by the wig or caftan and had thronged around him to squeeze his padded bra with great glee.

He didn't remember much of the play except that Lady Macbeth seemed to be forever washing her hands, and the chant that he had had to memorize: 'Double, double toil and trouble; fire burn and cauldron bubble. Cool it with a baboon's blood. Then the charm is firm and good.'

'What are you mumbling under your breath?' Dr Khan had shot him a curious look.

Gowda flushed. 'Something that I had forgotten all about suddenly popped up in my head.'

The corpse was never identified, and the body was handed over to one of the government medical colleges. But every now and then, the dead man's face came back to haunt Gowda. Who was he? How had he died? And here was one more dead man. Were these two deaths connected? He would know when the postmortem report reached him.

Gowda shifted in his seat. He darted a glance at Urmila. She was in animated conversation with the man sitting next to her. A corporate honcho type with his Omega watch and manicured hands, Gowda thought with a sudden taste of bile in his mouth. Her kind of man. And not like him, a middle-aged cop with no real prospects in sight.

Gowda looked away and through the window at the fat white clouds. The man next to him had his laptop open, his fingers flying over the keyboard. Gowda sneaked a look at the screen. It seemed to be a legal document. The man's elbow took up most of the armrest. Gowda glowered at him. Were all lawyers born assholes? Or did their profession turn them into one?

Dr Sanjay Rathore had definitely been one. Was that why he had been murdered? And then out of nowhere a young man had surrendered confessing to the murder. When Gowda had tried to question the legitimacy of the confession, a senior bureaucrat whom Gowda had tried to reason with flung his arms up in helplessness. 'You have no evidence to validate your accusation. What do you really expect me to do, Gowda?'

Gowda had flinched. Through most of his career as a police officer, he had had to wear the stigma of the moniker he was given: 'B Report Gowda'. The man whose cases came to nothing for want of evidence. Gowda had nodded and walked out of the room, seething with helpless rage.

A few more raids were conducted, and ten trafficked children were rescued, and a photo of Gowda was published on the fourth page of an English daily. Inspector Gowda became Assistant Commissioner of Police Gowda. They had bought him off by giving him a promotion that was long overdue. That's what they had done. A promotion ostensibly for the work he had done on the child trafficking case, but he had known it was to handcuff him and gag his mouth. For everything was the same—his duties and his ambit of power—but he was now ACP Gowda, no less and not very much more. He had hoped for a new boss, but they presented him with Vidyaprasad, who had been promoted to Deputy Commissioner of Police Vidyaprasad.

The pilot announced the aircraft's descent. Gowda straightened his seat and touched Urmila's elbow. She looked at him. He gestured to the seat-belt sign. She nodded and put her book away.

As the aircraft touched the tarmac, Gowda placed his right foot on the curve of the bulkhead.

'What are you doing, Borei?' Urmila laughed out loud. 'Are you trying to stop the plane?'

Gowda looked embarrassed and smiled. She shook her head in resignation. 'You are a nut job, Borei.' She giggled, and just like that, forgot to be angry with him.

'Are you afraid of flying?' Urmila asked.

He nodded. 'Petrified. I didn't want to grab your arm at take-off and landing. That's why...' He gestured to the aisle separating them.

'Oh darling...' Urmila said, and, throwing him a mischievous look, added, 'So you don't mind if I do this and someone sees us.'

She blew him a kiss as the plane came to a halt.

# 2

Head Constable Gajendra looked around him. His living room always filled him with a tremendous sense of pride. The wooden sofa with its intricate carvings and maroon velvet cushions, the 32-inch LED TV, the showcase filled with brassware and stuffed toys, including a cross-eyed hippopotamus his daughter had given him for something she called Father's Day. 'What ra, is your father only important on one day of the year?' He had teased her though he had been very pleased to receive a stuffed toy. He didn't think he had ever had a toy as a child.

At the sight of the empty space where the interlocked steel chairs had once been placed, he ran the tip of his index finger along the line of his moustache, back and forth. His daughter, who had started college five months ago, had insisted they move the chairs into the verandah.

'But why? I paid good money for them,' Gajendra had said.

'It looks like a dentist's waiting room,' she had scoffed. She took out her phone and showed him pictures. 'No one keeps these things in their hall.'

He had acquiesced but he had been on the lookout for a couple of stand-alone chairs to place there. Until then, the space niggled like the empty nest of a lost tooth.

The fragrance of ghee and jaggery filled the house. Gajendra's wife, Kamala, came into the hall where Gajendra was flicking an imaginary piece of lint from the velvet cushion. 'Why don't you eat your breakfast when it is still warm?' she asked.

He followed her into the dining room where on the chrome and glass table was a plate stacked with obattus. 'What's the occasion?' he asked at the sight of the sweet.

'Raji Akka may come by this afternoon and I don't want to offer her just biscuits.'

Gajendra nodded and put one of the obattus onto his plate. He whispered a thank you to his sister-in-law whom his wife couldn't decide if she loved or hated. But each time she visited, Kamala cooked something that was guaranteed to mellow her high-pitched complaining voice into silence.

The obattu was soft and flaky, its filling sweet and fragrant with cardamom. Kamala drizzled ghee on it and Gajendra tore a piece off and put it into his mouth.

'How is it?' she asked.

'Super,' he said through a mouth full of obattu.

'What?' Her voice rose in consternation.

He swallowed and said, 'Super.'

'You say that about everything I make.' She smiled.

'It's the truth,' he began when his phone rang. Gajendra looked at the number and frowned. He picked it up with his left hand hastily. 'Yes, what is it?' he asked.

Kamala watched Gajendra drop the piece of obattu he had in his fingers.

'What?' Gajendra barked. He listened even as he crumbled

the obattu on his plate. 'I am on my way,' he said, rising from the chair. He looked at the obattu longingly and hastily stuffed another piece into his mouth. Kamala sighed and took away the tattered obattu to nibble at while she prepared lunch.

The airport cab veered to the left at Sahakar Nagar. Gowda's gaze met Urmila's. It was in this vicinity that they had found Nandita, Gowda's maid's daughter who had been kidnapped. The investigation had led them into uncovering a sex trafficking ring that made no difference between children or adults, girls or boys. The child trafficking case had tainted their understanding of humanity, changing them forever. Urmila's hand reached for his. Not just Gowda and Urmila, but each one of them, Santosh, Ratna, Gajendra, Byrappa and Michael. Everyone who had ever had to deal with the rescued children would never be who they were. That much was certain.

'The real horror isn't what we discovered—the extent of depravity—but the fact that even at this moment, countless children are being trafficked,' Urmila said, her fingers tightening around Gowda's, speaking aloud what continued to haunt Gowda.

'I know,' he said, trying to gently extricate his fingers from her clasp. The driver had his rearview mirror adjusted so he could take habitual glances at them.

Gowda's phone rang. He felt Urmila tense. Usually, when Mamtha called, Urmila or he would leave the room as if to exorcize the spectre of adultery that wafted in.

Gowda glanced at the number. 'It's not her,' he said, and almost bit his tongue in exasperation. Had the driver heard him?

Urmila watched Gowda's face. The bland expression that sat on it when a work call came in changed swiftly to one of unease. His forehead furrowed, his eyes narrowed and his mouth tightened to a line. 'Does the deceased have a name?' Gowda asked.

'His name is Professor Raghava Mudgood.'

'Are you sure?'

'Why, sir? Who is he?'

'I'll be there soon,' Gowda said shortly and put his phone on the seat.

'Something has come up,' he told Urmila. 'I think you should drop me at my place and...' He paused, knowing that what he had to say would upset Urmila. The original plan was that she would stay with him for the day and night. 'And I think you should use the cab to head to yours,' he said in a rush, picking up his phone again.

Urmila looked outside the window and bit down the angry words that threatened to erupt.

Gowda was still officially on holiday, but Urmila knew him well enough to know that he had already transported himself to the crime scene. After almost six months of pushing files and trying to chase petty criminals, he finally seemed to have a big case on his hands. And nothing was going to keep him away. Not even her.

# 3

Assistant Sub-Inspector Ratna looked up as she heard the police vehicle drive in. She glanced at the woman who sat on a single-seater sofa. She hadn't spoken a word except to say, 'There,' gesturing towards the kitchen.

Ratna saw the Bolero pull up as she went to the verandah. Sub-Inspector Santosh and Head Constable Gajendra emerged from the police vehicle.

'Gowda Sir is on his way,' Gajendra said.

'Isn't he on leave?' Ratna asked, surprised.

'Not anymore,' Santosh said, his eyes darting around, seeking something to indicate a break-in. 'Let's take a look,' he said. Gajendra walked to the left of the house where a clump of trees grew while Santosh headed to the right.

A giant avocado tree stood very close to the house and around it was a paved pathway leading to the rear of the house. The back-yard was a wide, cemented yard with a low parapet wall. A few steps led down to the overgrown land on the next level. The land stretched past that as well. Through the dense trees and bushes, it was impossible to see what exactly lay beyond. Santosh walked towards the back door. He wound his handkerchief around his fist and pushed it open. It swung inwards and the smell of death came out in a sudden waft.

Half an hour later, Gowda rode through the open gates on his 500 cc Bullet. Ratna looked at him and sighed. No matter what you thought of the man, the bike had a way of imbuing an air of stability and strength to the rider, making it seem that this was a person you could depend on in a crisis. She wondered if she should consider buying a Bullet herself. When the bike spluttered to a stop and Gowda took his helmet off, Ratna felt that familiar sense of confusion the man evoked in her. There was so much she liked about him and so much she abhorred him for.

'Did he live here by himself?' Gowda asked by way of greeting.

'Apparently there is a live-in maid but she wasn't here when it happened,' Ratna said.

Gajendra emerged from the clump of trees and Santosh from behind the house.

'The deceased's daughter said that she had unlocked the main door. There seemed to be no indication of foul play,' Gajendra began.

'No, sir,' Santosh interrupted. 'We don't know that yet. The back door was not latched. And there are a few broken flower pots on the side of the house as if someone ran into them in the dark. Possibly while trying to flee.'

Gowda climbed the two steps onto the verandah. On one side hung bamboo blinds and in the alcove thus created was a wide, sturdy wooden table and an old-fashioned heavy wooden chair.

An anglepoise lamp sat on the table, which also contained a cup full of pens and a stack of notepads. Alongside the wall was an open bookcase with several books in it.

Gowda looked at the titles of the books. He hadn't heard of even a single one. 'He won the Rajyotsava Award two years ago. He is what they call a Public Intellectual.'

Gajendra swallowed. What on earth was a public intellectual?

'Who called to report the death?' Gowda asked, as he walked into the house, his eyes scanning the room. Old-fashioned wooden sofas and a rug, in the middle of which was the teapoy, though everyone called it a coffee table these days. There was a rosewood cabinet running the length of one wall. On it was a TV, several plaques bearing testimony to attendance at conferences and awards won and piles of papers and books. A few framed photographs stood with an air of uncertainty amidst such intellectual verisimilitude.

The curtains were thick and the room showed no signs of break-in and entry. On one of the single-seaters sat a woman with her head in her hands.

'That is the deceased's daughter. She called the control room,' Ratna said in a hushed voice.

Gowda cleared his throat. She looked up, a slightly blowsy woman, in her forties perhaps, dressed in a long-sleeved, apple-green silk kurta and white linen pants, and wearing adequate diamonds to suggest that while she may have several troubles, money wasn't one of them. He had noticed the red Skoda Octavia parked in the porch.

On the teapoy was a bag like the one Urmila had. She said it was a Louis Vuitton and cost enough to pay for a brand-new Bullet.

The daughter stood up and said in a voice that was flat and tinny, 'Inspector, I called about my father.'

Santosh butted in, 'It's ACP, not Inspector.'

Gowda waved the correction away with a flick of his hand. 'That's fine,' he said. 'You found him, Mrs...' he began.

'Mrs Janaki Buqhari,' she said.

Gowda hid his surprise. One of his colleagues at the BBMP local authority responsible for the city's municipal works had talked about a land-grabbing case and the accused had mentioned Buqhari Builders. But that wasn't all. Urmila had mentioned a fundraiser she had attended in the neighbourhood. It had been held by a Mrs Buqhari at the club in the gated community she resided in. Is this what they called six degrees of separation?

Gowda pulled his mobile out as he followed Gajendra into a passage that led towards the kitchen where the deceased had been found. The stench hit him even in the passageway. Gajendra stopped at the end of the passage. The door to the kitchen had been shut, and a prod with a pen opened it wide. Gajendra waited for Gowda to enter before following him.

Gowda had his kerchief to his nose, but he couldn't avoid gagging. The kitchen was filled with the putrid smell of decay; clogged drains and stale food, rotten eggs and rotting vegetables; and overlying it all, the reek of decomposing flesh and dried-up faeces. He shoved his nose and mouth into the handkerchief hastily. It was only then he saw the slumped man on the kitchen chair, his face submerged in a cauldron. At his feet were his shattered glasses. On the floor was a rust-coloured towel.

'What a ghastly way to go.' Gajendra's voice was muffled as it emerged through the handkerchief he clutched to his face. He turned abruptly on his heel and walked to the work area. The obattu churned in his stomach. A sour liquid filled his mouth. He willed it to return to where it had sprung from. Then, clearing his throat, he turned to Gowda, who, he noticed, was shooting pictures of the dead man on his phone.

'Sir, the work area door was shut but not latched,' Gajendra reminded him.

Gowda looked at the door. He took a picture of that as well. 'What about the kitchen door? Was it shut or open when the daughter found the deceased? Find that out, will you?' Then he looked at the photos and dialled a number. The Deputy Commissioner of Police needed to be informed. But he chose to call his DCP friend at the Central Crime Branch rather than his idiot boss. 'Hello, Stanley,' he said into the phone.

Gajendra saw Gowda smiling at whatever DCP Stanley Sagayaraj said. The two had been college mates, and some of the Gowda-haters had accused DCP Sagayaraj of being indulgent with Gowda when what he needed was a vicious rap on his knuckles.

Gowda took a deep breath and said, 'This is a work call. I am at the residence of Professor Mudgood. He is dead. Looks like a cardiac arrest but we'll know for certain when the postmortem is over. There is no sign of break-in and entry but the back door to the house wasn't latched. Nothing at this point to suggest death under suspicious circumstances. But I have sent you some pictures.'

There was a long pause as the voice at the other end took in the implication of the neatly inserted 'but'. 'Have you informed DCP Vidyaprasad yet?'

'Not yet.' Gowda's reply was just as terse.

'Do that. Meanwhile, we are on our way. And Borei, for now, don't let him know that the CCB is interested in the death.'

Gowda stepped outside. He needed to fortify himself before he contacted DCP Vidyaprasad, who picked up the call with a long-suffering tone. 'Yes, Gowda. What is it now?'

Gowda felt his fingers curl into a fist. 'I wanted to inform you about a death. Professor Raghava Mudgood. Prima facie, it looks like a cardiac arrest.'

'Oh,' said DCP Vidyaprasad. 'Look, I am getting my annual medical exam done so I am busy. Keep me informed.'

Gowda cut the call and slipped the phone into his pocket. Vidyaprasad hadn't recognized the name of the deceased and his connection to Buqhari Builders or he would have been rushing to the crime scene with a pack of newshounds. 'The CCB is coming in,' Gowda said, seeing Gajendra had followed him. 'They have an interest in the case,' he added quietly, seeing Gajendra frown.

# 4

Gowda went into the living room where the daughter sat. He heard a car door slam. Through the window, he saw a white BMW SUV pull up behind the Skoda. A tall, good-looking man wearing a navy-blue shirt and beige chinos stepped out of the passenger seat and ran up the steps to the verandah. He burst into the living room and came to an abrupt halt at the sight of the men in uniform.

'Jaanu, what happened?' he said, going to the woman's side. She shook her head and buried her face in her hands. 'Appa's dead...' she said through a bout of tears. The man patted her shoulder. She flinched involuntarily. He pretended not to notice and scanned the room. He quickly looked past Gajendra and Santosh and settled on Gowda. He stretched his hand out. 'Sir, I am Iqbal Buqhari, Professor Mudgood's son-in-law. What happened?'

Gowda nodded as he shook hands with him. The man was wearing the 'His' version of the watch the wife wore, he noticed. Together, the watches would buy a Harley. He also had a 4-inch gauze bandage on his right forearm. 'Assistant Sub Inspector Ratna will give you the details,' Gowda said softly. Ratna shot a surprised look at Gowda. She cleared her throat and spoke as if she were standing in the witness box: 'Control room received a call at 10.00 hours this morning from Mrs Janaki Buqhari. I was in a patrol vehicle and we arrived here almost immediately at 10.20 hours. Mrs Janaki Buqhari was here and she directed me to the kitchen where the deceased was.'

'May I see him?' Iqbal Buqhari asked.

A well-built man in his mid-thirties came to stand near Iqbal. Not alongside him but a few inches behind. He was dressed in a full-sleeved white shirt tucked into a pair of blue jeans with a brown belt and tan-coloured shoes. When he moved, his shirt clung to his muscles. The man looked like a boxer, Gowda thought, taking in the squashed nose and strong neck. He didn't seem like just another minion.

Iqbal gestured with his chin. 'My personal assistant. Right now, he's driving me around because of this...' He raised his forearm to show the bandage.

'What happened?' Gowda asked.

'A dog bite.' He turned to the man and said, 'Deva, you stay with Madam in case she needs something.'

When the man went to stand beside Janaki, she gave him a curt nod. Gowda saw Iqbal Buqhari's mouth tighten but he didn't say anything. Instead, he turned to Gowda and asked, 'Could I see my father-in-law, sir?'

'Yes, but don't touch anything,' Gowda said. He gestured for Santosh to go with the man.

'Why? Do you think it wasn't a natural death?' His face paled.

'Police procedure,' Gowda said, watching the man's gaze drop for a moment. What was he hiding?

Iqbal nodded and went with Santosh. When he came back, he was wiping his face with his handkerchief. He looked like he had strolled into hell and been disembowelled by the devil himself.

He slumped into a chair alongside his wife. A long moment later, he sat up straight. 'My wife and I tried to persuade him to move in with us. But he was stubborn about living alone. What do we do now, sir?' he asked, standing up.

Gowda looked into the middle distance. It sounded as if Iqbal was merely making appropriate noises.

'He wouldn't listen to anyone,' Janaki said. 'He wouldn't move in with us. So I came to visit him every day. And most days we ended up arguing about one thing or the other. But I should have remembered how old he is. In fact, that evening he had almost fallen and I had to help him steady himself,' she said staring at the floor. She looked up after a moment. 'Do you know what my last words to him were? Go to hell.'

Iqbal caught Gowda's eye and shrugged. A you-know-how-it-is shrug.

Gowda didn't acknowledge it. Instead, he turned to Janaki. 'Madam, did your father live alone?'

She shook her head. 'There is a live-in maid but she wasn't well and had been hospitalized.'

Gowda nodded. 'Once the formalities are over, the body will be released. Meanwhile, there is nothing you can do by waiting over here. I would suggest you go home, and we'll send someone to take your detailed statement.'

The husband went towards the wife. He offered her his hand. She ignored it and stood up. She turned to the kitchen for a fleeting second and then walked towards the main door.

'Something is not right in that marriage. I can bite the grit in the rice,' Gajendra said to no one in particular.

Santosh stared at the couple who were driving away in their individual cars. Then he gazed at Ratna, who took a deep breath and gave him a hint of a smile.

'Call me when DCP Sagayaraj gets here,' Gowda said to Gajendra, who had been considering leaving a PC in charge.


# 5


Gowda dragged his suitcase into the bedroom. Everything looked shipshape within the house. The newspapers had been placed neatly on the coffee table and the surfaces gleamed dust-free. His eyes widened in surprise. Shanthi, his maid, wasn't given to tidying frenzies. It was only when he would pointedly run a finger on a grimy surface that she flicked a duster with a snort, 'I just dusted yesterday... I can't help the construction work and dust settling on everything here.'

Earlier, when he had dropped his suitcase inside the door on his way to Professor Mudgood's house, he had noticed with delight that both his bike and car were sparkling clean. It was unusual for Shanthi to clean the vehicles without a reminder. Something was afoot, he had thought then. And now he was certain.

He had called Shanthi on his way to tell her that he needed her to make him lunch and she had said she was already at his home. And it had been half past eleven then. She usually left by nine-thirty in the morning and came back early evening to water the plants and cook his dinner. Whatever had happened to Shanthi? This new diligent version was more worrying than comforting.

He placed the suitcase near his bed and went into the kitchen. The fridge had bottles of water and his lunch in an assortment of Tupperware dishes. On the dining table was a jar that held half a dozen rava laddoos and another jar filled to the brim with Congress kadalekai. Gowda unscrewed the jar and shook a few of the masala peanuts into his mouth. When he had munched through them, he took out a rava laddoo and popped it whole into his mouth. He hoped that she wasn't going to ask for a week off or a sizable loan.

The doorbell rang. Gowda frowned and went to the door. He saw a familiar face on the other side through the peephole. Just why was Shanthi ringing the bell? She had a key. He opened the door.

'Namaste, sir,' Shanthi said as she walked in. 'Is everything all right?'

Gowda frowned. 'Why shouldn't it be, Shanthi?' he asked slowly.

'I meant the lunch I had cooked.' Shanthi's voice faltered.

'I haven't eaten yet. But you do know what I like, so what's the problem?' Gowda asked, sitting down. He fumbled for the cigarette pack in his pocket. Where had he left his lighter, he wondered as he patted his pockets. Then he remembered. It was in his suitcase.

Almost as if on cue, Shanthi brought a matchbox from the dining room. He lit the cigarette and inhaled. The morning had been overwrought with incident, and he needed this quiet moment to think and collect himself.

'So, Shanthi, tell me. What is it you want?' he asked, a good ten minutes later. 'All this—the kadalekai and laddoos—can't be for nothing.'

Shanthi, setting a mug of coffee before him, flushed. 'Since you were away, I had a lot of time on my hands and I decided to make a few things. That's all, sir.'

When Gowda continued to look at her, she added, 'It's just that my work here is done by ten and I was wondering if it's all right if I took up work in another household. I'll come back at four as I usually do.'

Gowda shrugged. 'As long as the work in this house doesn't suffer, I don't mind. Where do you have to go after here?'

Shanthi twisted the end of her sari pallu. 'Upstairs,' she said.

Gowda sat up. 'Have they moved in? Why wasn't I informed?'

Shanthi nodded. 'Two days ago. The young couple and the lady's brother. Apparently, he is here to help them settle down...'

Shanthi droned on. Gowda waved his hand to say yes, yes, do what you must. Shanthi would detail their horoscopes if he let her. It was best to shut her up when he could.

Vincent, the real estate broker, had arranged the tenants. A young couple—the husband worked at a software company and his artist wife—Vincent had said. 'They are very nice people. They will be no trouble at all,' he had added.

'Are they related to you?' Gowda asked him in a succinct tone.

'No, no... sir,' Vincent had stuttered. 'They came to me via a common acquaintance. I just met them then. But I checked the husband's credentials. All good... I told them you are a police officer and so no hanky-panky.'

Gowda had tried not to smile, wondering what constituted hanky-panky in Vincent's worldview. And so, the paperwork had been signed: an eleven-month lease to start and three months' rent as advance with a 5 per cent increase after a year.

'Are you sure the three months' rent as advance is enough? They are willing to pay up to eight months' rent. They seem to like the flat and area that much!'

Three months will do, Gowda had said, signing the papers.

'The broker came with them on the day you left and they asked if I could clean the house. By evening their furniture arrived. The lady's brother asked if I would work there. I said you wouldn't mind. "Gowda Sir is very understanding," I said but he said that I should get your permission first.'

'I suppose that explains why you went to all this trouble. Were you trying to bribe me, Shanthi?' Gowda smiled.

'How could you say that, sir?' Shanthi put on a suitably aggrieved face.

Gowda blew a perfect smoke ring. 'Get going.'

Shanthi hid her smile and walked to the door.

'Shanthi,' Gowda said. 'I am sure I don't need to tell you this, but you are not to discuss anything about me or my work or what happens here with the tenants upstairs.'

Shanthi nodded as she shut the door gently behind her.

# 6

He had barely eaten a few mouthfuls of his rather delicious lunch when Gajendra called to say that the CCB team had arrived and so had the forensics unit.

DCP Sagayaraj was talking to a member of the forensics team when Gowda entered the living room of the victim's house.

Sagayaraj nodded at Gowda. 'Give me a minute,' he said.

'What's going on, sir?' Gowda asked when Sagayaraj walked towards him with his hand thrust out.

'Belated birthday greetings,' he said with a smile.

Gowda blinked. 'Thanks, sir. But how did you know?'

'Facebook.' Sagayaraj smiled. 'It gives you birthday alerts. Do you ever even look at your Facebook account?'

Gowda grinned and then, clearing his throat, asked, 'Why is the CCB interested in Professor Mudgood?'

'Well, you do know that he has won the Rajyotsava Award as well as the Padma Shri. He was an important man.'

Gowda's eyes narrowed as he interrupted, 'What are you keeping from me?'

Sagayaraj shook his head at Gowda's impatience. 'Allow me to finish, Gowda. About a year ago Professor Mudgood published a series of articles on the Godhra riots. They were scathing attacks on what he called the emergence and consolidation of right-wing fascism in India. It offended certain people.'

'What people?'

Sagayaraj looked at Gowda steadily. 'You know who I am referring to. Things got a little out of hand. He was attacked at an event in Dharwad. And there were open threats. The Dharwad Superintendent of Police is a good friend of the Inspector General. He knew that the Professor had shifted base to Bangalore a few months ago and said that we needed to keep an eye on him.'

Gowda nodded, satisfied with the explanation.

'I am glad that you thought of calling me, Borei. It looks like he had a heart attack while doing a steam inhalation. That explains his submerged face in the water and the towel on the floor, but we have to follow the protocol. Once the postmortem is over, and the time of death ascertained, we'll release the body,' Sagayaraj added as they walked towards the vehicles.

'I don't know why, Stanley, but I have a feeling that something isn't kosher.'

'Something isn't what?' Sagayaraj stared at him.

Gowda flushed. 'Yiddish for "above board",' he said. 'Something the Jews say apparently!'

'Kosher,' Sagayaraj said in a bemused tone. 'Why is that? Because of the unlatched back door? We'll see.'

Gowda stood near the Bolero and glanced around him. Gajendra joined him. 'It's a five-acre property,' he said, seeing Gowda surveying the land around the house.

'How do you know that?' Gowda turned to Gajendra.

'One of the workers told me,' Gajendra said, gesturing to the farthest corner of the land. 'You can't see it from here but there are people living on this property. There is a line house built next to a corner of the rear wall. Once, this was a farm where grapes, maize and vegetables were grown, and cows and sheep were kept.'

'And now?' Gowda asked, setting out on a well-worn track through the trees. A coconut grove opened onto a fruit orchard. Gajendra followed.

'The Professor lost interest some years ago and sold the cows and sheep. Any vegetables grown were for home consumption. The people who live in the line house take up jobs as they find them, sir. Apparently the Professor let them stay for free and in return they were to keep the land from turning into a jungle.'

'Sensible idea if the men did their work to maintain it, which they don't seem to have,' Gowda said as he skirted a bush with vicious thorns. The track led around the house and to the back.

The land sloped down to a terrace dense with tall, brooding trees stretching over most of the area. 'This is almost like a reserve forest,' Gowda observed as he slid down the slope. He had spotted a path through it.

Gajendra looked around him nervously. What if there was a leopard lurking in the undergrowth?

The path suddenly opened into a small clearing on which was a cottage with a gabled roof and enormous windows. It looked like it belonged in a hill station. Gowda walked around the cottage and was taken aback to see a giant clearing of land on the other side. Farther away was the compound wall that stood seven feet high and was crowned with barbed wire. And as if that wasn't enough security, bougainvillea creepers in white, pink and orange climbed the trees along the wall covering everything in a riot of bloom. It was all beautiful while being unruly. The thorns on the creepers would deter anyone from climbing the trees to access the property.

Gowda turned to look at the cottage. Its front windows faced the compound wall. He could see the slanting roof, sturdy double doors and windows with frosted-glass panes. One of the window-panes had been replaced by clear glass. Gowda walked to the window and peered in through it. His eyes widened in surprise. 'Take a look,' he told Gajendra.

The Head Constable did as asked and then turned back to Gowda just as perplexed. 'It looks like Urmila Madam's hall room.'

Gowda smiled. 'Come to think of it, you are right,' he said, glancing at the bookshelves lining one wall, the luxurious leather sofas, the giant TV and the tables with pot-bellied lamps. 'Is this part of the property? Or are we trespassing?' Gowda asked.

'It's part of the Professor's property, sir. And something is not kosher, sir,' Gajendra said as he continued to look in.

A great big splutter of amusement emerged from Gowda's mouth. Gajendra had picked up the word from him. The thought of a bunch of provincial policemen from Karnataka, himself included, using a Yiddish word with such ease that it might as well have been Kannada, while he had had to explain its meaning to a DCP, choked him up with laughter.

'What happened, sir?' Gajendra asked.

'Nothing,' Gowda said. He took a deep breath. 'That's exactly what I thought too. Something isn't kosher here.

'How did the Professor get around?' he asked with a frown growing on his forehead.

'I doubt he had come this side in years. He was eighty-plus. I don't see him walking this far without help,' Gajendra said.

'Did he use a stick is what I meant.' Gowda turned towards the Head Constable who was still looking into the cottage through the window.

'I'm sure he did.'

'In which case where is it? I didn't see one in the kitchen where he was found, or anywhere else in the house. Did you?'

Gajendra shook his head.

# 7

Neelgubbi station was bustling with people and vehicles. Gowda glanced at his watch: 4 p.m. Once upon a time, the activity would have started winding up by late afternoon. But this was no longer the rural outpost it had been in 2006 when it was assigned to Gowda.

The new airport in Devanahalli and the tech park in the vicinity had turned the area into one of the fastest-growing neighbourhoods and hence into prime real estate. If once the villagers had fought over straying cattle or the colour of the serial lights for temple festivities, the sale and purchase of land was what drove crime in these parts now. Every farmer and shepherd wanted to sell what land he owned. 'The big real estate companies have moved in, and with the land gone and money in the bank, farmers and shepherds have turned into loafer magas with the time and leisure to gamble and drink. And to rake up past hurts and slights,' Gajendra liked to tell anyone new to the station.

The crackling of the wireless and messages punctuated the voices in the station. There was a new Station House Officer now that Gowda had moved up a rung. An ACP had important things to do and ought not to be bothered with the minutiae of managing cases and the case register. Or so the system believed. Gowda missed being in the thick of things. Paper-pushing wasn't what he had become a policeman for, he thought as he entered his room and saw the stack of files that awaited him.

He paused for a moment and surveyed his kingdom. The metal office table with its desktop computer, the pen-holder crammed with pens, pencils, a cutter and a small pair of scissors. The glass paperweight on a sheaf of papers. The swivel chair with black cushioning that had finally replaced the chair with a game leg. In his absence, someone had slung a new towel on its back.

He frowned at the appearance of this affectation of important men in government offices. It had always made Gowda cringe and he wondered which new fool had done this. The others knew him well enough not to.

On one side of the table were two sets of filing cabinets and a metal rack painted a regulation grey. Everything was as it had been when he was Inspector Gowda, except that now he had a name board which displayed his new designation: Assistant Commissioner of Police.

Gowda walked to the window and looked outside. Once again lorries had sneaked in the middle of the night and dumped another mountain of debris on the other end of the lake. Right under his nose, the lake was being filled up, and he could do nothing about it. The lorries belonged to MLA Papanna. A Member of the Legislative Assembly had powers that exceeded his and Papanna helped keep the government in power. A dying lake was a piffling matter that no administrator dared stick his neck out for.

More and more apartment buildings were being built everywhere. Tall edifices of matchbox homes and—as a sop for the mind-numbing sameness—zigzag pathways through the grounds with enough shrubs and flowering plants to warrant the word 'exclusive', along with a clubhouse with a pool and a gym to foster a sense of community. How was Bangalore going to withstand this erosion of green space and the water table, he shuddered. How was he going to cope living in this new Bangalore?

Real estate was the new mantra for quick and large returns. One day the bubble would burst but until then every farmer with ancestral land had turned into a real estate agent who talked only in terms of crores. Gowda had his doubts whether any of them even knew how many zeroes there were in a crore.

Janaki and Iqbal Buqhari were sitting on a diamond mine, he thought with sadness. More villas or flats would pop up on Raghava Mudgood's land, or perhaps a glitzy mall, since it was on the roadside. Gowda straightened his back to shrug aside his thoughts and pressed the buzzer by his table. A thin man with a bony face and a thick moustache appeared and saluted smartly. Gowda frowned. 'Are you a new appointment?'

The constable nodded vigorously. 'PC Gopal, sir. I was at the Yelahanka station.'

'Was it you who put this towel here?'

The man nodded again.

'Do you think that I come to the station to take a bath?' Gowda asked in a dangerously even voice.

Gopal stared in confusion.

'Don't put a towel on my chair. Ever. And don't nod. Say yes or no. That's why we were given mouths,' Gowda snapped, not knowing why he was in such a foul mood. 'Now send Sub Inspector Santosh in.'

Gopal nodded and muttered, 'Yes, sir,' and fled the room. The Station Writer Zahir had already told him to be wary of Gowda. 'Gowda was always an arrogant bastard, but ever since he became

ACP, it's like he's in a permanently foul mood. I can't imagine why. He could make some serious money if he wanted. But he won't and won't let us either. So be careful around him. Unless you want your head bitten off, that is.'

Santosh sat at his desk, staring at his desktop screen, reading the latest on the Dr Sanjay Rathore case. That it had been stretched out didn't surprise him, but it still felt like a kick in the balls. Nine months ago, when he resumed duty after a near-fatal episode, he had been made Child Welfare Officer and ASI Ratna Assistant CWO. Together they had thought they would make a difference, but their first child-trafficking case had gone south.

All of them, despite Gowda's promotion—which he said was a bribe so he wouldn't cause trouble—had sunk into a torpor of listlessness. The wilting of idealism begins thus... Santosh told himself, trying to feel enthusiastic as he made notes about a seminar Ratna and he had attended on the implications of the POCSO Act.

A constable came to him. 'ACP Gowda wants to see you,' he said.

'Are you PC Gopal?' Santosh asked.

Gopal began nodding, and then caught himself and said, 'Yes, sir.'

Santosh entered the room, wondering what Gowda wanted. He saluted.

Gowda looked at the fresh-faced young man in his crisply ironed uniform and gleaming shoes with something akin to affection. When Urmila teased him that Gowda was avuncular with Santosh, he would try to dismiss it by saying, 'He is an excellent police officer and as with Gajendra I would stake my life on his loyalty.' If it had been anyone else, Gowda would have punched that person for accusing him of favouritism. But deep down, he knew that Urmila was right. The young man meant something to him.

The sight of the scar on Santosh's throat always unsettled Gowda for a moment. He had literally dragged Santosh back to life. What was it the ancients said: once you save a life you become responsible for it. Santosh had recovered but the scar on his throat and his raspy voice was a daily reminder of what had happened that September night when Chikka also known as Bhuvana also known as Ramesh had shot his brother and slit Santosh's throat. It rankled that Chikka was still on the run despite Gowda's best efforts.

'All well?' Gowda asked.

Santosh shrugged.

'You look upset...' Gowda said, gesturing for Santosh to sit down.

'I just heard Krishna has been sent to the remand home. His lawyer produced a certificate to show he was only seventeen years of age, and apart from which Dr Rathore was accused of molesting Krishna. So he is suddenly a victim. What is the point in us doing what we do? The criminals walk away while we watch with our hands tied.' There was no mistaking Santosh's anger and frustration, Gowda thought as he took in the young man's flaring nostrils and narrowed eyes.

'You do know that we did everything we could,' Gowda said gently. 'Do you think I am not upset by what has happened? Do you think I like it?'

Santosh shook his head. 'I know that, sir, and that is why I haven't put in my papers.'

Gowda stood up. 'Come up with me,' he said, suddenly deciding to break his cigarette rule. A crisis of faith in a junior colleague warranted a ciggie, he told himself firmly.

Gowda and Santosh walked to the no man's land near the lake. A strip of land that stuck out into the lake and was not part of the station grounds but considered so by its sheer presence. A mango tree stood on it, and Gowda had marked this as his territory. No one else went there but him, which allowed him to smoke without being spotted. He lit the cigarette while Santosh watched disapprovingly.

'Had you heard of Professor Mudgood before this morning?' Gowda asked.

He took a long drag and let the smoke unfurl within him. The best thing to do would be to get Santosh involved in another case. He wondered what else there was in the case register he could assign him to.

Santosh took a step forward. 'I have, sir. It was a shock to discover that it was him this morning. My elder brother who's a journalist was his student.'

'Have you read his articles?' Gowda looked at Santosh curiously.

'I have read a few. He had a very acerbic point of view. But why, sir?'

'The CCB has an interest in this case. Apparently what Professor Mudgood wrote about the Godhra riots offended certain people and there were death threats against him. I want to find out what exactly he said in his articles,' Gowda said, watching interest flare up in Santosh's eyes.

'I can find the articles for you, sir. I'm sure my brother will be able to access them for me,' Santosh said, and then paused before saying, 'It doesn't look like a natural death, sir.'

'Everything points to that. Something doesn't sit right. That apart, I still want to read the articles,' Gowda said, stubbing the cigarette.

His phone rang. He glanced at the caller ID and then at Santosh.

'Yes, sir,' Santosh said.

From across the city, DCP Sagayaraj said, 'ACP Gowda, I just received a call from the forensic surgeon. I suggest you join me at Bowring Hospital. You were right. Something is not... what's the word you used?'

'Kosher, sir,' Gowda said. 'Let's say, I am not surprised at all, sir. I will leave right away.'

Gowda looked at the silent phone for a moment and turned to Santosh. 'That was DCP Stanley Sagayaraj. Apparently, the forensic surgeon thinks it wasn't a natural death. I'm going to Bowring where the body is.' Gowda paused. He wondered if he should ask Santosh to go with him, but then remembered how the boy had reacted when he had taken him to his first postmortem. In his current state of mind, it would be best to spare him this, he decided.

'Try and lay your hands on the articles ASAP,' he added. 'There are a couple more cases I need to talk to you about. But those can wait for now.'

Santosh looked relieved. 'Sir, I will do that. But I think I would like to go with you to the mortuary. And you can tell me about the cases on our way there.'

Gowda nodded. The boy would be all right, he told himself with a little blaze of relief. 'We need to leave immediately. Tell Head Constable Gajendra to join us.'

He read the curious look in Santosh's gaze. 'I don't want the CCB taking the case away from us. And three heads are better than one.'

# 8

Dr Khan looked up from his file. 'About time,' he said. 'I was surprised that the CCB was here before you.'

Gowda shrugged. Dr Khan was a fine forensic surgeon, but he had a fondness for gossip. If you spent your day with cadavers, it was probably only natural, this need to reaffirm the machinations of living. Nevertheless, Gowda was determined not to give him any juicy tidbits. 'The CCB has an interest in it,' he said without a change in expression. He pulled out a chair and sat down. 'Tell me,' he said.

Darkness had descended and the corridor lights were on. Little pools of yellow that only enhanced how dismal the place was. 'The PM report is being prepared. But to give you a gist: the time of death points to between 1 and 3 a.m. on 29 November. We found a head injury. Not strong enough to crack his skull but enough to make him unconscious. He also had a welt on his neck, bruises on his arm and wrist, and an open wound on his palm.'

Dr Khan waited to see the change of expression in Gowda's eyes. It was one of the most satisfying parts of his job. When he could turn the tables on what was seemingly a natural death and declare it to be an unnatural one. But Gowda, it seemed, was determined to deny him that satisfaction. Gowda glared back at him to say: Go on.

'There is a concussion spot on the left side of his skull and along his right arm, as if he hit the right side of his body as he fell.'

Gowda thought of the kitchen wall against which the table was pushed up. Had the Professor been killed before his face was shoved into the water to make it seem like an accident?

'So there wasn't any water in his lungs?' Gowda leaned forward to read the notes on Dr Khan's table. The man placed his hand on it.

'Naturally we did find water in his lungs and nasal passage. Scalding too, and fine froth over the trachea and bronchi. Since his face was submerged in the water, the froth had dissolved into the water, or at least wasn't visible. So a clear case of death by drowning and not a heart attack as presumed.'

Gowda drummed his fingers on the table. 'If he didn't slump into the water, how did he die by drowning?'

'Someone held his head forcibly down into the water,' Dr Khan finished with a flourish. 'The PM showed tiny flakes of paint beneath his fingernails, and his hands were badly bruised. It's quite possible that he was already weak from the blow and couldn't put up much of a struggle.'

'The blunt-force trauma... what do you think caused it?'

Dr Khan frowned. 'It wasn't a very hard blow. Just enough to stun him for a few minutes. It could be anything from a rolling pin to a walking stick to a ladle. And from the angle of the blow, it seems to me that the person was standing behind but further to his left and the weapon was wielded with both hands. As if it was swung wildly and so when the weapon made contact, it didn't do much damage.'

Gowda wondered what Stanley was planning on. In all probability the CCB would take the case away but Gowda was determined to put up a fight. He stood up. Dr Khan shuffled through the papers on his table, found what he was looking for and said, 'Gowda, wait, this isn't connected to this case but to your station. One of my colleagues did a PM and she mentioned the case was from your station precinct. The body of a young man.'

Gowda nodded. 'And?'

'And like the one found in the quarry four months ago, the cause of death was brain haemorrhage. What got my attention was she said the unidentified victim was a young, prominently muscular man,' Dr Khan added. 'I went to look at the body, and he could very well have been another version of the quarry chap. The same kind of injuries, and the cause of death is the same too. Cranial haemorrhage.'

Gowda stared at him in surprise. It had skipped his mind to ask Gajendra about the body found in the eucalyptus grove. 'I see,' he said.

'I think you need to check if there is a connection between these deaths.'

'Why do you say that, Dr Khan?' Gowda frowned. 'Couldn't it be a mere coincidence?'

'Somehow, I don't think it is. And there is something else. I was at a conference a month ago and the government forensic surgeon from the General Hospital in Tumkur was telling me of a corpse found by the railway track. Another man with the cause of death as cranial haemorrhage. After my colleague here

mentioned the same cause of death in the PM she conducted,
I knew I had to mention it to you. If you remember, we checked
if the organs had been harvested with the quarry chap. And there
was nothing like that. The surgeon at Tumkur and my colleague
said neither of the deceased's insides had been tampered with,'
Dr Khan said. 'Here,' he said, handing a printout to Gowda.
'It's almost like a pattern and most definitely not a coincidence.
I have asked the forensic surgeon at Tumkur to email the PM
report. I'll forward it to you. Most peculiar, this. So in case DCP
Sagayaraj takes away the Mudgood case, you have this to crack.'

Gowda threw Dr Khan a savage scowl.

'What's that for?' Dr Khan protested. 'I was only trying to
be helpful...'

'Indeed, you are,' Gowda said, suddenly feeling the ire fizzle
out of him. It had been a long day and he was exhausted. But
there was one more thing he needed to do.

The body was laid out on a steel table in the mortuary. The
postmortem was over, the place and the cadaver had been tidied
up. The viscera would go for testing, and thus a man would be
reduced to a case number and a police report.

Gowda looked at what had once been Professor Mudgood.
Did anyone remember what his first name was, he wondered; did
anyone even use it anymore? He remembered his father com-
menting about this once. 'No one calls me Chidananda anymore.
After a certain age, there is no one left who remembers you as
a person. Instead, you become Appa, Ajja, Chikappa, Father,
Grandfather, Uncle, etc. etc. Names for the roles you are meant
to play. Chidananda doesn't exist. Do you know how that feels?'

Gowda and his brother had exchanged glances then. It was
Roshan, Gowda's son, who broke the awkward silence. 'Shall
I start calling you Chidananda?' He had tugged at his grand-
father's cheeks.

His father had frowned at him and said, 'You rascal...'

＊

Gowda walked out of the mortuary, followed by Gajendra and Santosh. He was surprised to see DCP Sagayaraj in the corridor waiting for him.

'What made you think that Professor Mudgood's death wasn't natural?' the DCP asked.

The Head Constable met Santosh's eye as if to say, don't tell me I didn't tell you...

'Did you see the kitchen table?' Gowda asked.

Sagayaraj frowned. 'Yes, the paint had flaked like it had been scratched; I saw that, but there were numerous scratches on it anyway,' he said, trying to visualize it.

'But this was like someone was trying to grab on to it frantically to push himself up. It had comma-like furrows that weren't really noticeable, but they bothered me,' Gowda said. 'A few other things too. His broken glasses. The towel on the floor. If he had a heart attack the towel would be still on him and the glasses on the table. The unlatched door. The broken flower pots on the side of the house...'

He paused, stricken by the image in his head of Professor Mudgood's scalded face. No one deserved to die like that, he thought, imagining the man's last moments. Who could have possibly wanted him dead?

Out loud, Gowda said, 'So, what do we do next, sir?'

'They have collected samples from beneath the victim's fingernails. The viscera will be sent to the lab.'

'And we wait for the next two months before we get the results, I presume,' Gowda murmured. 'If we are lucky, that is.'

Sagayaraj looked at Gowda with a wry expression. 'Let's say I have my means and methods to expedite matters. So put that cynicism on hold for a bit.'

Gowda gave him a small smile. 'Whatever you say, boss.'

'The family is here,' Sagayaraj said.

'I will speak to them,' Gowda said.

Sagayaraj looked at him for a moment. 'Wait, Gowda,' he said, not quite meeting his colleague's eye. 'It's best I do that. This has all the potential of turning into a highly sensitive case. The CCB has to move very cautiously.'

Gowda stiffened. 'With all due respect, sir, this homicide happened in my station area, and we should be investigating it.'

Sagayaraj looked at Gowda. 'Why am I not surprised that you think so?'

'In which case...' Gowda began and paused as his senior officer held his hand up to stop him from launching into a tirade.

'We are going to have to set up a Special Investigative Team. Pick your people. We also need to call a high-level meeting with the Home Minister and the Chief Minister. The CM holds the intelligence-wing portfolio, as you know.'

Gowda took a deep breath. 'Thanks,' he said, well aware that this wasn't just another homicide investigation. The battle had begun.

Gajendra and Santosh stood by the police vehicle, watching Gowda and Sagayaraj talk. PC David sat inside. None of them knew what was going on yet but they already understood that Professor Mudgood hadn't died of natural causes.

'It could be a real-estate-linked murder,' Santosh said. 'He was sitting on a gold mine.'

'And probably it was one of the workers who did it,' Gajendra added. He hadn't liked the look of one of them. A luchha bugger with unkempt hair and beard, bloodshot eyes, a mouthful of tobacco and shabby clothes.

'Or maybe it was a revenge crime,' David added. 'Somebody who bore him a grudge.'

Gajendra snorted. 'I'm telling you it's something to do with land.'

When they saw Gowda approach, they went quiet.

*

Gowda stared ahead as the vehicle moved forward. He was exhausted but the adrenalin shooting through his system kept his thoughts tumbling one over the other. Was it just this dawn that he had woken up to see Urmila standing by the windows that gave them an almost 180-degree view of the waters of the Arabian Sea? It seemed another lifetime away. With Professor Mudgood's death ruled a homicide, he had to get cracking before the CCB wrested the case away from him.

As ghoulish as it may seem, the truth was everyone loved a high-profile murder case.

And then there were the dead bodies Dr Khan had mentioned. What on earth was going on? It wasn't an organ-trafficking racket. All the victims had had their organs intact. So why were they bludgeoned to death, and by whom?

Gajendra, Santosh and David maintained a studious silence. They knew Gowda well enough to see that he was deep in thought and wouldn't take kindly to having his flow of thoughts derailed by a banal query or chitchat. As the vehicle drew closer to Kelesinahalli, Gowda said, 'Santosh, don't forget to trace the Professor's articles. Gajendra, please have the house cordoned off if it hasn't been done already by the CCB. It's a crime scene. Check if the Professor used a walking stick. And if he did, look for it. If he couldn't walk without it, why wasn't it anywhere in the house? Where can it be?' He turned to look at the two of them. 'I don't need to tell you this but none of you are to discuss the case with anyone.'

The men nodded. 'That goes for you too, PC David,' Gowda added.

Santosh leaned forward, his mouth shaping a query. Gajendra, whose patent was an instinctive understanding of Gowda's silences, nudged Santosh to shut up. Santosh glared at him but didn't speak as the police vehicle covered the last stretch to the station.

# 9

The new high-rise across the lake was ablaze with light. Gowda stood under his mango tree, gazing at the building where once the horizon had stretched. The high-rise even had a helipad, he was told, just in case a corporate honcho preferred to hop into a chopper to get to the airport or wherever. If you gave it a cursory glance, you would think the condo apartments were all alive with people and life. When you looked carefully, though, you realized that most of the windows were wreathed in darkness; just the vestibules and hallways were lit up to give a sense of full occupancy. Nothing was what it seemed in this city. Not anymore, he thought with a flare of anger. Just as in the case of Professor Mudgood, which seemed to point obviously to murder for gain. Which probably meant it wasn't.

The mosquitoes buzzed around him, demanding, 'What do you think it is, Gowda?' They droned, weaving circles. But Gowda wasn't too perturbed. His fabric roll-on mosquito repellent was efficient enough. As for their incessant querying, he knew exactly how to deal with it. 'Fuck off,' he said as he took a deep final drag and shoved the butt into a cement pan filled with sand. 'Go find someone else to nag and suck on,' he added as a parting shot.

When he walked back into the station, he saw Gajendra and Santosh huddled together. They were looking into Santosh's phone. Gowda frowned. What on earth were they watching?

Gajendra flushed when he saw Gowda. 'This is...' he began.

'I have no idea what you are doing but if we are to be on top of this case, watching comedy scenes on the phone isn't the way to go about it,' Gowda snarled in a low voice. He could see the station writer Zahir, pretending to be busy, clacking away at his keyboard.

Santosh looked up at him with a pained expression. 'Sir, I found a YouTube video of Professor Mudgood speaking at a—'

he peered at the phone to double check the title—'"Secularism in Democracy" seminar in Dharwad.'

Gowda grunted. 'Let me see it as well.'

'I'll WhatsApp you the link, sir. You just need to click on it,' Santosh said.

Gowda nodded. Between Urmila and Roshan, Gowda had been tutored enough to know his way around mobile apps and use them with a fair amount of dexterity. He glanced at his watch. It was almost half past eight. 'Let's regroup at the earliest tomorrow before the SIT is formally announced. We need Byrappa and Ratna too,' Gowda said, walking to his room.

Santosh followed him. 'Sir, I have a suggestion.'

Gowda's eyebrows rose a fraction and Santosh felt his heart plummet to his knees. But he pulled himself together. 'Sir, I think we should ask one more person to join the team.'

Gowda's eyes narrowed. 'And who is that?'

'SI Aqthar Janvekar, sir. He is at the Dharwad city station. He was with me at the police college and he is a very sharp officer, sir. He will also be able to help us with the Dharwad part of the investigation.'

Gowda gestured to Santosh to sit. 'Why Dharwad?'

'Professor Mudgood is from there. He moved to Bangalore only four months ago.' Santosh leaned forward to stress his point. 'It's quite possible that the assailant is from Dharwad.'

'Makes sense. I will put in the request. But tell him to start first thing in the morning tomorrow. He will probably miss the first briefing but you can update him.'

Gowda liked to work with a tight unit. Both Ratna and Santosh had earned his trust, and though others had tried, he allowed very few people into his inner circle. So for him to agree so readily meant Gowda was perturbed.

# 10

The gate lights at Gowda's home were on. David said, 'Do you have guests, sir?'

Gowda frowned. Had he forgotten that Mamtha or Roshan were visiting? Then he saw that the house was in darkness, except for the porch light. 'No guests,' he said as the vehicle drew to a halt outside the gate. 'The tenant upstairs must have switched the lights on.'

Gowda walked in, latching the gate after him. As he had presumed, the gate lights and the porch lights had been turned on from the switchboard in the verandah. The potted plants had been watered as well.

From above, he could hear music playing at a low decibel. He glanced up and in the balcony saw a slight woman seated in a basket chair suspended from a hook in the ceiling. Gowda walked back towards the porch entrance and mustered up a smile to beam at Mrs Tenant. 'Good evening, I hope you have settled in,' he called out to her, not knowing what else to say. Besides, he had forgotten their names. 'It's a very quiet area,' he added in Kannada.

'I don't speak Kannada, Gowda Sir. We are Tamilians,' she said in English, rising from the chair and coming to the balustrade. 'Thank you for asking. We really like it here. My husband has been waiting to meet you.'

Gowda nodded. The husky note in her voice was pleasant enough. But he couldn't make out what she looked like. The light was behind her.

'Over the weekend, your husband and you should come over for coffee,' Gowda said, surprising himself. He was not given to hobnobbing with his tenants. But the little gesture with the lights and plants had touched him.

'That would be lovely,' she said.

Gowda wondered what Shanthi had told her about him. That he was a tetchy old bastard, perhaps, and not given to neighbourly acts of any sort.

'Goodnight,' he said as he climbed the steps to the verandah. The night air nipped at the tips of his ears and Gowda looked forward to a warm shower before doing anything else. He entered the house and turned the lights on one by one. It was as if he needed to dispel the disquiet of what he had seen in the morning, the ignominious end of a man living alone.

He turned on the hot water as he stripped his clothes off. Then, still in his undies and vest, he unpacked his suitcase, taking care to remove the airline and hotel baggage tags. He took them into the kitchen and threw them deep into the bin. They would lie buried under the debris from his plate once he was done with dinner. Caution wasn't being timid, it was being prudent, he told himself as he stepped under the shower.

Through the hiss of water, he heard a bike rumble to a stop to the side of his house where his bike and car were parked. Mr Tenant, Gowda surmised. In its own way, the thought of the couple upstairs made him feel less lonesome.

When he had showered, he poured himself a small drink and picked up his phone. Why hadn't Urmila called or messaged him all day?

Gowda stared at his phone: Should he call her or text her?

The phone in the hallway rang. He padded towards it, wondering who it could be. The landline instrument had turned into a paperweight beneath which old magazines waited for Gowda to eventually pick up and throw into the heap of old newspapers.

It was his father.

Since Chidananda Gowda seldom called, he felt the pit of his belly go hollow. 'Appa,' he said, trying to hide the worry in his voice. 'Is everything all right?'

'Does something have to be wrong for me to speak to my son?' his father retorted with an awkward laugh.

Gowda's heart sank. He knew precisely what the laugh was about and where it would lead to. He dropped into the chair by the phone and looked longingly at the drink that sat on the cabinet across the room.

Gowda waited for Chidananda to continue. 'Borei, how about if I come to stay with you for a few days? You must be lonely on your own.'

'When would you like to come, Appa?' he asked, and though he knew it would make no difference, added, 'I'm working on a new case. I will be very busy.'

Chidananda's voice became starchy. 'So you don't want me to come?'

'I didn't say that, Appa. Just that if you come when Mamtha and Roshan are here, you won't be on your own all day,' Gowda tried to explain.

Chidananda laughed awkwardly. 'I'll come again when they are there, but I feel like a change of air. Besides, does a father need a reason to spend time with his son?'

Gowda realized that his sister-in-law must have her relatives visiting and his father was feeling left out. This was Chidananda's way of telling Nagendra that he was annoyed with them. In a few days, he would demand to go back to Gowda's brother and the house he had built. But for now, he wanted to get away from the place that seemed overrun with strangers who flashed their teeth at him and then ignored him.

'When would you like to come?' Gowda asked again. For a fleeting moment, he wished his father had sought him out because he really wanted to see him and not because he was making a point to his brother and sister-in-law. But he quelled the thought, like he did all thoughts that made him want to run a fist through a door. He had learnt where such thinking led him: a hole-in-the-wall bar and binge-drinking. And he wasn't that Gowda anymore.

'Tomorrow?'

His father's voice had acquired a lilt, a chirp. He sounded excited, Gowda thought.

'Appa, I'll ask Nagendra to put you in a taxi and I'll be here at home to receive you,' Gowda said, trying to plan the day ahead.

'Why can't you pick me up?' His father was now the petulant child who had been told 'no sweeties till you finish your homework'.

'Appa, I'll do my best, but if I can't, please don't get offended. It's just that I'm working on a very important case and I have to be here.'

'All right then.' The old man didn't bother hiding how put out he felt at being denied the opportunity to make a statement of his departure from the house.

'Don't forget to bring your medicines and your warm clothes, and some reading material,' Gowda said, pretending not to hear the annoyance in his father's voice.

Gowda lit a cigarette in his living room with an almost angry flare of rebellion. In all fairness, his brother and sister-in-law needed a spot of respite; in all fairness, his father ought to be able to visit his son whenever he wished to. But in all fairness to him, he didn't have to roll on the ground kicking his legs in anticipation of the impending delight of Chidananda telling him how to eat, sleep, breathe and do his job.

Gowda took a deep draw of his cigarette and texted Urmila: Where are you?

When the phone screen stayed resolutely silent, he called her. The phone rang and rang. Then the screen lit up: You are a boor.

Gowda googled the word. A boor, he discovered, was a rough and bad-mannered person. Synonyms included lout, oaf, ruffian, hooligan, barbarian, Neanderthal... Gowda flinched. He cupped his lower jaw to see if it had the forward jut of the Neanderthal man. Gowda inhaled, wondering what his crime was. And then it struck him, the enormity of his doing. Or not doing.

Gowda left the light on and shut the door behind him. He was tired and his drink was untouched on the table. But a man must do what a man must do, especially when he has been called a Neanderthal...

As he closed the gate behind him, Gowda saw a curtain in an upstairs window move. He frowned. Was the woman one of those who liked keeping tabs on all comings and goings?

## 11

At half past nine, Hennur Road wasn't clear of traffic, as it once used to be. The incessant roadworks added to the congestion. Nevertheless, Gowda felt the familiar sense of well-being seep into him when he was on his Bullet. The thump of the bike and the cold fingers of air clawing the back of his neck. He stopped by the Ganesha temple at Hennur. The flower-seller was getting ready to leave, but Gowda persuaded her to weave him a string of jasmine buds. She raised an eyebrow at him. Gowda arched an eyebrow back but didn't say anything.

At the Outer Ring Road, he turned into the service road leading to Kacharakanahalli and then went over the Lingarajapuram flyover. Almost on a daily basis, everything about the route he took seemed to change. For a moment, Gowda wanted to stop at the bar across East Station.

Once, his bike would pause there on its own, as if it knew there was something about sitting on the terrace and watching the world go by while nursing a drink. He would watch the football game going on in the ground opposite and when it broke into a fight, he would continue to watch, unperturbed. But the Bullet no longer seemed inclined to slow down, and Gowda instead took a U-turn. On a whim, he drove through Mosque Road, which was bustling with people on foot. Suddenly ravenous, Gowda stopped at a tea stall. Freshly fried samosas sat on a plate, smiling at him coyly. He reached for one and bit into the flaky skin, then took a sip of the scalding tea. For the first time that day, Gowda felt a calm root within him. It seemed he had needed this—the explosion of heat, spice, oil, sugar and a few million bacteria to get his mind back on track.

Half an hour later, as he parked his bike in the basement of the apartment block on Lavelle Road, it occurred to him that she could have gone out. He sighed. He wasn't just a boor, but a presumptuous one at that.

But Urmila opened the door with an expression that would have frozen stiff even Genghis Khan and his hordes, Gowda thought.

'What are you doing here?' she asked.

'I am Borei, not a boor,' Gowda said, knowing how lame it sounded.

'Oh please,' she said. 'Your attempt at humour is pathetic.'

'I know,' he said, offering her the jasmine string.

'And the flowers are cheesy,' Urmila said, letting him in. Mr Right, Urmila's Maltese terrier, danced around Gowda's knees.

'I'm glad someone is happy to see me,' he murmured, taking the little dog in his arms.

'Shut up, Borei. You have absolutely no business sounding aggrieved. If anyone should be pissed off, it should be me. I am truly tired of this.'

Gowda listened quietly as Urmila told him exactly what she thought of him. When she was done, he took his hands in hers. 'I am truly, truly sorry, U, but you will understand when I explain.'

'Do you want a drink?' Urmila asked in a brusque voice. Gowda hid his grin. Despite the lambasting, she was secretly pleased to see him. Or the offer of a drink wouldn't have come.

He proffered a bottle of rum hastily picked up at an alcohol shop. 'This, please. Not any of your single malts.'

Urmila's smile was thin but she didn't say anything as she took the bottle.

Later, when they were sitting on the sofa, leaning into each other, with Mr Right on Gowda's lap, clinking glasses after every sip, he took Urmila's hand in his and wove his fingers through hers. She wore the jasmine in her shoulder-length hair and the fragrance of the flowers filled the room. 'You drink your Laguvulin, me my Old Monk,' Gowda hummed.

Urmila cocked an eyebrow.

'I thought you would be glad to see I haven't forgotten my Simon & Garfunkel,' Gowda murmured. She snuggled into his shoulder in response.

Everything felt right. Everything felt good. Gowda wished he could capture the moment forever. Something to hold on to; something to cling to before the Mudgood case sucked him in whole and tossed him this way and that. Gowda had no idea what the homicide was all about. But he knew for certain that it was going to be a tough one to crack.

'What was the "something" that came up?' Urmila asked. She nuzzled her chin against his arm.

'You are a very cat-like woman,' Gowda said with a rush of tenderness.

Urmila sat up straight and looked at him. She arched her back and shaped a silent meow with her mouth.

He reached for her. She moved away, asking again, 'Where did you go to after I dropped you home?'

He looked at her. 'When you make that silent meow, you know you are irresistible.'

Her eyes glinted. 'I know,' she said and meowed silently again.

Gowda knew this was her way of exacting revenge for having ignored her. 'Urmila,' he said. 'I know I should have called or at least pinged but I went straight to a crime scene from the airport. I think you know the deceased man's daughter, Janaki Buqhari.'

Urmila's hand flew to her mouth. 'Oh my god,' she whispered. 'What happened to Professor Mudgood?'

Gowda shrugged, unsure how much he could tell her. Then it occurred to him that he could tell her the bare minimum and see what she had to say. Urmila would offer a perspective that was not bound by fact or conjecture. Instead, it would be shaped by what she knew of the couple and her interactions with them.

'It's not a pretty story,' Gowda said, taking a deep breath.

'When is it ever?' Urmila said as she gulped her drink.

Gowda nodded. He rose and took their empty glasses. 'I need a refill. Do you?'

# 1 DECEMBER 2012, SATURDAY

## 1

Gowda woke up abruptly. Mr Right, who slept in the bed with Urmila and him, raised his head and watched him dress. Urmila was fast asleep, and he didn't have the heart to wake her up. Besides, he didn't want chitchat clouding his thoughts. So he shut the bedroom door quietly behind him and slunk out of the apartment.

The security guard pretended not to see him as he rode up the ramp. Gowda smiled. Was looking away a dereliction of duty, or merely a nod to the that's-none-of-my-business attitude? Either way, Gowda didn't particularly care. He had too much going on to ponder on the moral dialectics of a man pretending not to see him.

He wondered what the security guards made of his nocturnal visits and if it would cause trouble for Urmila. Though she seemed very blasé about it, he tried to be as discreet as possible. But security guards were notorious gossips and he was certain they were being discussed. Gowda shrugged. He was too old to care about what anyone thought of him.

The nip in the air made Gowda glad that he had remembered to put on his biking jacket and riding gloves. But despite the blade-like edge of the wind, Gowda felt awash with the thrill of being on his Bullet at that hour. No one, but no one, except true bikers would relate to that feeling.

At half past four, the thump of the four-stroke engine echoed along the street. The headlamp threw a beam of yellow on the shadowed empty roads. No one seemed to rouse in Bangalore earlier than half past six in the morning. Here and there he saw vendors gather at newspaper and milk depots, otherwise all life that was there on the streets came from the occasional glint of the tiger's eye along the medians. The air was clear of exhaust fumes and dust. Gowda let the calm and quiet texture of Bangalore that resembled the city he knew and loved, and which only existed at Brahmamuhurtam, seep into him. To quote one of those WhatsApp forwards, he was ready to make lemonade of whatever lemons life threw at him.

Gowda laughed aloud.

Forty minutes later, as he pushed open his gate, he saw a light come on upstairs. So they were early risers. A point to be noted for future reference, Gowda told himself.

He switched off the porch light and went inside. After looking at the untouched drink for a moment, he hastily tossed it down the sink. Then he made himself a mug of filter coffee. Shanthi kept some decoction in the fridge for him to use for his 'bed coffee', as she called it. Though how the coffee was going to make itself, leap onto a tray and find its way to his bed on its own was something neither he nor she had figured out yet.

He looked away from the bed resolutely and sat at his desk and switched his laptop on.

When Urmila had said Gowda should buy a laptop, he had dismissed it with a glib 'U, police work doesn't happen on screens. It happens on the streets.'

When Roshan had called him a dinosaur for still using a stodgy old desktop, he pretended it didn't bother him. Then came the day when Mamtha looked up from her own laptop and said, 'Roshan, leave Appa alone. If he doesn't want to use a laptop, why do you insist that he does? Not all of us can take to new technology naturally.'

That stung. But it was Mamtha's smile of mild denigration that had made him drag Santosh to the nearest mall the next morning to help him buy a laptop.

The blank screen stared back at him. His fingers hovered over the keyboard and, with great deliberation, he typed: MOTIVE.

It felt like he was playacting at being a sleuth. So Gowda minimized the page and instead opened the link Santosh had emailed him along with the set of articles authored by the Professor.

The video was of Professor Mudgood addressing a group of Rationalists in Dharwad. It was a sizable crowd. Gowda took a sip of his coffee. Were there so many Rationalists in the country? Who knew.

A few minutes into the Professor's keynote address, the crowd seemed to stir. There was some commotion at the end of the hall, not covered by the camera. Professor Mudgood paused, took a drink of water and began speaking again. He had just started on Hosur Narasimhaiah and the black magic curse of Banamati when a balloon flew through the air and landed on him, splattering him with cow dung. The video ended with the resultant chaos.

Gowda took another sip of his lukewarm coffee and stared blankly at a YouTube advertisement for a German car that he had no intention of ever buying. He could retire and start a goat farm if he had that sort of money.

Urmila had filled him in on a few things. A couple of months ago, Janaki had confessed the following to her circle of friends one drunken evening as she tossed one vodka tonic after another down her throat.

Iqbal Buqhari was in financial trouble. And he hated his father-in-law. Janaki Buqhari felt torn between the two men, not knowing where her allegiance lay. She had been able to deal with it as long as there were 500 kilometres between her husband and her father. But no one had expected the Professor's wife to die of jaundice almost a year ago. Janaki had felt compelled to bring her father to Bangalore. She was his only child, after all. Besides, that had always been the intention and he had made his retirement plans accordingly.

The Professor had moved to Bangalore four months ago but had insisted on living in his own house. Janaki wasn't happy about it, but the old man did not budge. Iqbal wasn't thrilled at this either. He had been eyeing the property for a while and had already found prospective buyers—all of those plans had to be scrapped now.

It seemed several people wanted Professor Mudgood dead, but who would actually go ahead and murder him? Gowda was still pondering this when he realized it was time to get ready to leave for the station. When he emerged from his bathroom, he heard noises from the kitchen. He sighed in relief. That meant breakfast on the table and probably a cup of freshly brewed coffee.

Shanthi smiled at him and gestured to the table. 'Nashta is ready.'

Gowda ate his ragi dosa and peanut chutney in silence. When he was done, he pulled a 1,000-rupee note from his wallet. 'Appa will be coming this evening; cook some mutton for the night and buy vegetables and any groceries we have run out of for the rest of the week.'

'Why is Appa coming now? Did Madam ask him to?' Shanthi asked, not bothering to hide the curious gleam in her eyes.

Gowda shrugged and then parroted his father's words, 'Does a father need a reason to visit his son?'

Shanthi nodded. 'True... don't worry, sir, I will make sure that he doesn't want to return to his house ever.'

Gowda shuddered at that prospect but said nothing. The sound of the police vehicle pulling up outside the gate allowed him to make a hasty getaway. Mr Tenant's bike was gone. He must have left for work, Gowda thought with relief. He was in no mood for chitchat. As he walked to the gate, he cast a covert glance at the upstairs window, and there it was again. The slight parting of the curtain. He thought he saw a man quickly retreat into the shadows. Gowda shook his head. That must be Mrs Tenant's brother. What was wrong with this lot? Didn't they have anything else to do?

## 2

Head Constable Gajendra and Sub-Inspector Santosh were at his room door even before he had time to sit down. 'Please come, sir... We want to show you something.'

Gowda followed them down the corridor, more than a little puzzled.

There were four inmates in the lockup. One of them was seated, leaning against the wall. Two others were curled up on their side. And a fourth was pacing the cell.

'Dacoity attempt,' Gajendra said. 'Two women were alone when these rascals turned up with sickles. They locked the women in a room. But the commotion and their dog's barking woke up the neighbours, who called the control room. They were apprehended before they could leave.'

Gowda nodded. 'Check on their whereabouts on the night of 28 November,' he said.

'These are novices, sir,' Gajendra said. 'I doubt if they have the meter for murder.'

'That may be so, but check it anyway,' Gowda snapped. 'Now what is it you wanted to show me?' He didn't bother to hide his impatience.

Gajendra stopped in his tracks. 'Sir, I read the PM report.'

'How?' Gowda snapped. 'I am yet to read it.'

Gajendra looked into the air behind Gowda and mumbled, 'I have a friend at the hospital morgue. Sir, what I wanted to tell you was the Professor died in the early hours of 29 November.'

Gowda frowned in annoyance. 'So? We already know that.'

'Sir, the 28th was a Wednesday. That's when the sante market takes place at Doddagubbi. A lot of strangers and their wares— vegetables, fruit, clothes, fish, spices, toys—you can buy everything there. And it is always crowded. We need to take that into account too.'

Gowda was quiet for a moment. Then he said, 'You are right, Gajendra. We should check that angle as well. Though God only knows how we will, given how short-staffed we are. Now what is it you wanted to show me?'

HC Gajendra and SI Santosh had commandeered a room for the SIT. Two tables had been pulled together and chairs arranged around them. No hierarchy between the CCB and us, it said decidedly. There was a jug of water and a few paper cups stacked next to it. And a whiteboard on the wall. Where on earth had they managed to unearth it from? Gajendra and Santosh's gaze followed his.

'It would be better if we get prepared before the CCB get here,' Gajendra said, switching the fan on.

Gowda nodded. 'Good idea,' he said, drawing a chair out. 'Where are the others?'

The wireless on the table hissed to life. Byrappa's voice rang out amidst the crackle.

'We have a problem, sir. People from various parts of Karnataka and neighbouring states have begun gathering outside Professor Mudgood's residence. We may have a law-and-order situation on our hands.'

Gowda looked at Gajendra and Santosh for a moment. He picked up his mobile and called DCP Sagayaraj.

'We are on our way,' Sagayaraj said in lieu of a hello.

# 3

A group of young men and women stood outside the gate of Professor Mudgood's residence. On either side of the road were more people. All of them seemed stunned into a state of disbelief. Gowda wondered what they were going to say to the restive crowd as he saw the television vans arrive and press photographers dashing this way and that.

'The CCB vehicle is behind us, sir,' David said, glancing at the rearview mirror, 'and, sir, DCP Vidyaprasad is behind them.'

Gowda nodded. The circus had begun. Two constables stood within the gates, trying to hold the crowd at bay. Gowda could see fists being raised to go with the war-cry-like slogans.

The Bolero pulled up to the gate, honking loudly, causing some people to disperse with an angry hiss. 'Was that necessary?' Gowda frowned at David.

'The mob is a mindless monster,' David said.

One corner of Gowda's mouth lifted in a laconic curl. 'Which movie did that come from?'

David grinned sheepishly. 'Sir, there are just two constables, and they won't be able to hold the crowd for long. This is the only available entrance, sir.'

'That's true,' Gowda agreed as his eyes scrutinized the rearview mirror to see if the CCB vehicle and DCP Vidyaprasad had caught up with them.

Gowda got out of the car and started walking towards the gate. DCP Sagayaraj and DCP Vidyaprasad were doing the same.

'This is a police matter; please allow us to do our duty.' Gowda tried to speak to the heckling crowd. Who were these people? And where had they come from?

Vidyaprasad turned towards the crowd, holding his hands up and flapping them as if he were shooing crows. 'I am DCP Vidyaprasad, the senior officer in charge,' he hollered, trying to sound as stentorian as he could.

Something sailed through the air. Gowda ducked. The egg flew into Vidyaprasad's face. A howl emerged from his mouth. For once, Gowda felt a qualm of pity for the man as the stench of rotten egg rode up his nostrils. Vidyaprasad was a vegetarian who gagged at the mere thought of sharing a table with anyone eating an omelette.

Gajendra rushed to the assistance of the DCP, who looked like he was going to burst into tears and throw up at the same time. David, stupefied at the sight of Vidyaprasad with egg dripping down his face while bits of shell clung to his thick hair, offered the car-washing cloth to him. The crowd tittered and Gowda roused himself with a roar. 'Have you come here to mourn Professor Mudgood or act like hooligans?'

DCP Vidyaprasad's vehicle roared away. Gowda glanced towards it and thought he was probably fleeing to the nearest bathroom.

DCP Sagayaraj came to stand beside Gowda. 'Calm down,' he called out to the crowd. A blue police van with reinforcements turned into the road, but it was still some distance away.

'How do you expect us to calm down when a thinker like Professor Mudgood is murdered?' a young woman called out.

'Do you have any idea who the assailant may be?'

'Was it a political murder?'

'Do you think it was the real estate mafia?'

Journalists had taken over the frontline.

'We will be calling a press conference later in the day. Professor Mudgood's body will be placed for public viewing at the Town Hall and you can pay your respects there,' Sagayaraj said.

'This is a crime scene,' Gowda added. 'Let us do our duty; please cooperate.'

The police van pulled up and a posse of policemen armed with bamboo lathis and shields stepped out. Gowda and Sagayaraj looked at each other and exchanged a small smile of relief. The contingent would handle the crowd, leaving them free to do their work.

'Now that we are here, we may as well take another look,' Gowda said.

Sagayaraj nodded. 'The dog squad will be here soon, though I don't know how effective they will be.'

Gowda shrugged. 'We haven't let anyone enter the premises, and sir, we need to speak to the daughter and her husband.'

'Speak or question?' Sagayaraj stared at Gowda, who held his gaze. He frowned. 'You don't think it is a political murder?'

'It could be, or it could be disguised to look like one,' Gowda said.

He stood at the gate and took a picture of the driveway leading to the house. The distance was a little more than 150 metres, which set the house deep within the compound. It was mostly camouflaged by trees.

Sagayaraj watched with barely concealed amusement. 'The police photographer has it all, why bother?'

'I think the word is perspective,' Gowda said with a grin to soften the sting of his words. 'He won't see what I do.'

'Indeed,' Sagayaraj said. Gajendra swallowed hard on hearing their exchange. There was no telling what Gowda Sir would say next. Fortunately, Sagayaraj and Gowda were college mates so the DCP gave him a long leash.

'Sir, what about the outhouse?' Gajendra asked hastily to dispel any awkwardness.

Sagayaraj frowned. 'What outhouse?'

'It's a cottage on the other side of the main house and closer to the compound wall on the rear side of the property. Gajendra and I saw it last morning but it was locked.'

# 4

'How big is this property?' the DCP asked as they skirted the house and walked through the dense orchard of fruit trees.

'About five acres,' Gajendra said.

'This land is worth a lot, considering it is on the main road,' Gowda said.

Sagayaraj nodded. 'This must be worth a hundred crores at least. I see what you mean. This could be a set-up to make it look like a political murder.'

Gowda shot a few more pictures, walking deep into the wooded area.

'Look at this,' Gajendra called out. He was concealed by a giant clump of bamboo.

The two men walked briskly towards Gajendra, who stood looking down into a shallow pit filled with ashes. A few half-burnt slivers of cardboard and bits of aluminium foil glistened amidst the ashes. Gowda clicked another picture.

'What do you think?' Gowda asked, pulling out a twig from a stack of dried branches under a tree. He nudged a piece of cardboard out and examined it.

'Keep walking,' Sagayaraj sniggered, poking through the pit with another twig from the stack.

'I don't understand.' Gajendra frowned.

Gowda raised his head and looked in Gajendra's direction. 'DCP Sir was using the slogan for Johnnie Walker whisky. That's a Black Label carton. And all the cartons are empty. If you check the garden shed or somewhere behind the house, you will find the bottles, I'm sure. Someone probably wanted to sell them to the skriap man. But they didn't want the empty cartons found or any of the debris to be discovered. So they burnt it all. Let's do a quick search to see if they dropped anything.'

They found cigarette stubs, an aluminium foil case that still held remnants of food, a soiled paper napkin with the name of a restaurant printed on it, and a ball of bloodstained cotton wool stuck on a thorny bush. 'Looks like someone had a big party here and it ended in a fight,' Gajendra said.

'Probably just about two to three days ago. All this doesn't look too old. It would have disintegrated to nothing,' Gowda said.

'Not the cigarette butts. They take eighteen months to ten years,' Sagayaraj said.

Gowda threw him a surprised look. When did Stanley become an enthu cutlet? Accruing useless trivia to be spouted at opportune moments.

The DCP noticed Gowda's expression. 'I read it in a magazine last night,' he offered lamely.

Gowda turned to Gajendra. 'Do you have a clean plastic bag?'

Gajendra pulled one out from his back pocket. Gowda gathered the napkin into it.

'One more?' he asked. Gajendra offered Gowda another.

Sagayaraj asked, 'How many plastic bags do you carry on you?'

'Usually three,' Gajendra said. 'When you are in the field, there's no knowing when you'll need one.'

'Good idea. I must suggest it to other station HCs too.'

Gowda shoved the bloodied cotton ball and the cigarette stubs into separate bags. He twisted the top of the bag to make another compartment and dropped the food remnants into it as well. Then he said, 'Sir, I think we need to get the forensics people to come again and search the grounds as well as the cottage.'

Sagayaraj sighed. 'I will get that going.'

'One other thing.' Gowda glanced at his watch. 'We need to question the family right away. I know this may sound insensitive but the first twelve hours after discovery of murder is crucial. After that the family clams up, begins to hide things. Grief at its rawest makes people talk. And we are already late.'

The DCP looked at his phone. 'The body will be released by noon. It would be best if we do so now.'

Gowda called up Santosh. 'I am sending some photos; have them printed out and stick them up on the wall. Have ASI Ratna go to Professor Mudgood's daughter's house.' He looked at Gajendra and added, 'I want you there as well. DCP Sagayaraj and I will join you there.'

'What about me?' Gajendra asked.

'Stay here with the forensics team until they leave.'

'They don't need a babysitter,' Sagayaraj smiled.

'They don't but they need Gajendra,' Gowda said.

Later, Gajendra would tell Santosh and Byrappa, 'When Gowda Sir said that my chest became breasts.'

# 5

Gowda and Sagayaraj exchanged a glance as they drove past the gated community where the lawyer Dr Sanjay Rathore had been murdered. A homicide that had led Gowda and his team into witnessing depravity like they had never known or seen before. 'I still wake up in a sweat remembering the children we rescued,' Gowda said.

The DCP nodded grimly.

'The team lost their morale at how that case went, Stanley,' Gowda said.

'You got promoted, Gowda,' Sagayaraj said. 'Isn't that a commendation of your ability?'

Gowda's laugh was mirthless. 'You know as well as I do that it was just a sop to shut me up.'

Silence hung between them. Sagayaraj broke it with a softly exclaimed 'Idiots' as three boys on a bike zipped past. 'How is your Bullet? You still haven't considered giving it to your son?'

Gowda understood the question for what it was meant to be: Let's change the subject.

'No way!' Gowda said. 'He is too young to ride a Bullet.'

'How old is he?'

'Twenty-two,' Gowda said and then smiled. 'I know. I was riding your bike when I was twenty-one.'

The driver stopped at the ornate gates manned by half a dozen security guards. A board read: 'In the Orchard of Silence'.

Gowda snorted. 'Bloody fools!'

Sagayaraj glanced at him.

'The builder hasn't spent a dawn or a dusk in this area. You can't hear yourself think between the sound of borewells being dug during the day and the mosquitoes whining at night. Not to forget all the garbage lorries trundling past looking for a place to dump their loads. In the Orchard of Silence. Who comes up with these names?' Gowda shook his head.

The gates opened smoothly, almost magically, at the sight of the police vehicle. 'This is a very exclusive property. HNI among the HNI lot,' Sagayaraj said as Gowda took in the well-laid roads between houses and the CCTVs at every crossing.

There were no children playing cricket or bicycling around. There weren't even any cars visible; all of them were probably in the double garages attached to each villa. None of the residents were outside, except for an anorexic woman walking an overweight Labrador. This could be a ghost town. What did the people who lived here do with their messy emotions? Gowda wondered. The honking of a vehicle behind snapped him out of his tangled thoughts. Santosh and Ratna had arrived.

'I think we should have a quick chat before we go in,' Sagayaraj said as they stepped out of the vehicle.

Gowda nodded. 'Let's leave the cars here,' he said, gesturing to the visitors' parking lot which was well away from the house they were going to. 'An element of surprise is always good.'

Santosh and Ratna joined Gowda and Sagayaraj. 'We will walk to the house,' Gowda said.

'Don't any people live here?' Santosh asked, taking in the silent roads, the silent homes.

'Everyone here is an HNI among HNIs,' Gowda said.

'What is HNI?' Santosh asked.

Gowda bent to tie his laces.

Sagayaraj said, 'High-net-worth individual.'

Gowda stood up, hiding his relief. So that was what HNI meant.

'What does that mean? Celebrities?' Ratna asked.

'Very, very rich people,' Gowda said, his eyes darting towards Stanley. 'That's DCP Sir's way of saying it.'

Sagayaraj cleared his throat. 'Brief them, Gowda.'

# 6

The gates of the house were ornate without being ostentatious. The garden was perfectly landscaped, with a tinkling fountain, a gazebo that had a brick barbecue pit, a lone wrought-iron garden bench and many trees. A flock of mynahs chattered on the lawn, and a crow pheasant sat on a low branch, filling the silence with its deep, throbbing call. The house bespoke an elegance and a quiet charm.

Gowda looked towards the porch where a beagle sat, gnawing on what looked like a hide bone. It raised its head at the sight of people at the gate. Then it bayed as only beagles know how to and rushed towards them. The dog leapt at the gate and whined.

'It seems to like you,' Sagayaraj said with amusement.

'For some reason, dogs do,' Gowda muttered, thinking of Mr Right.

A side door opened and someone stepped out. Gowda recognized him as the man who had been with Iqbal Buqhari. Deva. 'Stop it, Bootz,' the man said sternly. Bootz gave him a baleful glare while being led away.

Was this the dog that bit Iqbal? It didn't look like it could say boo to a crow, let alone maul anyone, Gowda thought as he opened the gates.

The four of them walked in, and as Santosh reached out to ring the bell, Deva came running out again from the side door. 'We are from the police,' Gowda said even though Santosh's uniform said as much.

Deva nodded. 'I know, sir. I saw you at the Professor's house. Let me open the main door,' he said, disappearing into the side entrance again.

A few minutes later, the double doors opened, and Deva led them into what seemed to be a vestibule. In one corner was a tall Chinese vase with umbrellas and walking sticks in it. Right in the middle of the vestibule was a round wooden table on which was a giant glass vase of flowers. So this was how HNIs lived, Gowda thought, taking in the silk drapes and the long, expensive-looking carpet that stretched like a runner across the room.

'We need to speak to Iqbal Buqhari and Mrs Buqhari,' Gowda said.

'Please follow me, I will inform them,' Deva said, leading them to a well-appointed room.

A maid wearing an apron over her sari appeared with glasses of water on a tray. Behind her was Iqbal Buqhari.

'Good morning, DCP Sagayaraj... I wasn't expecting you...' he said with a weak smile.

Sagayaraj nodded. 'My condolences again...' he said. 'I suppose you have already met my colleagues.'

Iqbal nodded, stretching his hand towards Gowda and giving the same weak smile to the others. Gowda took his hand and copied the DCP. 'My condolences.'

Sagayaraj sat down on a sofa. 'How is Janaki?' he asked, his eyes darting to the corridor.

'She had many disagreements with him, but at the end of the day he was her father. And she loved him. He was her hero,' Iqbal said.

'And the children?'

'They are shaken, of course, but they weren't particularly close to their grandfather.'

Santosh looked up, startled. He thought of his Ajja, and how his grandfather had always been at his side through his childhood, reading out to him from newspapers and coaxing him to get on with his lessons. His silver-haired Ajja would take him to the shops on his evening strolls. He would buy him a treat every evening: a cone of salted peanuts or a lollipop or jeera mittai. His mother would complain, 'The boy will lose all his teeth by the time he is thirty.'

'I have all of mine,' Ajja would say and flash his teeth.

Santosh looked around to see if any of the others were as startled by Iqbal's admission, but Gowda seemed to be more interested in a painting of a horse and Ratna in a houseplant that seemed to have been fed on a combination of whey protein and steroids. Santosh took a sip of water and put his glass on the table close to him. He saw Iqbal's eyes dart towards the glass and the tray placed on the other table. Was he expected to leave it on the tray? Well, he wasn't going to, Santosh decided.

Gowda turned to Iqbal. 'How is the hand?'

He looked at his bandage and said, 'Getting better.'

'Did the beagle bite you?'

'No, no... Bootz is too much of a clown to bite anyone.' Iqbal smiled. 'My sister's dog.'

A cloud of perfume arrived first. Behind it came Janaki Buqhari, her face drawn, eyes swollen. She was wrapped in a blue and grey shawl and carrying her handbag. 'Are you sure you are up to this, jaanu?' Iqbal asked, rising to his feet and going to her side with a solicitous air. She pretended not to hear him, then, as if realizing that the people in the room were trained to note such details, she touched his elbow and said, 'I am fine.'

She sat on a sofa and Iqbal joined her there. 'Hello, Stanley,' she said in a low voice, turning to the DCP.

'I am sorry for your loss,' Sagayaraj said. She nodded, gazing at the floor. She raised her eyes to greet Gowda. 'I didn't know Urmila and you know each other, ACP Gowda,' she said.

'We were in college together.'

'We were all at St Joseph's at the same time, though I was their senior,' Sagayaraj added, and then with a quick shift in tone he began, 'Janaki, this may be painful but we need to know about the last time you were with the decea... your father.'

She let out a loud sob, then reached for a wad of tissue from a carved wooden box and patted her eyes dry.

'I visited him most days; sometimes in the morning, sometimes in the evening. On that day, I went there by about six in the evening. Iqbal is at the club most evenings but that day he had a golf game at the KGA and the children had a tennis lesson. So I decided to stay and have dinner with my father. He was very irritable. More than usual. I thought it was because Gurunath, his assistant, had gone back to Dharwad. I don't know what happened between them but Mary, the live-in maid, said they had had a very loud argument earlier in the day. My father had dinner, and he and I had a disagreement, and I left very upset with him. It was about 9.30 p.m.'

'What about the maid? Didn't you say that she lived there?' Ratna asked.

'She was unwell. So I sent her home,' Janaki said after a pause.

'Could you tell me what the argument was about?' Gowda asked.

'He made a comment about my appearance. He said I looked like a Dalda tin and...' she stopped abruptly.

There was silence in the room. 'And I said go to hell. Those were my last words to him.' A fresh bout of tears erupted.

'I knew he was alone and he would have difficulty managing alone. But I was furious with him. So I didn't call or go over the next day. Then yesterday morning I started feeling uneasy. He hadn't called. He wasn't picking up my calls either. And Mary who had been discharged was still at her own home. I grew worried. And in all honesty, I felt guilty too. So I decided to go over and check on him and then...'

Janaki's grief, even if a tad on the histrionic side, seemed real, Gowda thought, watching her crumple another ball of tissue paper.

Iqbal patted her shoulder. 'Do you want to lie down, jaanu?'

Gowda leaned forward. 'Is there anyone you think might have wanted to hurt your father?'

Janaki sniffed.

'The world and his mother,' Iqbal said from the corner of his mouth.

Janaki shot him a venomous look. 'My father had very strong opinions and he offended many people with his views.'

'He had also squabbled with his siblings and cousins on a family property dispute,' Iqbal added.

As if unable to stop herself, Janaki butted in with, 'And with my husband. Iqbal wanted him to sell the property. But my father wouldn't.'

'Jaanu, it wasn't anything like that... I thought that would make him move in with us.' Iqbal's protest rang through the room.

Janaki was bristling, and before she spoke, DCP Sagayaraj stood up abruptly. 'Janaki, Iqbal... that will be all for now.'

Gowda stared at him in surprise. He saw Santosh and Ratna exchange glances. Why was DCP Sagayaraj terminating the interview just when it was getting interesting?

'Sir...' Gowda couldn't help rage streaking his voice. A baton of fluorescence that demanded what the fuck was going on.

But Sagayaraj refused to be intimidated by indignation, self-righteous or otherwise. 'Thanks, Janaki, for talking to us. We will need to do a detailed interview, of course. But we can do that later.'

He looked pointedly at Gowda, who had no option but to rise and follow the DCP.

At the door, Gowda paused. 'Just a quick question. Did your father use a walking stick?'

Janaki nodded. 'It should be at the house,' Iqbal said. 'He was seldom without it.'

Gowda saw Janaki Buqhari's eyes fall on the multiple walking sticks and umbrellas sticking out of the tall Chinese urn. Then she hastily looked away. What was she hiding, he wondered.

# 7

At the gate, Gowda muttered under his breath to Santosh, 'Don't say anything... just walk ahead with Ratna.'

Then he turned to Sagayaraj. 'With due respect, sir, why did you terminate the interview? She was just getting ready to tell us more...'

The DCP grinned. 'Gowda, man... I am so glad to see this new improved version. I thought you would collar me and thupify me, as my daughter Esther calls it.'

'I don't spit at people. I'm not a camel,' Gowda snorted. 'But you still haven't answered my question. Is it because you are friends?'

The DCP stiffened. 'That was uncalled for. I have my reasons.'

'Well then, explain them to me. The SIT is not going to make any headway if my team and yours won't share what we know.'

'It has nothing to do with this case.' Sagayaraj's terseness riled Gowda to a pure white rage.

'With all due respect, sir, that is not for you to decide on your own,' Gowda snapped.

The DCP sighed. 'We have been investigating instances of high-stakes betting in the city for some time now. We have seen a spike and then a name came under the radar and Iqbal's name is on his call list. I didn't want his guard going up.'

Gowda flushed. Urmila was right. His natural cynicism had become more acute on this job.

'Iqbal is not a fool, Gowda. He is very shrewd and one of the smoothest bastards you will find on this planet.'

Gowda looked at the DCP. 'Remember the whisky cartons and all we found on the Professor's land? Do you think Iqbal is using the premises for such activities?'

'Quite possible. In fact, that's the first thing I thought of when we found the burnt debris.'

Gowda nodded. 'It would be helpful if you loop me in on everything that has to do with Iqbal Buqhari, even if it looks like it is not connected with this case. With all due respect, sir, that is!'

Sagayaraj cocked an eyebrow. 'What's with the "all due respect, sir" business? Coming from you, it sounds like an insult.'

Gowda grinned at the DCP. That's the idea, the grin said.


Santosh and Ratna watched Gowda and Sagayaraj walk towards them, deep in conversation.

Ratna frowned. 'Do you think he's on the take?'

'Who? The DCP?' Santosh asked.

'Yes.'

'No, no... Gowda Sir respects him, and that means the DCP is clean,' Santosh said.

'Why do you think he ended the interview then?' Ratna rummaged in her bag for a boiled sweet. She had recently acquired a taste for the orange-flavoured candy.

'I'm sure Gowda Sir will have asked him why,' Santosh snapped.

'No need for you to get so tetchy... How do you know the DCP hasn't got ACP Gowda to join in his deal?' Ratna snarled back.

'You don't know what you're saying, ASI Ratna. You're talking rubbish.' Santosh pulled himself to his full height and glared at her, offering the best proximation of a furious Gowda he could muster.

'Do you light a lamp before his photograph every morning? I'm curious about how you worship him,' Ratna shot back.

'Looks like a fight has broken out in your nursery school,' Sagayaraj muttered to Gowda.

'They must be arguing about why you stopped the interview abruptly,' Gowda muttered back. 'They probably think you and Iqbal have a personal equation.'

'In which case...' Sagayaraj strode towards the young officers.

Gowda watched him have a quick chat with Ratna and Santosh. Ratna looked embarrassed, while Santosh seemed relieved. He didn't have to think very hard to realize what conclusions his colleagues had arrived at. In all honesty, he had thought the same.

'DCP Sir was just telling us why he cut short the interview.' Santosh turned to Gowda as he approached.

'I think we should get back to the station for our first briefing,' Sagayaraj said, looking at his watch.

Gowda nodded. 'There's a lot of ground to cover and we need to get going.'

'Santosh, we need the CCTV footage of that night. Check what time Mr and Mrs Buqhari got home.' He paused and then added, 'Deva too. And check for any CCTV footage you can find for the road leading to the Professor's house. And around it.'

'Already on it, sir,' Santosh said.

Ratna opened her mouth and then shut it again. 'What is it, ASI Ratna?' Gowda asked, groaning inwardly. She was a smart officer but sometimes lost track of the goal, blinded by her own need to be proved right.

'The deceased's daughter visited a hospital on 28 November. The thing is, sir, she went there by about 10 p.m.'

They looked at her in surprise. 'Where did that information come from?' Gowda asked.

'One of my sources saw the news about Professor Mudgood. Apparently the TV channels were running pictures of his family. She recognized the daughter and called me.'

'Have you looked into it?' Gowda asked.

'Not yet, sir. I received the information just an hour ago,' Ratna said. 'But I'm going there in the afternoon. The duty doctor who was in the casualty ward on that night has his shift from 2 p.m. this afternoon.'

'Excellent. I will see you at the station,' Gowda said, walking towards the vehicle that the DCP was already seated in.

# 8

It was a little past twelve noon when the team assembled in the briefing room.

A young man with a clean-shaven face and a square jaw stood next to Santosh. Ratna looked at him curiously. He looked like a movie hero in a policeman's uniform. He wasn't as tall as Santosh but then none of the Bollywood Khans were over 5 feet 5 inches—or so she had heard—so this one could very well be Amitabh Bachchan, towering over them. He also looked like all he did was rub cotton pads with toner into his skin and then work in some nourishing cream each time he had a moment to spare.

'ASI Ratna, this is my friend from the Dharwad crime branch. SI Aqthar is joining our team,' Santosh said.

Ratna smiled at Aqthar and was rewarded by a grin that crinkled his face into a devastating handsomeness. Ratna felt her heart flip. Santosh frowned ever so slightly. He had forgotten the effect Aqthar Janvekar had on people, especially women.

Unable to help himself, Santosh blurted, 'Aqthar is here on assignment. His wife and children are back in Dharwad.'

'Child,' Aqthar said. 'The second one is still on its way.'

Ratna nodded and walked towards Gajendra who was wrestling with a whiteboard placed against a wall. Gajendra stood beside it, trying to prop it up to make it stand straight. He smiled at her as it slid again to dangle crookedly. 'Useless thing,' Gajendra said, shaking his head in annoyance. 'I have to put another nail in the wall.'

Ratna rummaged through her handbag. Then she left the room to return with a wad of papers which she slid between the board and wall and adjusted it.

Gajendra moved his palm upwards as if it were a climbing vine and warbled, 'Aaahahahaha.'

The others looked up at Gajendra's exclamation of appreciation, as did Gowda, who had been followed into the room by PC Byrappa. The DCP had dropped him off and gone to meet someone, he had said. Gowda didn't ask who the someone was. And neither did the DCP volunteer the information. It was understood that he was going to pay his respects to MLA Papanna.

'What was that about?' Gowda asked. He had caught the tail end of Gajendra's exclamation of wonder.

'Ratna Madam made the whiteboard stand straight,' Gajendra said. 'And we didn't even need to add another nail.'

Gowda frowned at them as if they were errant children. 'Right, now that we have got past the most important thing on our list, let's work on the case,' he said, making no effort to couch the sarcasm in his tone.

Santosh darted a look at Aqthar as if to say the bark was worse than the bite. SI Aqthar took the cue and saluted smartly. 'Sir, SI Aqthar reporting.'

Gowda did a double take at the movie-star lookalike standing in front of him. He looked like he belonged on the silver screen rather than this rathole with a dodgy whiteboard. 'I wasn't expecting you until later in the day.'

SI Aqthar smiled. 'I left Dharwad at two in the morning, sir, and was here by 10 a.m. I have relatives at Frazer Town. So I had time to freshen up before reporting for duty, sir.'

Gowda nodded. 'Take a seat, everyone. I think it's time we did a reconnaissance of what we know this far,' he began and paused, looking pointedly at SI Aqthar, who was staring into his phone screen. Aqthar suddenly became aware of the silence that had crept into the room. Everyone was staring at him with different degrees of disbelief: Bloody fool! Is he out of his mind! Aqthar, bro, what are you doing! Why the fuck are you here if you are not interested. Ratna offered a tiny snort of disdain: You won't last too long here, it said.

Aqthar reddened. 'Sir, I was checking the meaning of the word "re-connai-ssance".'

Gowda wanted to kick himself hard. He really ought to stop watching American cop shows.

'Recap. That's what it means...'

He took a marker and wrote on the whiteboard. RECAP.

Then he turned to the team. 'If you have a doubt, a thought, the slightest of hints on a lead, bring it up. Don't hesitate. As you all know, the CCB is also part of the SIT, and that is because this case is quite unlike any other we have worked on.'

Gowda saw Aqthar tap something into his phone. His mouth tightened. Was he actually texting someone in the middle of a briefing? He swallowed his ire and continued, 'We thought it was a natural death at first. But there are two other angles that have emerged. Professor Mudgood, the deceased, had offended certain right-wing Hindu elements. We need to know everything about the Professor's life in Dharwad. And this is why, SI Aqthar, you are here.

'Then there is Iqbal Buqhari, who is seemingly a successful real estate developer. However, he has been hit by the economic slump, like everyone else, and is looking to develop new properties now that the market is picking up. Anyway, a five-acre property in this part of the city is a gold mine. Two obvious reasons. And it's easy for us to assume it's one or the other.'

'What else could it be?' Santosh asked.

'That's for us to find out,' Gowda said. He knew he was doing exactly what DCP Sagayaraj was afraid he would. Sidelining the findings and going off on a wild-goose chase. Gowda turned to the whiteboard and wrote: MOTIVES. Beneath it he wrote:

POLITICAL
REAL ESTATE
X

'We are going to examine the first two motives, but we will also keep our radar open for X. Having said as much, I want you to understand that the CCB is not going to be part of the X line of enquiry till I say so. I expect full discretion from each one of you.' Gowda erased the X carefully.

He then proceeded to bring them up to speed on everything that had happened from the moment the call had been made to the control room. At the end of it, he paused to drink some water. 'For the benefit of SI Aqthar, HC Gajendra and PC Byrappa, this morning we went to the deceased's daughter's home. And that's where it stands,' he finished as the door opened and DCP Sagayaraj and his four-member team entered the room.

Gowda watched the play of emotion on his own officers' faces and felt something shift in the air. A coiling of breath, a tensing of muscle, a quickening of pulse. It occurred to him that it was like college, when the district basketball team was being chosen. Some of the players were familiar faces from district matches but they had never played as part of the same team. And that changed the entire dynamic. Everyone was on guard.

He saw his officers eye the CCB team warily to see how cocky they were; and the CCB trying to gauge just how provincial and clueless the local boys were. He saw their eyes widen at the sight of Ratna. It wasn't that they had never worked with women officers, but perhaps not on a case like this, when their days and nights would merge into the single-minded pursuit of a criminal or a gang of criminals. That was the thing. There was no knowing.

Gowda tried to hide his smile. They didn't know Ratna and how she could hold her own. As if reading his mind, Ratna met his gaze. He knew what she was thinking: Both teams were almost evenly matched in terms of number and designation but the CCB didn't have a woman on theirs. She shook her head ever so slightly.

Byrappa stepped out to bring in a few more chairs. When everyone was seated, DCP Sagayaraj moved to where Gowda had been standing just a few minutes ago. Gowda introduced his team, pausing at Aqthar. 'SI Aqthar is here on deputation from Dharwad. I wanted him to join the team.'

Sagayaraj frowned. 'I have seen you before. Aren't you the off-spinner who took four wickets in the Police Shield Tournament semi-finals last year?'

Aqthar smiled shyly. 'Yes, sir!'

The DCP nodded his head at him. 'Let me introduce you to my team. This is Inspector Natraj. This is SI Papa Nayak, ASI Albert Prakash and Constable Jaishankar.'

Gowda recognized Natraj, who had been especially useful in the serial killer case. He shot him a smile of acknowledgement.

Gowda saw the DCP's gaze dart to the photographs Ratna and Santosh had taped to the wall. He took in what was written on the whiteboard and said, 'I have already briefed my team. We don't need to go over it again right now. What about the CCB?'

Sagayaraj said, 'They have been briefed as well. What's happened to the CCTV footage from the security gate of the gated community? Please hand it over to us. And you can take a look if you want after that.'

Gowda was about to protest but the DCP beat him to it. He said firmly, 'We'll conduct the investigation on two levels. The macro angle, which the CCB will undertake, and the micro angle, by ACP Gowda and his team.'

Gowda looked at his fingernails and took a deep breath. He didn't want to accuse the DCP of pulling rank, but it seemed to him that that was exactly what he was doing. What on earth was this micro level he was supposed to investigate? The number of times Professor Mudgood moved his bowels in a day and where Janaki Buqhari got her pedicures done? When he had managed to swallow his annoyance, he met the DCP's gaze and said, 'Yes, of course. If we are done for now, my team and I would like to do some micro-level investigation.'

Sagayaraj pretended not to hear the taunt and said, 'There's one other thing.'

Gowda clenched his jaw. He waited pointedly for the senior officer to finish.

'The media.'

'Well, sir, I think you are the best person to handle that,' Gowda said.

Gajendra winced and looked at the DCP. Sometimes Gowda forgot that he was now an ACP and his job profile had been expanded to include interaction with the media vultures. The truth was that Gowda was petrified of public speaking.

'Actually, no, Borei. This operation is split into two parts so that the CCB's role in it is off the radar. I don't want any rumours being fuelled by the media. There is too much at stake here. Potential threat of unrest and violence included.'

'Why don't you get rid of them with our standard the-investigation-has-just-begun line?' Gowda said.

Sagayaraj looked stern. 'You are going to handle them. Give them just enough so their reports straddle fact and speculation. We don't want the perpetrator, whether he did it for political reasons or not, getting spooked. We want him thinking that we are clueless so he gets complacent. For me to address the media might get him thinking that we consider it a bigger case than a regular homicide investigation.'

Ratna raised her hand. 'Sir...'

Santosh felt his intestines coil into a tight ball. Was she going to offer to handle the press?

Sagayaraj paused. 'Yes?' he said.

'How do you know it's a he?' Ratna asked.

He leaned back and folded his arms. 'I don't. But "he" is a mere figure of speech.' The DCP drew quotation marks in the air.

Gowda glared at Ratna, who had her face set in a mutinous expression. Being feisty was one thing but being mulish was a sure way to kill your career before it even took off. Ask me and I will tell you all about it, young lady.

'While I handle the press, the CCB team can scoot. If the media asks, I will tell them that the CCB was here for another case,' Gowda butted in before Ratna said something else to upset the DCP even further.

# 9

Gowda briskly ran his fingers through his hair—more bristles than anything else—as if to restore order. Gajendra drew closer to him and murmured, 'You look tiptop, sir.'

Just outside the station, a clutter of media persons had collected. Once, there had been no more than a handful of reporters who diligently took down notes. Now there were television vans and news reporters, stringers for news websites and crime reporters from various publications. All of them had an insatiable monster to feed: the twenty-four-hour news cycle ruled by breaking news.

Microphones were thrust into Gowda's face. He flinched. He had been part of press briefings before but he had never led one. His job was to just stand next to the main speaker with his arms folded and a grimly purposeful look on his face. Now that had changed.

'Sir, how was Professor Mudgood murdered?'

'Was it a political murder?'

'Do you have the list of suspects?'

'Who is leading the SIT?'

Gowda held up his hand to silence the clamour. He cleared his throat, and from the corner of his eye caught DCP Sagayaraj's vehicle driving away. What didn't kill him would only make him stronger, he told himself for the nth time since he had been left with a microphone to hold. 'We received a control room call last morning about Professor Mudgood. He had been found dead at his house by his family. Professor Mudgood lived alone. The initial findings and postmortems revealed that it wasn't a natural death. We are investigating, and at this point we really can't share anything beyond this. Thank you.'

The reporters stared at him and murmured among themselves. He had begun his statement as if he was going to reveal every forensic finding but had then said nothing beyond that.

Gowda walked back to his room, hoping the line of sweat beads on his face wasn't visible. He went into the attached bathroom and looked at himself in the mirror. Thus begins your life as a master of duplicity, he told his reflection. Then he washed his face and patted it dry with the hand towel. He took the body mist which Urmila had given him and sprayed himself. In the mirror, the Gowda who stared at him looked as if nothing would faze him.

DCP Vidyaprasad stared at the fresh-faced and fragrant Gowda. 'I say, Gowda, what's this I hear about a press briefing? You can't call one without following the protocol!'

As Vidyaprasad launched into a tirade on officers who didn't know their place it occurred to Gowda that the man resembled a baboon trying to reinstate himself as the alpha male in the troop. His long canine teeth were on display. Gowda waited for the loud 'wahoo' bark but instead DCP Vidyaprasad hmmphed, unable to still his fury.

Gowda looked at him without reacting. You didn't engage with a baboon. Period.

A moment later, he said carefully in his most patient tone, 'I was merely following DCP Sagayaraj's orders, and it wasn't a press briefing. We just needed to get rid of the media people who had come here to sniff out a story.'

The morning had been a disaster for DCP Vidyaprasad from the time he had woken up. He had heard about the new developments on the Professor Mudgood case from his Mole No. 1 at Neelgubbi station. Zahir had woken him with a series of persistent calls. The station writer had told him what he heard on the station grapevine. 'The CCB is coming in on this case, sir. I just wanted you to know.'

Vidyaprasad had felt a tight ball of fury lodge just above his diaphragm. He had snapped at his orderly, kicked the dog and barked at his teenage daughter. Most days he wanted to wring Gowda's neck but this time he wanted to wring DCP Sagayaraj's as well. Those two were in cahoots, and he didn't like being left out. His Mole No. 2 had told him that there was trouble at the Professor's residence, where he had made his way, only to have a rowdy activist fling an egg on him. He thought the day couldn't get any worse. But then he had walked into the Neelgubbi station only to discover that Gowda had been speaking to the media. Gowda was getting too big for his boots. He needed to be pulled down a few notches.

'Sir,' DCP Vidyaprasad snapped.

'I don't understand,' Gowda said, opening his eyes wide.

'You have to address me as "sir",' the DCP snarled. 'You may be an ACP now but I am your superior officer.'

'Yes, of course, sir. Like I said, sir, it was just a tactic, sir, to get rid of the media, sir.' Gowda stressed the word 'sir' each time he mouthed it.

DCP Vidyaprasad scowled at Gowda. 'Next time let me know first. The media are our friends and we must maintain a close and cordial relationship with them. There is a knack in how to handle them. It's not for everyone. Unless you have been trained at the National Police Academy, Hyderabad... we are taught many things there unlike the state police academies.'

Gowda wondered if it was against the police code of behaviour to box a senior officer's ears. It probably was, he decided, and he put on his most attentive expression and asked, 'Speaking of Hyderabad, have you eaten the haleem at Paradise restaurant? Oh, I forgot, you are a strict vegetarian. I can't even imagine how you felt when the egg broke on your head.' Gowda made whickering noises to suggest heartfelt pity.

He saw the DCP's face redden and a pulse begin to throb at his carefully coiffured temple. A little nerve that popped up and down. Gowda decided that he ought to stop messing around with the baboon and shut up. He didn't want the man having a stroke.

Gowda stared into the middle distance as DCP Vidyaprasad burst into a torrent of recriminations. He wondered if the crack on the wall behind the DCP was a horse or a dinosaur. By the time he had decided that it was the Eiffel Tower, the DCP had run out of breath and words.

Gowda waited for Vidyaprasad to reach for the glass of water on the table and then said, 'We have some developments in the Professor Mudgood case.'

Vidyaprasad frowned. 'Why didn't you say so before? I thought you told the press that we have no suspects.'

'DCP Sagayaraj instructed me to say so,' Gowda said, careful to hide his glee.

'Oh well... tell me what we know.'

'Sir, I suggest, sir, that we, sir, go to the SIT room.' One last time, he promised himself, and added, 'Sir.'

# 10

The old man glanced at the clock again. It was almost 3 p.m., and none of them had come home yet. His daughter-in-law and her noisy family had gone to visit a friend and had promised to be home by 2 p.m.

Borei had said he would pick him up. But Chidananda Gowda knew his son well enough to know that in all probability, it wouldn't happen. So he had gone ahead and booked himself a cab. He wanted both his sons to realize that he wasn't a doddering old fool as they thought he was. He glanced at the clock again.

The sight of the taxi driver sitting in the car and laughing into his phone added to his irritation. The idiot had been told to arrive at 3 p.m. and he had got here half an hour early. What was it with people? No one understood the meaning of punctuality, he mumbled to himself. Either they were late or too early.

From the window, he could see the gate with the two coconut trees that stood like guardsmen on either side, one for each son. The right one for Nagendra and the left one for Borei. He had planted the saplings on the advice of an elderly relative. 'They will serve as a reminder that your sons are no longer your little boys. You have to understand that one day they will be grown-up men. Taller than you, perhaps, and with minds of their own.'

The only problem was that he wasn't entirely sure if he could ever stop being a parent. And Borei worried him. His wife and son lived away in Hassan. Strangely, Borei seemed to be least perturbed about living alone. When his wife died, Chidananda Gowda had felt as if someone had chopped his limbs away. But Borei seemed perfectly happy on his own. It was time he did some investigation of his own, the senior Gowda decided.

His older daughter-in-law's sister and family who were visiting had provided him with a cast-iron excuse to visit Borei. But he had dithered until last evening, when he decided he couldn't take any more of watching his daughter-in-law's sister wipe all the counter surfaces every half hour, and her husband and teenage children fight over the remote. He couldn't even read his newspaper in peace. His daughter-in-law wore the expression of someone thrown into a room full of lunatics, and he couldn't bear to see her helpless rage, either.

Chidananda decided he had waited enough. He stood up and took his hold-all. He waited until the clock struck the hour. When the chimes had retreated into silence, he stepped out of the house and latched the door shut.

The driver was a young man, perhaps only as old as his grandson Roshan, but he had a string of jasmine buds encircling the little Ganesha on the dashboard. And that had reassured Chidananda to some extent. No God-fearing man could be a reckless driver.

At first Chidananda thought the driver was talking to him, until he saw the earphones and realized he was on the phone. He sighed. It was the same everywhere. People seemed to prefer speaking to disembodied voices rather than the person sitting beside them.

When the cab paused at a signal near Lal Bagh, he turned to the driver and said, 'My son is an Assistant Commissioner of Police.'

The driver darted a look at him, as if he had said his son had an extra head. A look that said: And how does that matter to me?

Chidananda frowned. Bloody fool, he thought. Then, watching the driver mutter into the speaker of the headphones, he touched the driver's shoulder and said, 'Stop talking on the phone and pay attention to how you drive. My son will have your skin hanging from the clothesline if something happens to me.'

The young man snorted but cut the call and didn't make any more for the rest of the ride. Chidananda told the driver about his kidney stones, of his memories of the old Bangalore, and how road rage was the direct consequence of listening to music that sounded like someone was pounding areca nuts in a mortar. 'Listen to a Kanakadasa-krithi or even a bhavageetha and see how it relaxes you.'

By the time the cab turned into the road that led to Green Park Housing Colony, the driver felt a huge wave of sympathy for the policeman who was going to have to endure this garrulous old man for 'a week, ten days, a month, probably the rest of my life', as he had been informed.

# 11

It was a little past six when the official vehicle pulled up outside Gowda's gate. Music was playing from upstairs. Akaashe Neeliyadalle. Bhavageethe. It was his father's particular favourite. Gowda's eyebrow rose. His father was going to be ecstatic when he discovered the tenants liked his kind of music.

He opened his door and entered, switching on the lights as he went in. He took his shirt off and, still in his vest, he lit a cigarette. When the bell rang, he frowned. He opened the door with the cigarette in his hand and found Chidananda on the verandah. He saw his father's expression change from a beaming smile to a frown.

'When did you start smoking?' he snapped.

'How did you get here?' Gowda asked, hiding the cigarette behind his back. Why was he behaving like a four-year-old caught with his hand in the candy jar? Gowda thought, utterly disgusted at himself.

Gowda walked towards the coffee table, on which was a glass ashtray. Urmila had given it to him. It apparently came from a ship that had once sailed the Indian Ocean.

'At least the ashtray has seen more places than you,' she had said when Gowda baulked at the thought of international travel. He stubbed the cigarette in the well-travelled ashtray. 'As if you don't know I smoke,' he muttered. Chidananda pretended not to have heard.

'I took a cab. I knew that if I waited for you, it could be tomorrow, the day after... God knows when. You are such a busy man these days.'

Gowda ignored the barely veiled complaint and instead looked over his father's shoulder. 'I didn't hear the car.'

'My hold-all is hidden behind the chair outside. Would you bring it in?' Chidananda walked into the house.

Hold-all, Gowda cursed under his breath as he drew the bag out of its hiding place. Why couldn't he call a suitcase a suitcase?

Chidananda was frowning when Gowda walked back into the room with the suitcase. 'When did you get a tattoo?' he asked, looking at the wheel with wings inked on Gowda's forearm.

Gowda shrugged. 'A long time ago.' He looked at his father and asked, 'Did you just get here, Appa?'

'I got here more than an hour ago. Your tenant took me upstairs, gave me coffee and murukku. Very nice girl. So talented too. She paints replicas of Ravi Varma paintings. There is a huge market for them, she says.' Chidananda beamed.

Gowda frowned. He didn't like it when tenants got over-familiar. He gave himself a mental shake. Stop this paranoia, this inability to accept a kind gesture for what it is. Gowda had always let himself off the hook by telling himself that it was an occupational hazard of being a policeman, the fact that suspicion dogged your every step and thought.

'Would you like some coffee?' he asked, not knowing what else to offer his father.

'I told you that I just had coffee. A second cup at this time will aggravate my acidity. And I will have to endure heartburn all night. What I need to do now is my evening puja. Do you even have a puja room? I have forgotten. It's been so long since I came here,' Chidananda said as he followed his son to the guest room.

Gowda hoped Shanthi had remembered to clean the lamps and the other puja paraphernalia in the little cupboard that constituted the puja room. Or there would be another lecture on how godlessness had led the world to what it had become—a cruel, corrupt, lawless hell—and that Gowda was on his way to becoming its team leader.

*

Shanthi had done him proud. The guest bedroom was squeaky clean and the bed had been made with fresh sheets. A brown-and-red-checked blanket draped the foot of the bed. On the bedside table was a bottle of water and a glass, and for some reason she had borrowed the desk lamp from Roshan's room and set it up on the table by the window. There was a bunch of roses in a vase on the table. Gowda blinked in surprise, wondering where those had come from.

Gowda placed the suitcase on a low stool near the wardrobe. 'I am in the living room, Appa,' Gowda said.

'What's the living room? Don't you live in the other rooms?'

'Hall room, Appa,' Gowda said, trying not to grit his teeth. 'Call me if you need anything.'

'I am not your guest. I am your father and I know my way around your home,' he said.

Gowda turned on his heel and went to move his much-travelled ashtray to his bedroom. He was going to lie down on his bed and finish his much-deserved smoke. He had just lit his cigarette when the doorbell rang. Gowda stared at the ashtray with disgust and asked it, 'Is this why you were kicked off the ship?'

He stubbed the cigarette and left it in the ashtray. Stay, he told it, as if it were a boisterous dog inclined to jump out and follow him. He pulled on a shirt hastily and lumbered to the main door to find his father had already opened it. It was Ratna. Gowda's heart sank. His father would now lecture him on how inappropriate it was for a young woman to visit him after the sun had set. Then, over Chidananda's shoulder, he saw Santosh, and smiled at him with the warmth of relief.

'Appa, they are here to see me,' Gowda murmured.

He saw Chidananda give them a close look, as if to ascertain they were not villainous door-to-door salespeople pretending to sell blankets, plastic containers and roti-makers.

'This is my father, Chidananda Gowda, and this is ASI Ratna and SI Santosh,' Gowda said, hoping his father would take the hint and go back to whatever he was doing.

Santosh rushed to take the old man's hands in his. 'What an honour it is to meet you, sir!' he gushed. 'I have heard so much about you from ACP Sir.'

Gowda didn't think he had ever mentioned his father to Santosh or any of his colleagues; nevertheless, he was pleased to see his father preen, and something tugged at his throat. How little it took to delight a parent after a certain age! And how seldom we give them what they need—instead we ply them with medicine, health drinks, woollen vests and temple visits, when all they need is to know they are still relevant to our lives.

Gowda pulled himself together and said, 'Appa, we won't disturb you. We will sit in the verandah.'

Chidananda shook his head as he moved from the doorway.

'No need. I will finish my puja and meditation. You don't need to sit in the verandah and get chewed by the mosquitoes. What do you feed them? Horlicks? I have never seen such enormous ones...'

Ratna giggled. 'Sir, you should see the ones in the station... they are twice as big.'

Chidananda smiled at her and left the room. Then he came back with a bottle of water and three glasses. Gowda blushed but said nothing. He knew that in his father's worldview, a man in a home without a woman was as helpless as a one-handed man hanging from a cliff and wanting to scratch his balls. This was Chidananda's way of making his point. He saw that Ratna and Santosh were embarrassed too. When his father left the room, Gowda turned to Santosh and said, 'Thank you.'

Ratna darted a glance at Gowda. She had thought he would snap Santosh's head off for being such a prat.

Santosh smiled. 'I know how happy it makes my father when my brother's colleagues mention that Nagendra had praised him. That's all, sir.'

Ratna examined her fingernails, while Gowda poured himself some water. He took a sip and said, 'So tell me, what brings the two of you here?'

# 12

As always, Providence Hospital was bustling with people. Every patient seeking medical help was accompanied by two or three people. The MD had liked it at first. The hustle and bustle made it seem like a busy hospital, one that patients sought. It encouraged new patients to come in.

But Dr Tehrani wasn't sure anymore. 'This looks like a fairground,' he muttered to his wife, Dr Zohra Tehrani. 'We need to do something about this,' he said as two shrieking children ran around a row of chairs.

Dr Zohra shook her head. 'Best to leave it as it is. You know how Iqbal gets if you ask him for administrative changes,' she said.

Dr Tehrani grimaced. 'I wish I hadn't agreed when he offered us this hospital to run. We are no better than hired help here.'

Farhad Tehrani, an Iranian doctor, and Zohra had met while they were medical students at Manipal. After they got married, Farhad had stayed on in India, and Iqbal Buqhari, his brother-in-law, had played big brother and set up this hospital for them.

It was technically their hospital but Iqbal held the strings that decided how they should run it. Farhad knew there was nothing much he could do. Besides, all that was asked of him was to turn a blind eye to some of the goings-on at the hospital. He ran his hand along the bonnet of his new Audi A6. The truth was that the conscience didn't prick too hard when the best of German engineering ferried it around.

Ratna and Santosh walked straight into the casualty area. They had chosen to be in mufti. Gowda had been very clear about the need for discretion while following any leads pertaining to the case.

Amidst all the comings and goings, no one gave a second look to the young couple with a rather determined step entering the hospital. It was a few minutes past 4 p.m. and a woman walked past them with a tray of plastic beakers. Tea.

The casualty nurse who had the night shift on 28 November was taking her tea break. She looked up from her teacup with a frown. Ratna put her arms on the counter and leaned forward. 'We are from the police.'

The young woman sat up straight. 'Yes, ma'am,' she said, placing her half-full cup down abruptly, inadvertently splashing a few drops on the surface of the table. Ratna gave her a brief smile. She realized the woman was nervous. The mention of police unnerved most people. She had been the same until she had become a policewoman herself. As for the uniform, it lent a make-believe sense of authority—as if it would brook no sense or logic, or know pity and shame. 'Is Dr Gireesh in?' she asked in her softest tone.

The nurse gestured to a tiny cubicle at the end of the ward. A man in a white coat with a stethoscope peeking out of his pocket sat on the edge of a table, scrolling on his phone.

'We are in the middle of an investigation and we need to see the list of patients admitted here on the night of 28 November,' Santosh said before Ratna could speak. Ratna frowned.

The nurse pulled out a register. 'Is this the accident case? The head injury...' she asked, flipping the pages backwards.

'That and another case,' Santosh said, taking the register. He found the relevant page and started reading. Then he looked up, puzzled. There was no mention of Janaki Buqhari. Ratna caught his glance and turned to the nurse with a smile. 'I haven't seen you before. Are you new?'

'Yes, I joined just ten days ago.'

'You must be a very experienced nurse,' Ratna said. 'Dr Zohra is very careful about whom she posts at the casualty ward.'

The nurse's face lit up. She touched the strap of her watch in an unconscious gesture. 'Six years, madam, I was at a hospital on Coles Road. Do you know Dr Zohra?'

'Yes, of course.' Ratna's reply was a half-truth. Yes, Aswathamma is dead. Aswathamma the elephant. 'In fact, I think I saw the two of you here on 28 November, Wednesday night, and Dr Zohra's sister-in-law too.'

'Oh yes, she brought her maid here. The woman came with an alleged snakebite. You should have seen the scene she made. It was as if a king cobra had bitten her.'

Santosh looked at the register again. There it was, case no. 36.

Name of the patient: Mary Susheela

Age: 35 years

Time of admission: 10.10 p.m.

Santosh took a picture of the case notes. On a whim, he also clicked some of the pages before and after.

The nurse frowned, not sure if he had the authority to do so.

'And was it a king cobra?' Ratna asked.

The nurse shook her head. 'It wasn't a snakebite, whatever it was.'

Santosh saw Dr Gireesh approach them. He walked towards him, holding out his hand. 'I am SI Santosh from the Neelgubbi station,' he said.

The doctor nodded. 'Any problem, sir?'

'There has been an attempted dacoity, and the robbers escaped and crashed the car. So we are looking at casualty patients in hospitals and nursing homes in the area,' Santosh said. 'And Sister here was telling us of a snakebite case that wasn't a snakebite.'

'Oh, that one.' The doctor smiled. 'It was the most curious thing. The skin was punctured and there were tooth marks that seemed more human than an animal or snake. In the end, we gave her a tetanus shot, an anti-rabies shot, and when her husband demanded we send her home, we had to let her go. I gave her a prescription of sedatives to calm her down.'

'Oh, I see,' Santosh said.

'Did you find what you came for?' the nurse asked.

They were interrupted by the door to the casualty ward being flung open, and a stretcher being brought in with a boy bleeding from his abdomen. The doctor and the casualty nurse rushed towards him.

'We came straight from the hospital to you, sir,' Ratna said.

'Good job, you two,' Gowda said. Then he looked at Santosh. 'WhatsApp me the pics of the case notes you took.'

Santosh sent him the page, and on a whim decided to add the photographs he had taken of the hospital register.

'Let's meet at 7 a.m. tomorrow,' Gowda said. 'I want you two to get a good night's sleep. There are too many loose ends to this case, and I want to tie them up first.' He stood up.

'Why do you say that?' Ratna asked. Santosh sighed. Ratna knew as well as him that Gowda's king sense always saw a pattern emerge from what appeared to everyone else as a jumble of loose ends and jagged edges.

Gowda shrugged. 'Nothing is what it seems.'

Santosh followed Gowda to the door, hoping that Ratna would take the hint. 'Goodnight, sir,' he said emphatically.

# 13

As Gowda walked past the guest room, he saw his father sitting on the bed, staring blankly at the window on the opposite wall. Gowda wondered what he was looking at so intently. The only thing beyond the compound wall on that side was a row of empty and overgrown plots. A line of tall silver oaks separated each plot of land from the next. Some nights Urmila and he would lean against the headboard and watch the tops of the trees wave at the full moon.

But it was overcast tonight. He went into the room and noticed his father was now looking at the curtains. 'What are you doing, Appa?' he asked.

Chidananda turned. 'Nothing.'

'Why didn't you come to the hall?'

'I didn't want to disturb you,' he said. Gowda tugged at the curtain and opened the window. A gentle breeze wafted in. Chidananda shivered and pulled his shawl closer around his shoulders.

Gowda saw his father as though he was seeing him for the first time. When had he become this frail? His years had always sat lightly on him, but his cheeks were sunken now, and the bones on his shoulders were visible through his parchment-like skin. Where had all the flesh melted away? Gowda wanted to wrap his arms around Chidananda's shoulders and hide him from Yama's noose. But he knew that the God of Death was a cat burglar with oiled skin. He would enter by stealth so no one knew that death had come and gone, taking what he sought. Gowda swore to himself that he would rein in his irritability and be his best self with his father. The days with him were precious and he wanted each one to count.

Gowda went back to the hall and switched the TV on. 'Why don't you come here, Appa?'

When Chidananda had been seated in a comfortable chair and his favourite TV channel found, Gowda brought his laptop and sat down in another chair. His father looked at him. 'I see you have a laptop now. Do you know how to use it?'

He wanted to retort, 'Why would I have one if I didn't know how to?' But his resolution to not snap at his father held good. Gowda nodded. Chidananda shot him a disbelieving look but didn't say anything. Gowda looked at the screen. What had he opened this damn thing for?

He messaged Santosh to email him the reports. He would read them on the large screen again and see if that prickling at the back of his neck at the first cursory read occurred again. In two minutes, his mailbox lit up. Gowda put on his reading glasses.

> Mrs Mary Susheela, 35/F, was brought to casualty at 10.10 p.m. with alleged H/O snakebite at about 9.45 p.m. on 28.11.2013 while doing household work.
> Informant: Mrs Janaki
> Relation to patient: Employer
> O/E: PT: Conscious, alert, oriented
> B/P: 140/90 mmgh
> PR: 92/min
> Regular V&T good CVS: NAD CMS: NAD
> Local examination: Bite mark seen 2 cm above lateral malleolus of L ankle; no active bleeding or ooze. No discolouration. No local reaction or swelling.

He scrolled down to read the discharge summary.

> Patient was discharged at 8 a.m. against medical advice and taken home by husband Mr Paul Selvam.
> Hospital stay uneventful.

Everything seemed above board, though Gowda decided to speak to the doctor himself. This hasty hospital visit probably explained why the back door had been left unlatched. But why had it all happened the same night? Was it a mere coincidence? Why hadn't Janaki mentioned it? She had merely said her maid had been away, as if she knew nothing about what was wrong with her.

Gowda decided to park his speculations about the maid episode and began reading Professor Mudgood's articles. He had just started on the third one when he raised his head and saw Chidananda staring at him. Gowda realized he had been muttering under his breath. He sat up straight involuntarily. His father had once threatened to tie a ruler to his back when he was a teenager if he ever caught him slouching. 'You are going to be a tall man, and you have to make the choice now. Are you going to be a man who stands straight? Or one with a permanent stoop and apologetic expression?'

'I didn't realize you use reading glasses.' Chidananda sounded surprised.

Gowda grinned. 'I'm fifty-one years old, Appa. I have been using them for eight years now.'

He saw Chidananda's gaze go to the clock on the wall. It was a quarter past eight. Gowda groaned inwardly. He had forgotten that his father ate early. 'I'll get dinner ready,' he said, shoving his glasses back into his pocket and walking towards the kitchen.

Gowda put the Tupperware boxes into the microwave one by one. As he laid out plates and glasses of water, he hoped his father was ravenous. Shanthi had cooked enough to feed him for a month. However, Chidananda wouldn't touch a morsel of food that had been cooked the previous day. He would have to explain this to Shanthi.

Chidananda's previous visits had coincided with Mamtha's, and she had taken over the kitchen's reins even before unpacking. This was the first time his father was staying over when Gowda was on his own, and he wasn't quite sure how to go about things. 'Appa, the food is ready,' he said, going to the hall where his father was watching a show called *Beastly Foods*.

'Five minutes more,' Chidananda said, his eyes glued to the screen in morbid fascination. Considering he thought even beef unclean, Gowda wondered at what was making him watch a ponytailed young man with several piercings crunch on fried grasshoppers.

'The food will go cold, Appa,' Gowda said, thinking of how Mamtha would once tell seven-year-old Roshan the same.

Gowda shook his head in bemusement and went to the dining table. His father followed him and lifted the covers off the boxes on the table. 'Did you make all this?'

Gowda laughed. 'Shanthi did. If you relied on my cooking, it would be rice, rasam and egg bhurji.'

Chidananda was not given to showing much emotion. But when he had had his last mouthful, he said, 'I can see why you don't miss having your wife around.'

'A wife is not just a cook,' Gowda began and stopped.

'I have to set out my night-time medicines.' Chidananda stood up.

Gowda watched him leave, and with some relief served himself all the food he wanted. He didn't know why he couldn't savour a meal unless he ate alone. Or at a crowded table like at a wedding feast where everyone was intent on shovelling food into their mouths rather than making conversation.

Urmila despaired of him and his inability to converse while eating. 'I might as well prop a book up and read it while we eat,' she had said once.

'You should,' he had retorted.

'Doesn't your wife ever complain?' she had asked, surprising him. Urmila took great pains to never mention Mamtha.

'She makes a plate and sits in front of the TV,' Gowda said. 'There is no question of conversation ever.'

'And Roshan?'

'He takes a plate to his room,' Gowda had said, shredding a lettuce leaf into ribbons of green.

Gowda meticulously licked each finger one by one. The joy of eating alone was you didn't have to tread carefully around the landmines called table manners. You could burp and belch, lick your fingers and pick your teeth, no holds barred, and not worry about what others at the table would think or say.

Gowda put the rava laddoos on a ceramic plate and took it

into the living room. 'Dessert on porcelain and not steel, Borei,' Urmila had taught him.

His father had laid out rows of pills in different colours and shapes.

'Why do you need so many medicines?' Gowda's eyes narrowed. How ill was Chidananda?

'This one is for digestion.' Chidananda pointed to a round white pill. 'This blue one is my blood-thinner and this one is for cholesterol. The capsule is for my knee pain and this mustard-like one is for sleep.'

Gowda had a sinking feeling. Was this what lay ahead? Watching *Beastly Foods* and popping pills like candy? Were his sunset years going to dwindle into the same?

'Are you sure you should eat the sweet then?' Gowda asked.

'Who says I can't.' His father's voice rose at the thought of being denied dessert. 'I am not diabetic.'

That was the other thing. Old age seemed to have opened up a hitherto sealed vault in his father's system: his appetite. Or was it greed? Gowda was going to have to speak to Nagendra and find out more about Appa's state of health. He was disgusted with himself for being such a distant son.

'Priorities, priorities, Borei,' Urmila hissed in his ear.

He hadn't yet let her know that he had new tenants and that his father was with him, and that she couldn't pop in whenever she felt like it. He knew Urmila would be upset, and that it was going to raise all the ghosts he had managed to stake. Which was why it was best conveyed in person. The thought of how much it would hurt her bothered him, but he didn't know what else to do. For a moment, a distant school lesson resurfaced.

Gowda as Sisyphus trying to push a composite rock called his life up a hill. One part always gave way and rolled back. Urmila. His father. Mamtha. Roshan. The cold cases that waited at the back of his conscience. And now Professor Mudgood's homicide.

Where did a man begin? And how was he to make the rock stay at the top of the hill and not hurtle down?

Gowda sat down, overwhelmed. For now, there was nothing to do but follow his father's lead and eat a laddoo.

# 14

Ratna told Santosh once they were back at the station, 'I think we should pay Mary Susheela a visit.'

'Shall we go now?' Santosh asked.

'It's late. I thought we could do it tomorrow.' Ratna was shocked. Santosh wasn't exactly given to impetuosity.

'I think we should go now. I remember Gowda Sir saying it's best to interview the immediate family as quickly as possible. After a few days, they either embellish or hide details. In some cases, they forget too.' Santosh rose from his chair. 'Give me a moment. I'll change my uniform shirt to something else. I don't want neighbours speculating about Mary Susheela.'

Ratna smiled. This was the Santosh who made her heart flutter once in a rare while. The kind, sensitive police officer.

'Do you know where in Neelgubbi Colony the house is?' Ratna asked.

Santosh nodded. 'I have a house number.'

Ratna got off the bike and looked around. It felt as if she had suddenly entered rural Karnataka. Fields. Tiled houses. A tractor with a tiller attached. Two donkeys tethered to a stake in the ground. A cold wind rushed through the fields and trees. Ratna shivered. Santosh saw her wrap her arms around herself. 'Are you cold? Do you want my jacket?'

Ratna shook her head.

Santosh blushed. Ratna wished she hadn't refused his offer. To fill the silence that had crept in, she spoke quickly, 'So the sante market that Gajendra mentioned starts from this point and goes down the road for almost half a kilometre.'

Santosh didn't speak, eyeing the stretch with dismay as he parked his bike near a hardware store. How were they to get a fix on who the regulars were and who had come in just for the Wednesday market on 28 November? It was going to be a lot of legwork but it had to be done. He should know better than to mooch around, he told himself.

'Let's go,' Santosh said, walking towards the settlement.

Neelgubbi Colony was a little maze spread around an old Shiva temple covered in scaffolding. Slabs of granite lay around it and near the giant banyan tree. A couple of vans were parked alongside an autorickshaw. Even though it was almost eight in the evening, there were people bustling around the temple.

'Have you observed this sudden trend to restore old but perfect temples into something enormous and garish?' Santosh muttered under his breath.

'I was thinking the same,' Ratna murmured.

Santosh smiled at her. 'Let me ask for directions at the bakery.'

'No, no...' She touched his elbow. It stopped him in his tracks as if he had touched a live wire. 'Don't. I will ask at one of the houses. It's better that way.'

Santosh nodded and walked ahead.

Ratna had knocked on a door that was already open. A woman, possibly in her twenties, with a baby perched on her hip, came from an inner room. Ratna smiled at her and said, 'Could you tell me where Mary Susheela lives? Her house number is thirty-four.'

The woman frowned. 'Why?'

Ratna knew the villagers were clannish. Gajendra had already warned her. 'It's difficult to get a word out of them about a neighbour. It doesn't matter whether they are Hindu or Christian, everyone has the other's back. Why do you think those loafers get away with all the illegal activities?'

Ratna touched the snotty baby's cheek first. Then she put on a worried expression. 'Is Mary Akka all right? I wanted to check if she is fine. I heard she was admitted to the hospital.'

The woman pushed the baby higher on her hip and appraised Ratna carefully. Then, as if satisfied, she said, 'She is better. Turn left after the barber shop... after about ten houses you will see a plastic tray on a low wall. Her house is beyond the wall. The third house.'

She stood there, watching Ratna walk away. Santosh moved away from the shadowed side of the road and joined Ratna. 'She is calling Mary Susheela, I think. I can see her speaking on her phone,' he said under his breath.

The street was narrow and the houses squat and small. Clothes dried on wires strung up between walls jostled against potted plants. A water tanker stood parked by the side, taking up most of the road. A scruffy spitz ran busily ahead, and two young men sat on a parked bike, looking at a mobile screen. A toddler in a frilly yellow net dress that made her look like a chrysanthemum stood with her finger up her nose, watching a baby goat tethered to a rope, grabbing at leaves hanging from a hook on the wall. An old couple bundled in blankets sat leaning against the wall. Snatches of conversation and theme music from TV soaps escaped the doors, all of which were wide open so no one inside would miss any of the goings-on in the street. Everyone looked at the two police officers in plain clothes as they passed.

Ratna turned to Santosh. 'I feel like I've stepped back in time. It's hard to believe this is a part of the same city we live in.'

Santosh smiled. 'They don't think they are part of Bangalore either. When they go into the city, they refer to it as Bengaluru.'

'What language are they speaking? It isn't Kannada. Do you know it?'

Santosh nodded. 'Tegulu, it is a dialect that mixes Tamil and Telugu.'

'I've never ever heard of it.'

'I didn't know about it either. Gajendra Sir told me about it. He says that's one thing that binds them together.'

Ratna shook her head in amazement. 'You read about places like this, with its own unique dialect. Maybe customs too. And secrets perhaps.'

Santosh shoved his hands into his pockets. 'Not all that unique. There are some other pockets too in Bangalore where Tegulu is spoken.'

'Who do these people vote for? What's their political leaning?' Ratna asked. They crossed two temples that seemed to be part of a house.

Santosh snorted. 'Papanna is their man. He is one of them. No matter what anyone else has tried to do to swing the vote their way, they have failed. On polling day, the entire population of the area turns up, every single one of them who has a vote, to keep him in power.'

New Star Hair Dressers was at a corner that curved into a narrow lane. The plastic tray the woman with the baby had mentioned was a broken shower tray rescued from God knows where. It sat on a low wall overrun with creepers. The tray had turned into a planter, with marigolds growing in it. The road curved into a narrow, darkened alley. The third house was set back from the dirt road and was surrounded by several trees. A naked bulb hung from a wire, casting a pool of light from the broken gate to the doorway. An enormous dog on a chain barked as they approached.

A short burly man wearing thick soda-bottle glasses came to open the door. Santosh stepped forward. The man looked at him and said, 'I suppose you are from the police department, and it is about the old man's death.'

Santosh asked, 'Are you Paul Selvam?'

He nodded.

'ASI Ratna and I need to talk to Mary Susheela.'

'She is my wife,' the man said. 'Come in.'

They followed him into the front room which held two plastic chairs, a padded bench, a double-seater couch draped with a bedsheet, and an old woman wrapped in a blanket sitting on a camp cot. A flat-screen TV was mounted on a wall from which an evangelist preached in the cadence unique to evangelists everywhere. Paul looked for the remote, and not finding it, turned the main switch off. The old woman crumpled onto the bed and pulled the blanket over her head.

'Please sit down,' he said, gesturing to the couch. 'I will call her.'

Santosh and Ratna opted for the plastic chairs. A middle-aged woman in a bright blue maxi dress with white frills and flounces on the bib limped into the room. She wore chunky gold earrings and what seemed like a dog chain in gold around her thick neck. Her hair was pulled back into a knot and a patina of talcum powder covered her face. She saw Santosh and Ratna and almost on cue began wailing. 'He was tiptop even on the night I was bitten.'

Ratna nodded, pretending a sympathy she didn't feel for this loud woman. Then she looked at her ankle pointedly and asked, 'You are limping... what happened?'

'I got bitten by a snake,' Mary Susheela began.

'We don't know that,' the husband interrupted. 'For all you know it could be that mad old man.'

Mary Susheela snorted. 'He is eighty-two and not eight to crouch at my feet and nip at my ankle.'

'Why do you say that, sir?' Ratna asked, turning to an irate Paul. 'Professor Mudgood was a highly regarded scholar and a very respected man.'

Santosh watched Ratna in admiration as she threw him the bait.

'Highly regarded scholar, huh?' Paul snorted, taking his glasses off and polishing the lenses on his shirt.

'Don't you think so?' Ratna started reeling in the line.

'Tell them, Mary... tell them how he used to trouble you. He would demand she make him hot water at two in the morning, refusing to keep a flask near him. But that's all right. What was unbearable was how this great Professor couldn't keep his hands off my Mary. He'd use his stick to pull off the dupatta Mary wore over her maxi and say, "What are you hiding? Let me see." Then there were the massages he demanded she give him. Mary used to work at a hospital so she is used to cleaning up any mess. My Mary never complained about that but this... This was not right.'

Paul paused, unable to speak further. 'What did he do to Mary?' Ratna asked.

'He would take all his clothes off except for his kaacha and ask me to massage oil into his skin. I didn't mind the head and shoulders, the arms and legs, but he insisted I touch him around there as well.' Mary gestured to her groin.

'Bloody pervert,' the husband growled. 'But I put an end to it. I got Mary a waistcoat to wear over her maxi and I said no more massages. I talked to Iqbal Sir about it. You should have seen his expression. He was disgusted.'

'Oh, I see.' Santosh joined in. 'How do you know Iqbal Buqhari?'

'I used to work for his company as a painter. Then I had an accident and couldn't climb ladders anymore. So when Janaki Madam offered this job to Mary, I encouraged her to take it up. I wish I hadn't.'

'It was very good money, and we have children in school. I got a day off every Sunday and it was close to home.' Mary sighed. Then, as if unable to contain the simmering resentment, she erupted. 'So I would ignore his constant cribbing about food and coffee. It wasn't just me. He would pick quarrels even with Janaki Madam and say the most horrible things to her. He fought with everyone. The cab drivers, the odd-job man... my mister used to come there but he refused to go anymore after the Professor accused him of spying on him for Deva Sir.'

Before Mary could finish, Paul interrupted her. 'It's been two months since I saw that dirty old man. I told my Mary that I won't ever come there again.'

Mary wiped her tears. 'That afternoon Gurunath also left after a quarrel.'

'His assistant Gurunath? What sort of a man was he? Did the Professor have several guests?'

Mary snorted. Both husband and wife snorted a great deal, Santosh thought. He wondered if it was a local affectation. David did that with great effect too.

'Gurunath was just fine. He cooked his own food. He was a strict vegetarian who didn't approve of the Professor who liked his eggs and ate one every day. But there were other guests too. Quite a few. Old men, young men and women—they all trooped in and out as if it was a church and the old man a bishop. Not that they stayed long. Usually these visits ended with an argument of some sort. But Gurunath Sir was very patient. He was the old man's PA or some such thing, and the only one who could stomach his madness. And me...' Mary snorted again.

'If you ask me, sir, it is good riddance to bad rubbish,' Paul said as Santosh and Ratna rose to go.

'I will come with you to your vehicle. The village people are not especially fond of police who come snooping around,' Paul said, untying the chain and using it as a leash to lead the dog.

Ratna strode ahead. Santosh looked nervously at the dog, which appeared to be a Rottweiler. 'Does it have a name?'

'Rocky,' Paul told him.

# 2 DECEMBER 2012, SUNDAY

## 1

Gowda woke up with a start. He had heard a movement outside his room. His heart stilled, as he instantly remembered the time he had been ambushed right outside his door. He had been returning late in the evening on his bike when an SUV had emerged from the shadows and run him off the road into a ditch. Before he could get back on his feet, three men had descended on him. They left him with a broken nose, two bruised ribs and a concussion. The bike headlight was smashed as well. Until this incident, Gowda hadn't even considered his life could be threatened by the criminals he was working to put away. But ever since, he had been twice as cautious. When he heard shuffling feet and dishes rattling in the kitchen, Gowda lay back on the pillow with a relieved smile. It was Chidananda rummaging around, putting on some water for coffee perhaps. The clock struck a quarter to five. Gowda groaned and rose from the bed. He padded into the kitchen where his father stood in front of the hob, puzzled.

'Good morning, Appa,' Gowda said, turning on the ignition switch.

'I was wondering how to light this.' Chidananda examined the ignition switch.

'Nagendra has the same hob,' Gowda said, placing a saucepan of water on the burner.

'I don't enter the kitchen in my home. Your sister-in-law ensures I don't need to,' the old man mumbled. 'Warm water for me to brush my teeth and clean my dentures, and piping hot filter coffee, all at my bedside by 5.30 a.m.'

Gowda poured hot milk into a steel jug and made filter coffee with the decoction in the fridge. He hoped to hell that Chidananda wouldn't complain that the decoction wasn't freshly made. He was going to have to call up his sister-in-law to find out his father's routine. He opened the cabinets, looking for a steel tumbler and its matching basin. His father didn't approve of coffee in anything but its traditional glass and davare. Gowda added a flask of warm water to the tray and carried it all to the guest room.

He placed it on the bedside table. 'I have put the geyser on so there is hot water in the taps. Breakfast will be on the table by 7 a.m. Is that fine?'

Chidananda nodded. 'Thank you,' he added.

'No need for thanks, Appa. It's my duty,' Gowda said dutifully. He wondered if it was the first time his father had ever thanked him for anything. Chidananda belonged to a generation for whom using 'please' and 'thank you' with family was considered pejorative. You used such expressions of courtesy only with strangers and outsiders.

At half past seven, Gowda vroomed out of his gate. His father stood on the verandah, watching him. Gowda felt his eyes bore through the back of his uniform even though he realized he couldn't really be seen. There was something disconcerting as well as comforting about having your father watch you leave for work. Someone watching you leave meant someone waiting for you to come back.

He had also seen the woman upstairs peeking through the curtains again. Didn't she have anything better to do, he thought in disgust. Well, at least she knew he was away and would keep an eye on his father.

David stared in surprise as Gowda entered the station. 'Sir, I was on my way to your home,' he said, wondering if he had misheard the pick-up instruction.

Gowda waved him away. 'Not an issue. I decided to come in early.'

He walked into his room and stood by the window. His team was yet to appear, and his mouth thinned in irritation. He took a deep breath allowing the crackle of the wireless, the sounds of people talking from the other rooms in the station, the rattle of vehicles arriving and leaving, and the voices of students from a school nearby as someone played 'Una Paloma Blanca' on a keyboard, to lull him into something akin to calm. Gowda felt his shoulders relax.

'Sir,' a voice said. A constable stood at the door with a plastic beaker of tea.

'Come in, Gopal,' he said, moving towards the chair. 'Let me know when HC Gajendra comes in.'

'HC Gajendra and everyone else—SI Santosh and SI Aqthar and ASI Ratna and PC Byrappa—are all in the SIT Room.' The constable beamed, which made him look more furtive than usual. Like a cartoon rat, Gowda thought.

'They came in at 7.30,' Gopal continued. Seeing Gowda in what seemed to be a genial mood, he asked, 'Sir, I was wondering if I could be part of the SIT?'

Gowda was surprised. It was a very forward request from a constable who had just been transferred. He grunted, not knowing what else to do.

Gowda walked into the room to see everyone huddled around the table. There was a palpable excitement in the air.

'So,' Gowda began without going through all the requisite pre-mumble. 'I can see that you have something to share. Shoot.'

He listened to Ratna and Santosh take turns to narrate the interview with Mary Susheela and her husband.

Gowda doodled on a pad as they spoke. He looked up when they finished. 'So what do you think?'

'Sir,' Ratna said. 'We need to put down Paul Selvam as a suspect.'

Santosh nodded his head vigorously in support. 'I agree, sir.'

Gowda stood up and went to the whiteboard. 'We may as well use this,' he said, taking a blue marker. He turned back to them and said, 'We also need to check on this Gurunath, more importantly.'

'Sir, according to Mary Susheela he left on the morning of the murder,' Ratna said.

'Do we know that for sure?' He wrote the names one by one.

Paul Selvam
Mary Susheela
Gurunath

'For now, I want all their movements checked. Find out as much as you can about their actual relationship with the deceased,' Gowda said, dropping the blue marker on the table.

He picked up a red marker and added to the list.

Iqbal Buqhari
Janaki Buqhari

SI Santosh cleared his throat. 'Iqbal Buqhari is a definite suspect. But Janaki Buqhari, sir?'

'You think daughters are not capable of murder?' Gowda asked.

'There isn't a motive, sir. She is rich and she has no other siblings. When he dies, all his property will come to her anyway. I don't see how...' Santosh asked, unwilling to back down.

'Indeed, and a valid point. As you know, the walking stick is still missing. When we were at the Buqhari residence, I asked about it and it triggered a peculiar reaction from Janaki Buqhari.

That bothers me. Maybe she is covering for Iqbal. So she must stay on the list.'

'What about Deva?' Ratna asked.

'He was out of town for a whole week, in Udupi. He returned only on 29th morning,' Gajendra said.

Gowda shook his head. 'We need to confirm that as well. So he goes on our list too.'

Aqthar cleared his throat. Gowda looked at him and said, 'Yes, Aqthar?'

Aqthar stood up, as if he was in class. 'Sir, I think your hunch about Gurunath is right. He is well-known to us as a student troublemaker. Who knows what happened for him to leave in a huff?'

'Santosh and Ratna, I want you to check on Iqbal and Janaki. Aqthar, you will look into Gurunath. Gajendra and Byrappa, I want you to check on Deva, Paul as well as those families living at the edge of the property. We need to move quickly. DCP Sagayaraj thinks it could be a political assassination. But I believe there is no way of knowing until we actually eliminate each one of the suspects. All of them have a motive. But is it strong enough to commit murder?'

When all of them rose to leave, Gowda gestured to Gajendra to stay back. He listened with a frown as Gowda told him about PC Gopal's request to be included in the SIT. 'What do you think?'

Gajendra crossed his arms. 'I understand that he is looking to fast-track his promotion but, sir, I know you won't like me saying this, he is a member of the Lingayat and our DCP Vidyaprasad is one too. And that makes me wonder if he is doing this on the DCP's orders.'

Gowda nodded.

'And yet we can't ignore his request,' Gajendra added. Then his face lit up as if he had found a solution. 'He is a local man, unlike Byrappa and me. So I'll take him with me to meet Paul Selvam. We'll evaluate what his agenda is as we go along. And after that, I'll put him and Byrappa to check on the 28 November sante. If there was anything unusual that happened, who were the strangers there, etc.'

Gowda grinned.

'Before I get down to that, sir, I want to try something,' Gajendra said, carefully erasing Gurunath's name on the whiteboard and adding another.

Gowda grinned. There are more ways to catch a rat than one, he thought.

The summons came an hour later. It was a quarter to eleven on a Sunday, which meant it was possible to reach the DCP's office in thirty minutes.

A flat-screen LED TV was playing a music video when Gowda knocked on the door. Gowda pushed it open and walked in as the DCP hastily changed to a local news channel.

'I say, Gowda,' DCP Vidyaprasad growled in greeting.

Gowda offered him his village idiot smile in response.

He saw the startled expression in Vidyaprasad's eyes and continued to give him the benefit of his flashing teeth.

'I say, Gowda,' Vidyaprasad resumed, trying to regain the thread of the tirade he had wanted to bury Gowda under. 'What is this nonsense about your putting down Papanna as a suspect in the Mudgood murder case? Do you realize who you are accusing of what?'

Gowda sat down, even though he hadn't been invited to. 'Sir, do you think MLAs can't commit murder?'

'Gowda, don't play the fool with me,' Vidyaprasad snapped. 'You know what I mean.'

'In which case, sir, stop treating me like one. You don't need a mole to report to you on what's going on. All you have to do is ask.' Gowda stood up. 'If that's all...' He glared at Vidyaprasad. 'I will take my leave. I have a homicide to investigate.'

Vidyaprasad continued to sit. He didn't know if the MLA was really a suspect or if Gowda had played him. But it would be prudent to warn Papanna that he could be under suspicion. And the man wasn't going to take kindly to it.

## 2

A political party is only as strong as its workers. Papanna knew that more than anyone else. He had risen from the lowly rung of a faceless party stooge all the way up to being who he was now. The maker and breaker of governments.

Papanna had begun life as a garbage-truck driver. He had worked for a man who had an understanding with the municipal corporation about garbage disposal. Papanna was older than the corporator, but like everyone else, he too had called him Anna. Corporator Ravi Kumar had taken to Papanna very quickly. 'We have the same humble beginnings,' he would tell everyone.

One evening Anna asked him to accompany him to a political meeting in his neighbourhood. Papanna had nothing better to do and this had seemed like a good way to spend time without having to dip into his wallet to buy a round of drinks. Anna had promised him a full bottle of brandy.

Papanna found himself drawn into the world of politics. He also realized he had a certain flair for it. Anna had explained that politics was a lot like garbage collection. Anyone who worried about getting their hands dirty or being splattered with filth shouldn't be involved in it. This made perfect sense to Papanna.

And so, even when he was still finding his place in the system, Papanna had learnt how to whisper perfectly pitched insinuations into various ears to crank up paranoia. When tides of power were afloat, a word here accompanied by a cup of sweet milky tea, a phrase there with a cutting of whisky changed the course of destinies.

Then came the day when after a party meeting, Papanna overheard a conversation between a nobody and a certain political-leader-in-the-making. The man glanced at Papanna and mumbled, 'Papanna is a blessing. A fantastic party worker. If he had a bit of flesh on him, I may have included him in my inner circle. Right now he looks like one of the scrawny garbage-pickers in his truck.'

'He is a good fellow,' the crony mumbled back. 'Gets things done efficiently and almost effortlessly.'

'I know, but people evaluate a politician by his appearance. A substantial-looking man makes them think of stability, lineage, etc. Papanna looks too hungry, and hence unreliable. And those scars on his face, he looks like chappar class.'

The crony looked at him with amazement.

'What? You don't believe me? Name one scrawny-looking politician from any part of India,' the leader-in-the-making said.

The crony couldn't think of anyone. Nevertheless, not wanting to appear ignorant, he said, 'What about Gandhiji?'

'And look what happened to him!'

Papanna thought a great deal about the conversation he had overhead. The leader-in-the-making was an idiot, but for once what he had said had struck him hard, like a punch in the jaw. So Papanna joined a gym in the neighbourhood where college boys and thugs worked out to define their musculature.

It didn't happen as easily as it did in the movies. But Papanna was determined to not remain that scrawny chappar-class creature he had been dismissed as. In a year's time, he had filled out and acquired an unmistakeable swag, a mean uppercut and an inner circle of his own, boys and men who were ready to lay down their lives for him.

Anna helped Papanna acquire a fleet of garbage trucks that collected the refuse of a city bursting at its seams with people and everything they consumed with the fervour of hungry rats. Disposable income had changed lives and consumption patterns and Papanna understood this long before economist doyens held seminars and TEDx talks on the subject.

Garbage was Papanna's weapon and he didn't have to shed a drop of blood to amass the acreage that he coveted. All he had to do was make his trucks deposit mounds of garbage until the stench drove landowners away and forced them to sell their land at throwaway prices. Then Papanna would move the garbage to another zone. Anyone who protested was dealt with ruthlessly.

He was soon ready to join active politics. He stood as an independent candidate and won every election he contested. From panchayat president to councillor—once Neelgubbi came under the city limits—and from there to MLA. His value was magnified with the customary horse-trading after every election.

Papanna was shrewd so he didn't chase a ministerial position as he knew it would limit his powers. As an independent MLA, his liabilities were minimized while he had the entire Cabinet do his bidding. This was the man Gowda was accusing of homicide, DCP Vidyaprasad rued as he drove to the MLA's residence.

Everyone who was anyone was in the breast pocket of Papanna's crisp white shirt along with the Mont Blanc pen he kept there: real estate and liquor lobbies, politicians and the press, charge-sheeters and the police. It was quite possible that the MLA had already heard about his name being on the suspects' list, the DCP worried. He called up his wife. 'Priya,' he said, trying to keep the concern out of his voice. 'Is everything all right?'

'Why wouldn't it be?' his wife retorted.

'No garbage troubles...?'

'When did you get so interested in garbage?'

Priya's laugh grated on his already tattered nerves. He took a deep breath and persisted. 'I mean, no one has dumped garbage at our doorstep?'

'Have you been drinking?' his wife demanded in her meanest voice.

'No, Priya. I just wanted to know. There was some talk of police officers being targeted,' he tried to explain.

'Hang on, let me check,' she said as she walked to the door. He heard the door open and then the creak of the gate. 'So far, so good.'

'All right then,' he said, cutting the call. He exhaled. Papanna made his displeasure known in multiple ways. But the first warning was always a mountain of garbage at your doorstep. Vidyaprasad shuddered at the very thought. Apart from the stench and unsavouriness of food waste and leaking plastic bags, broken plastic and all kinds of refuse blocking his gate, there was also the embarrassment of his neighbours and colleagues speculating on what had led to this. For once, he thought with some relief, the MLA's jungle drums hadn't tom-tommed yet.

The road to Papanna's home was lined with vehicles and people, as always. Bella Mane. A white house in which lived the man who dressed only in white. The gates were wide open as usual, and the fleet of white cars were all lined up except for the yellow Porsche that, if he remembered right, was awaiting its registration papers. In all likelihood, Papanna's son must have taken it out. He hoped that the idiot wouldn't have an accident, or worse, mow somebody down. When Papanna called in a favour and you didn't comply, there was hell to pay. And when it came to his son, he would make no exceptions.

Vidyaprasad took a deep breath as he took the key from his car. He wondered if he should have called first, but he had thought it prudent to do this face-to-face rather than on the phone.

## 3

Papanna had been surprised when his son thrust his own phone into his face. 'Here, a call for you.'

'Who is calling me on your phone?' The MLA had frowned even as he held it to his ear.

Both surprise and fear jostled within him when he heard the voice at the other end. 'Chikka,' he yelped.

'Don't call me that again. My name is Ramesh. Time everyone remembered that,' the husky voice said firmly. 'I am on my way to see you.'

Papanna handed back the phone to Sagar. 'Why did he call you?' he asked after a few seconds.

'Probably because he thought you wouldn't pick up. Or he must be afraid that your esteemed colleagues in the Cabinet are tapping your phone.' Sagar laughed aloud.

Papanna smiled. There was so much his son didn't know about him, and Papanna wanted it to stay that way.

'Have you had your milk and saffron?' he asked, changing the subject. 'Sunil Rai wants to meet you.'

Sagar beamed. His father was bankrolling his debut film but he didn't want just anyone to direct it. And, Sunil Rai didn't take on projects just like that. 'Daddy, but how?' he asked.

Papanna fondled his son's cheek. 'What is the point in me being who I am if I can't do for you what you want...' he said softly. 'And don't forget to use sunscreen when you go out,' he added as Sagar left the room.

Papanna wondered what Chikka wanted. The man had a lookout notice in his name. He wondered if he should call that fool Vidyaprasad and tell him to grab the criminal. But that would be neither here nor there. If Chikka had asked to see him, that little bastard must have a secret weapon to protect himself. So he abandoned the thought of calling the DCP and instead left word that a visitor named Ramesh was to be brought into his private office as soon as he arrived.

Papanna looked at the slight young man with his curly hair and a squint in his eye. He seemed to be doing quite all right for a fugitive on the run.

'What are you doing here?' Papanna asked as he led Chikka

towards a sofa. 'You know there is a lookout notice for you. Is it even safe for you to be here in Bangalore?'

'I need to get a few things done and I need to be here,' Chikka said, holding the older man's gaze steadily. When Papanna looked away, he dropped down into the sofa and sat daintily at its edge.

'I thought you would have got some plastic surgery done. Altered your looks,' Papanna said, wondering if it was nail polish he saw on Chikka's toes. Even as a boy he had been a little strange, Papanna remembered. There had been all kinds of rumours about him but nothing concrete.

'I will when the time is right,' Chikka said. 'And that is why I am here.'

'What can I do for you?' Papanna asked.

'I need cash. And as quickly as possible.'

'How much?'

'Two crore for now.'

'That's a lot of cash.' Papanna swallowed. He wasn't sure his gratitude stretched to that many zeroes. 'Let me see what I can do.'

'I need it soon.'

'How soon?'

'A few days. I need it in a week.'

'Raising that kind of cash isn't going to be easy but I have a plan,' Papanna began.

'I need the money so your plan better work,' Chikka said.

'Where are you staying?' Papanna asked.

'Why?'

'I am not your enemy. Your brother was my guru.' Papanna injected a sincerity into his voice which he hoped would convince the Peanut about his earnestness. 'Do you hear me?'

'With my cousin. She lives in this area.'

'Does she?' Papanna asked, surprised. He hadn't known that.

'She just moved here,' Chikka said, amusement lighting up his eyes.

Papanna's mouth tightened. What was so funny about that? He turned his gaze to the window to collect his thoughts. His eyes crinkled with surprise as he saw the DCP's car screech through the gates. He thought the man a fop and a fool; nevertheless, DCP Vidyaprasad was his person, and you didn't ever denigrate your person. Even the smallest piece of garbage had its use.

Chikka saw Papanna's frown and wondered what was going on. 'Who is that?'

'ACP... no, he's DCP Vidyaprasad now. Why is he coming here? He never does without informing me.'

'So it's not a coincidence that he's here to see you when I'm in the room with you,' Chikka said in an even voice.

Papanna felt a shiver run down his spine. Anna had a way of intimidating people, but it seemed his brother was a hundredfold more menacing without even raising his voice.

'Don't you still trust me...' he began.

'I don't trust anyone, Papanna.' Chikka got up from his chair and stepped into an adjacent room. 'Get rid of him quickly.'

Moments later, the door opened.


'What is your interest in Professor Mudgood?' Vidyaprasad demanded as he strode into the MLA's office. 'Unless you tell me what's going on, how can I help?'

Papanna let it pass. The belligerence was from agitation rather than anything else, he realized.

'Calm down, DCP Sir. What is the issue?' He registered the beads of sweat on his forehead and the flared nostrils.

DCP Vidyaprasad sank into a chair and took a deep breath. He tried with not much success to put into effect what his yoga master muttered every alternate day: inhale-exhale-inhale-exhale.

'Did you have any connection with Professor Mudgood?'

'I heard that old idiot died in suspicious circumstances. Is it true?' Papanna said, rolling the wart on his jaw under his finger. It seemed to have sprung up from nowhere.

'Are you telling me you know nothing about it?' The DCP was unable to help himself.

'Why would I? I know his son-in-law very well. That's about it. When did that become a crime, Vidyaprasad Sir?'

The MLA's laugh sounded genuine enough, Vidyaprasad thought. 'You had no interest in his land?'

'I am interested in every piece of land. I had wanted to acquire the land adjacent to his to convert to a public park. Do you know we don't have one in the Neelgubbi area?'

DCP Vidyaprasad smiled in relief. 'That must be it then.'

'That must be what?' Papanna's voice acquired a raspy timbre.

'Your name on the list of suspects,' Vidyaprasad said, rising to go.

'Sit down, DCP Sir. Tell me what's going on.' Papanna locked his gaze with the policeman's. 'Who is the officer in charge? Start with that...'

'Gowda.' DCP Vidyaprasad sighed.

'I see...' Papanna said. He listened as Vidyaprasad detailed the findings of the case.

When the DCP left, the MLA's visitor returned to the office room. 'How is that man still in service?'

Papanna shrugged. He didn't think it was any of the Peanut's business.

Chikka stared at Papanna in a distant manner. His squint became more pronounced and Papanna felt afraid.

'What about the money?' Chikka asked abruptly.

'The old man's death is going to cause some trouble. You have to wait,' Papanna said.

'What does the Professor's death have to do with my money?'

Papanna rolled his wart some more. A wart needed to be removed without affecting the skin around it. It would pop back after a while. But for now both the wart and the Peanut across the table needed to be dealt with. It seemed that Gowda had given him the perfect excuse to remove this irritant from his life.

'Everything I need to do to raise the money will have to be put on hold,' he said. 'You must have heard what was discussed. So, Gowda, ACP Gowda now, who is in charge of the case, has put me on the radar. He is a tenacious bastard. But you know that better than me.'

Chikka reached across and brushed aside Papanna's hand from his wart. Then he pinched the skin around it. An abrupt snapping of fingers that sent a shooting pain up Papanna's jaw. 'What are you doing?' he yelped.

'Nice try,' Chikka said in his low, husky voice. 'I need my money. It isn't your family wealth that I'm asking a piece of. It is what is mine and is only one per cent of what my brother gave you for safekeeping. And don't bullshit me by saying it's all invested. You don't want to upset me, Papanna. I know you don't want to do that.'

Papanna looked at his desk calendar. The dates danced in front of his eyes as Papanna wondered what it was the Peanut had on him. Anna and he had been partners in several deals, most of which were illegal. Part of which Anna had documented and in all probability, it was all in his name. Which was why the Peanut was so aggressive, he realized.

'I'll see what I can do,' he said quietly.

When Chikka left, Papanna sat for a moment gazing at his hands. He wasn't afraid of that little Peanut, he told himself sternly. He dialled a number. 'We need to talk,' he said.

There was a long silence at the other end. 'Boss, can't it wait? You know that there is some trouble and I need to lie low,' the man said.

'We have to, Military. And right now,' Papanna snapped. 'Don't fuck with me. I expect you here between 1 and 3 p.m. We have a bheegara oota this afternoon in my mother's memory. It will be crowded. No one will notice you. You will be just one among hundreds out there filling their bellies.'

# 4

Gowda was just rising to leave when he heard a knock on the door.

'Come in,' he said, wondering if he was going to have any of this Sunday left for himself. It didn't matter much otherwise but with his father at home... Gowda looked at the clock.

Papanna entered the room with folded hands and a smarmy smile. 'Namaskara, ACP Sir,' he said with an obsequiousness more apt for an IG rather than a lowly ACP, Gowda thought with amused disgust.

'How can I help you, sir?' Gowda sir-ed him back. Two could play at this game.

The MLA moved a chair from where it was as if to say I sit where I please and not where you tell me to. He sat down straight backed and placed the heel of his palm on his knee. 'It's my mother's birth anniversary and we have organized a feast. I wanted to invite you to it. Also, I hadn't come by to congratulate you after your promotion, and then I heard about Professor Sir's murder and thought I would come by to assure you that you have my full support. He was our state treasure; a gem of a man. His murderer must not go unpunished.'

'Indeed.' Gowda's tone was dry. Wanting to terminate Papanna's fishing expedition, he added, 'Thank you, sir, and thank you for stopping by.'

He let the period stretch into a long silence. The MLA's smile faded and he stood up. 'I don't want to take more of your time. It is a Sunday after all. Though we public servants have no Sundays or holidays. Speaking of which, you must come to the New Year's Eve party at the Orchard of Silence. You know that gated community, right? I will have them send an invitation for the missus and you.' He paused and added, 'Plus one.'

Gowda's heart skipped a beat. Had Papanna referred to the plus-one for Roshan? Or was it Urmila? What was he insinuating? But he kept his face pleasantly blank as he muttered, 'Thank you. New Year's Eve is one night public servants like me don't celebrate.'

What did Papanna want from him? He wasn't someone who got rattled by the appearance of his name in a suspects' list. Papanna had at least four criminal cases pending against him.

He watched the MLA shut the door behind him. Had Gajendra's bait lured a monster out from the murky bed of the lake?

Later that evening Gowda decided that he would go for a long bike ride. It would open up threads of thought that somehow never seemed to pop up when he sat at his desk being an ACP.

# 5

Military looked at the teeming crowds with astonishment. Where had all these people come from? On one side of Papanna's house, a giant white tent had been raised. Rows of long, narrow tables were laid out, with chairs dressed in shimmery white satin-and-blue sashes. The first set of guests were still eating; behind them stood the next set, waiting to pounce on the first available seat. Each leaf was so laden with food that it could have fed a whole family of four. And yet, everyone stuffing their faces kept asking for more. Some chicken here, some mutton there, biriyani here, ragi mudde there...

'Follow me,' a man said, discreetly arriving at his elbow.

Military frowned. 'How did you recognize me?'

'Boss said that you would be dressed like a soldier. Do you see anyone else like that here?'

Military didn't say anything but followed him to a table not far from where Papanna sat holding court. 'Sit down,' he gestured. 'Bring him a leaf and serve him,' he said, turning to one of his many minions.

As the food was being served, Papanna casually made his way over to Military. 'We have just a week,' he began. 'And it has to be high-stakes so we need a surprise element.'

'I can't do it in one week. I need more time than that. I need to look for another place. A month at least,' Military said, examining the fried fish. 'Is this some local fish?'

'I don't have a month. Ten days max,' Papanna replied. 'And no, it's not local fish. I don't want to poison my guests. It's seer fish at 800 rupees a kilo. Bannur mutton, Kadaknath chicken—I want only the best items served to my guests... so eat without fear or shame,' he added as he moved away.

A few minutes later, Papanna ambled back towards him as if to check if his banana leaf plate had to be replenished. He gestured to the mutton curry man to serve Military. 'Get that Manipuri fellow in. Everyone knows that the Manipuri is good so they will place their bets on him. He has a few dedicated fans including my son and his friends. But we need someone new. Someone who will make that Manipuri sweat and so everyone will wonder at his form. So when we bring in Sumo Mani in the last bout the bets will be divided but I am certain it will favour Sumo Mani. Everyone knows what a monster he is. Sumo Mani will take care of the rest.'

Military looked at Papanna uncomprehendingly. Papanna gave Military a little pat on his back and muttered, 'The Manipuri will be a happy man. Do you understand now?'

Military folded his leaf over and stood up. Papanna must be really in need of funds if he was going to rig the fight. He stopped at the paan counter and took a couple. He stuffed both paans into his mouth and as it flooded his mouth with an explosion of juices, he told himself, as long as he got what was due to him, he didn't particularly care why Papanna needed the money or how he went about making it.

# 6

'What the hell!' Gowda cursed aloud as he turned the corner leading to his house and spotted a car outside his gate, blocking the way. When he realized it was Urmila's Audi, he felt the insides of his mouth go dry. What was she doing here? He parked his bike outside the gate. It was shut but not latched and he could hear voices from within as he walked towards his front door. His father's and Urmila's.

He pushed the door open gently and saw the astonishing sight of Mr Right on his father's lap. Gowda blinked, but before he could speak, Mr Right hurled himself at Gowda's legs, prancing around them and whining as if he hadn't seen Gowda for several months instead of just the previous morning. Gowda bent down and picked up the dog.

'He is very fond of Borei,' Urmila said, keeping her eyes on Mr Right.

Gowda pulled in his core to stop his stomach heaving. He summoned a bland smile. 'Hello, Urmila, what a surprise...' he said, and, turning to his father, added, 'Appa, Urmila and I went to college together. And Michael. And DCP Sagayaraj too.'

'Yes, yes... Madam was just telling me.' Chidananda beamed.

'Mr Gowda, please don't call me madam.' Urmila leaned forward with mock annoyance and tapped his arm.

'In which case you mustn't call me Mr Gowda.' Chidananda smiled. Gowda had never seen him smile with such an indulgent gaze, not even at his grandchildren. It was time to break this mutual admiration society, he thought as he sat down holding Mr Right.

'I was on my way to Janaki's. All of us, our circle of friends, have been taking turns to be with her. She is very distraught. I didn't realize she was so attached to her father. I was taking Mr Right along since he gets along with her dog. But another friend called as I was reaching Ring Road and she said that Janaki collapsed this morning. She has been refusing to get out of bed or eat any-thing. I don't want to take Mr Right there in these circumstances. I thought I would leave him here for a bit,' Urmila said.

Gowda realized that Urmila had also meant to surprise him and was now trying to make her visit, in her own words, kosher.

Gowda saw his father take his spectacles off and shine them carefully. What was he thinking about? Chidananda put his spectacles back on and said, 'He seems very fond of you, Borei...'

As if he had understood, Mr Right arched his neck backwards and licked Gowda's chin. Gowda smiled. 'Urmila brings him around when she comes to this side of town. Do you remem-ber my friend Michael? The three of us catch up very often...' Gowda rambled while Urmila watched his face with a bemused expression.

As he saw her to the gate, she muttered under her breath, 'Why didn't you tell me your father's here?'

'Didn't I?' he sighed. 'I thought I did. I thought I had come over to tell you about my father visiting. How could I have forgotten?'

'I have never seen you so distracted,' Urmila said. 'What's bothering you, Borei?'

Gowda wished he could tell her what was making him feel perplexed, restless and uncertain all at the same time.

'Tell me if you see anything unusual at the Buqhari residence.'

'Are you asking me to spy on my friend, Borei?' Urmila snapped, defiantly sticking out her chin.

'I said if you see something unusual... not to keep tabs on her. Someone did kill her father. And it is my duty to ensure that the murderer is caught,' Gowda said in his patient voice and then regretted it. He knew it riled Urmila. She called it his 'mansplaining voice'.

'What I meant is I have this feeling that all of us are chasing phantom killers while the real one is lazing in his easy chair watching us make fools of ourselves,' he added hastily. 'I'm not entirely sure about Iqbal Buqhari. There is something about him...'

'Is it because he's Muslim?' Her voice sounded strained.

'Whoa,' he said. 'That's unfair. Do you even realize what you are accusing me of?' Urmila's gaze dropped. She touched his arm apologetically. 'I'm sorry, I don't know why I'm being so argumentative,' she said as she slid into her car seat.

'Wait, U... could you very casually ask Janaki about her father's walking stick?'

She didn't even turn to wave at him as she drove away.


Gowda glanced at his trustworthy HMT watch. It was almost two. He walked back into the house hastily to fix lunch. The thought of his father putting him through the third degree about Urmila loomed over his head. But Chidananda appeared more intent on talking to Mr Right.

'Shall we have lunch, Appa?' He was relieved that the dog was taking up all his father's attention.

'Urmila left a bag. She said it has his treats and a water bowl, and his favourite toy,' Chidananda said, his eyes twinkling behind his glasses.

Gowda found the bag and took out some things. Later, when they had finished eating and given Mr Right some scraps from their plates, Chidananda retired to his room. Gowda put Mr Right on a leash and took him out. He smoked a cigarette as he walked the dog.

He wondered how the CCB team was faring. It was half past two on a Sunday afternoon and he didn't think DCP Sagayaraj would appreciate being interrupted as he tucked into his chicken biriyani. But a homicide was a homicide, Sunday biriyani or not, so Gowda quelled his reservations and decided to call.

Almost as if on cue, his phone burst into life.

'We are on our way to Dharwad,' DCP Sagayaraj said. 'How's it going at the local end?'

Gowda briefed him on what the team had come up with. Then, suppressing a laugh, he told him about adding Papanna's name to the suspects' list. 'So, here's the thing. We did that to flush out the rat at the station, but it turns out Papanna is indeed rather perturbed. And that makes me wonder why.'

'Oh God,' Sagayaraj sighed. 'Oh God, Gowda...'

'What's wrong?' Gowda knew what was coming.

'Are you going to get me into trouble with the Home Minister? You know Papanna pretty much keeps this party in power.'

'That doesn't make him above the law, sir.'

'It doesn't, Gowda. But tread very carefully. Do you hear me?'

'I do, I do, sir.' Gowda paused, wondering if he should mention Gurunath, the Professor's assistant. 'I'll keep you posted, sir,' he said and ended the call.

He looked at Mr Right, who was raising his leg against the lamppost. 'Mr Right, if I tell Stanley about Gurunath, they'll bring him in, and before you know it, this case will go into the hands of the National Security Advisor and turn into something else. We don't want that, do we?'

Mr Right wagged his tail in response.

Gowda wondered if he had time for a nap. The afternoon sunshine was making him sleepy. When he got home, he took the leash off Mr Right, who leapt onto the sofa by the window. It gave him a vantage spot from where he could stare at nothing with great intent. Gowda took his work clothes off and slipped into a T-shirt and track pants. It was tempting to get under the quilt but he was afraid that if he did he would wake up only a day later. So he lay down and crossed his hands beneath his head.

When the phone rang, he groaned loudly. Urmila. 'I was just leaving to pick Mr Right up,' she said.

'No, don't,' Gowda said hastily. He didn't want his father mentioning Urmila's visits to his wife. He was unable to shrug off the guilt that shadowed their relationship. In his line of work he had seen the best and the worst traits in people, and he knew that no one was perfect. Neither was he. He had eventually come to terms with the fact that he was now a trope of sorts: the middle-aged married man finding solace in the arms of his ex-girlfriend who happened to be his college sweetheart, but he didn't want to flaunt what Urmila and he shared; certainly not to his father. 'I will drop Mr Right back to your place.'

'Are you afraid I'll blurt out something about us to your father, Borei?' Urmila's voice dripped ice.

'It isn't that...' He tried to placate her ruffled feelings.

'What is it then?'

'I'll tell you when I come over.' And because he knew that it would make her feel less insecure, he added, 'I need to see you. Please.'

For a moment, he thought he saw a shadow lurk near the door.

'When is the funeral?' he asked loudly.

'Tomorrow afternoon. There is a public viewing planned in the morning.'

He slipped his phone into his pocket, wondering if he had imagined it or if his father had been eavesdropping.

# 7

For a moment, Gowda wondered where he was. The room was wreathed in shadows, and it was chilly. His mouth was dry and his eyes felt gritty. He glanced at his watch. A quarter past five. He leapt out of bed, cursing himself for not setting the alarm.

His father was in the kitchen, pouring coffee into two mugs lined up on the granite counter. He gave Gowda a smile. 'You were sleeping so peacefully,' he said. Gowda walked to the drying cabinet and pulled out a steel tumbler and davare.

'Here, Appa, use this for yours,' he said, smiling sheepishly at Chidananda. 'I slept through the alarm. I wanted to make you your evening coffee at 4.30.'

'That's all right. I am still capable of brewing some coffee.'

Gowda took his mug and mumbled thanks.

'What's all this thanks business?' Chidananda frowned. 'Am I a stranger to you? We don't say thanks to each other within families...'

In the living room, Gowda sat in his chair, staring at the silent TV. Mr Right lay on the sofa with his snout on his paws. Gowda would have liked to go out on a bike ride. But he felt lazy at the thought of putting on his biking gear and setting out. Gowda laced his fingers and leaned back into the chair. He stretched his feet on the table. He wondered what his team was up to. Probably sleeping off their Sunday lunch, he thought. Or probably not. He picked up his phone and called Santosh.

'I was just about to call you, sir.' Santosh's voice was quivering with excitement.

'What's up?' Gowda asked. 'What's happened?'

'We got a tipoff, sir. I can't believe that this has been going on right under our nose.' Santosh's raspy voice rasped some more.

'Tipoff about what? Get to the point,' Gowda said impatiently. From the corner of his eye, he saw Chidananda walk down the passage back to the kitchen.

'Cockfights, sir. Apparently, there's heavy betting involved.'

Gowda snorted. 'What? A goat?'

'More like 50,000 rupees and upwards, sir, and they have a bookie system going on for those who are not allowed to be there,' Santosh said, trying hard not to crow.

'Are you serious?' Gowda sat up.

'Never been more serious, sir,' Santosh said. 'There is one happening this evening.'

'When? Where?' Gowda barked into the phone. Suddenly, he noticed both his father and Mr Right were watching him. 'I'll see you at the station at six,' he said, cutting the call.

'Do you have to go?' Chidananda asked.

'I have to, Appa, it's work...' Gowda said, trying to ignore the hurt and affronted looks coming his way from both man and dog.

'Can't it wait?' his father demanded. 'It's Sunday, after all.'

'You think criminals say oh it's Sunday, let's take the day off?' Gowda snapped. He saw Chidananda's face fall and hastened to make amends. 'I wouldn't go if it wasn't really important, Appa.'

'What about the dog? What if he needs to do number one or two?' His father gave Mr Right a worried look.

'I'll let him out before I go. And once I return, I'll drop him off,' Gowda said, scratching Mr Right under his chin.

'Why don't you ask your friend to pick him up?' Chidananda persisted.

'Appa, Urmila has gone to make some arrangements for the public viewing of Professor Mudgood's body. Do you expect her to drive all the way into town and then return here for Mr Right? Have a heart, Appa,' Gowda said and then, to emphasize his point, added, 'She is a woman after all.'

Urmila would have slit his throat if she had heard him, but a man must do what a man must do, Gowda thought. He didn't want his father and Urmila spending too much time together.

'Won't Urmila Madam's husband mind if you go there this late?' his father asked, not quite meeting his eye.

'Urmila's husband lives in the UK and they are separated,' Gowda said. He took a deep breath and asked, 'What do you want to know, Appa?'

'Nothing, nothing. I don't want to know anything.' His father's voice rose as he turned and walked to his room.

Gowda sighed. He knew the honeymoon was over. But he had had a lifetime to get used to his father's moods and so he tucked his mixed feelings into a box called 'Complexities of Dealing with Appa' and shoved it into a dark corner of his mind.

The station was quiet. It was a Sunday night, and though he had been sardonic when he told his father about criminals not taking the day off, the truth was there were fewer petty crimes on Sundays—most people were home in the evenings preparing to go back to work on Monday.

Santosh and Gajendra were waiting for him, as was a belligerent-looking Ratna. 'Do so many of us have to follow this up?' Gowda frowned.

'Precisely, sir, that's what I was telling ASI Ratna,' Santosh said, ignoring her frown.

'So tell me about this tipoff.' Gowda turned to Gajendra, who seemed unmoved by the crackling tension between Santosh and Ratna.

'Sir, it was actually me who alerted SI Santosh,' Ratna burst out before Gajendra could speak.

Gowda cocked an eyebrow enquiringly at Gajendra, who reiterated, 'It was Ratna Madam who got the tipoff.'

Ratna said, 'I wouldn't call it a tipoff. More like the person blurted out the information without realizing it.'

'Even so, it's not safe for a woman to be there,' Santosh said loudly and firmly in a tone he had heard his father use with his mother.

Gowda was inclined to pull and twist Santosh's ears but he opted to make his point with a brusque tone. 'Stop fretting like a hen, Santosh. She is a police officer. Just as you are. End of discussion. Besides, ASI Ratna is not going on her own.'

Santosh's jaw set mutinously but he didn't speak.

'We'll take my car,' Gowda said. 'Less conspicuous than the police vehicle.'

Gowda hadn't actually meant to go with them. He had just wanted to get away from home as twilight fell. The thought of sitting at home watching TV alongside his father on a Sunday evening was depressing. And when Santosh called, Gowda had his perfect excuse to make his escape. But now that he was here, he decided that he may as well go along. Who knew what it would lead to?

*

Beyond the big banyan tree, on the Kannur–Bagalur route, the road swerved to the right. They passed a building which housed a few shops. Narrow lanes on either side led to clusters of small houses. Thereafter, the road turned left and onto a path lined with eucalyptus groves on either side. The officers parked in a dark spot between two distant streetlights. The narrow road was dense with trees. Several vacant plots with granite slab fencing were on both sides of the road, enclosing trees and tall grass. An owl hooted, then another one took up the call. Gowda tapped the steering wheel impatiently as Gajendra and Santosh stood by a fence looking for a place to vault over.

'How did you hear about this?' Gowda asked Ratna, who sat at the back.

'Mary Susheela, sir. I went to meet her again a little while ago. I called her on an impulse in the morning and she said to come over by four in the evening. Her mister wouldn't be there, she said. I thought she would open up about the Professor if he wasn't around.'

'And did she?'

'She didn't say much about the Professor but a great deal about her husband. How he's a compulsive gambler and a cockfight enthusiast.'

# 8

'Look at him,' Mary Susheela had said, mopping away a stray tear. 'It's a Sunday, and instead of going to church or even staying at home, he's gone to set up a cockfight in the jungle near Ramapura. He has to buy rice and meat for the biriyani, he said. He has to set up the shamiana and do this and that. I thought he was helping someone with a function and then that loafer tells me it's for a cockfight and that he won't be home for dinner.'

Ratna tried not to show her growing interest as Mary Susheela keened about marrying a compulsive gambler. She and the other police officers would occasionally get wind of these cockfights, but no one had pursued the leads, probably considering it too inconsequential.

'Oh,' Ratna had said, putting her notebook away. She hadn't ever seen a policeman or woman use a notebook except in movies. But she thought Mary would expect her to do so. So Ratna had carried one to fit the movie template.

'Is there a cockfight every Sunday?'

'No, no... once in a few months. There's a lot of money in it,' Mary Susheela said, pulling her shawl around her. She realized she might have said too much, and thereafter clamped up and refused to divulge anything further.

A girl in her teens came up to them with a tetra pack of juice for Ratna. 'Akka, is that Hero Honda Splendour outside yours?'

Ratna nodded.

'You ride a bike, Akka?' The girl seemed wonderstruck. 'Can you give me a ride?' she asked.

'Hush, you idiot,' Mary Susheela said. 'Madam is from the police.'

The girl's mouth became an O and she left the room hurriedly.

'I would have given her a ride,' Ratna said. 'It's no trouble at all.'

Mary Susheela didn't respond except to sink her head onto her arms.

'Soon it will be time for Rosalyn to get married, but with such an irresponsible man for a father, how will we find a decent boy?'

'When will he be back?' Ratna asked.

'Not till dawn, and he will be drunk. If his rooster wins, he'll drink to celebrate; if his rooster dies, he will drink to console himself. Drunks just need a reason to drink.'

'I thought you said the cockfight is now.'

'No, no... it'll be after 8 p.m.'

*

'I left soon after that,' Ratna finished. To her surprise, she saw Gowda drop his head on the steering wheel and hit it a few times.

'Did you tell Gajendra about this?' he asked quietly.

'No, sir.' Ratna stiffened. 'I told SI Santosh and we had both seen that the husband was a volatile man and it fitted his profile. I didn't feel the need to cross-check with HC Gajendra as Mary Susheela herself gave the details.'

'Next time, talk to Gajendra first... he would have spotted holes in the story. They have big day-and-night cockfights in places like Vijayawada but here they are done quietly and it isn't a big party as Mary Susheela indicated to you. They played you, Ratna...' Gowda said gently.

'What do you mean, sir?'

'They just wanted to engage our attention. And you were the pawn they used to accomplish that. Mary Susheela must have told Paul you were coming over in the evening and he knew that if he mentioned the cockfight, she would tell you.'

'Are you sure, sir?'

Ratna sounded desolate, Gowda thought. He didn't bite her head off as he wanted to.

Gowda called Gajendra. 'Come back... there is nothing there.'

The two men returned to the car. 'I think Mary Susheela's husband set us up,' Gowda said as he started the car.

Gajendra and Santosh were silent as he told all of them what he thought of police officers who set off on trails without determining all the facts first. 'Sir, it's my fault,' Gajendra said. 'I should have verified with ASI Ratna first. But I didn't.'

'No, Gajendra Sir, I should have asked you but I think I put two and two together and came up with six,' Santosh interjected.

'If you have finished deciding who is to blame, can you shut the fuck up?' Gowda said, unable to stem his irritation. There was a stunned silence. For a while now, Gowda had been true to the office he held, careful to rein in his temper and use of expletives, behaving exactly as an ACP should behave. Dignified. Measured in voice and expression. And completely unlike the previous Gowda, Gajendra decided that he was more relieved than shocked at Gowda's reversal to his usual form.

Almost as if he regretted his outburst, Gowda sighed. 'This case has tied us all up in knots. It is as if we have little control over what happens and we get distracted easily. But let's take a step backwards and ask why they pulled this stunt.' Gowda started the car. 'Who would want us distracted and why?'

'Sir, someone took an educated guess that one of us would go back this morning,' Ratna said. 'Or perhaps they would have found another way to feed us that information. Instead of which I presented myself at their doorstep.' She sounded furious with herself.

'And they fed us a cock-and-bull story that would have us out of the way,' Santosh added. 'Very, very smart!'

Gowda stared at the grim-looking Santosh. 'I guess they wanted us busy for a couple of hours.'

'I think we should head to the Professor's house, sir,' Gajendra said, sounding determined.

'Neither Paul nor Mary are real criminals to have planned this ruse. So that leads us to the boss. Iqbal Buqhari,' Gowda said, taking the turn to SK Halli. A streetlamp threw a pool of light onto the gate. But the rest of the Professor's property was in darkness. The two constables on duty stood to attention as they recognized Gowda's car.

The gates were locked and the police seal on them was intact. The forensics team hadn't yet examined the cottage. Until that was done, the constables were expected to be there. A property of that size would need at least half a dozen policemen on duty but there weren't enough policemen to spare. Even these two had been specially requisitioned. Gajendra stepped out of the vehicle to speak to them.

'They may have leapt over the compound wall somewhere.' Gajendra came back to the car and gestured to the granite fencing. He looked at Gowda. 'The constables claim that no one has come this way. Not even a fly or a crow, according to one of them.'

'Tell them not to open the seal. Let's not call any attention to our presence here,' Gowda said, parking his car.

'How do we get in, sir?' Santosh asked.

'You only need the gates open if you are moving furniture.' Gowda touched the seal. 'It's easy to climb over them.'

Santosh didn't know what shocked him more: the sight of an ACP jumping over a gate, or a woman police officer doing the same. As he hesitated, Ratna turned to him and asked, 'Aren't you coming?'

Santosh followed quickly. The four of them switched on their phone torches and walked stealthily towards the house.

The house was locked and the police seal on the main door was intact as well. Silently, Gajendra and Santosh went around to check the back door while Ratna waited by the front. 'Come,' Gowda said to Ratna as he ran down the steps of the verandah to go towards the copse of trees.

He flashed the phone torch into the dense vegetation. There was nothing. Suddenly, he heard a crackling of twigs underfoot. 'I hear someone or something moving that way,' Ratna called as she ran back towards the front of the house. Gowda followed her. They heard the sound of leaves crunching once more. Then there was a commotion, as if someone had stumbled on a metal object. Gowda and Ratna hurried in the direction of the sound. But everything was silent again. 'Do you think it was a dog or a jackal?' Ratna asked Gowda.

'I don't think so.' Gowda shook his head as they walked back towards the house. 'It definitely sounded human.'

Gajendra chewed on his lips for a moment. 'Someone was here... Someone who saw the car stop by the gate and must have run to the back. But when we went to the rear of the house, he must have run towards that side of the property,' he said, pointing his phone torch to the left of the house. The beam picked a lone rubber flipflop and an upturned wheelbarrow beneath the avocado tree. 'We must have passed him as we walked to the back of the house,' Gowda spat in disgust at his own lack of alertness.

They walked slowly towards the house.

'The house seems untampered. All windows are latched and the back door is locked too,' Santosh said. He was cold and hungry. His phone showed the temperature to be 14 degrees Celsius and the sight of the digits made him feel even colder.

'Should we do a thorough search right away?' Santosh heard himself ask.

'Organizing one at this hour isn't going to be easy,' Gowda said. 'And even if we bring in the two sentries, the six of us won't be able to do much without proper lights. By which time, whoever is here or was here would have fled. There is no point in hanging around here. Let's go back.'

Much as he was fond of his team, he had decided to return here on his own. He knew he overlooked things when others were around. He didn't say much as he drove them back to the station. 'I'll see you in the morning,' he said brusquely and left.

# 9

Gowda left the car engine running and went to the doorway of his house. The curtain in the window upstairs stayed still and he didn't know if that disappointed or pleased him. He shoved his key into the lock and was relieved to hear it click open. He had been afraid that his father would have latched it from inside, which would have led to the elaborate production of him opening the door with a complaint—an old man like me needs his rest, etc.—and ending with Gowda snapping, 'Why do you have to latch the door? That's why I had to wake you up.'

It was a quarter past nine and his father had clearly retired to his room. Mr Right was waiting by the door, dancing on his hind legs. Gowda laughed at the dog. 'I wish your mistress would be half as delighted to see me...'

He tucked the dog under his arm, gathered his things and left as stealthily as he had entered. Either his father had fallen asleep or he had taken his hearing aid off, Gowda thought as he whispered a prayer of thanks.

As he drove through the quiet roads, he felt the knots in his shoulders unravel. He turned the radio on to soak in the silence. 'You don't mind, do you?' he asked Mr Right, who seemed to have no objection. 'I supposed you don't like Hindi songs, like Urmila,' Gowda said. For the first time in two days he finally had the headspace to think things through.

Why had someone gone through the elaborate ploy to send him and the team to a fictitious cockfight? Was there an agenda or was it done merely to confuse? Had they just needed to make sure that he and his team didn't rush to the Professor's property in case a control room call came through of trespassing? Who was the person who had run away from the Professor's property? What was he doing there? It was someone who knew the lay of the land. It wasn't a flat stretch, and with its multiple levels could cause a nasty accident, or at least a stumble and fall. The queries whirled and twirled in his head.

Gowda hit the steering wheel with the palm of his hand. When he realized he was almost at Urmila's block of flats, he wondered if he should continue driving around for a bit longer to clarify his thoughts, which finally seemed to be going in the right direction. But Mr Right, as if sensing that his home and Urmila were close by, began whining.

Gowda turned into the basement parking.

Urmila received him with a frosty glare and gathered Mr Right into her arms with a goofy smile. 'Have you missed me? Have you missed me, darling boy?' She baby-talked the dog while ignoring Gowda.

'Of course I missed you, darling,' Gowda whispered loudly.

She gave him a dirty look. 'I wasn't speaking to you.'

'I know,' Gowda grinned. 'I just thought I would answer for him.'

'Shut up, Borei,' Urmila said and let him in.

'Look, U, I need to explain,' Gowda began as he dropped into a sofa.

'What are you going to tell me that I already don't know? That you don't want your father finding out about us; that you don't want to mess things up, etc.' Urmila's tone was devoid of emotion.

Gowda shrugged. 'When you do get it, what are you so upset about?' he asked, unsure why he was being subject to such indignation.

'I don't have to like it even if I understand the situation,' Urmila said, sounding weary, the fight suddenly gone out of her.

Gowda stood up and went to her. He pulled her to him and held her tight. 'Do you think it doesn't bother me, U? Don't you know that I want to be with you?'

She wrapped her arms around him and so they stood for a long moment. That's all they had, Gowda knew, the here and now.

As if Urmila sensed this, she loosened her clasp and pulled his head down for a long kiss. When she moved away for air, he grinned at her. 'What was that?'

'An angry kiss.' She grinned back.

'Oh well, I think I should get you angry more often.' Gowda darted a sly look at her.

'Stop being cute, Borei, and kiss me,' Urmila growled.

Later, as they sat with their feet up and spooning muesli drowning in milk into their mouths, Urmila said, 'You are right, Borei, something isn't right at Janaki's home.'

Gowda turned to her, his spoon poised midway to his mouth. 'Why do you say that?'

Urmila chewed on a raisin. 'It's so strange. I used to watch Iqbal and Janaki together and feel envious of what they had. They were madly in love. She eloped with him because neither of their families approved or accepted their relationship.

'Once they were married, things did get better. Iqbal's family took them in, and Janaki's parents let them visit. But something felt off today. Janaki didn't mention Iqbal even once. I mean, she used to find it difficult to even start a sentence without saying Iqbal said this or Iqbal said that.'

'Maybe...' Gowda began and popped the spoonful of muesli into his mouth to bite down his words.

'Maybe... what?' Urmila frowned as she leaned sideways to place her bowl on a table.

'Maybe he had an affair,' Gowda said. 'And she found out.'

'You think so? I can't pinpoint what it is. Anger, fear or disgust. She seemed to shrink into herself when he came anywhere near her. That disturbed me.'

Gowda remembered Janaki being just as uncomfortable when Iqbal had put his arm around her on the day she found her father dead. He thought of the long-sleeved kurta she was wearing on that day and when they had visited the Buqhari home, and the make-up plastered on her face.

'Unless she comes forward and makes a complaint about him, there is little the police can do, U,' Gowda said gently. 'Who else was there at their house?'

'Some family. Lots of press, colleagues and several politicians. Papanna was bustling around as though he was the son-in-law and not Iqbal,' Urmila said. 'I asked Janaki about the walking stick, by the way. I said maybe we should keep it alongside the casket with his books, etc.'

'And?' Gowda sat up.

'She was vague about it. She said she didn't have the headspace to find it and just wanted the ceremonies to be over and done with. If there's anything else I remember, I'll call you.'

The clock had struck the half-hour chime. 'You need to leave, Borei. It's almost midnight. If your father wakes up, he'll wonder why you haven't come home.'

Gowda dug himself deeper into the sofa. 'Do I have to?'

Everything felt so right at this point. Gowda knew the moment he stepped out of Urmila's elegant doorway, the chaos and mess that constituted his days would fling itself at his face.

'You must, darling,' Urmila insisted, even though her eyes told him that she understood his reluctance to leave.

'In which case...' He rose, enveloped her in a hug, tickled Mr Right under his chin and left.

# 3 DECEMBER 2012, MONDAY

## 1

He had been unable to sleep. This was unusual for him as he was usually out cold even before his head touched the pillow. But he had stayed awake, unable to decide which thread of thought to follow: the missing assistant, Gurunath; the cockfight they had been lured away with; Janaki's behaviour around Iqbal; the walking stick that seemed to have mysteriously disappeared—and through it all, the puzzling question of the intruder on the Professor's property. Who had left the slipper behind and pushed aside the wheelbarrow to make enough noise to alert them to it? Was everything a charade to mess with their heads? Who would go to such lengths? And why was the woman upstairs so interested in his movements? He tossed and turned, trying to make sleep override the chaos in his head. Go to sleep, Gowda, he had told himself sternly.

He woke up a little past 4 a.m. He dressed hurriedly and went into the kitchen to put the coffee on for his father and himself. He laid out two flasks on a tray, one with warm water and the other with coffee. He set it on a tray and tip-toed to his father's bedside and placed the tray on the table there. He gazed at his sleeping father, who had his hands crossed at his chest and his mouth open. His chest rose and fell. Gowda had an overwhelming desire to caress his father's brow. But he resisted the impulse. He wanted to leave before Chidananda awoke and snared him into making small talk.

It was a quarter to five when he left.

A thick mist engulfed everything and the sun was nowhere in sight. Gowda's Bullet thumped through the road towards the Professor's house. It was silent and sombre and the thumping sound of Gowda's Bullet echoed as his headlights cut a swathe through the mist. The cold penetrated his jacket and gloves and chased all grogginess away.

The two constables, dressed in thick jackets and wearing monkey caps, were fast asleep, seated on their plastic chairs. Even the sound of his bike didn't rouse them. Gowda parked a little away so the Bullet was out of sight and looked at them in disgust. He knew that the cold and boredom had lulled them into sleep, but surely they had to wake up at the mighty sound of the Bullet. For a moment, he wondered if he should tell them exactly what he thought of policemen who slept while on duty. Then he decided to save it for later. He took a picture of them—one had drool stains on his chin and the other's palms were tucked between his thighs.

He vaulted over the gate, just as he had done the previous night. He wondered if it had been locked on 28 November. Not that it mattered. Anyone could jump over it easily. He made his way over to the place they had found the flipflop and upturned wheelbarrow. The slipper was gone but the wheelbarrow stood on its head.

They had debated about the flipflop last night, whether to leave it there or take it with them. Santosh had sniggered at Ratna, 'We still don't have the technology to match it to footprints.'

Ratna had glared at him but hadn't said anything.

'Do you think there's any point in taking this?' Gajendra looked at Gowda.

'No,' Gowda said. 'Absolutely no point. God knows how many millions of slippers Bata alone manufactures every year. Where do we even begin? Most people own a pair.'

'And some people keep the intact one of a pair,' Gajendra said, thinking of the mismatched pair of chappals he wore when watering his plants.

Gowda switched on his Maglite. Michael had given it to him saying, 'You need this more than I do.' Gowda would never pay as much for a torch, so he had accepted it gratefully.

In its powerful light, he saw a set of footprints beneath the avocado tree. Gowda bent to look at what had once been a grassy verge along the paved path. The shade of the tree had killed the grass and it was now mostly mud. The footprint markings were from a pair of boots. None of them had gone that way last night, or worn boots.

Gowda nibbled on his lower lip. And here was the question: had the slipper been there before last night? Had the owner retrieved it between then and now? Or had someone else—maybe the person wearing the boots—taken it away? Or had these footprints been there last night and gone unnoticed? It had been dark, and they had to make do with their phone torches. He hadn't thought of keeping a flashlight in his car.

No more using phone torches, he decided. They didn't cover as much area as a regular torch. He was going to put a circular out to that effect that everyone needed to carry a flashlight in their vehicles at all times.

He lit a cigarette and decided to take a walk along the perimeter of the property. He would go in the direction that the intruder had taken. That was where he would begin. Meanwhile, he would call Gajendra and ask him to get here ASAP.

Gowda set out from the left of the main gate, which had a granite fence along its entire length. After about 150 metres, the topography of the land changed, the dense tree cover making way for sparser vegetation. Cement posts on which remnants of vines grew suggested that this had once been a vineyard, and probably a flourishing one—it appeared to stretch for acres. At about 50 metres from the last line of cement posts, the fence turned the corner. Bougainvillea laden with pink, white and orange flowers grew in lush opulence along it.

Gowda walked its length till he reached the next property, a convent which also had a home for elderly persons and a vocational institute for orphan girls, Gajendra had told him. The nuns had grown bougainvillea shrubs along their side of the wall, which was about seven feet high. The bright flowers hid thorns on their branches that were an inch long. No one would try to jump over the fence unless they wanted to be tattered to shreds. It was better than having a guard dog or an alarm system. The intruder had certainly not scaled the wall from this point. Gowda walked along the convent wall that abutted the Professor's land. He wanted to see how far the bougainvillea stretched. Almost at 500 metres the convent grounds ended. The bushes had been trimmed a few feet after.

The granite fence now abruptly became a barbed-wire fence. On the other side was an empty tract of land overgrown with trees and shrubs and giant anthills. In the middle of the land was a little structure. The pump house, Gowda thought, taking in the several water tankers parked on a dirt track. In the distance were giant gates made of sheet metal.

Gowda stood on his toes to look as far as he could into the property. The well must be near the pump house, he thought as he scanned the land. Suddenly, he felt the cement post he was leaning on give way. Gowda managed to jump back as it began to topple.

He reached out and pushed it back, hard. The post corrected itself like a drunk man trying to stand upright. Gowda collected a few rocks and propped it up. As he brushed the soil off his hand, he bent down and touched the soil on the ground. It was still loose, as though it had been freshly dug. He examined the soil around the posts on either side. The two posts on the left as well as two on the right also looked like the soil around them had been dug recently.

A pale, watery sun had emerged by then. Across the fence Gowda saw a man walk to the gate. In the distance he could hear the sound of a tractor approaching.

Gowda took a few photographs of the cement posts and the land beyond it. From where he stood the Professor's house wasn't visible. The side of the cottage was, though. In fact, it wasn't too far from the fence. He took a photograph of that as well.

He continued to walk along the fence which had again turned into granite slabs. He paused and took another photograph of the change in fencing. A query had begun germinating in his head. The granite slabs ran the entire length of the property. On the other side of the granite fence was a eucalyptus grove. What lay beyond that? More land or a road?

There was a break in the fence for a tall metal-sheeted gate wide enough to let a small truck in. It was locked from within. Gowda stood at the gate and surveyed the property. A flattened piece of ground indicated a carpark. The line of thick trees that edged the clearing covered most of the cottage and it was barely visible from that angle as well. Gowda continued to walk. The fence suddenly turned at a right angle, and a few metres further stood a line of rooms with asbestos sheets as roofs. Three doors led off a narrow verandah and he saw a makeshift shack that had been erected to the side of the building. Beneath it was a TVS 50 and a CD100 Honda. Behind the shack was a narrow gate just wide enough for a bike to pass through. The gate opened into the eucalyptus grove, through which a tarred road was visible in the distance. If one looked carefully, that is, Gowda thought.

A man stood outside the line of rooms, brushing his teeth with great vigour. There was a well nearby and a woman was drawing water from it. They stared at Gowda, astonished to see a stranger on the premises. The man walked towards him, his toothbrush dangling from his foam-filled mouth.

Gowda pulled himself up to his full height. The man stopped in his tracks. He had seen enough policemen in his life to identify Gowda as one. Just in time. He had been about to demand who the fuck he was.

Instead, he pulled the toothbrush out of his mouth, wiped his lips with the back of his hand and said through the foam, 'Give me a minute, sir.' The woman offered him water to rinse his mouth.

'Sorry, sir,' the man said. 'Is anything the matter?'

'Not really,' Gowda drawled, 'except that a man was murdered here four nights ago.'

The man flushed and dropped his gaze.

'What's your name?' Gowda asked.

'Muniraju, sir.'

Gowda gestured to the woman. 'And she?'

'Kavitha, my missus.'

'And you live here?'

Muniraju nodded.

'Did you notice anything unusual on the night of 28 November?' Gowda asked, knowing very well that Muniraju would deny any knowledge about anything.

'I already told the police I was away.'

'He already told the police we were away,' the woman echoed from near the well.

'Tell me again,' Gowda said, pinning Muniraju to the spot with his narrowed gaze.

'I came back from work by eight.'

'Where do you work?'

'The Plaza Supermarket in Kothanur. I usually finish work by ten and reach home by ten-thirty. The next morning, I leave by ten; that's my usual routine.'

'So why did you take off early that day? And what about you?' Gowda turned to the woman.

'I was in the village,' she said. 'And he was with me.' She gestured to Muniraju.

'Did you notice or hear anything unusual? Some noise from the Professor's house? A dog barking? You were here until almost nine, right?' Gowda persisted, turning back to the man. Even consummate liars were known to blurt things out when they were asked the same question over and over again.

'Dogs? What dogs? We are not allowed to keep dogs here. We had to give ours away,' the woman called out.

Muniraju turned to frown at her, and Gowda without a change of expression lit another cigarette. 'Who doesn't let you keep dogs?'

The man looked at Gowda's cigarette yearningly. 'Deva Shetty, sir. He said the Professor disliked dogs and couldn't stand their barking. But it wasn't as if the Professor could walk this far. Even within the house, he used a stick. And no, sir, we didn't hear anything.'

'Are you from around here?' Gowda asked despite having guessed from the accent.

'We are from Hoskote, sir. We came here five years ago,' Muniraju said. 'My wife and I were in our village that night.'

'Anything special happening at your village? Why did you leave so late in the evening?'

'My mother was very unwell, so we went there to be with her,' Muniraju said.

'Where in Hoskote?' Gowda asked, blowing out a perfect smoke ring.

'Not too far from that biriyani fellow's place, sir. You know, where everyone from Bangalore City queues up to buy from. At six in the morning, can you imagine, sir?'

'How is your mother now?' Gowda asked.

'She is fine, sir,' Muniraju said, and then, unable to help himself, asked, 'Sir, do you have a cigarette to spare?'

Gowda thought of the last three sticks in the packet. 'Don't you know smoking will kill you,' he said through a whorl of smoke.

Then he offered the packet to the man and said, 'If smoking doesn't kill you something else will. Enjoy!'

Muniraju and his wife grinned and stood there watching him as he continued to walk along the last bit of fencing.

The granite continued, as did the dense tree cover. The cottage wasn't visible from any other side. Gowda took one final set of photographs, then walked back towards the gate. It was a quarter to seven—where the hell was Gajendra? Just then, he saw the police vehicle approach. By now the constables must be awake and quaking in their shoes at the sight of his bike. Or so he hoped.

Gowda placed a bet with himself.

The jeep pulled up and Gajendra stepped out and walked towards the gates. Something on him glinted—the flask slung over one shoulder. Gowda smiled. Sometimes a man deserves to be right. One extra drink tonight was his reward.

He saw Gajendra speak to the constables as they fumbled with the lock and seal. Gowda crossed his arms and stood there watching. He was too far away to hear what was being said but he was certain Gajendra would be stripping their skin into ribbons with his tongue. He had a special brand of ire reserved for constables caught sleeping on duty.


# 2


David drove towards the porch and pulled up under it. Gowda walked towards the jeep.

'Good morning, sir,' Gajendra said, stepping out and saluting him. Gowda saluted him back. It was a tradition between them from a long time ago.

'Do they do it every day?' Gopal asked under his breath.

'Every single day,' David muttered.

'How did ACP Gowda reach here?' Gopal asked.

'Didn't you see his bike parked outside?'

'Are you saying he jumped over the gate?'

David grinned. 'I don't think he can fly yet.'

Gopal wondered if one had to be insolent to be eligible for Gowda's team.

Gajendra looked in their direction. 'Bring the jute carry bag,' they heard him demand.

As David and Gopal walked towards the others, Gopal asked in his most artless voice, 'Do you know what's going on?'

David shrugged. 'Absolutely no idea,' he said.

'Leave the bag here and return to the station,' Gowda said. 'Gajendra can ride back with me.'

Gajendra gestured to the jeep. 'Bring me the spare helmet, will you?'

As Gopal walked towards the gate with David following in the police vehicle, Gajendra opened the bag and started placing food parcels on the bench beneath the avocado tree. 'Why don't we eat first before we get down to work?'

Gowda frowned and was about to tell Gajendra he should get his priorities right, when he saw Gajendra extract a forensics kit from beneath the food parcels.

Gajendra grinned. 'I didn't want Gopal here, sir. I don't trust him fully. That boy has eyes like a rat, darting this way and that way all the time.'

'What's the kit for? The CCB and the forensics team have scoured every inch of the house,' Gowda said as he opened the tiffin box lined with a banana leaf to find a set dosa. Gajendra opened a steel box filled with sagu.

Gowda looked at the vegetable curry with delight and dismay. It was one of his favourite combinations on a wintry morning, but the thought of Mrs Gajendra slaving in the kitchen filled him with guilt.

'You shouldn't have put your wife to such trouble,' Gowda said. 'You could have picked up something from a Darshini restaurant.'

Gajendra poured coffee into the mug built into the flask lid. 'No trouble at all, sir. And which Darshini opens at this hour? Useless fellows. They start sweeping the floors only at seven.'

Gowda started eating, knowing Gajendra wouldn't begin until he did. The first mouthful made him feel like he had died and gone to heaven. He hadn't tasted food this delicious.

Gajendra looked at his rapturous expression with delight. For a few minutes there was silence as they ate and drank. When Gowda was done, Gajendra pulled out a bottle of water. Gowda took a big sip. All he needed was a smoke and they could get to work. He reached for his pack in his trouser pocket and remembered he had handed the last three to Muniraju.

Gowda looked at Gajendra and said, 'Now if you could produce a cigarette, I might just marry you.'

Gajendra blushed and reached into the depths of the bag. He pulled out a pack of Classic Milds. 'I won't hold you to your promise, sir.' He grinned.

Gowda grinned back as he lit the cigarette. Inhaling slowly, he said, 'I suppose you want to check the wheelbarrow for prints.'

'I do, sir. There will be several, I know, but I want to check if there are any that belong to Paul Selvam.'

Gowda stood up.

'The slipper's gone, by the way,' Gowda said. 'And there is a set of footprints. Looks like a boot. The thing is, I don't know if it was here already, what with so many people having walked through the property, or if the person from last night left it.' Gowda took a photograph. He placed his foot alongside. It was a size bigger than his. That made it size ten.

Gajendra busied himself trying to fingerprint the wheelbarrow. He had done a refresher course in forensics, and had been itching to give it a shot after a new forensics kit had been brought to the station just last week. When he was done, Gowda asked, 'What about the cottage? Weren't you here when the forensics team looked at it?'

'Well, sir, they did. But they just gave the cottage a cursory look. It isn't a scene of crime. And there was that double murder crime scene in Jakkur they needed to get to. It was a job hastily done, if you ask me. Should I call SI Santosh and ASI Ratna, sir?' Gajendra asked, walking towards the house.

Gowda paused. 'What about the sniffer dogs?'

'The dog squad didn't find anything conclusive either.'

'Let's go check this cottage.'

They went towards the cluster of trees through which the path ran towards the cottage.

'Check that man Muniraju's story about his and his wife's whereabouts on 28 November,' Gowda said.

Gajendra frowned. 'I am inclined to put Byrappa on this. But we are already so short-staffed.'

Gowda nodded. 'No need. I'll have someone from the Hoskote station check out that end of it but first get Byrappa to check if Muniraju was on duty at Plaza Supermarket that night, and what time he left.'

It took them a few minutes to reach the cottage tucked deep into the property.

'You can't see the cottage from any of the perimeter walls or the main gate. But you can from the property with the well.' Gowda showed Gajendra the photographs on his phone. 'I know Byrappa has brought us details of the adjacent properties. But dig a little deeper into the well property.'

In the distance the sound of tractors approaching and leaving shattered the quiet with a constant drone.

Gajendra produced a key.

'Where did you get that and the gate keys from?' Gowda asked, sounding worried. It seemed like his bending of the rules was a contagious affliction.

'The forensics team gave it to me for safekeeping until they were done. I took them happily. I sort of knew that you would like a good look at whatever it is you would want to look at.'

'Let's walk around before we go in.'

On the eastern side of the cottage was a line of French windows opening on to a long deck lined with tubs of palm. The deck was furnished with two cane chairs upon which sat fat green cushions, and a cane table with a glass top. Thick beige curtains hid the room, but one end of a curtain had a long tear, almost as if someone had pulled hard in their haste to close it.

The row of geraniums planted in the ground along the deck had been trampled. Gajendra bent down to look at the broken stalks and crushed florets. 'Someone was here last night, sir... look at this!' Gajendra straightened and asked, 'What do you think there is in here, sir? For them to go through that elaborate drama to get us out of the way...'

Gowda pulled at the bridge of his nose. 'I'm sure this cottage was never used by the Professor. It's too far for him to get here. So who used the place?'

Gajendra nodded.

Gowda said, 'I think we should call Santosh and Ratna.'

Gajendra looked up with a smile. 'Sir, they are already on their way. I informed them.'

The two of them looked at the photograph on the screen. 'So you think the murderer came in through the well property to get to the Professor's house?' Santosh turned to Gowda.

'What about the small gate near the row of rooms?' Gajendra asked.

'The assailant could have come from the front gate too. Jumped over like we did,' Ratna said.

'Who locked the gate at night? Did the Professor do it?' Gowda asked. 'I'm not sure he would have been able to walk even that far. Even if he could, I don't think he would have,' he added. 'Somehow I don't see him doing it. I know his type. Going on all day about women being marginalized and at home not lifting a finger to even fetch himself a glass of water.'

Ratna nodded. For once she was in total agreement with Gowda. 'Mary Susheela would lock the gate and latch the back door at night. But she wasn't sure if she did or didn't on 28 November after all the commotion of her being bitten. She also said the latch was faulty and that she placed the kitchen chair against the door to hold it in place,' Ratna said.

'Which means the gate wasn't locked on 28 and 29 November. Check with Janaki Buqhari if it was when she came in here on 30 November.'

'The forensics team must have gone over the place with a fine-toothed comb. What do you think we are going to find?' Ratna whispered to Santosh.

Santosh whispered back, 'Sometimes he gets a hunch and it usually leads to something. When I first started work I had heard about Gowda's instinct. The Head Constable at Meenakshipalya station had called it his "sakkath sense". He made it sound like an extra set of arms that allowed Gowda to hold a phone and a cup of coffee while writing out a report. When the sakkath sense nudges him, you know the case is coming to an end. "Deal time aagithe, sir," Muni Reddy would say.'

Ratna frowned. 'Sakkath? Do you think that's his way of saying sixth sense?'

'Whatever... it means the same,' Santosh shrugged, his mind still on Meenakshipalya Station.

'Muni Reddy said something else too. That Gowda was fearless and intelligent. Which, according to him, is a terrible combination for a policeman. He goes looking for trouble.' Santosh sighed.

'Are we stepping into trouble?' Ratna sounded worried.

Gowda looked at the two of them. 'What is the matter?'

Like schoolchildren caught sucking on candy in class, they flushed and said, 'Nothing, nothing at all, sir.'

'Let's enter the cottage, sir.' Gajendra led the way to the front

door. 'The forensics team is yet to go over the cottage properly.
Do keep that in mind, everybody.'

# 3

The door opened into a large living room with a luxurious leather
couch, a giant TV, bookshelves and a rolltop desk. 'It looks like
the workspace of a writer in an English movie,' Santosh said.

Gowda smiled at him. 'That's exactly what I thought when
I saw it through the window. It looks like a movie set. And now
you just gave it context. It is meant to suggest a man of letters
and means. Namely, our deceased Professor Raghava Mudgood.'

Gajendra walked towards the windows one by one, checking
the latch on each of them. Santosh and Ratna started examining
the furniture. Gowda went towards the desk. He paused at the
bookshelves. Row after row of leather-bound books ran from
end to end. Pulling out one at random, he was startled by its
lightness. He flicked it open—it was a school textbook bound in
leather with gold-embossed lettering on its spine. Gowda took
out a few more books. School textbooks, university textbooks,
pulp fiction—anything that fit had been suited and booted and
shoved into the bookshelf. 'Look at this,' Gowda called out.

The others rushed towards him. Gowda handed them each
a book. They opened it gingerly and Gowda saw their faces take
on a myriad of expressions: a perplexed Gajendra, an excited
Santosh and just-what-the-fuck-is-going on Ratna.

'It really is like a movie set,' Gowda said.

'I know this sounds ridiculous, but do you think this house
is given out for film shoots?' Santosh ran a finger along a row of
books.

'Probably. And probably not. Let's check the rest of the house
and we'll decide.' Gowda opened the rolltop desk. Again, it had
all the markings of being used by a writer. A few notebooks, a

tray with a fountain pen and a bottle of ink. Gowda opened a notebook. It was blank.

Above the desk was a cabinet. Gowda opened it to find bottles of alcohol. A few single malts, a bottle of gin and a bottle of vodka. He took a photograph.

The living room led to a passage, beyond which was a bedroom with a canopied four-poster bed and an en-suite bathroom that would overwhelm even a decadent Roman emperor. It had a stand-alone bathtub and a circular shower cubicle. The taps were golden and light fixtures vintage bronze. Gowda opened a built-in cupboard and saw towels which were neatly rolled and stacked. The washbasin counter was laid out with a vast array of toiletries.

Gajendra gazed at the bathroom in disbelief. He had never seen anything like this, not even in films.

'Sir, I think this is a love nest,' Gajendra said, eyeing the tub with the jacuzzi and the corner of the ceiling with the glass-tiled roof and rain shower.

'Or maybe where they shoot porn,' Ratna said.

Santosh frowned. How did Ratna know of such things?

Gowda stepped away from the bathroom and said, 'Do you see that not one of the toiletries has been used? And everything is spick and span... the water in this area has a high limescale content and it leaves residue on all fixtures. No sign of that.' He was thinking of his home and the bathroom fixtures that were covered in a patina of white.

'What do you think they are hiding?' Ratna asked, looking around the bathroom again.

'What could be hidden in this cardboard house?' Santosh asked, stepping into the corridor. At the end of it was the kitchen. They went there next.

'Now this looks familiar,' Gajendra said. 'Similar to what I've seen on cookery shows.'

'What?' Gowda frowned. 'You have the time to watch cookery shows?'

'Not me, sir. My wife,' Gajendra hastened to explain. 'She watches a cooking show where the chef seems to specialize in food for rabbits. Everything she makes is raw, leafy and crunchy.'

Gowda opened the overhead cabinets. Everything they contained seemed new and unused, all the jars and bins filled to the brim with rice and wheat; lentils and spices...

'Do you think at least this is real?' Gajendra opened the jar of rice. He sniffed at it. 'It isn't.' His horror was palpable.

The dining room was an extension of the kitchen. The French windows opened to the deck. Gowda looked at the torn curtain which looked as if someone had tugged at it rather than use the motorized cord. Someone who didn't know how exactly to draw them close, perhaps, or someone in a tearing hurry.

So what was that someone—maybe a person who wore flip-flops—doing in a house that was already spotless and didn't look like anyone lived in it? If he had come to change a lightbulb, why do so in the dead of night? What else was there for him to do?

Gowda saw a door on one side of the kitchen. 'What's there?'

Ratna pushed it open. It led into a passage which had a wide staircase leading down at its end. A secret room? Wooden planks were stacked alongside a wall of the passage. 'You need to see this,' Ratna called out with unconcealed excitement. Gowda reached the door before Gajendra and Santosh had the time to register her summons.

Gajendra stared at the staircase in shock. 'We didn't see this when I came in with the forensics team.'

Gowda bent to look at the stack of wooden planks. 'This is why,' he said. 'These planks were used to board the entrance of the staircase. The staircase is too wide for a door and besides a door that size would be conspicuous. See, they are numbered. If you turn them around, I'm sure they will be the colour of the walls,' Gowda said. 'What do you think is down there?'

'A drug lab making illegal substances?' Santosh asked.

Gowda walked towards the head of the staircase and paused. 'Gloves on, everybody,' he said, unaware that the others were already pulling theirs on. Gajendra offered him a pair. Gowda wore them, switched on his Maglite and started descending the wooden staircase. He came to a small landing and a second flight of stairs.

Gowda stood at the foot of the stairs and gaped at the expanse of the basement. He groped along the wall for a switchboard. The lights came on. Wall lights in all four corners and one in the centre of the ceiling as if it were a stadium. The basement looked even more vast and desolate with all the lights on.

'But there is nothing here,' Santosh said in an astonished voice.

Like the emperor's new clothes, Gowda thought. Nothing at all but the machinations of a cunning mind.

'I thought we would find an illegal meth lab or some drugs or something here,' Santosh said. 'What's that?' At the farthest end of the basement hung a punching bag.

One wall had a stack of plastic chairs against it. Gajendra looked at Gowda, puzzled. 'Do you think this is a place for prayer meetings?' One of his neighbours, a devout Pentecostal man, held a prayer meeting in his living room every few weeks and he remembered seeing stacks of plastic chairs being hired for the occasion. His eyes fell on a pile of folded gunny bags on the topmost chair as Santosh walked towards it.

'Sir, do you think this is a terrorist sleeper cell?' Santosh asked, not quite meeting Gowda's eyes. He knew that Gowda could very well snap his head off for that. 'Iqbal Buqhari—he is Muslim, after all.'

'Terrorists have no religion.' Gowda glared at Santosh. 'They worship their own immortality by killing or dying. If Iqbal Buqhari is a terrorist, it's not because he's Muslim.'

Silence crept into the room. Gajendra cleared his throat while Ratna examined the punching bag. Santosh swallowed loudly.

Gowda pointed to a door. 'Santosh, check that door.'

'It's a room, sir,' he called out as he pushed the door open.

Gowda followed Santosh into the sparsely furnished room. A peculiar reek greeted them. A composite of several smells, but it was disinfectant and room freshener that fought with each other to dominate. Gowda spotted the bottle of room freshener on a table behind a stack of toilet rolls. He picked it up and sniffed at it. It reminded him of the library at the Buqhari residence.

The room had a table, a chair and a bed. The walls were bare except for a mirror. A steel cupboard was placed in one corner.

'Odd place for an almirah,' Gowda said, twisting the handle. It was locked. He began pushing the cupboard to one side, and Gajendra and Santosh rushed to assist him. Behind the cupboard was a door which Gowda pushed open.

It was a bathroom with a shower cubicle of frosted glass, and a WC. An entire wall was a mirror with a crack running through it. On the washbasin counter was a much-squeezed tube of toothpaste, a bottle of handwash and a bottle of Dettol. A cabinet on another wall had cotton pads, a tube of Soframycin and a box of band-aids.

Gowda opened the door to the shower cubicle. His eyes widened. Someone had made a hasty attempt to clean up blood, but missed a few drops which were lodged in a corner. Gajendra and Santosh peered over Gowda's shoulder to see what had caught his eye. 'I suppose this is what they were trying to clean up,' Gajendra said.

'What do we do about this, sir?' Santosh asked.

'For now, let it stay between us,' Gowda said, feeling a strange reluctance to let the department or DCP Sagayaraj in on it.

'But don't we need the forensics staff to check it?' Ratna asked.

Gowda smiled. 'We do. And I know someone at the Madiwala lab. I'll ask him to come at the earliest. After he collects all the physical evidence he can find, we'll enter the discovery in the case diary and then forensics can make one more official visit.'

None of them said anything as Gowda fished out his phone and took pictures of the bathroom. He WhatsApped the pictures to his contact at the lab. When he put his phone back in his pocket, he said, 'Simon will be here in an hour. I want one of you here.'

Gajendra cleared his throat. 'I'll stay, sir. As you know I did this refresher course in forensics evidence collection but that was just classroom learning. Observing him will be helpful, sir.'

Gowda nodded. 'Get Simon to examine the basement. Every square inch of it.' Then he turned to Santosh and Ratna. 'I want you to go to the records office and check something. Find out what this building is registered as. I'll bet you a thousand bucks that it will be a godown or warehouse. Get a copy of the blueprint as well. And go to all the hospitals in a three-kilometre radius to check if any medico-legal cases are registered. Another thousand bucks says you will find none.'

To his disappointment, neither of them were inclined to challenge him. His certainty was too daunting to refute.

'How is any of this connected with Professor's Mudgood's murder?' Ratna asked when they were back in the kitchen. 'Maybe there was a brawl of some sort here, but it could have nothing to do with the murder.'

Santosh looked at Ratna as much in admiration as outrage. None of them would dare question Gowda on why he wanted something done. Ratna was too feisty for her own good. He waited for Gowda to snap at her. Instead, Gowda shrugged. 'Right now I can't tell you why but I want to be certain that Professor Mudgood's homicide isn't linked to his politics. Murders of high-profile victims always come attached with a political narrative. This one will be no different.'

The others read his expression: End of discussion.

'Ratna and Santosh, I want you to check with Janaki Buqhari about the gates as well,' Gowda said. He checked the time. It was a quarter to nine. 'Talk to Muniraju, the man in the line house, Gajendra,' Gowda said. 'He knows more than he is telling us.

Simon will call you when he is at Kothanur. You can give him
directions from there. And he'll drop you back at the station.
We should get the results of the scrapings from beneath the
Professor's fingernails soon, I hope.

'One other thing. We need to examine the house and grounds
thoroughly once more. The Professor's missing walking stick has
to be here somewhere. He used it all the time. Where has it gone?
I think the head injury he had was caused by his walking stick.
The assailant probably wanted to weaken him first.'

Gajendra nodded and waited for all of them to step out.
Santosh and Ratna watched Gowda as he hurried away. 'Where
do you think he is going?' Ratna asked, wondering what he wasn't
telling them.

'Home, probably. His father hasn't left yet,' Santosh said as
he started the bike. 'Do you want to stop for breakfast on the
way?' He turned to look at Ratna who sat astride the pillion. He
was now used to occasionally giving her a lift on his bike but it
still didn't feel right.

Ratna nodded. 'I'm so ravenous that I could eat an elephant.'

Santosh grinned. 'Me too. I might need a camel as well.' He
was rewarded with a finger jabbing him in the ribs.

'Get going unless you want me to ride the bike,' Ratna said,
adjusting her helmet strap.

# 4

Gowda rode away, wondering if he should go home and check
on his father. He had called Shanthi and asked her to come in as
early as she could. Another half hour would make no difference,
he thought, taking a left.

He needed to find the narrow road he had seen beyond the
property after the Professor's house. He wanted to see for himself
what was on the other side of the perimeter wall. He wasn't sure

what he was hoping to find, or what bearing it had on the case. But he knew that in this new Bangalore, 60 per cent of crimes were real estate linked. Find a reason and you will find the murderer, he told himself.

It took him a while and he had to go through a labyrinth of little lanes before he found himself on a road that seemed to lead towards Horamavu on the right. He took a left and continued down the road. He saw a board that read: This way to El Dorado. A thick black arrow indicated the way ahead. He rode past a eucalyptus grove and a couple of coconut plantations, the El Dorado billboards rearing their heads at every 500 metres. Then to his left he spied a giant arch painted yellow. Beneath it were big metal gates. The arch was painted with the letters *El Dorado*.

Gowda slowed down, idling the bike. He was somewhere in the vicinity of the Professor's property. He honked. The gates stayed shut.

He stopped his bike and looked through the metal bars of the gate. In the distance he could see the Professor's back gate. Within El Dorado, there was nothing but plots marked for property development.

As Gowda turned into the lane that led to his house, he felt a familiar sense of trepidation. This was how it had been when he would reach home after school basketball practice, knowing that along with the lime juice followed by coffee and tiffin would be his irate father demanding where he had been and what he had been up to. 'Have you seen the time?' Chidananda's expression would curdle an old man's blood and be the death of babies.

Gowda no longer thought about it, but he had been unable to shake off the sense of foreboding that haunted him whenever he returned home to someone waiting for him. A fear that he would be castigated for no reason, with the only certainty being that somehow it was always his fault.

Gowda saw his father seated on the verandah reading the newspaper as he rode into the side porch where he parked his vehicles. He noticed Chidananda's frown was in place for the torrent of recrimination that was about to begin.

'Good morning, Appa,' Gowda said as he unclasped his helmet.

'You can fry your good morning and eat it as a snack,' his father began. 'Do you know what time it is? Where were you? Is this how a responsible police officer behaves? I am not surprised that Mamtha ran away to live in Hassan. Which wife is going to tolerate this sort of behaviour?'

Gowda walked into the house without saying a word. He heard his father fling down the newspaper and follow him. When Chidananda was furious, Gowda noticed, he didn't hobble or shuffle. He strode around, rage lending agency to his gait and demeanour.

Gowda turned and looked at him. He pointed to the clock. 'It's a quarter to eleven and I have been up and working from four-thirty in the morning. It's because I am a responsible police officer that I have to go when my team needs me or if there is a development in the investigation. As for Mamtha, that's between her and me,' Gowda said in his most patient but stern voice and walked into his room. For the first time he understood why Roshan would bang the door of his room after an argument. But he was a fifty-one-year-old ACP and he couldn't do the same. He gently shut the door on his father's frown.

Gowda pulled his clothes off and, despite the nip in the air, turned on the cold water tap, letting the icy jets calm him down. It felt like he had been awake forever and climbed a mountain or two.

When he had dressed in a fresh set of his uniform that Shanthi had thoughtfully left on a hanger hooked to the wardrobe knob, he felt human again. And ready to face his father's wrath. Chidananda Gowda wasn't a man to take an altercation lying down.

But it was a benign father who looked up when Gowda walked into the living room.

'Why don't you eat lunch before you leave?' He smiled.

Gowda hid his astonishment well. If his father wanted to pretend that no words had been exchanged, he would play along.

'I will do that,' he said. 'How about you? Would you like to join me?'

'Why not?' Chidananda said, rising from his chair. 'Bhuvana asked if I wanted to go to a movie with her. It's best I eat early.'

'Who is Bhuvana?' Gowda blinked in surprise. The name sent a shiver down his spine. She had left a trail of victims and disappeared into thin air. They still hadn't been able to find a lead even though Gowda hadn't yet given up.

You are paranoid, he told himself when his father burst into laughter. 'Don't you even know your tenant's name?'

Gowda grinned at his father. 'I think of her as Mrs Tenant.'

'She's a wonderful person,' his father said. 'Very concerned about you. She came down now a little while ago to ask if everything was all right. Apparently she saw you come in a little after midnight. I thought you left last night with the dog and were coming home now,' Chidananda said. 'I thought it was Shanthi who had prepared my coffee,' he added.

In his father's lexicon, this constituted an apology and Gowda accepted it. Though it rankled that the woman upstairs had had to vouch for him.

He walked into the dining room and sat at the table. His father followed. Gowda began telling him about the Professor's homicide. Chidananda listened quietly. 'Old people shouldn't live alone,' he said. 'Do you remember the double murder in Jayanagar? The retired couple? The maid they had trusted for years let in a man who killed them. No one can be trusted, Borei. That's the fact we have to learn to live with.'

Gowda nodded. He didn't dare tell his father that the man who had killed the elderly couple had been hired by their son to do so. 'With the Professor, there could be other reasons too,' he added.

'That's true. He wrote a lot of nonsense and annoyed many people. I am surprised that he wasn't bumped off before. You can't offend people's sentiments without consequences,' Chidananda said, adding rasam to his plate of rice.

'I didn't know you were familiar with the Professor's work.'

'I read a book of his on Basava and liked it. I started reading his column in *Prajavani*. But in the last two years I have had my doubts about his sanity,' his father said, gulping down a glass of water.

'Why is that, Appa?'

'Anyone can choose to be an atheist but you can't mock people who believe. You can't ridicule people for their faith. I understand how religion is being used to manipulate things. But that doesn't give him the right to reduce faith into what he called "fairytales for grown-up children". He wanted all temples, churches and mosques to be demolished and instead have meditation centres in their place open to anyone.'

'I see,' Gowda said, not seeing it at all. He had heard these sentiments repeated before and the men and women who had made them were still alive. 'I should get going, Appa. One of my colleagues should be returning now from Dharwad with the Professor's assistant,' Gowda said, trying to clear the table. 'I may be late again tonight.'

'As long as you keep me informed, it doesn't bother me what time you come and go,' Chidananda said. 'You may be a fifty-one-year-old man, Borei, but you are still my child and I worry when I don't know where you are.'

Gowda nodded. 'I understand, Appa. Enjoy your outing. Call me if you need anything,' he added, knowing it was expected of him to say that.

# 5

The station house was busier than usual for a Monday. There were several people by the gate as well as inside.

'Why are there more people here than at Shivaji Nagar bus stand,' Gowda muttered under his breath to PC David.

He kept a straight face. 'It's been like this since daybreak, sir. Some altercation between two property owners and things got out of hand. One of them ran a machete through another's thigh and now members of both families are demanding justice.'

Gowda grunted. Land ownership did strange things to people. It turned them into adventurers or pioneers, monsters or megalomaniacs. And some men would do anything to grab a piece of land. Perhaps even murder. Was that what happened to Professor Mudgood... But most people, including his father, thought it was the Professor's controversial views that had led to his death.

No one from his team was in, except for Gopal, who was lurking by his chamber, hoping to catch his eye. Gowda ignored him and went into his room. A stack of files sat on his table. Aqthar and Byrappa would arrive in about a couple of hours, along with Gurunath, the Professor's assistant. All hell would break loose when Sagayaraj discovered that Gowda's officers had whisked away the assistant right under his nose. Meanwhile, it would be best to deal with the files. Sometimes, there was something therapeutic about looking at the mundane details of police work.

An hour later, Gowda had cleared half a dozen files. It was time for a smoke, he decided as he walked to the mango tree. The skies were an indecent blue, with tiny puffs of clouds here and there. At 33,000 feet high, the world was a beautiful place, but down here the rot festered. Its stench was the rank odour of decay rising from the drying lake, settling on everything and everyone. He heard movement behind him. It was Gopal holding a beaker of tea.

'I thought you might need this,' he said.

Gowda shot him a semblance of a smile.

'Sir, did you find anything this morning at the crime scene?' Gopal asked, seizing the moment.

Gowda felt his face freeze. Without batting an eyelid, he shook his head. 'Nothing at all. I have a feeling we are wasting our time. The CCB is in control of the investigation. It's best they take over.'

Gopal said nothing, Gowda noted. He didn't think Gopal believed him. Time to throw him a bone to take to his master.

'The maid's husband is still under scrutiny. His wife hinted about a possible cockfight to ASI Ratna and the team went looking, but when they got there... nothing at all.' Gowda shrugged. 'Though there are two constables on duty there, I thought we should check on the crime scene. Again, nothing at all...'

Gowda hammed disappointment and frustration. He hoped his acting skills had improved considerably since his last theatrical appearance.

Gopal suddenly seemed in a hurry to leave. 'Sir, I have to go to the site of the land dispute. ASI Prakash wanted me to go with them. Sir, have you thought about my request? I really want to be part of your team.'

'We may not have a team if the CCB takes over this case. Let me see... thanks for the tea, Gopal,' Gowda said carefully.

Gopal trotted away. Gowda noticed he took out his phone and began tapping away even before he was out of Gowda's sight.

After his smoke break, as he walked into the station building, he saw Santosh and Ratna arrive on Ratna's 100 cc motorbike, which she wouldn't let anyone else ride. Santosh had had no option but to ride pillion. His face was a study in fear, anxiety and embarrassment, Gowda thought with a secret laugh.

*

Gowda was waiting for them in his office.

'Who wants to go first?' he said, feeling curiously like his school headmaster who liked to greet student committees or warring parents with this query.

Santosh and Ratna turned to look at Gajendra hopefully.

'Mr Simon was on time, sir,' Gajendra said, clearing his throat. 'He did a thorough study of the place and took samples. He also fingerprinted the basement floor and the bathroom.'

Gowda nodded.

'One other thing. I asked Mr Simon to also look at the main house and the scene of crime. He sees things we don't.'

Gowda rested his chin on his clasped hands. 'Excellent thinking,' he said. 'Anything of interest?'

Gajendra nodded. 'The punching bag, sir... Mr Simon thought he would look for fingerprints and DNA samples on that as well.'

'And now we must wait to see what he comes up with,' Gowda said.

'You were right, sir,' Santosh began. 'The plan for the cottage shows it as an agricultural storeroom.'

'I thought as much. But how did they get permission? It had ACs, as we saw.'

Ratna smiled. 'The Professor was a partner in a flower export business and a flower storeroom requires ACs to keep them fresh.'

Gowda wondered how they had managed to extract such detailed information in a couple of hours. 'What about the well property?' Gowda asked. 'Anything about that?'

'It belongs to someone called Naga Reddy. We have his details,' Ratna said.

Santosh read Gowda's expression as he played with the glass paperweight. 'Sir, I'll check on him...' He began and paused at the knock on the door.

Gowda waved them in. Aqthar and Byrappa were accompanied by a slender bearded man wearing glasses. Everything about him screamed as if marked out with neon strips: academic. Intellectual.

Gowda gestured for them to sit as he studied the young man's darting eyes, pinched nostrils and the stiff set of his shoulders.

'This is Gurunath Badige,' Aqthar said. 'Professor Mudgood's assistant.'

Gowda gave him a brief nod and said, 'I am very sorry for your loss.'

Gurunath relaxed. 'Thank you, sir. I was his assistant for the last four years. We were very attached to each other. When he died, it was as if I lost both my mentor and my anchor.'

Gowda nodded. He let the silence stretch. Then he looked up and asked without changing his inflection, 'And yet you didn't even attend his funeral. Why did you stay away, Gurunath? Didn't you want to see him one last time?'

Gurunath stared at the floor.

'I suppose you would like to freshen up. Have you eaten anything?' Gowda asked, changing his tone.

Aqthar looked at Gowda with admiration. Interrogation didn't always necessitate force. In less than a minute, Gowda had managed to put Gurunath at ease, then churned him up again and finished on an avuncular note of concern. Gurunath would be so unsettled that he would be unable to lie with ease now. Gowda had ensured that.

Gowda turned to Gajendra. 'Take him to the interrogation room and get him some lunch. We will join you in about half an hour.'

Gajendra nodded. He understood that Gurunath was not to be let out of sight. Byrappa got up and went along with them. He knew something was afoot and there would be no time for a debriefing.

Gowda looked at Aqthar. 'How did you find him? And more importantly, how did you convince him to come here?'

Aqthar smiled. A complacent smile that started at his eyes and ended at his mouth, making his face gleam with mischief. 'I have my sources, sir. And I had put someone on the job even before we started from here. I didn't want to waste time. Just as I thought, Gurunath had gone to his village, about 40 kilometres from Dharwad. PC Byrappa and I went there straight.'

'And?' Ratna leaned forward.

Santosh frowned. Gowda narrowed his eyes at the two of them. One was behaving like a besotted calf and the other was playing Othello. Fortunately, Aqthar seemed completely impervious to the drama unfolding before him.

'Gurunath, I discovered, has been accepted for a PhD programme in the US on a full scholarship. I told him that a police complaint could throw that plan out of the window and it was best he come with us rather than be hauled away by the CCB.'

'Very smart move, that.' Gowda smiled.

'How did you evade the CCB? They are looking for Gurunath too,' Santosh asked, not certain how he felt about Gowda's words of praise for Aqthar. Gowda seldom took to anyone, everyone knew that. And he had always been told by Gajendra that Gowda had a soft spot only for him. He wasn't inclined to share that soft spot.

'There is a late-night train which starts from Dharwad, sir. I boarded it from there so anyone watching would see just me getting on board. Byrappa stayed with Gurunath and they boarded the Vasco Da Gama Express from Hubli instead of Dharwad. And here we are.'

'Excellent,' Gowda said, standing up. 'Law enforcers mustn't break the law but there are many ways to skin a cat. And now let's talk to Gurunath. But first I need to make a call. I need to skin a cat too.'

Gowda looked at his phone, uncertain how to phrase what he had to say. DCP Sagayaraj was sure to give him an earful, but there was no escaping it.

'Hello, Stanley,' he began. 'How's it going?'

Sagayaraj gave him a list of everything that was going wrong. The hotel was all right but the food way too bland. His team wasn't making much headway in Dharwad. 'As for that Gurunath, he seems to have disappeared. We have to put out a lookout notice,' he concluded.

Gowda knew there wouldn't be a better opening. So he waited for the DCP's tirade to end and said, 'Sir, Gurunath is here with me in the station.'

'Are you serious?' Sagayaraj thundered. 'How did he land up there?'

Gowda pulled at the bridge of his nose, wondering what to admit to. 'SI Aqthar, the police officer on deputation here, had gone back to Dharwad to visit his family and met him while he was there. He persuaded him to travel with him to Bangalore. He is here now.'

'Is that so?' The DCP's sarcasm was evident, but Gowda pretended not to recognize it for what it was.

'Well, keep him there till I get back. He's one of the prime suspects in this homicide. Don't let him out of sight till I get back tomorrow,' Sagayaraj said. 'We are heading to the Professor's residence in Dharwad and will start back immediately after.'

When the DCP cut the call, Gowda exhaled. He walked back to his room where the three officers were waiting.

'It's best that only SI Aqthar come with me into the interrogation room,' he said.

'Sir?' Ratna protested, voicing Santosh's irritation as well.

'Gurunath will need to be coaxed to talk, and it's best that I go in alone. And since SI Aqthar is already known to him, I want him there,' Gowda said, cutting Ratna off.

'I wish we lived in a country with interview rooms with one-way glass and both camera and audio facilities. You could see and hear what's going on,' Gowda finished, thinking of the interview room which had once been called an office room when the station was still a house. A little room with blank walls and a window that overlooked the five-foot-high rear compound wall.

Santosh shot Gowda a strange look. 'That's fine, sir. As you said, there are many ways to skin a cat.' Turning to Aqthar, he said, 'If you record the interview on your phone, we'll be able to see it too, even if a little later.'

Gowda grinned back at him. 'That could come back to bite us. There will be the official recording, of course, but if you want to watch it live, what you can do is use Skype and call Aqthar. If he leaves the call on, all of you can watch it as it happens.'

Santosh stared at him in surprise. Skype. Gowda knew about Skype? When had the dinosaur become a geek? Gowda pretended not to see the expression on Santosh and Ratna's faces. Nor did he reveal the glee he felt.

Gajendra cleared his throat. 'Byrappa is very upset about how we were played last night, sir, and has gone to dig a little deeper into the illegal cockfighting. He said he has a source but hasn't really kept in touch with him. But now he's decided it's time he took a chance,' Gajendra said.

Gowda shook his head in resignation. 'Byrappa has decided, has he? Well, good... he's better than a bloodhound once he gets the scent.'

# 6

Gurunath sat with his head in his hands. Gowda's eyes bore into him. The slight young man didn't look like he had the strength to squash a cockroach, let alone hold the Professor's face down in a vessel of hot water. And yet there were too many factors weighing against him. He would be putty in the hands of those looking for a scapegoat.

Gurunath looked up. 'Why am I here, sir?'

'Gurunath,' Gowda said gently. 'Don't be afraid; you know you are not guilty of any crime.' He paused and added slyly, 'Or are you?'

Gurunath gasped. 'Of course not, sir!'

'Good. We just want a few answers from you.' Gowda pulled himself a chair and sat across from Gurunath.

Aqthar walked in. Gurunath looked at Aqthar popping his phone into a cup as he went to sit beside him.

'Why am I here, sir?' he asked again.

'We have a few questions. If you can answer them then the CCB will know we have interviewed you first and let you go with minimum fuss. Or we can keep you in custody and let the CCB deal with you. They are used to dealing with very serious crimes—terrorism-related, for instance—and have their own way of extracting information.' Gowda's voice was veering on the impatient, a fact that wasn't lost on Gurunath.

Gurunath said, 'I want to cooperate with you, sir. But my scholarship funding is at stake here. Please understand, sir.'

Gowda nodded. 'Gurunath, you're a sensible young man. Answer truthfully and share everything you know. You're a highly intelligent man, but I have found that the problem with such people is that they think they know how to speak half-truths and get away with it. So don't take me for a fool and try to do the same,' he said in his most level voice.

'What do you want to know?' Gurunath asked, putting his arms on the table along with an earnest expression on his face.

'How long did you know Professor Mudgood?' Gowda asked.

'Four years now, sir,' Gurunath said. 'I had joined Karnatak University in Dharwad for my MA in Ancient Indian History and Epigraphy. One of my professors there said Professor Mudgood was looking for a part-time assistant. It was a paid job. I come from a lower-middle-class family so I agreed without even asking what the job entailed.' Bitterness had crept into his tone.

'And what did it entail, Gurunath?' Aqthar leaned forward.

'At first it was professional assistance and I was learning a great deal from him. In the last two years something changed, sir. He was always an eccentric man but after his wife died, I think he became a little mad.' Gurunath pointed to his temple and moved his forefinger in a little circle.

'As in?'

'As in insisting that I don't come to work with pavitra budi on my forehead or that I never wear a saffron-coloured shirt. As in expecting me to eat chicken when I am a strict vegetarian. So many things, sir. In both his work and personal life, his madness was visible. It was like he had no more filters left. He said and did what he felt like without ever thinking what repercussions it could have or whom he hurt. I was glad when his daughter insisted he move to Bangalore.'

'And you continued to work for him after he moved to Bangalore?' Gowda asked.

'He wanted me to move to Bangalore with him but I wasn't keen on doing so,' Gurunath said, drumming his fingers nervously on the table.

'And why was that?' Aqthar said. 'I would have jumped at the chance to leave Dharwad.'

Gurunath's smile was grim. 'Oh, if I did, I would have ended up being his nurse. He was eighty-two years old. How can you say no when someone that old asks for help to bathe or pretend to not see when he is mixing up his medication?'

He looked down at his fingers and said, 'I worked for him remotely. And once a month I spent two or three days with him in person going over the research I did for him and collating his notes. Even in that short time, he wouldn't let me sit for a moment. Fetch me this; find me that. Or listen to his endless diatribes on everything that was wrong in the country, his daughter and grandchildren...'

'Where did you stay?' Gowda asked.

'With the Professor. And each time I was more and more convinced that I had made the right decision in not moving to Bangalore.'

'In the main house or the cottage?' Gowda interrupted.

'Main house, sir. I had asked if I could stay in the cottage and the Professor said no. He said it was pointless if I stayed that far away and besides his son-in-law had built the cottage and he didn't want any favours from him. Apparently, it's a set for a TV serial which is used ten days a month or so. That's what the Professor said.'

'Which one? Would you know?' SI Aqthar asked.

'I don't watch TV serials. That's for bored housewives and pensioners who have nothing else to do.' Gurunath's smirk of disdain made Gowda want to reach across and smack him hard.

'And yet you didn't think of quitting?' Gowda asked.

Gurunath shook his head. 'I needed the money.'

'I heard he was a cranky old man,' Aqthar said.

Gurunath sighed. 'Sir, my grandfather who is older than the Professor can be called cranky. I understand how old people are. In fact, the Professor used to say that no one was as patient with him as I was. But you couldn't just call him cranky. He was turning irresponsible in a malicious way. Aqthar Sir, don't you remember that incident at Kadapa Maidan?'

Gowda frowned. 'Is this the one where he was attacked?'

Gurunath nodded. 'It was meant to be a Rationalists' conference. The Professor was talking about how religion had changed the political discourse in India. The session ended abruptly when someone threw a balloon filled with cow dung at him as he was speaking.' He hastened to add, 'And in all honesty, I think he deserved it. I am a secular person, sir. But this blatant attack on Hinduism was something I couldn't accept. He made it sound like being a Hindu meant being irrational, toxic and a terrorist. He made Hinduism out to be a bad thing.'

'And you don't think it is?' Gowda asked.

'I think that all religions have poison embedded in their teachings which self-serving fanatics pounce on. The Professor was known to be a person with sound ideas. You should read his articles and books. He exerted a huge influence on students and people in general. So he should have known better than to spout such nonsense.'

Gowda thought of what his father had said. You can't offend people's sentiments without consequences.

'Once he moved to Bangalore my interaction with him was limited. I made excuses to not visit him. From once every two weeks I began visiting only once a month. I was due to visit him in mid December, sir. But I needed a reference letter from him and so I came to Bangalore. He wanted me to read his notes for the talk he was to give at the Town Hall. I was appalled by the venom in his notes when I went through them. We argued, and he told me to get out of his sight. He refused to give me the reference letter and called me a fool who thought licking a White Man's boots in a White Man's university would further my academic prospects. I told him to stuff his letter with his opinion up his backside and left.'

'And you took the bus to Dharwad,' Aqthar said.

Gurunath nodded.

Gowda leaned back in his chair. 'Gurunath, what did I tell you about telling me half-truths?' he asked in his coldest voice.

Gurunath flinched. 'I went to Yeshwanthpur to catch the bus. But I didn't get on it. I was very angry so I returned to his house. My plan was to destroy his notes and leave. I knew he would fumble and make an ass of himself without being able to read from them. I wanted to humiliate him.' He dropped his gaze.

'And?' Gowda probed.

'I reached the Professor's residence at around 11 p.m., sir. His workstation is on the verandah. His notes were in the drawer in the table. I took them and left. I had been covering for him for the last few years and I thought it's time the world knew he was nothing but a delusional old man.'

'Where are the notes now?' Gowda asked.

'In my lodge at Dharwad,' Gurunath said. 'I can have my roommate send them if you like.'

'Do that,' Gowda said.

'Did you notice anything unusual at the house?' Aqthar asked.

Gurunath shook his head. 'Nothing at all. The lights were off, except for the one in the verandah. The table lamp in the sitting room was on but it was always left on at night anyway.'

He paused and said, 'Well, I don't know if this was unusual, but the gate was wide open. Usually, the maid locks it. I don't know why it wasn't locked that night.'

'What did you do then?'

'I went back to Majestic and boarded the first bus out to Dharwad.'

'How did you get back to Majestic?' Gowda asked.

'I walked to the main road and found the autorickshaw I had come there in still waiting for a fare. I asked him to drop me back,' Gurunath said.

Gowda checked his watch. It was a little past four. 'SI Aqthar will take all the details from you including the name of the bus service you travelled by. The CCB will interview you tomorrow. And then you should be free to leave. It is best you cooperate with them as you did with us.'

Gurunath stared at the table. Aqthar felt pity for him. All he had wanted was to ridicule a cantankerous man and now he was facing such dire consequences. Even if he had nothing to do with the homicide, the machinery of the state and other vested interests just needed someone to pin the blame on. Gurunath was tailor-made to be the fall guy.

Gowda glanced at Aqthar. 'The nearest hotel is at the Ring Road. Take a room for the night. And keep him with you,' Gowda said. Aqthar nodded.

'Get some rest.' Gowda turned to Gurunath. 'If there is anything you have left out, tell SI Aqthar about it. We will be looking at your call records, of course. So, if you are covering for someone, you might as well mention it right away.'

Gurunath looked at Gowda, 'When will I get my phone back?'

'When we are done with it,' Gowda said, not taken in by Gurunath's righteous indignation. He was certain that Gurunath still wasn't speaking the full truth.

'What next, sir?' Santosh asked Gowda. They had all assembled in the SIT room once Gurunath and Aqthar had left.

Gowda was lost in thought. He tried to shake off that strange but distinct feeling that he was missing something. 'Did you manage to check the hospitals?' he asked.

'Not yet, sir,' Ratna answered.

'In which case, get down to that,' Gowda said. 'Santosh, I want you to speak to Iqbal Buqhari about the cottage. Find out who dealt with the shoot and how it was organized. We need to know who else used it. And how was the property accessed? The rear gate opens into El Dorado, a new layout that is the other side of the Professor's property. Does Iqbal have a stake in El Dorado?

'By the time the CCB comes back, we need to fill in some of the gaps. I'm quite certain that Gurunath isn't the culprit. But he was present at the scene of the crime on the same night. Everyone needs a perpetrator, and he fits the profile. It is on us, the burden of proof, to prove that he wasn't the actual murderer. At the most, he was an accomplice who facilitated the crime in some manner.'

'And you are that certain?' Santosh asked, unable to help himself. Gowda nodded.

'A thousand guilty may go unpunished, but even one innocent person mustn't be punished,' Gajendra said.

The three of them stared at him. 'I got that from a movie,' Gajendra grinned.

Gowda threw him a black look and went back to his room.

# 7

They had made a list of medical institutions within a ten-kilometre radius. There were about forty-three hospitals, nursing homes and clinics. Ratna and Santosh looked at the list in dismay.

Santosh cleared his throat. 'I'll call Byrappa in. Let's divide the list among us and get going.' He looked at his watch. 'The clinics will be open now as well.'

'Why bother with clinics?' Ratna asked.

Gajendra answered, 'Some of the clinics are attached to doctors' homes. Since hospitals ask too many questions, patients may choose to go to a clinic for first aid or in an emergency.'

'We have to add doctors in this area to the list?'

Ratna sounded overwhelmed, Gowda thought, as he stepped into the SIT room. 'Investigating a case is like running a marathon. Everyone begins with a great sense of purpose and urgency but as you hit the middle, everything falters and begins to slow down—energy, leads, evidence—but you have to remember there is no reaching the finishing line till you survive this middle phase,' Gowda said.

He waited to see his words bring on a determined expression on his colleague's face. But it was not to be and that made him snap. 'Policing is a lot of grunt work based on leads and sometimes mere hunches. Nothing is ever offered up on a platter. The CCB team will be in tomorrow morning and we need to have as much information as we can by then.'

'Are you sure this is not a political murder then?' Santosh asked, still not convinced that it was anything else.

'As certain as I can be at this point,' Gowda said, sauntering away abruptly and ending the conversation. He didn't want to badmouth the department. As his father said, decorum was everything.

*

Gowda walked to the mango tree. He had some paperwork to finish before the morning meeting. But he wasn't inclined to huddle over files sanctioning leaves of absence and signing circulars assigning beats. He thought of Urmila, who meditated every day and told him to do the same, to fix his mind on an object and concentrate. A flame, the top of a tree, a cloud in the sky. 'That will help you focus and clarify your thinking,' she had said.

He lit a cigarette. The flame extinguished before he could gaze at it. He looked at the top of a tree. Its leaves moved ever so gently. It was almost hypnotic. The movement sought to calm the chaos in his head. Just then, a crow unfurled from among the leaves and flew purposefully towards the clouds. Gowda ground his cigarette into the cement pan that served as his ashtray and strode back into the station. Bloody crow, he thought.

# 4 DECEMBER 2012, TUESDAY

## 1

Stanley Sagayaraj studied Gowda carefully. But he was giving nothing away. The DCP had called the night before saying that they should start early. It was a quarter to eight and they sat facing each other across the table in Gowda's room. Gowda switched on his desktop and turned it to face the DCP.

'We recorded the preliminary interview and I thought you might like to see it.' He increased the volume on his computer.

The DCP watched the video and made a few notes. When it ended, he told Gowda, 'He is still a prime suspect.'

Gowda wondered if he should spout Gajendra's 'a-thousand-guilty-can-go-unpunished-but-an-innocent-mustn't-be-punished' line but he was wary. His college basketball captain and now DCP might cuff his ears for mouthing movie dialogues.

'Well then, it is up to us to prove him innocent.'

'I thought our job was to find the Professor's murderer slash assassin,' the DCP retorted, rising to leave.

'Yes, sir, but I am not convinced that it is Gurunath.' Gowda stood up as well.

'Sit in on the interview and you may change your mind.' Sagayaraj walked to the door.

*

The CCB team's hostility was apparent in the stony looks they all threw Gowda's team members as they walked past them to the SIT room.

'What's with them?' Aqthar asked.

'They are pissed off that we got to Gurunath first.' Santosh frowned.

'And that we are part of the SIT,' Ratna added.

Gajendra watched Gowda accompanying the DCP to the room. His phone pinged. He read the message and turned to Santosh. 'Gowda Sir is going to be at the interview. And he wants us to gather as much information as we can by the time it ends.' Gajendra paused and added softly, 'I don't think things are looking too good for Gurunath.'

A good night's sleep had cleared Gurunath's face of some of the fatigue, and he sat straight and tall in his chair. Gowda nodded at him.

The CCB lot ignored Gurunath and talked among themselves. One of them adjusted the recorder. Gowda realized that they would throw all kinds of red tape his way if he were to ask for the recording. So he moved to a corner of the table and switched on the video recorder of his phone. He took his cue from what he had seen Aqthar do and placed the phone against a teacup. No one paid much attention to what he was doing. The younger men assumed that he wasn't tech savvy enough, Gowda realized with some satisfaction.

DCP Sagayaraj started the interview with questions Gurunath had already answered. Gowda realized that the words and phrases Gurunath had used were exactly the same ones with which he answered Gowda and Aqthar. Gowda felt the back of his neck prickle. While he had been prepared for Gurunath to repeat what he had said yesterday, the use of the same phrases right down to pauses and exclamations made him think it sounded rehearsed. As if he was mouthing a script someone had carefully put together.

As the interview drew to an end, Gowda wondered if he should share his suspicions with the DCP.

Gurunath took a sip of water and asked with an earnest expression, 'Sir, I hope you are satisfied that I had nothing to do with the Professor's death.'

Sagayaraj threw a sweet smile back. 'I am not.'

'But, sir, why? What can I do to convince you I am innocent?'

'You could start off by telling us about your association with the Bhartiya Seva Sangh. You are a card-carrying member is what we hear...' DCP Sagayaraj said.

Gurunath immediately became defensive. 'I used to be when I was an undergraduate student. And that was a long time ago. How does that matter?'

'Firstly, why would someone like you, with your ideology, work for someone like the Professor who routinely attacked the BSS in his writings?'

'I told Gowda Sir about this. I needed the money and I thought working for the Professor would widen my network. You need to have a good one if you have serious academic aspirations.' Gurunath's indignation was carved into his features. But Gowda no longer trusted him.

'I see,' Sagayaraj muttered, disbelief all over his face.

'Sir, I have been his assistant for four years now. Why would I wait this long to kill him if that was my intention?'

Gurunath was not the same timid creature Gowda had seen the previous day. It was as if he had undergone a transformation overnight. A certain cockiness had crept in. Nevertheless, Gowda was still certain that Gurunath had nothing to do with the murder. But what if he was covering for someone?

And then, as if someone had rapped their knuckles hard on his skull, Gowda suddenly remembered Constable Byrappa's midnight call. Gowda hadn't been convinced with Gurunath's story of how and when he got back to Dharwad and had asked Byrappa to verify the details.

'I made some enquiries and found the bus attendant. He had something very interesting to say,' Byrappa had begun and narrated the entire conversation detailing every pause and sigh.

Gowda had been unsettled by the information. His hunches seldom failed. He had wanted to believe that this wasn't a political crime and his bullheadedness had blinded him. It was probably best he left Gurunath to the CCB and let them proceed with the case, he had thought as he fell asleep. He had meant to loop in the DCP on the new information, but had forgotten all about Byrappa's call in the chaos he had woken up to a little later. His father's retching.

Chidananda was still in the bathroom when Gowda rushed to his father's room.

'Appa,' he hollered, banging on the bathroom door. His father had opened the door looking pale and exhausted.

'Must be gas,' he said, rubbing his abdomen. Gowda had waited until his father had settled in and pulled his blanket to his chin. 'Turn the fan off. It's chilly,' Chidananda said.

When Gowda went to check in on his father a little later, his father was running a fever. He placed another blanket on his father. It was a little past six. He had a busy morning ahead apart from the early-morning meeting with the DCP and for a fleeting moment he had toyed with the idea that he should call his brother Nagendra and ask for help. But he had quelled the thought and called Shanthi.

He coaxed his father to have a watery cup of coffee. 'I'll get some rehydration salts. Even if you don't eat, you must at least have that.'

Chidananda drifted back to sleep and Gowda had left for work at seven knowing his father would bring up his leaving as soon as he was able to sit up. It didn't help that he felt like a piece of shit for doing so.

Byrappa's call had slipped his mind entirely until something about Gurunath's demeanour had raised his ire.

Gowda scribbled on a notepad: Ask him about the journey back to Dharwad on 28th night.

Sagayaraj shot him a grateful look. 'You told ACP Gowda about how you took the notes and left. When did you reach the bus stand and what time was your bus? And which bus service?'

Gurunath fished out a paper with a ticket printed on it and waved it in his face. 'As you can see, it was booked through an app. I took a printout. I am not the person you are looking for.'

Gurunath would do well on stage, Gowda thought. Even though he knew he would invoke the CCB's displeasure, he asked, 'Do explain how you reached Dharwad on this bus because the bus conductor remembers that the seat stayed vacant.'

'He is mistaken,' Gurunath said without a change of expression.

'I don't think he is. He remembers it distinctly because the passenger in the seat next to yours was a lady and she had asked for a change of seat. But you didn't turn up.' Gowda enunciated slowly to let Gurunath know whose version he believed.

'I am telling you he is confusing me with someone else, sir,' Gurunath persisted. He took another sip of water.

Gowda looked at Gurunath and decided that it was time to leave him to the CCB. But he wanted to rattle the cocky bastard before he left the room. So he gave him a cold smile and asked, 'Which means you would know the name of the movie they played on the bus.'

'I don't watch films so I don't know which one it was. Besides, I slept the whole way.'

Gowda turned to Sagayaraj. 'Sir, he is all yours. Gurunath wasn't on that bus. They didn't play any movie that night. The DVD player wasn't working. Byrappa said the bus office has a CCTV so I am sure you can take a look at the footage and see if he actually did check in at the bus office.'

To Gurunath, he said softly, 'Boli magane, you fucked up. I told you not to bullshit me and you did... now enjoy the consequences.'

*

Gowda played them the video he had recorded on his phone. They watched the interview in silence. Gajendra gasped once. Aqthar took his eyes off the screen to look at Gowda's face. And Byrappa's eyes sparkled with triumph.

'So where does it leave us, sir?' It was Santosh who bit the bullet.

Gowda shrugged. 'We will continue to assist the CCB. The SIT is still an active unit. But we mustn't forget the cottage basement. It may have nothing or everything to do with the Professor's murder. But that is up to us to prove. If nothing, we may have stumbled upon an unreported crime. So to answer the question on each of your minds: that's where we stand.'

The door opened abruptly. DCP Vidyaprasad stood there, frowning. 'I hear the CCB has a suspect in custody,' he snapped at Gowda. All the others stood up and saluted the senior officer. He beamed at them and glared at Gowda.

'Sir,' Gowda said. 'They are going to investigate the suspect's alibi. But he hasn't been charged with anything yet.'

One by one all of them left the room as the DCP watched in dismay. It was best to deny him an audience when it came to him berating Gowda, they knew. He tended to be even more vicious with Gowda if his team members were around.

'The SIT is still active,' Gowda concluded.

'Take me through your findings,' DCP Vidyaprasad said as he moved to pull Gowda's chair from behind him and planted himself in it.

For a moment Gowda sought his isle of calm. He tried to think of the tops of trees, the colour white, monkeys' tails and whatever else... instead, all he could envision was DCP Vidyaprasad crouching in a corner between two steel almirahs while Gowda advanced towards him wearing shoes with steel spikes. He could feel skin tear and hear the crunch of bones splintering as he kicked and stomped on the howling DCP. Gowda exhaled slowly. It always helped.

'It would be best if we went into the SIT room where the CCB are, sir,' Gowda said with his biggest fake smile.

# 2

The already crowded SIT room now seemed like a fairground with the entry of DCP Vidyaprasad. He looked at the blank whiteboard and smirked. 'You haven't got very far, Gowda?'

'We don't leave our thoughts on the whiteboard, sir,' Gowda began in his blandest voice.

Sagayaraj cleared his throat to tell Gowda he should stop baiting Vidyaprasad.

'Sir, this is an SIT and we have to be careful that our findings in an ongoing investigation don't get leaked. This is a very sensitive case and has much to do with national security so it is best that only the actual team know what the developments are,' Gowda ad-libbed.

Sagayaraj inserted himself into the conversation with a silky suggestion. 'Vidyaprasad, why don't you take a seat? We'll update you...'

Gowda looked at him to ask—are you sure? Sagayaraj gave him an almost imperceptible nod. Gowda responded with a tiny shrug.

The two teams watched DCP Vidyaprasad as DCP Sagayaraj took him through the findings. They all knew that if Vidyaprasad was peeved with them, he would try to derail the investigation. And they didn't need that.

'So what are you waiting for?' Vidyaprasad asked. 'We should charge the rascal, lock him up and call the media. Let's tell them the news.'

Gowda looked thunderous. The baboon was hungry for publicity. A political murder would make national news. He wanted to be present when microphones were thrust towards them and flashbulbs popped in their faces.

'Not yet, Vidya,' Sagayaraj said. 'The fingernail scrapings are in the forensics lab. We should have the results soon. I have told them that time is of the essence. But you know what they say, foreign DNA starts to disintegrate within six hours and our victim was found almost thirty-six hours after he was killed. By the time the postmortem was done, it must have been at least forty-two hours. So we need to proceed cautiously. And Gurunath is just a cog in the wheel. We need to find the mastermind. Arresting and charging Gurunath will send whoever it is underground.'

'Yes, yes...' Vidyaprasad nodded. 'Of course, this is going to shake up the country. It's best we proceed cautiously.' He mouthed Sagayaraj's phrase and spewed it back at him.

Vidyaprasad added, 'And we must take great care that we don't send the criminals behind this into hiding.' He stood up and stared straight ahead at Aqthar. 'Congratulations, young man! You brought Gurunath to us, I hear.'

Aqthar opened his mouth to clarify that he had merely transported Gurunath, but Vidyaprasad drowned out his words. 'Don't be so modest. I'll be keeping an eye on you from now on. The force needs smart officers like you.'

Vidyaprasad hummed under his breath as his car sped towards Papanna's residence. The MLA would be pleased to hear that he was no longer under suspicion. Vidyaprasad was thrilled that he had managed to undermine Gowda in front of his colleagues by giving Aqthar all the credit. Nothing gave him a greater sense of satisfaction. He would send someone to pick up bottles of Johnnie Walker Black Label, one to send to Papanna, and one for himself.

'What's our next course of action, sir?' one of the CCB officers turned towards Gowda and asked. None of them cared much for DCP Vidyaprasad and his tactics of divide and rule. This was their way of telling Gowda that no matter their differences they knew him for what he was: a fine policeman and a decent bloke.

Gowda smiled at Inspector Papa Nayak, one of Sagayaraj's most trusted lieutenants. 'I think DCP Sagayaraj should tell us that.'

'And he will,' the DCP said, making a note of the new dynamics in the room. 'Just so you know, the fingernail scrapings results aren't conclusive. They are running a few more tests to see if they can find anything concrete.'

Gowda stared at him, nonplussed. 'So we have nothing much to go on. Meanwhile, sir, I need to tell you all something.'

Gowda proceeded to take the CCB team through his team's explorations of the Professor's property and what they had found at the cottage. He switched on his laptop and showed them the photographs. Everyone looked on in silence. 'Do you think the blood in the bathroom is connected to the Professor's death?' Sagayaraj asked, scrolling through the pictures again.

'In all honesty, I don't know, sir. They could be two separate incidents or one might have led to the other,' Gowda said.

'What's going on in your head?' Sagayaraj probed.

'Perhaps the Professor witnessed something he shouldn't have. And so he was eliminated.' Gowda spoke carefully. It was a rather slender straw. And yet they had to begin somewhere.

Sagayaraj shut the laptop. 'Here's what we'll do. Get the forensics team to come in right away. How could they have missed the basement? Meanwhile, we'll pursue the Gurunath lead. And you and your team can see what comes up from the forensic evidence. Knowing you I am sure you have already begun.'

Gowda grinned. 'This is not a competition. We are a team here and we need to find who the perpetrator is; and that should be our sole guiding purpose. Can we agree on that?' The DCP looked at his team and Gowda's.

'We do a debrief every morning, and if someone makes a discovery, it needs to be shared ASAP. Everyone in this room must know what the others are doing. And that goes for me as for you, Gowda,' the DCP finished.

'What about Gurunath, sir?' Aqthar asked.

Sagayaraj ran his fingers through his hair. 'We'll take him with us. Give him a taste of our hospitality. And once he talks, we'll decide on what next.'

He paused and looked at Aqthar's frown. 'Don't worry, we are not going to torture him. We know how to break suspects without laying a finger on them.'

Gowda tried to decide his next course of action once the CCB team left with Gurunath. It was already half past twelve. Twenty-four hours had gone since Simon had collected samples from the cottage. Gowda stood up, impatient to get things moving. But forensics didn't work that way. Nevertheless, Gowda picked up his phone and called him.

'I don't have to tell you what you already know, sir. This is going to take some more time. At this point all I can tell you is that there are three different samples. That much is evident.'

Gowda cut the call. Not far from him, Santosh swatted a mosquito hovering by his forearm. And something fell into place. Iqbal Buqhari's bandaged arm.

'So here is what we are going to do,' Gowda said, speaking with a renewed sense of purpose.

'I am going to divide the investigation up. Aqthar, I want you in charge of forensics.' Gowda saw the hesitation in the younger man's eyes. 'I know that your exposure has been limited. But now is a good time to start. Aqthar, I want you to ensure the documentation at the cottage is done and the chain of custody of the evidence is unbroken.

'Santosh and Ratna, I want the two of you to check all the hospitals, clinics and doctors in a two-kilometre radius of the Professor's property. Look for inpatients and outpatients with injuries, wounds—especially stab wounds—on 27, 28 and 29 November. You also need to get the details on who uses the cottage and when from Iqbal Buqhari.

'Gajendra and Byrappa, I want you to pursue details of the well property and all the other properties around the Professor's including that layout El Dorado. Who are their owners? Are any of them in the process of being sold? What's the real estate buzz? I want every whisper of information even if it isn't on paper... And I want it all by noon tomorrow. I hope I have made myself clear.'

'What about Gopal, sir?' Gajendra asked. 'We need to give him something to do.'

Gowda smiled. 'I am inclined to ask him to count every tree in that compound and then start on their leaves. But since I can't, Gajendra, I want you to set him onto the sante trail. Byrappa, maybe you can give him some tips on how to go about it.'

'What do you think he is going to do?' Ratna asked her colleagues as Gowda strode out of the room.

'I am sure he has something planned,' Santosh said.

'And he'll tell us when he can, so don't second-guess him,' Gajendra finished and turned to Byrappa. 'Let's get going.'

## 3

Gowda went home. He needed to check on his father.

When he reached the house, he saw the front door open. Gowda frowned and raced in. He heaved a sigh of relief when he heard voices from his father's room. For a moment, he hadn't known what to think, and the image of the Professor with his face in a cauldron had sprung to mind.

'Appa,' Gowda called out. His father was seated on the bed, propped up against pillows. A woman with her back to the window sat by the bed, spooning food into his mouth. Gowda thought he looked like a baby bird.

The curtains had been pulled shut and the only light in the room came from the desk lamp. Gowda couldn't see her face clearly in the darkened room.

'Hello, sir,' the woman said. 'We haven't met. My name is Bhuvana. Your tenant.' He heard the laughter in her voice and then she continued, 'I heard uncle coughing all morning. I think it must be the AC at the movie theatre that's affected him. So I thought I'd bring him the special rasam my mother used to make,' she said in a low voice as she spooned the last mouthful into the old man's mouth.

Gowda nodded. 'Thank you. You are very kind.'

'Why don't I put a light on?' Gowda walked towards the switchboard.

'No, no, let it be, the light hurts my eyes,' Chidananda croaked.

Bhuvana offered Chidananda a napkin to wipe his mouth and took back the soiled napkin. She stood up.

'Please don't leave because I am here,' Gowda said, trying to see her face better. It was still in the shadows but Gowda could see she was a petite woman. He decided to follow her into the living room. Almost as if she had read his mind, she said, 'Sir, I'll see myself out. Please don't hesitate to call me if you need me to sit with him. I know you are a very busy man.'

Gowda stood by his father's bedside, not sure what to do. There was something about her that was familiar but he couldn't place it.

'Such a kind girl,' Chidananda said once Bhuvana had left the room. 'And so caring. It's been, what, two or three days since I got here, but I feel like I've known her forever. That is our atmabandham.' He tried to sit up.

Soul connection. Gowda wanted to grunt. What next?

'Borei, I need to pass urine. Please help me to the bathroom,' Chidananda muttered, touching his arm. 'Bhuvana called Mamtha to ask about medication to bring down my temperature. I said a paracetamol would do but she insisted she speak to Mamtha first to find out if there's anything I shouldn't be taking. You are fortunate to have her as your tenant.'

'What do you know about her?' Gowda asked his father, giving him his arm to hold as they walked the few steps to the bathroom.

Chidananda paused to glare at Gowda. 'For once, stop thinking like a policeman. Do you have to be suspicious about everyone and everything?'

'Occupational hazard, Appa,' Gowda said quietly.

'Nonsense. Do schoolteachers cane their own children at home or make them stand on tables if they misbehave?' the old man croaked furiously. 'When you are home, you are just Borei. Not a policeman. I came to stay with my son. And not with ACP Borei Gowda.'

His father did have a point. Urmila had told him as much. Suspicion had become second nature to him. But it wasn't easy shedding that state of mind when he stepped across his threshold at home. He would have to try harder, he decided, as he waited by the bathroom door while his father peed into the toilet bowl in fits and starts, and shuffled to the basin to wash his hands.

He offered his father a towel once he was done.

'I'll rest now,' Chidananda said. He looked very frail.

'I'll sit here with you, Appa.'

Within a few minutes, it was Gowda who had fallen asleep while his father sat looking at him in amusement.

# 4

Gowda woke up with a crick in his neck. The skies had darkened, and the small lamp on the desk in Chidananda's room was on.

His father was nowhere in sight. Gowda sat up straight and kneaded the muscles of his right shoulder. What time was it? His mouth felt dry and parched. He stood up and stretched. He could hear sounds from the kitchen.

Gowda walked to the living room where his father sat wrapped in a shawl, sipping a mug of coffee. 'I am sorry, Appa... I fell asleep. You should have woken me up.'

Chidananda smiled. 'I enjoyed watching you sleep, Borei. I probably saw you sleeping last when you were in your cradle.'

Gowda grinned. 'I have grown since, Appa.'

'You have,' his father muttered. 'You have.'

'How are you feeling?' Gowda asked.

'A lot better. Bhuvana's rasam, whatever was in it, worked, I say.'

'I can see that,' Gowda said, sinking into a chair. He stared in surprise when Shanthi came into the living room bearing a tray with coffee.

He took his cup and asked Shanthi, 'What are you doing here?'

'Bhuvana Madam called and asked me to come over. She said you were home and that as Ajja wasn't well, I need to be here.'

Gowda took a deep draw of the filter coffee. After the tepid over-sweetened dishwater they passed off as coffee at the station, this was gloriously delicious.

'What do you want for dinner, Ajja?' Shanthi asked.

'I am not your grandfather. You can call me sir. Or uncle as the whole world does anyway!' Chidananda growled. Gowda remembered that moment when a random stranger somewhere had first addressed him as uncle. He had suddenly felt deflated; the greying hair, the slackening belly, the slouch in posture and the occasional lapse of memory—all to be his soon. Along with knowing that there was no going back to the young man he was.

Gowda watched his father tell Shanthi exactly how he wanted his broken wheat upma made. 'Don't drown it in oil.'

When the doorbell rang, Gowda got up to answer it. He opened the door to discover Roshan standing there with a broad grin on his face, carrying a backpack.

'How come you're here?' Gowda asked.

'It's customary to say hello first, Appa.'

Gowda enveloped him in a hug. The boy was no longer a boy, he realized, feeling the muscles on his back and the rasp of his beard against his cheek.

Chidananda's face lit up at the sight of Roshan. 'Ajja,' the boy said, extricating himself from his father's embrace and rushing towards his grandfather. 'Amma said you were unwell, so I took the afternoon bus. Are you all right?'

For a moment, Gowda felt left out. Then he gave a mental shrug and told himself that the arrival of Roshan, an almost-doctor, meant there was no need for him to babysit his father.

Gowda sat with them for half an hour so that his father and his son wouldn't throw him the 'bewildered dog' look as he left.

'Roshan, why don't you call for pizza, and don't forget to make sure Ajja eats a proper meal,' Gowda said as he buttoned up his shirt.

Roshan watched him from the door of his room. 'Where are you going?'

'I am working on a very important case. That's all I can tell you.' Gowda smiled as he buttoned the cuffs.

'Like this? In formal clothes?' Roshan's tone was disbelieving.

'Undercover. And undercover doesn't mean I have to look unkempt and wear torn clothes.' Gowda examined his face in the mirror one last time.

'What time will you be home?' Roshan demanded.

'Are you my father?'

From the hall, Chidananda called out, 'No, he isn't. But I am. What time will you be home?'

Gowda walked past Roshan, who followed him into the hall. 'I will be home when I am done with what I need to do.' Gowda's smile dripped a fake sweetness. He pulled on his leather jacket and swung his bike keys from his forefinger as he walked out.

Urmila gasped. 'I don't think I have ever seen you in a full-sleeved shirt, Borei Gowda. What is the occasion?'

'Undercover.'

'Like this?' Urmila's tone had the same incredulity as Roshan.

Gowda sighed. 'What's with the world? Why does a man have to look like he is homeless to be undercover?' He picked up Mr Right and nuzzled him.

'If you are undercover, ACP Gowda, why are you here?' Urmila asked, watching Gowda as he moved his face this way and that to avoid the dog's exuberant licking.

'Gosh, woman, can't you say hello before you put me through the third degree?' Gowda sat on the sofa.

Urmila joined him. 'Tell me what's going on. And why are you here?'

Gowda grinned at her. 'Because I need your help. You can be Robin to my Batman! Or is it the Penguin. I can never remember who is who.'

Urmila frowned. 'Never mind that. So what does this Robin have to do for you, Batman?'

'Take me to the club. You are a member and I need access,' Gowda said, his tone now serious. 'Unofficial access.'

'I suppose this has to do with Iqbal.'

Gowda nodded.

'I can't remember how often I've asked you to go with me. And you always had an excuse. But here you are...'

'Aren't you pleased?'

Urmila gave him a withering glance. Gowda took her hand in his. 'I wouldn't be comfortable at the club, U. I am just an average hick policeman and I don't want to embarrass you. That's why I always make excuses.'

Urmila covered his hand with hers. 'You always know how to make it seem almost plausible. Give me a few minutes and I will put some lipstick on.'

When Urmila emerged ten minutes later, she was dressed in a pale-yellow chiffon sari and a blouse that was no more than an embellished bra. It made him want to tear her clothes off and make urgent love to her. But the all-pervasive sense of duty was better than a cold shower, Gowda decided.

'You look amazing,' he said. 'The blouse is a little too bold, no?'

'Hardly, Borei. Besides, when you are with me, what do I need to fear?' Urmila's eyes twinkled.

Gowda shut up. Urmila knew what was right for her and he wasn't the callow twenty-two-year-old who had once tried to change her into someone else, telling her that her jeans were too snug, her blouses too revealing and her lipstick too bright.

Urmila said they would take her Audi. 'Easier this way. I have the club sticker on it. The two of us arriving on your bike might be a little too conspicuous. That kind of attention I don't need.'

Gowda was going to ask what she meant by that but they were already turning into the members' parking lot. 'I will sign you in,' she said. 'How do you know he will be at the club?'

Gowda shrugged. 'I don't, but his wife mentioned he is here most evenings.'

She paused for a moment. 'I just hope he isn't at the Gentleman's Bar. You need to wear a jacket to enter that part of the club.'

Gowda grimaced. As they approached the main club building, he said, 'I don't think we're likely to find Bukhari here. Is there an open space perhaps?'

Urmila nodded. 'The lawns.'

'That's the one. The most open space, hence the most discreet,' Gowda said as his eyes took in the club's architecture. The columns and stately arches. The lovingly maintained facades of the different buildings. The perfectly pruned shrubs and plants. The expanse of the lawns.

Urmila and Gowda walked past Gazebo, the bar that was bursting with people deep in conversations, talking, laughing, drinking, smoking, seemingly without a care in the world.

One of the stewards greeted Urmila like a long-lost friend. 'Find me a table, Kenneth,' she murmured. 'Not in the centre but somewhere away from the noise.'

He nodded and led them to one such table. She turned to Gowda. 'What will you have? Would you like a single malt?'

Gowda smiled at her persistence in converting him into a single-malt drinker. 'I will have my usual. A large Old Monk and Coke, with a piece of lemon in it.'

Urmila ordered a vodka tonic and gave the waiter her club card. 'What's on the specials tonight?'

As Urmila and the steward discussed what was best on the special menu, Gowda scanned the lawns. Then he saw Iqbal Buqhari walk past the bar and head towards a table not too far from where they sat.

Gowda cleared his throat. Urmila followed his gaze. Her eyes widened. 'Damn, Borei, you almost scare me with how you are a step ahead of people.'

Gowda grinned. 'I have been doing this a long time, U.'

'What now?' she asked. 'What were you planning to do once you saw Iqbal here? Ambush him with accusations?'

Gowda threw her a searing glance. 'Hardly. We wait.' He took out his cigarettes. 'He will come to our table.'

'Why would he?' Urmila frowned.

'To let me know that he has seen me here with you,' Gowda said, lighting up.

Urmila stared at him. 'But why? What does he get from that?'

'I am a cop. I am having a drink with a "woman who isn't my wife". It's a nice little tidbit for him to preserve if he needs a favour from me. He is a businessman, U. They see opportunities where you and I see nothing.'

Urmila nibbled on her lip and then leaned forward to take a cigarette from Gowda's pack.

'Why do you even bother, U? You are wasting a ciggie. You don't even inhale,' Gowda said but held out his lighter for her.

'I like a smoke once in a while.' She smiled at him as she took a long drag.

The drinks arrived along with a plate of kebabs. 'We should have asked Michael to join us,' Gowda said.

'I was thinking the same. Next time,' Urmila said, and almost choked on her drink as she saw Iqbal coming towards them.

'Hello, ACP Gowda,' Iqbal said, approaching them with his hand outstretched.

Gowda managed an amiable smile and stood up to shake hands.

'What a surprise to see you here, and with Urmila.' Iqbal darted a sly glance at her.

Urmila offered him her hand, which he enveloped within his palms instead of shaking it.

'Urmila, how are you?'

She smiled at him. 'Borei, or ACP Gowda, as you know him, and I were in college together. Another friend was to have joined us but he couldn't.'

Iqbal nodded. His expression changed as his eyes met Gowda's. 'Any developments, sir?'

Gowda gestured for him to sit. Iqbal looked at Urmila. 'Are you sure? I am so sorry for barging in...'

'Don't be,' Urmila said, standing up and picking up her handbag. 'I have to use the ladies'.' She walked away.

'We are not sure yet. But everything points to a political assassination,' Gowda said, choosing his words carefully.

'Oh my God...' Iqbal's response was almost theatrical. 'May I have a smoke?'

Gowda pushed the pack towards him.

Iqbal took out a cigarette and lit it. He inhaled deeply as if to steady his nerves. Gowda watched him hamming it up, like in countless scenes in countless movies: hands trembling as the actor lights a cigarette, takes in a deep breath and leans forward conspiratorially. 'What makes you say that, sir?'

Gowda shrugged. 'I can't reveal the details yet, but we will once everything is clear. Protocol!'

'My father-in-law wasn't a very nice man. At first, I thought he liked me because he was supportive of my marriage with his daughter. Then I realized that for him I was just a talking point. What he liked about me was just my religion. I was a living testimony to his secular image. He was a manipulator. He would introduce me as his son-in-law and casually insert that I am Muslim. And I would see the flicker of respect in the person's eyes. Professor Mudgood walked the talk, etc. He was a cruel man; he knew exactly what to say to inflict a wound that wouldn't ever heal.'

Gowda didn't speak. He was afraid of breaking Iqbal's stream of thoughts. From the corner of his eye, he saw Urmila threading her way towards them. When she paused at a table, he exhaled in relief.

'And yet...'

'And yet...' Gowda prompted.

'He didn't deserve to die like that. I'll wait to hear from you, ACP Sir.' Iqbal stubbed out the cigarette and stood up as Urmila reached their table.

'See you around, Urmila,' he said, leaving to join two other men at his own table.

Urmila dropped into a chair once he was gone. 'Did you get what you wanted?'

'Well, I will now.' Gowda took out a paper napkin and pulled out a stub from the ashtray. He wrapped it carefully and dropped it into a small Ziploc bag he had in his wallet.

'So, this was what it was all about?' Urmila said.

Gowda smiled at her.

'How do you know which one was his?'

'Your stub has lipstick stains. Mine is usually pinched around the filter. That left his.'

'Do you still want to hang around? Can we leave?'

'Let's go,' he said.

# 5 DECEMBER 2012, WEDNESDAY

## 1

Gowda woke up with a goofy grin plastered on his face. He felt ridiculously happy, and he wasn't sure why. Could it be because he had managed to extract Iqbal Buqhari's DNA without him realizing it? Or was it because Roshan's presence at home made the responsibility of having his father around less overwhelming? Or was it the way the previous evening had ended?

He closed his eyes and tried to picture the frantic lovemaking, reminiscent of the early days of their relationship. When he had never been able to gauge whose hunger was sharper as their passions seemed evenly matched. A kiss for a kiss; a caress for a caress. White-hot and with each nerve end a conduit leading to the little death and blessed release. As time went on, they had sought each other with a lessening of hunger. Familiarity and a certain sameness had crept in. But last night there had been an almost frantic edge to how Urmila had sought to pleasure him and demanded what she wanted him to do for her. Gowda hadn't yet seen an Urmila who was both confident and vulnerable at the same time. He had responded with an excitement that he hadn't felt for some time now.

He heard the clock as it struck six. Barely four hours of sleep but he felt rested and awake. Gowda sat up and stretched. Knots deep within his shoulders unravelled and he felt like he was ready to take on whatever the day threw at him.

Gowda padded around the house softly to check on his father. It was chilly and he shivered a little. The house was dark when he had returned at almost two in the morning. He had kicked his shoes off and fallen into bed fully clothed.

He paused outside Chidananda's room and looked in to see his father sleeping soundly. Gowda arranged the blanket around his legs. Next, he went to Roshan's room and noticed the boy had left his door open. He was touched by Roshan's thoughtfulness. His grandfather could call out to him at night if he needed anything.

Roshan was curled into a comma-shaped bundle under the bedspread. Gowda sighed. Why hadn't the boy taken a razai or a blanket? He knew what Roshan would say: 'But I didn't know where it was, Appa.'

But this morning Gowda was not going to let his irritation with Roshan's habitual bewilderment at life and living corrode his mood.

He put the water on to start making coffee, trying to be as silent as possible. He didn't want to wake up his father. No need to fret about Roshan, who he was quite certain would sleep through a nuclear holocaust. He wanted a mug of coffee and some quiet time to go through his thoughts, all of which were like bits of string making up a ball. If he could lay them out, he would be able to examine the logic of each thought and sequence them.

Gowda took his coffee to the verandah. The sky was dark and a mist wreathed the trees. He placed the mug on the cane table. Arranging one of the two chairs the way he wanted, he sat down and put his feet up on the verandah railing. Then he pulled out a little notebook from his pocket and the slim pen stuck into the elastic band. Urmila had given it to him as he left last night. She called it a Moleskine. 'This is too fancy, U,' Gowda had mumbled but slipped the notebook into his pocket anyway.

'In which case you can give it to Shanthi,' Urmila had said in a huffy voice. 'She can list out the clothes you send for ironing.'

'Don't be like this, U,' Gowda had said. 'I didn't mean to offend you.' He held her tightly and felt her ire melt away. 'I am still learning how to receive gifts, so bear with me.'

She had cupped his arse cheek in response and given it a resounding slap. He laughed out loud; the memory of that moment had travelled with Gowda and now lingered as he opened the notebook and began jotting down the multiple threads of thoughts floating in his head. Forty-five minutes later, Gowda had smoked three cigarettes and filled up five pages with every detail of the case that was inconclusive and yet pertinent. Once he was with his team, they would go over it.

Gowda stood up and stretched. It was now a quarter past seven and he headed inside to check if his father was awake. He heard Chidananda hawking and spitting from the bathroom. Gowda had left him a flask of hot water and he knew his father would need coffee as soon as he was out. He made him a steaming cup, laid out a couple of biscuits on a plate and took it all on a tray to his father's room.

Chidananda was pleased to see the coffee. 'How are you feeling, Appa?' Gowda asked as he placed the tray on the bedside table.

'I am fine.' Chidananda noticed the biscuits. 'I don't like Marie biscuits.'

Gowda didn't respond. The petulant tone reminded him of Roshan the child demanding chocolate cream biscuits instead of the orange cream ones in front of him. 'I'll get some cream biscuits today, Appa.' Gowda spoke as he did to Roshan when he had been a child throwing a tantrum. And just as he used to with Roshan, he diverted Chidananda's attention. 'Appa, I went to the club yesterday.'

His father's eyes shimmered with interest. 'Did you? Mr Rangarajan took me there just before I retired from service.'

'Did you like being there?'

'Very impressive building and all high-society people. I had a nice time but I was glad to leave as well.' He nibbled at a biscuit.

Gowda smiled. 'I know that feeling, Appa.'

He had twenty minutes before PC David arrived at his gate to pick him up. 'I have to get ready to go to the station, Appa.'

He saw his father start to speak and then bite down the words. 'What is it?'

'Well, now that Roshan is home, don't come home so late. He is going to wonder where you are.'

Gowda felt his intestines descend to his knees. Did his father have suspicions about him and Urmila? Gowda gave himself a mental shake. He was fifty-one fucking years old and it was his life to do with as he pleased.

'He knows, Appa, and understands,' Gowda said in an equally ambiguous tone.

'What?'

'That a police officer keeps crazy hours,' Gowda said as he turned to go. He knew exactly the conclusion his father had almost come to.

Gowda stood under the shower, which seemed weak and ineffectual after the tingling cascade that was the rain shower in Urmila's bathroom. He would also get one installed, he told himself as he rubbed shampoo into his scalp. Sometimes he wished he had a Man Friday to carry out all his instructions, someone who would be a faithful shadow like Iqbal's Deva.

That got him thinking. Deva had seemed very familiar with Professor Mudgood's house. Who was Deva? he wondered. And what did he actually do for Iqbal Buqhari?

Gowda looked at his team gathered in the SIT room. 'Where is Gopal?' he asked.

'Out chasing Gurunath's accomplice,' Gajendra said.

Gopal had been sent off to the Majestic bus stand after an elaborate charade. 'It's quite probable that Gurunath had an accomplice. I don't see him doing anything on his own,' Gajendra had said, giving his moustache a slight twirl at its tips.

Gopal had nodded, 'Yes, sir, I got that impression too.'

'Gopal, I think it's time we looked for the accomplice.'

'But where do we start, sir?'

'Here is what you do: go to the Majestic bus stand or VRS Travels—that is the bus office—and get a list of passengers who travelled on both 28 and 29 November. We start there,' Gajendra said. In his best avuncular tone, he added, 'I'll show you how we draw out a list of possible suspects once you bring me the full passenger list.'

Byrappa, watching the goings-on, grinned in admiration. Gajendra wasn't happy though. It was wasting manpower but maybe Gopal would find something, he hoped.

Gowda drew out the cigarette stub and paper napkin that Iqbal Buqhari had wiped his fingers on. He had retrieved that as well.

'This is a DNA sample of Iqbal's. It has to reach Simon ASAP. Aqthar, did forensics find anything?'

'The cottage had been swept clean when they went, sir. As though someone was expecting it to be combed by forensics,' Aqthar said, looking perturbed.

Gajendra, seeing Gowda's frown, added, 'Aqthar Sir called me and I went across. It was not as we had left it. Someone had cleared it up.'

Gowda's frown deepened. 'Even the basement?'

'Yes, sir,' Gajendra said. 'I showed Aqthar Sir photos of the basement from when we went there. Let me show you what it looks like now.'

The pictures showed a spick-and-span basement and bath-room. The shattered mirror had been replaced and there were no bloodstains.

'And?' Gowda asked.

'Well, Aqthar Sir was insistent that forensics extract whatever was possible...'

'I suggested they use luminol and was told not to tell them how to do their job. They seemed upset that I knew luminol existed. But they did a thorough job, sir. And the luminol showed up the blood spatter. They were able to harvest a sample from the ridge of the shower cubicle,' Aqthar said.

'Look at this, sir,' he continued, showing Gowda a series of photographs on his phone.

'Do you think whatever happened in the cottage has anything to do with Professor Mudgood's death?' Aqthar asked.

'Maybe the Professor was murdered because he saw something he shouldn't have, as Gowda Sir indicated earlier,' Ratna said slowly.

'And Iqbal Buqhari has a bandage on his forearm,' Santosh added.

Gowda smiled to himself. He was waiting to see who would bring it up first. Mentors couldn't have favourites, he knew. But as much as Santosh annoyed him with his orthodox views and small-town ways, Gowda felt a deep affection for him. And it pleased him immensely when Santosh displayed his observation skills.

'Indeed,' Gowda said. 'What about the hospital reports?'

'Two more this morning, sir, and by lunchtime I'll give you a full report,' Santosh said.

Byrappa spoke up. 'Sir, we are going to need a little more time. Gajendra Sir and I have been doing our best to dig up all the details about the adjoining land but we are hitting a wall. Nobody seems to know who the actual owner is. It's not Naga Reddy.'

'I see,' Gowda said. He had been afraid of that. Something about the property and the cement posts that seemed to walk a few feet on their own every now and then suggested a connection of some sort to Professor Mudgood's property.

'What about me, sir?' Aqthar looked apprehensive.

'How are your acting skills?' Gowda asked.

'I don't understand, sir,' Aqthar muttered.

'There is a chance one of us will be recognized. You are not from here, so you are going to pretend to be a real estate scout and visit the place where the water tankers are filled. We need to employ whatever methods we can.'

Aqthar looked baffled, then quickly regained his composure. 'I think I can manage that. The relative I am staying with is a real estate developer too. Apart from the half a dozen businesses he seems to run.'

'In which case I suggest you get down to it.'

## 2

Aqthar put on a white kurta pyjama and wore a skull cap on his head. He applied some surma in his eyes, smudging it a bit so it seemed as if it had been applied the night before. Something in him baulked at the image in the mirror. All his adult life he had tried to distance himself from the stereotype of the Muslim male but it seemed to be the best disguise at hand.

He went to his uncle's room, from whom he had got the clothes and skull cap. 'I need some attar,' he said.

His uncle looked at him approvingly. 'Now you look like one of us,' he said, handing over a flagon of the perfume.

Aqthar daubed the attar at his pulse points. 'If this doesn't convince them, nothing will,' he told himself as he mounted his bike.

Gowda had told him of the road on the rear side of the Professor's property. It could be reached from Horamavu Main Road. He hadn't spotted anything that looked like a layout yet. Bangalore people were strange, he thought. They called housing colonies 'layouts', drank their coffee as 1/2 and acted as if jowar rotis were exotic cuisine.

Despite the signboards every now and then, there was no sign of El Dorado. He was running out of patience when suddenly amidst the eucalyptus groves and coconut plantations he spied a giant arch with metal gates. El Dorado. Alongside it was a mud path on to which a tractor with a water tanker attached to it turned. Aqthar followed.

The mud path was so narrow that the water tanker brushed against the lantana that grew densely on either side. The fragrance of the bruised lantana bushes filled the air. Beyond these bushes were clumps of giant trees. Aqthar felt as if he were going down a forest road.

The tanker rattled on. Aqthar accelerated. Soon, the water tanker approached a set of giant gates clasped together with a steel chain, strong enough to tether an elephant. A little path ran alongside the barbed-wire fence of the property and along the Professor's property compound wall. The Professor's compound wall was El Dorado's back wall. Aqthar remembered Gowda mentioning a gate near the workers' quarters. They probably used this path.

Aqthar pulled to one side and parked the bike. He gestured to the tanker driver that he would open the gates. He smiled and waved his hand for the tanker to go through. He shut the gates behind him and rode his bike in.

The man was waiting for Aqthar near the borewell with a wide smile. The man at the borewell pump looked at him and said nothing. 'Thanks, bhai,' the tanker driver said.

Aqthar flinched. There it was again. Muslim man = bhai. But he smiled back and walked towards him.

'No problem,' he said.

'I am Praveen,' the man said, lowering a pipe into the tanker's barrel. 'Are you looking for someone?' he asked.

Aqthar gave him his best lopsided and affable grin and said, 'Not someone. But something, land...'

'This land isn't for sale,' the borewell operator said from the corner of his mouth.

'You are not from here, I suppose,' Praveen said, taking in Aqthar inch by inch. 'Your Kannada sounds different.'

'Good catch. I am from Dharwad,' he said. 'I have joined my relative's real estate company. It's a big one. Dilawar & Co. Have you heard of it?'

Praveen shook his head. 'I have heard of the Prestige Group and the Puravankara Group. They have properties in this area. Not this company. They can't be big enough.'

Aqthar put on an offended look and snorted. 'We build offices and tall towers for corporate real estate. Not like these fellows and their matchbox apartments. Imagine two to three times the height of the Salapuria building at Kothanur. That's what my family has done.'

The tractor driver was impressed. Aqthar could feel the bore-well operator's eyes on him as well. 'We need land with adequate water supply. So I decided to scout around. Who did you say the owner of this land is?'

Praveen shrugged. 'No idea. This used to belong to Gowrappa Reddy. But I don't know whose it is anymore. Do you know, Raja?' He turned to the borewell operator.

The man shrugged. 'I am just a worker here. As long as I get paid on time, I don't care if it's Gowrappa or the Mysore Maharaja.'

'What about any other land around here?' Aqthar persisted.

'How should I know?'

'What a pleasant fellow he is,' Aqthar muttered. Praveen laughed.

'He isn't usually this foul tempered. He lost 10,000 rupees last night in a cockfight. You can't blame him.'

Aqthar had heard about the phantom cockfight chase Ratna had led them on. He wondered if there had been some truth in it after all. 'Cockfight! I haven't been to one in years. My uncle in Dharwad used to rear fighting cocks.'

The borewell operator came closer. 'Is that true? You must be an expert. Can you pick out winners?'

Aqthar shrugged. 'I can't identify a winner but I can tell you what are the signs that will make a rooster tear open its opponent.'

'Bhai, sit down and tell me more,' the borewell operator said, all smiles.

'So you do know how to smile,' Aqthar quipped.

'Bhai, I am willing to dance too if you want.'

Praveen guffawed loudly. 'Our Raja is a riot once he gets going...'

Aqthar grinned. 'Look, I need to call my colleague first,' he said as he walked towards a stone slab bench under a tamarind tree. 'I was to have met him at Bagalur.'

He pretended making a call and sending some messages and then ambled back to the duo. 'I can't get through to him. I have to leave soon. You do know, don't you, how to pick a winner? Not because you like the rooster's height or tail feathers...'

Raja looked at him blankly. So Aqthar threw him some basic trivia he had gleaned off the internet moments ago. 'One of the ways to identify a rooster who won't give up is its beak. Look for a short, curvy beak...'

'How short?' Praveen asked.

'Look, why don't you call me next time and I'll help you pick a good fighter,' Aqthar said, glancing at his watch. 'Here is my number.'

The two men exchanged a glance. The borewell operator nodded. 'Bhai, I'll give you a missed call. Save my number and I will call you soon.'

Aqthar waited for his phone to ring. When it did, he saved the number. He got Praveen's number too.

As Aqthar turned to leave, the borewell operator mumbled, 'Don't mention it to anyone. The owner of this land is a woman called Sarasamma.'

Aqthar lowered his voice. 'Why is it such a secret?'

The man shrugged. 'I don't know, bhai, but I found out by accident. The man before me was kicked out for asking too many questions.'

'The real estate world is like that. I understand,' Aqthar said, 'I'll send you some pictures of the roosters my uncle reared,' Aqthar promised as he started his bike.

It was half past twelve and Aqthar felt his stomach rumble.

He decided it would be best to stop for a meal before heading to the station. He looked this way and that for an eatery where he wouldn't be conspicuous. A bike thundered past him and the pillion rider turned to look at him and holler, 'Bhai, stop thinking of your khuska and kebab and get going. You are holding up traffic.'

Aqthar accelerated his bike and stopped at a bakery. He wolfed down two buns smeared with butter and jam and drank two cups of coffee. For a moment, he wished he was back in the station at Dharwad where everything was familiar and the people civil.

He had been excited and also astonished that ACP Gowda, of whom he knew a little through Santosh, had asked for him to work on the case. This was his big break, he had told his wife as he prepared to ride to Bangalore.

He wasn't so sure of that now. And yet he knew that this investigation was like nothing he had done before. Even though the discoveries he had made that morning were neither here nor there, Gowda would probably see something he couldn't.

Aqthar rode into the station conscious of the looks that came his way. He opened the carrier box on his bike and pulled out his uniform. From the bottom of the box he drew out his belt and shoes. He had wedged in a grooming kit as well. He ran up the steps and walked into the main hall. As he moved towards the corridor that led to the bathroom, a constable stood in his way. 'Where do you think you are going?'

Aqthar paused and pulled his ID out. The constable glanced at it and suddenly straightened to salute him.

'I am on ACP Gowda's SIT. You can check with him if you like,' Aqthar said in his coldest voice though he knew the constable had every right to stop him.

'Sir, I am sorry. I didn't recognize you. I am really sorry, sir.' The apologies followed him into the bathroom.

Aqthar washed his face but the surma in his eyes was going to take a while, he realized. His black-rimmed eyes stared back at him in the mirror. He wondered if he could ask Ratna what to do about it. Santosh, he realized, might not like it. Santosh seemed to behave as if Ratna was his private property. It would be best to call his wife, he decided. He washed away as much of the attar as he could. Changing his clothes reduced the intensity of the perfume but he wondered what the team would say when they saw him with smudged eyes and smelling of roses.

He walked to the SIT room and sat at the table, trying to sort through the information he had collected. He had made several discoveries but how much was relevant to the case, he wondered as he chewed on the tip of his pen.

The door opened and the other officers trooped in one by one. Ratna's eyes widened and her jaw dropped at the sight of Aqthar with kohl-rimmed eyes. Gajendra sniffed the air.

Aqthar grinned at them. 'Say what you will but the surma and attar opened mouths...'

Gowda, who had just walked in, asked, 'And what did the mouths say?'

'Sir, the borewell operator's name is Raja.'

Both Gajendra and Byrappa leaned forward curiously. They had discovered as much but Raja Reddy was a reticent man. He had feigned ignorance about everything outside the purview of his job.

'The land used to belong to someone called Gowrappa,' Aqthar continued.

'That's what we heard too, sir,' Byrappa said. 'But no one seemed to know who owns it now.'

'Actually, it's a lady called Sarasamma,' Aqthar said. 'Do you know who she is?'

'I don't know who she is. But Papanna's wife's name is Sarasamma,' Byrappa said.

'What do we know about the MLA's wife?' Gowda asked.

'Nothing much, sir,' Gajendra said. 'She is a quiet lady busy with house and family. However, I do know that she is a local woman and her father was a cucumber farmer. So Gowrappa probably was her father.'

'Tell me,' Gowda said, 'how did you extract this information?'

'Raja Reddy, the borewell operator, and I hit it off, sir.' Then Aqthar paused. 'He talked to me because he thinks I am a cock-fight enthusiast. I told him my uncle had reared Aseel fowl—that's an indigenous variety used in cockfights—and that I can help him pick winners. It's a betting game, sir. He lost ten thousand rupees at a cockfight last night, I was told.'

'Aqthar, we have been trying to catch these betting men in the act but we haven't been successful,' Santosh said. 'This might be the break we have been looking for.'

Aqthar nodded. 'I thought so too.'

Gajendra looked at Gowda, waiting for him to snap and say something to the effect of not talking about bananas when the problem was elephants. Instead, Gowda took a deep breath and said, 'Simon called. And he said that the bloodstains weren't human.'

'What?' All their voices rose in unison.

'That was precisely my reaction,' Gowda said.

'Do you think they held the cockfights on the Professor's property?' Gajendra frowned.

'In which case why the blood in the basement bathroom?' Santosh asked and paused with his mouth half-open. 'I know. To mislead us.'

Gowda nodded. 'Quite possible.'

'But why, sir?' Ratna asked.

'Do you remember the cotton wool with blood along with the booze cartons and food packets? We found them in a pit near the cottage. DCP Sagayaraj had called to tell me the forensics people had most definitely identified the blood on the cotton as human,' Gowda said. 'Someone is worried about that. And this is a good way to divert our attention from whatever is going on.'

There was a moment of silence. Then Santosh spoke, 'Sir, we have the findings from the hospitals...'

'Go ahead,' Gowda said.

'In a radius of five kilometres from the Professor's property, we discovered twelve hospitals, fourteen clinics and nineteen doctors with private practices,' Ratna began.

'And?' Gowda asked, suddenly impatient.

'Nothing at all, sir. We checked all the outpatient and inpatient registers. There were, of course, several accident cases, vehicle accidents, home accidents and even four cases from a brawl in a village. And all of them checked out,' Gajendra said.

'So we have nothing then?' Gowda muttered, twirling a pen on the table. Then he looked up and asked, 'What about Providence Hospital? I know it's not in the area earmarked...'

'That's what we were coming to,' Santosh interjected, his voice wobbling and crashing in excitement, so all that emerged was air and a syllable.

Gowda pushed a glass of water towards him. 'I didn't mention Providence Hospital though I have had my suspicions about the place right from the beginning. The hospital belongs to the Buqhari family and the cottage as well. It's very easy to see the connection. But we needed to be careful or we will be accused of going after an individual. This is why I suggested we do the area search,' Gowda said, giving Santosh time to recover his voice and composure.

Ratna opened a file and pulled out photocopies of pages from a hospital register. She placed them in front of Santosh, who cleared his throat and began again. 'The night after the Professor was murdered, that is 30 November, a little past 2 a.m., a John Yaangba was admitted with fourth and fifth metacarpal bone fracture, lacerations and a dislocated shoulder. He also had a blackout caused by a concussion so was kept under observation for twenty-four hours and then sent home.'

'And you think this John Yaangba has something to do with our case?'

Santosh nodded. 'Sir, please look at the name of the person who admitted him... the attendant, I mean.'

Gowda read the name out aloud. 'Paul Selvam.'

Santosh nodded. 'We need to bring him in, sir. I think he knows more than he is revealing.'

Gowda gave Santosh a celebratory thump on his back. 'Excellent work!'

Aqthar thought Santosh's expression was that of a cat after it had caught a rat and laid it on its human's doormat as an offering. Pride vying for place with a sense of triumph.

'What next, sir?' Byrappa asked. 'We have the cart but we don't have the horse.'

SI Aqthar stared at him surprise. He hadn't thought Byrappa would have the balls to say what all of them had been thinking.

Gowda said, 'I have an idea. Send for bondas and coffee. I missed my lunch.'

# 3

Gowda looked at his Mysore bonda one last time before he returned to the SIT room. He had gone back to his own room ostensibly to sign some papers. The truth was he needed a little time on his own to process all the bits and pieces of information he was given. There was an invisible thread connecting them all and he couldn't see it yet. Byrappa had come to him a few minutes later with two bondas on a paper plate and coffee in a plastic beaker.

He had sipped at his coffee, saving the bondas for later; he didn't want crumbs smearing the documents. He was just about to take his first bite when his phone rang. Sagayaraj informed him that he and his team were approaching the station grounds. Gowda knew he had to speak to Santosh and the others before they blurted out their discoveries.

When Sagayaraj and his team entered the SIT room, Gowda and his team were waiting. Sagayaraj took in their composed faces and the tense sets of shoulders—a dead giveaway. Something was afoot, he realized, but Gowda wasn't ready to share it with him yet. He wondered what it could be for a moment and then parked his thoughts as he saw Gowda rising to his feet. 'Good evening, sir.'

Sagayaraj nodded. 'I wanted to debrief you on what we have. Gurunath admitted to having stayed back in Bangalore on 28th and 29th night. He came clean once I confronted him with all the evidence, including his call records and emails.'

Gowda looked up, startled. 'And?'

'He stayed back to meet an acquaintance in Kengeri, he said.'

'Let me guess; another card-holding member of the BSS,' Gowda said.

'Yes. We brought him in for questioning. Gangadhar Patil. That's his name.'

Aqthar interrupted. 'Sir,' he said.

Sagayaraj turned towards him, along with everyone else.

'Sir,' Aqthar continued. 'Gangadhar Patil. Age thirty-two. He has a mole on his chin. Tall and well-built?'

Sagayaraj nodded. 'Do you know him?'

'Yes, sir. We picked him up for questioning six months ago. We had found a cache of country guns while investigating a murder and his name had come up. The investigating officer let him go because he said there was nothing to link him to the guns except that he was a friend of the victim's brother,' Aqthar said, not bothering to hide his disgust at what had transpired.

'Let me guess. The IO was ACP Rajat Trivedi,' Sagayaraj said.

Aqthar nodded. Rajat Trivedi had quit the force a month later and joined the BSS in Meerut, his hometown. He would be contesting elections soon.

'We have had our eye on Gangadhar Patil for some time now. I did ask Gurunath about him. He said that Gangadhar and he are classmates from nursery school and wanted to know if there was a law against meeting friends,' Aqthar added.

Gowda looked up from the pad he had been doodling on. 'Gurunath's turned aggressive. So all that butter-won't-melt-in-the-mouth demeanour was an act?'

Sagayaraj shrugged. 'Maybe. Maybe he just keeps that side of him very quiet.'

'Gurunath and Gangadhar are also relatives, sir,' Aqthar said. 'They keep that very quiet too.'

Sagayaraj's mouth narrowed. His men dropped their gaze, embarrassed. They hadn't known this.

'And you think they had something to do with the Professor's homicide,' Gowda asked, not certain anymore where the investigation was heading.

'We don't know yet, Gowda Sir. But the last email that Professor Mudgood sent was to Professor Shirish Jugande. He wrote that he had something very confidential to tell him about Gurunath, which he would when he called him the following afternoon,' one of the CCB men said.

'And he was killed before that...' the DCP concluded. There was a heavy silence in the room. Gowda saw an opportunity to get his hands on what had eluded him. 'What about the security camera footage from the gated community?' he asked in a silken voice. 'Has anyone looked?'

He knew he was being offensive but he was tired of pussy-footing around the CCB. Before Sagayaraj could respond, Papa Nayak fished out a pen drive. 'Here it is. Nothing at all there, sir,' he said with a dismissive gesture of his hand. 'Mrs Buqhari returned at 10.45 p.m. Iqbal Buqhari came in at about 12.45 a.m. He paused at the gate so we definitely know it was him. We saw Mrs Buqhari's car leave at about 1 a.m. and return at 2.15 a.m. At about 3 a.m., Dr Tehrani and Dr Zohra Tehrani came to the Buqhari residence. They left only around 7 a.m. We checked on the late-night trip and Mrs Buqhari had gone to Providence Hospital to check on her maid who was admitted there, she said. We are having that verified, of course.'

'We would still like to take a look at it,' Gowda retorted, just as casually.

'So what is the POA?' Santosh asked, wondering if all their efforts had been in vain.

'We have to check the grounds to see if there are any hidden firearms there. Gurunath has visited Bangalore several times in the last few months but he's been to see Professor Mudgood only three of those times. One time Gangadhar Patil travelled with him and he didn't return to Dharwad thereafter. One plausible theory is that the Professor knew or found out something and was finished off before he could make it public.'

'And our theory is that the Professor stumbled on something illegal happening in his backyard and was killed before he could raise an alarm,' Gowda said to his team's delight.

'Tell me the basis for your theory,' the DCP asked in a firm voice, realizing that Gowda probably had more information on hand than he was letting on.

'I will, sir. Give me twenty-four hours and I will be able to present my case,' Gowda replied.

'We are going to start a ground search...' the DCP said and abruptly turned to Aqthar. 'What did you use when you unearthed the guns in Ashoka Colony?'

'Sir, we used a GPR—ground penetration radar—a metal detector and a magnetic locator.'

Gajendra was impressed. The boy had more up his sleeve than he had reckoned.

'Borei, do you need everyone on your team?' The DCP turned to Gowda.

'I do, sir. But there is one member of the team who isn't here. You can have Constable Gopal all day. I understand that you have five acres to cover. The others will come in, of course, but won't be able to stay there all day or however long it takes.'

Santosh and Ratna sighed in relief. They had no field experience in using geographical detection methods. This would be an ideal opportunity to see for themselves what exactly was done.

'Good,' Sagayaraj said. 'I'll put in a requisition, and we start first thing tomorrow.'

When the CCB team left the station, Gowda gathered his team for a hasty huddle.

'Check the CCTV footage. That's something I want you to look at carefully,' Gowda said, handing over the pen drive to Santosh. 'I wonder why they didn't bother investigating if Janaki Buqhari was at Providence Hospital. They are so convinced that Gurunath and this Gangadhar fellow are linked to the homicide that they aren't thinking straight. We don't have much time and DCP Vidyaprasad wants us off this case. So we need to work twice as hard,' he added.

'Do you think they will find weapons on Professor Mudgood's property?' Gajendra asked.

'Even if they do, it won't mean anything,' Gowda said with a certainty that none of the others felt.

'What now?' Santosh asked.

'What have you found out about the El Dorado layout? And the details of the TV shoots at the cottage? These may seem insignificant but trust me, in a homicide every detail matters. As for the rest of you, head to the sante. Not you, Aqthar. You will stick out with your Dharwad Kannada. But everyone else, try and find out everything you can about strangers and regulars. Did Gopal have anything to say about the sante? Didn't he go there earlier this morning?' Gowda asked.

'Nothing at all, sir,' Gajendra said. 'He said they were still setting up the shanties. And none of the people were very forthcoming.'

'The idiot must have made it very obvious who he is,' Gowda muttered under his breath. From within the station, the clock struck five.

'Pretend you are there to buy things. I don't need to tell you how to go about it. I want answers, not excuses,' Gowda said with a face like a thundercloud.

Gowda's mobile rang. He glanced at it and was surprised to see Urmila's name. She knew well enough to never call him on his official number. His phone, he had explained a long time ago, could be with just about anyone.

'Hi,' he said, picking up.

'Borci, you need to come home. To my home.'

'Why? What happened?' Gowda tried to hide the consternation in his voice.

There was a pause. 'It's Janaki,' Urmila said. 'She wants to meet you. She seems very distressed and needs to talk to you.'

'Can it wait?' he asked. 'It's not the most convenient time. But I can have a woman officer speak to her right away. Has Iqbal hurt her?'

'She is fine, physically, I mean. But I think you ought to hear her out. She won't tell me what it is about, but I think it is urgent and important, she says.'

## 4

Urmila sat on a sofa across from Janaki. Neither of them spoke. The dogs played with each other, impervious to the silence that hung heavy in the air.

'It will be fine,' Urmila said when the clock began striking the hour. She looked at the door.

Janaki held a tissue to her face. 'I know it won't be fine.'

Mr Right suddenly paused in his attempt to pull a toy out of Bootz's grasp. His ears perked up and he whined. Urmila stood up and put leashes on the dogs.

'He is here,' she said as she picked up her phone. 'I'm taking the dogs out.'

Urmila opened the door as the lift door closed, having let Gowda out. She managed a small smile. 'She is in there.'

Gowda nodded. He touched her wrist fleetingly. 'Don't worry...' he whispered.

Janaki was still as a statue, except for her hands that twisted and balled up a wad of tissue.

Gowda asked, 'Why did you want to see me, Mrs Buqhari?'

Her hands stilled. She looked up and offered him a wan smile. 'Urmila said you would get to the truth one way or the other.'

Gowda shrugged. 'The truth always reveals itself. There is no escaping that.' He paused. 'But what is it you want to talk to me about?'

She dropped her gaze and then after a long pause began to speak.

## 5

It was a little past midnight when Janaki drove through the gates of the Orchard of Silence. She took the third left and then the second right to the cul-de-sac at the apex of which was House No. 40. Her house. Janaki sighed in relief as she parked on the road. Iqbal wasn't home yet, and she needed to take the car out in the morning to go to the hospital. Once he arrived, he would have to park behind hers. She would message him and tell him as much. All she wanted to do was take a hot shower and crawl into bed.

The evening's events had worn her out. Her father was growing more and more cantankerous by the day and she hoped that Mary Susheela would resume work in a day's time. She would go back early tomorrow and spend a couple of days with him until Mary Susheela was back, she decided.

The porch light and garden lamps cast little pools of warm yellow light on a night that was particularly chilly. Janaki shivered as she groped in her bag for her house keys. She couldn't find them no matter how much she searched. She went back to her car to check. That was when she remembered that she had taken out the house keys in her father's kitchen while looking for the emergency ciggie in her bag. She could go back but was reluctant to face him after the words they had exchanged just a short while earlier.

She wondered where Iqbal was. He had a meeting at one of the golf clubs, either BGA in the city or KGA beyond the old airport. Deva was away. So was the live-in house help. The children were at a friend's place for a sleepover. They had taken Bootz along. She was locked out until Iqbal arrived home.

Janaki sighed and went back to the front verandah. She wondered if she should call him. Her phone lit up just then. Home in twenty, the message said. Janaki smiled.

Iqbal hadn't changed from the time she would sneak out of her hostel at Mounts to meet him. He would be waiting some distance away on his bike. There had been no mobile phones then but he had always found a way to send her a message, just as cryptic as the one he sent now. She needed to rekindle the old fires, she thought. And she needed to get back in shape.

A mosquito whined in her ear. Then another one. She pulled out a mosquito repellent tube and smeared the oily cream on her face, arms and feet. She lay down on the cane chaise and propped two cushions beneath her head. She was dozing off after a few minutes, exhausted by all that drama with Mary Susheela. She woke up on hearing Iqbal drive up. A look at her watch told her he was late by almost an hour. She heard him park in the driveway and start walking towards the door.

Janaki had turned off the verandah light to keep away the insects. Iqbal had no idea she was there as he spoke into his phone while approaching the house. He was whispering sweet words of love to someone. 'Goodnight, my queen,' he murmured as he opened the door and made his way in.

Janaki stiffened in shock. Her limbs had turned to stone. One part of her wanted to race after Iqbal. She wanted to accost him with what she had suspected for a while and was now certain about. Another part wanted to smash everything around her.

And there was yet one more part that made her want to crawl into a dark hole and never emerge. She didn't know what to do or where to go. If her mother was alive, she would have rushed to her and buried her face in her lap and wept. Her father was disapproving of any emotional excess but even he wouldn't be indifferent about her husband's infidelity. She would go to him. No matter what had taken place between them, he was her father and he would be there for her.

Janaki had waited for Iqbal to enter the house and shut the door behind him before she got into her car. She started driving, and as she neared her father's house, she saw that the gates were ajar, as she had left them. He really shouldn't be living on his own anymore, she thought as she parked. She found the spare key hidden behind a painting on the inner wall of the verandah.

The table lamp was giving out a soft glow in the living room. A passage light was on as well. Janaki closed the door behind her gently. The house was as silent as it could be. She put her handbag on the table and sank into a chair. It was a chair she remembered fondly from her childhood—her mother's favourite. As Janaki sank into the worn and faded cushion, she felt strangely comforted. The tears came then. Rage and humiliation. Hurt and self-recrimination. And through it all a profound sense of remorse that she had let this happen. She decided this time she would tell Iqbal that it was over.

There was only so much a woman would take. She had pretended for so long that the pretence had started feeling like reality. She had become a cliche. The quiet, docile wife who turned a blind eye to her husband's flings. The quiet, docile wife who let her husband treat her as if she was his chattel.

She heard her father coughing. She retreated deeper into the chair. She didn't want to frighten him. A few minutes later, she heard him coughing and then the sound of his walking stick tap-tapping on the tile floor of the passage.

She held her breath as she heard him enter the kitchen. A clanging of vessels followed. She heard running water as he filled a vessel. What was her father upto, she wondered? Through the silence, she heard a litany of filth: Fat bitch. Fucking bitch. Cock-sucking bitch. Whore. Fucking bald whore. Janaki felt her hand go to her mouth. What was wrong with her father? Who was he raging and cursing at? She sat up and took a few deep breaths, as her pranayama teacher had taught her. She wiped her face with the back of her hand and decided to tell her father she was here.

She heard him mutter again: 'Fat bitch. Leaving me all alone here.' He was railing as the water bubbled on the stove. 'When her husband dumps her for looking like a fat fucking hippo, then she will come crawling here. Then she will need her father...'

Janaki stood in the shadows for a long moment. How could her own father dislike her so much? All her life she had tried to please him. Even her only act of rebellion—marrying Iqbal—had been eventually met with his approval, if not her mother's. But he had found a way to make it all about him. He was the liberal Hindu man of letters performing his daughter's civil wedding with a Muslim man. After the wedding he had taken her aside and said, 'You have chosen this life. Stick with it now. And don't humiliate me further with a divorce.'

Janaki had been aghast. It was as if she was seeing her father for who he was for the first time. He was a pompous hypocrite, she had realized. For all his talk about every religion being equal and how one must never be bound by societal norms, he cared a great deal about what people thought of him. When she had told Iqbal how upset she was, he had smiled and held her. 'I am here for you. I am always here for you,' he had murmured. She had wrapped her arms around him and whispered back, 'You are my man. I don't need anyone but you.'

It occurred to her now that it had been a mistake to confide in Iqbal. Neither her husband nor her father gave a flying fuck about her. She was on her own. Her entire life had been wasted pandering to them and their whims and moods.

Professor Mudgood took the cauldron of boiling water and tottered to the table. He put his head under a towel as he inhaled the steam rising from it. Janaki stood at the kitchen door and saw her father raise his head. She saw him put on his glasses. She heard him ask if anyone was there. She stepped back into the shadows. Her father pulled the towel over his head again.

As though she was watching herself from outside her body, she saw herself reach for the walking stick he had slung on the kitchen door handle. She swung it around and hit him on the head.

She turned and walked back to the living room. She waited to feel something. Fear. Remorse. Guilt.

Nothing at all. She took the walking stick with her and went back to the living room, and collected her keys and handbag. She shut the door, placed the key back in its hiding place, and drove home. The gates were open, as Iqbal had left them. She drove straight into Iqbal's two-month-old BMW. Almost immediately, the lights in the house came on. When Iqbal rushed towards the cars, Janaki reached for the secateurs she had in the glove compartment and stepped out. 'You lying bastard,' she hissed, slashing at his throat. But Iqbal deflected the blade's edge, and it slashed his arm instead.

He grabbed her hand and made her drop the weapon. Then he slapped her hard. A few times. When she began hitting him with her fists, he dragged her into the house and shoved her onto the bed in the downstairs bedroom. He locked the door and went to attend to his arm.

A few minutes later, he returned to a room that had been wrecked. Everything that could be smashed or ripped had been smashed and ripped. The floor was covered in broken glass. Janaki rushed at him with a shard of glass but this time Iqbal was ready. From the wardrobe upstairs, he had pulled out what seemed like a scarf. He grabbed her and twisted her hands behind her. She struggled to push him away, but he was stronger and managed to tie her wrists together.

He was panting with the effort but didn't pause. He pushed her towards the bed and threw her on it, then sat astride her and wrenched the runner off the bottom of the bed and tied her legs together with it. He taped her mouth, afraid she would scream even though the heavy curtains and closed windows made the house almost sound-proof. When he was certain she couldn't move or scream, Iqbal looked at the bleeding gash in his arm. The cotton wool and plaster he had covered it with had come off, and there was blood on Janaki as well. She had stopped struggling and turned still. A catatonic stillness that frightened him. He called his sister, Zohra.

'I don't really remember much after that. I know they tranquillized me. I know that when I woke up, it was the dawn of the 30th. Everything that had happened to me and all that I had done seemed like a dream. And I was back to being the quiet, docile daughter and wife. Except I had killed my father and attempted to kill my husband,' Janaki finished, staring straight at Gowda with a glass-eyed expression.

Gowda sat there, trying to wrap his head around what he had just heard. It explained the hostility between husband and wife. It also explained her grief.

'I prayed for a miracle, that somehow my blow to his head hadn't really hurt him. But he hadn't called or texted and I knew. I drove back there and my father was where I had left him. I thought at first that no one would find out. That it would be considered a heart attack maybe. But when I heard that the postmortem said murder, I knew it was only a matter of time. I thought of how your eyes had gone to the Chinese urn in the lobby of my house. I knew you were looking for a walking stick.'

She turned to the side of the sofa she was sitting on and reached for something on the ground. It was the stick wrapped in bubble wrap. She handed it to him quietly.

'It was in my car. Here is the murder weapon, ACP Gowda,' she said. 'I suppose you will arrest me now.' She stared at him as if suddenly struck by the enormity of what she had done.

Gowda wondered what to do next. He knew he ought to call DCP Sagayaraj and ask him for counsel. He also knew that Janaki was not the murderer. Professor Mudgood had died of drowning and not from blunt-force trauma. Dr Khan had categorically said that the blow had probably only stunned the victim.

'Listen to me,' he said. 'What you did was a crime but you didn't kill your father. I want you to know that.'

Janaki looked at him, perplexed. 'If I didn't, who did?'

'That's exactly what we are trying to find out. For now I want you to go back home and not mention this to anyone. Not even Iqbal. I will take the walking stick with me. There will be consequences for what you did. Do you understand that?'

She nodded.

'Get yourself a good lawyer, and when it is time for us to enter your name in the case file, we will take your statement. You can ask your lawyer to step in then. Until then, no leaving town, not even to Mysore. Do you understand?'

Janaki wrapped her arms around herself as if in readiness for the impending storm she was about to be hurled into and fixed her eyes on the floor.

# 6 DECEMBER 2012, THURSDAY

## 1

Aqthar picked up Gajendra from outside his gate. He looked a little bleary-eyed. 'All okay, Gajendra Sir?' he asked as the older man adjusted his helmet. 'Did you get any leads last evening?'

'I can tell you the price of tomatoes will drop to almost half by closing time. The pakoda man is from Kolar and the jalebi man came from Uttar Pradesh four years ago. The fisherwoman claims the fish is from lakes nearby and special vegetables like broccoli and mushrooms are sold out in less than two hours' time. Apart from that, nothing.' Gajendra sighed.

Aqthar met his gaze in the rearview mirror. 'So a wasted trip?'

'This case is peculiar, sir,' Gajendra said. 'Each time I think we've reached somewhere, I discover it is nowhere.'

Aqthar raised the throttle as he overtook a garbage truck that was scattering garbage on the road. 'Santosh and Ratna had to go to a children's home near Narayanpura. A child from there called the helpline,' he said to Gajendra, who was gesticulating at the garbage truck driver.

'After what we have seen and heard, none of us take cases involving minors lightly, Attar... er, Actor Sir,' Gajendra said, who struggled with Aqthar's name each time he said it.

Aqthar darted a glance at the rearview mirror. 'Sir, it is not Attar or Actor, it is Aqthar.' Then trying to soften the sting in his words, he quickly said, 'Tell me about the trafficking case, Gajendra Sir.'

When they reached Professor Mudgood's property, the gates were open and the CCB officers were already there. Constable Gopal, looking very self-important, was taking a beaker of tea to the DCP.

'Constable Gopal has found his calling,' Aqthar muttered.

Gajendra smiled at him. 'Don't be so dismissive of chaiwalas, sir. They know how to buy and sell favours.' He got off the bike and looked at the young man's face. 'You think he'll come to power?'

Aqthar shrugged. 'What do I know, sir?' He wanted to end the conversation. Why had he broken his own rule of never bringing up politics with colleagues? He had seen the mildest of people froth at the mouth when politics and political affiliations were being discussed. And there was no way of knowing where Gajendra's sympathies lay.

Sagayaraj waved them over. Aqthar sighed with relief.

'We'll start in the next five minutes,' the DCP said as they walked towards him.

Aqthar and Gajendra saluted and went to stand near him uncertainly.

'Where are Gurunath and Patil, sir?' Aqthar asked.

'At Patil's home,' the DCP said. Pre-empting Aqthar's follow-up query, he added, 'We can't keep them after twenty-four hours have passed, as you know. But two of my men are with them and we'll take a call on what next based on what we find here.'

Gajendra wandered away towards the CCB officers. They were sharing a smoke while Gopal hovered near them. Gajendra gave him a mirthless smile and asked, 'How's it going?'

'I want to move to the CCB,' Gopal murmured. 'Sir...' He gestured to the gate.

A Bolero had entered the gates and was parking. Three men got out from the rear seat and from the back of the vehicle a constable and a German shepherd emerged.

Gajendra looked at the young man and the dog curiously. He didn't recognize him. He knew the entire dog squad and wondered who this was. 'Apparently he's just back from the NTCD after a year's training,' Aqthar said.

'The young man or the dog?'

'Sir, at the National Training Centre for Dogs the handler too has to be trained.' Aqthar laughed.

'Where is the centre, sir?' Gajendra couldn't stop looking at the dog, who seemed very composed despite the presence of strangers.

'Tekanpur, Madhya Pradesh,' Aqthar said, walking towards them.

Gajendra shook his head. 'That dog is more widely travelled than me, sir. The farthest north I have gone is Hyderabad.'

When the group broke up into teams, Gajendra decided to go with Sheba the dog and her handler, Pratap. Aqthar went with the team using the electromagnetic detectors.

Sheba sniffed out the first cache within half an hour. She pawed a spot and whined. 'Has she found something?' Gajendra asked, as excited as Sheba.

'Looks like it,' Pratap said. He called one of the men with the detectors. 'Check here, sir. Sheba seems to find this spot very interesting.'

A probe was brought there to verify the exact location. Gajendra watched in fascination as they created a grid around the area Sheba had whined at. A reedy man resembling the probe ran it in an X pattern over the area. At the point where the probe beeped the loudest, he stopped. 'Here, sir,' he said and paused.

A stake was planted at the spot. All very well, Gajendra thought, but someone needed to dig there. Jaishankar, one of the CCB officers, came there with two shovels. 'We need to start digging,' he said.

Gajendra looked at Gopal. 'Take a shovel and dig.'

Gopal glared but took the shovel.

Gajendra called Gowda. 'Sir, the super dog is here...'

Gajendra grinned as he heard Gowda say, 'I say, Gajendra, you can't call DCP Vidyaprasad a dog.'

Gajendra hastened to explain. 'No, no... a real super dog, sir. With a tail, sir. Her name is Sheba and she seems to have sniffed out something. Gopal has been told to dig up the area. I thought I should keep you posted.'

'Good,' Gowda said and hung up. Soon, he arrived there with Santosh, Ratna and Byrappa.

Sheba and Pratap noticed their arrival. Gowda walked towards Sheba, who had stood up on her hind legs, smothering Gowda with several wet licks.

Pratap saluted Gowda. 'Sir, I didn't expect to see you here.'

Gowda grinned and said, 'And neither did I, Pratap. I didn't know you were with Special Intelligence now.'

'Sheba was transferred recently, sir. Now that Sheba has become one of the best bomb detectors we have. So where Sheba goes, I go. She is adept at sniffing out firearms too though she's still learning.'

'Sheba, you clever, clever girl,' Gowda said, bending down to pat the dog again while Gajendra looked at Sheba with admiration.

As Gowda walked towards the others, the excitement was palpable. Sagayaraj looked at him. 'Looks like we are moving in the right direction,' he said, indicating the site.

At a depth of about one and a half feet, Gopal had stopped. He was sweating profusely and seemed dazed by exhaustion. Gowda looked at him, concerned. Was Gopal going to collapse? He was about to ask someone else to step in when Byrappa jumped into the ditch and took the spade from Gopal. 'I am a farmer's son,' he said by way of explanation to a curious Ratna. 'All through my childhood, I would go to the fields before school and after school. My father couldn't afford to hire workers. There is a method to how you do it.'

He dug at a steady rhythm that wasn't as manic as Gopal's had been but was far more efficient. At a depth of three feet, a tarpaulin-wrapped bundle was found. Byrappa stepped aside.

The tarpaulin bundle was opened to reveal four country pistols and two machetes.

Sagayaraj looked at Gowda, who stood with his team flanking him. He gestured for Gowda to come along with him.

'Looks like we have the evidence we need to arrest Gurunath and Gangadhar,' he said.

'Looks like,' Gowda agreed.

'You are still not convinced, even with the firearms.' The DCP's tone was tetchy.

'To be honest, sir, I am not,' Gowda said quietly. 'In all probability you might even find fingerprints on it that are Gurunath's or Gangadhar's or both. But if they hid the weapons here, why would they kill the Professor? Something doesn't sit right...'

'Maybe he saw them burying it and threatened to expose them,' Sagayaraj snapped. Then he pulled himself together and said, 'Is it so hard to accept that you could be wrong, Borei?'

'DCP Sagayaraj, our ACP Gowda is stubborn as a mule at times,' a honeyed voice interjected. The two of them turned to see DCP Vidyaprasad. Gowda glared at his superior officer and wondered if he could plant a hard kick on the man's backside and ascribe it to his mulish behaviour. Almost as if reading Gowda's mind, Sagayaraj inserted himself between a belligerent Gowda and a smug-faced Vidyaprasad. 'I didn't expect to see you here.'

'Nothing happens in my area of control without my knowledge,' Vidyaprasad said. 'I heard about the search and was sure you would discover something. I have been suspicious about that loafer Gurunath right from the time you brought him in. Congratulations, DCP Sagayaraj... I think we can safely assume that you have the culprits and sufficient evidence to take them into custody.' Vidyaprasad had the relieved air of a man who had thwarted a disaster.

Gowda didn't speak. He had this horrible suspicion that Vidyaprasad would prefer the case to be taken over entirely by the CCB and for the SIT to be disbanded. He looked at the site where the firearms had been found.

It was closer to the cottage than the main house.

Professor Mudgood had been sprightly enough at eighty-two years, he had been told. Nevertheless, he wasn't a stupid old man to go exploring the grounds on his own. Especially when he had to climb down the slope to the third terrace on which the cottage was located.

Gowda took a deep breath and forced the ghost of a smile on his face. 'Evidence is everything. I understand that,' he said and sauntered away, leaving one DCP puzzled and the other reassured.

## 2

A couple of hours later, Gowda found Gajendra sitting in the SIT room, staring at the whiteboard, looking as forlorn as a kitten abandoned in a ditch. He sighed loudly, unaware of Gowda standing behind him.

'What's that long sigh for, Gajendra?' Gowda asked.

Gajendra turned, startled. 'I hate seeing a case slip out of our hands.'

'Who said the case has slipped out of our hands?' Gowda shot him a sly grin.

Gajendra stared. 'What are you saying, sir? The evidence...'

'Evidence for what?' Gowda's eyebrow cocked.

'Sir, we all saw the firearms...'

'That we did, but the most obvious detail didn't strike DCP Sagayaraj. As for DCP Vidyaprasad, he is so determined to prove that this is a political murder that he isn't considering any other motive.'

Gajendra asked, 'Shall I call in the others?'

Gowda nodded.

Ratna entered, followed by Aqthar and Byrappa.

Gowda gave Gajendra a questioning look. He read his senior's silent query with an ease which baffled Aqthar.

'Gopal has gone with the CCB team, sir. He seemed to have asked DCP Vidyaprasad for sanction, which I hear was readily given.'

Santosh walked in, chewing his lips. He ignored the others and blurted out, 'Sir, the soil was as hard as a rock...'

'What soil?' Gowda frowned. 'Take a deep breath and tell me... slowly.'

Santosh obediently took a deep breath, paused and took one more. A little boy about to recite the poem he had rehearsed all day, Ratna thought with suppressed amusement.

Byrappa thumped the table with excitement. 'Santosh Sir, I noticed it too. But it never occurred to me to bring it up. I guess that's why you are an SI and I am a constable...'

Santosh darted Byrappa a piercing look. 'Next time question it if something troubles you.'

Gowda remembered telling Santosh something very similar once.

'I suppose you are referring to the soil where the firearms were discovered. You were the one who dug it up, Byrappa... you thought so too?' Gowda asked.

'Yes, sir,' Byrappa said. 'If the firearms were buried just a few days ago, the soil would have been more crumbly. But this was like cutting into a rock.'

'And there was grass on it,' Ratna interrupted.

'Weeds, madam. They are demon seeds. They grow overnight,' Byrappa said. 'And they grow as if they are fed on Complan.'

'And you would know because...' Ratna persisted.

'Because he is a farmer's son,' Gajendra said.

Ratna flushed and subsided into silence.

'I had my own reservations about the homicide and the fire-arms being linked. This reinforces it,' Gowda began.

'What made you think that, sir?' Santosh asked.

Aqthar pulled his notebook out. He had decided to switch to one after Gowda had admonished him for constantly looking into his phone.

'Look at the lay of the land. The Professor was eighty-two years old. Do you see him sliding down to the next terrace to spy on what was going on at the third level? And that too in the night. My father is younger. And I see how unsteady he is on his feet even in broad daylight outside the house. Secondly, the Professor's vision. His glasses were on the floor, shattered. But we could see that they were thick as soda bottles.'

Gowda gestured to indicate the thickness by holding his thumb and index finger apart. 'He wouldn't have been able to see that far, especially at night. And Gurunath, who had been his assistant for several years, knows that well enough.'

There was silence in the room. Gowda wagered a bet with himself on who would bell the cat. When Ratna raised her hand to ask the question that none of the others dared articulate, Gowda drew a big blue tick in a box in his head.

'Sir, why is the CCB so determined to make it out to be a political murder?' she asked. 'Hasn't all of this occurred to DCP Sagayaraj?'

'Who knows what pressure he is under, Ratna?' Gowda's query was cryptic and rhetorical.

Santosh blinked furiously at Ratna to shut up. She pretended not to see and continued to probe. 'You mean political pressure...'

'I didn't imply anything. You are free to read whatever you choose to into it.'

Gowda's mobile rang, loudly, stridently, breaking the awk-ward pause that had crept into the room. His face lit up when he saw who was calling. 'I need to take this,' he said, leaving the room.

Gajendra gave Ratna a sympathetic look. 'Madam,' he said gently. 'I speak to you from experience. You don't need to question everything. Sometimes it is best to watch and wait. The answer will occur to you on its own.'

Ratna chewed on her fingernail. Santosh wished he could give her shoulder a comforting squeeze. Instead he murmured, 'He should have some consideration; he is talking to a lady.'

'Why?' Ratna snarled.

Byrappa said, 'Gowda Sir makes no distinction at all... whether it is a man or a woman who is shooting their mouth off.'

Aqthar made another squiggle in his little notebook: No gender bias when pointing out stupidity.

Gowda walked back into the room, looking pleased. 'That was Simon, the forensics person. He is sending the official results but he will also drop in by 4 p.m. I think he has something unofficial to share. We should have a clearer picture once he does.'

Something clicked in Aqthar's mind. It dawned on him that this must have been what Gowda was waiting for when he had asked DCP Sagayaraj for twenty-four hours' time.

Gowda decided to head home. His father was still unwell. Roshan had assured him that he would keep an eye on him but he still didn't trust his son entirely. The boy seemed to have cleaned up his act, but he wasn't sure if that was an act as well. Besides, it was a quarter to one and he was hungry.

The house seemed empty, Gowda thought as he unlatched the gate and rode in. No noise from a blaring TV or Roshan's music that sounded like someone was pounding rice in a mortar. He frowned as he felt his insides curl into a tight little ball of dread. He opened the door and went in. 'Appa... Roshan...'

He rushed to his father's room. The bed was made and the bathroom was dry. He went into Roshan's room. The bed seemed hastily made and there was a blob of toothpaste stuck to the washbasin in the bathroom.

Gowda was just about to call up Roshan when he heard a peal of laughter followed by Roshan's excited voice. He grimaced. What the hell!

He went to the verandah, took a mighty breath and hollered, 'Roshan!'

A minute later a beatific face rose above the balcony wall. 'Appa, are you home? I didn't hear you come in. We are just coming down.'

Roshan's smile sent warning signals down Gowda's spine. He plonked himself in a chair to wait. Gowda wondered if Roshan was using again. He didn't mind his son smoking the occasional joint but the problem was it never stopped there. He would have to keep an eye on him once again. Sometimes he wondered if it was his fault that Roshan had turned out the way he did. And yet there seemed to be nothing wrong with him. His grades were decent, his manners no more atrocious than kids of his generation, and he was an affectionate boy when he forgot to be surly and bad-tempered.

Gowda sighed. Had he really been stretched out on a king-size bed a few days ago with not a worry except how to decide whether to have karimeen pollichathu or Alleppey fish curry for dinner. Urmila hadn't texted him all day. She must be pissed off as hell. Gowda sighed once again.

A few minutes later Chidananda, Roshan and a youngish-looking man appeared.

'Hello, sir,' he said. 'I am Shashank. Your tenant.'

Gowda stood up to shake his hand. Shashank was of medium height and build with a clean-shaven jaw and a nose that seemed to have been surgically altered. He caught Gowda's curious look and touched his nose. 'It was smashed in an accident and the plastic surgeon decided to gift me a perfect nose.' His smile was open and disarming.

'Please sit down.' Gowda gestured to a chair. The smile stayed on Shashank's face, and Gowda wondered if that too was sewn on by the plastic surgeon. Urmila had told him of women whose Botox injections gave them a look of perpetual surprise.

Something about Shashank seemed familiar. He couldn't figure out exactly what made him think so. But it would come to him. Eventually, Gowda asked, 'I hope you like the house and the area...'

Mr Tenant nodded, still smiling. 'Everything is tiptop.' He spoke in a soft voice and in Kannada.

Gowda frowned. 'You are not Kannadiga?'

Shashank shook his head. 'I moved here when I was twenty-two but I am originally from Vellore, sir. But how did you know?'

Gowda shrugged. 'Training.'

Shashank's smile seemed less ardent suddenly, but he made up for it with an effusive invitation. 'Sir, please come over for lunch this Sunday. All of you. My missus is a very good cook.'

'Bhuvana gave us dosas this morning, Appa,' Roshan said. 'They were paper-thin, and so crisp.'

'Yes,' Chidananda interjected, seeing Gowda's frown. 'As for the korma she made... what can I say. Just so good.'

Shashank continued to smile.

'I would love to but I'm not sure about my schedule,' Gowda said, wondering why Shashank and Bhuvana's presence made him uneasy. He really should have met them before agreeing to rent out the upstairs to them but he had been lazy or was it sheer complacency? What is it they say about a cobbler's child never having shoes of his own. 'I am very busy with a few cases,' he said abruptly.

'You are always busy,' Chidananda said.

'He is a very important police officer.' Shashank rushed to Gowda's defence to his annoyance.

'We'll make up for you, Appa,' Roshan chirped.

Did the boy have a crush on the woman? Gowda groaned. First his father, now his son... He didn't particularly want to share a meal with his tenants but he did want to see what had his family hovering around Mrs Tenant like flies buzzing around overripe fruit.

'Let me see...' Gowda said and glanced at his watch pointedly.

Neither of them were hungry, Roshan said after Shashank had left.

Gowda frowned. 'So are you going to skip lunch?'

'Appa, I'll eat at three,' Roshan said, while tapping away at his phone. He was on his phone a little too much, Gowda thought. Perhaps it was time for one round of snooping.

'What about you, Appa? You can't miss meals... you know that.'

'I will have some rice and rasam later,' Chidananda said.

Gowda took a deep breath. Don't raise your voice, he told himself. 'Well, it would be sensible to not eat between mealtimes... And I don't like the two of you spending so much time with the tenants.'

'Why?' Roshan looked up. His aggrieved expression made Gowda want to box his ears.

'I don't like it,' Gowda said as he began heating his lunch.

'Do we need to get police verification before we can be friends with someone? Bhuvana is a lovely person and so interesting to talk to.' Roshan looked at his grandfather for support.

'Borei, we need to have good relations with the neighbours. In the absence of a family, they become our de facto family,' Chidananda began.

'We went up to meet Bhuvana's brother who's visiting. Ramesh Anna is amazing.'

'A very nice young man too, with no airs about him,' Chidananda said, seeing Gowda's sullen expression.

'He is like Shakuntala Devi.'

'Who?' Gowda looked up.

'The human computer,' Chidananda said impatiently.

'You mean he can multiply twelve-digit numbers in a matter of seconds?'

'I think he will be able to. I asked him some really tough questions and he got it right each time, Appa,' Roshan said. 'I wanted to share on Facebook a short video I made while we were there but Ramesh Anna said no.'

Gowda ignored the two of them and hastily gobbled his lunch. He shouldn't have bothered coming home. The two of them seemed like they could fend for themselves.

'I'll see you when I see you,' Gowda said as he cleared the table and stacked the dishes in the sink.

'We'll probably go for a walk in the evening,' Roshan said.

'Don't tire your grandfather out.' Gowda glanced at his father who sat with his eyes closed.

'I am old, not decrepit,' Chidananda said, not opening his eyes. 'And don't talk about me as if I am not in the room.'

Gowda didn't respond. It occurred to him that his own brand of terseness was an inheritance from his father. He would tell Urmila that. In fact, he would try and surprise her if the forensics report turned out the way he hoped it would.

He was going to have a meeting with Stanley if the unofficial forensic findings needed to be made official. There was going to be a matter of chain of custody but he hoped that it would only be one of the corroborative pieces of evidence he was gathering.

Gowda picked up his bike keys. He had planned to call David but changed his mind. He didn't trust Roshan—he might just take his bike out for a spin.

# 3

Simon looked at the eager faces around him. Only ACP Gowda seemed less interested in knowing his findings. Simon knew him well enough to know that this was an act. He was probably the most eager of the lot.

'Well, sir, I have the results here,' Simon said. 'It's a curious matter. The first set of samples that I took are here...'

Simon thrust a sheaf of printouts towards Gowda. 'Let me give you the official version first. The house contained numerous fingerprints at various places. At least about half a dozen. We matched them with the family members and the staff. As was to be expected, the Professor's daughter, the live-in maid and her husband Paul Selvam and Iqbal Buqhari's assistant Deva—all their prints were found.'

'What about Iqbal Buqhari?' Gowda asked.

'His as well.'

'But it is to be expected. He is the son-in-law,' Ratna said.

'What was surprising, though, was that the main door had been wiped clean. As was its handle. Not a trace of anything,' Simon said as he pulled his glasses on.

'What about the back door?' Santosh asked. 'It had been left unlatched.'

'The door handle was wiped clean. The door itself was a mess of numerous prints, as all of us know. But that's not all, sir. As you know, there were some traces of the perpetrator or perpetrators in the tissue found beneath the Professor's fingernails.'

Gowda asked, 'Did you find a match?'

Simon shook his head. 'The time lapse had been too long and we were not able to establish anything conclusive except that some of the substance belonged to a human. Strangely, there was a lot of soil residue too beneath his fingernails as if he had been playing in mud.'

Gowda twirled the paperweight on his table. He wanted to fling it at the wall.

'There is something that's conclusive,' Simon said, hastily reading Gowda's expression. 'The cotton wool found on the grounds matched with the blood in the cottage.'

'The shower cubicle?' Aqthar asked.

'Actually, no... I found a blood smear on the steel almirah.'

'So all the blood we saw in the cottage was animal blood to deliberately mislead us,' Gajendra growled. 'This is a very clever criminal, sir.'

'The bathroom was first messed up and later cleaned to mislead even further.' Gowda's expression sent a chill down Santosh's spine. He looked like he wanted to pulverize a few things.

'I suppose there is very little that's different in the unofficial version,' Gowda said after a long pause.

'Yes, sir,' Simon said. 'I wish I could say otherwise but...'

'What do we do now, sir?' Santosh asked Gowda when Simon had left.

'We start from scratch with what we have now, and look at every shred of evidence again. The forensic findings will be our framework.'

His phone trilled to life. Gowda cut the call. It was an unknown number. When it rang again, Santosh saw Gowda frown. He watched him swipe the accept icon.

'Hello, ACP Gowda here,' he said carefully.

'Hello, sir, this is Janaki Buqhari.'

Gowda's voice was soft as he responded, 'Hello, Mrs Buqhari... how can I help you?' He walked slowly out of the room.

'I need to speak to you, sir... should I come to the station? It isn't about what I told you last evening,' she added hastily. 'This is something else.'

Gowda stood up. 'My team and I will come to your residence. We will be there in the next half an hour.'

Gowda slipped his phone into his trouser pocket and returned to join the rest of his officers. 'Janaki Buqhari wants to meet us. Ratna and Gajendra, I need you to come with me.'

Bootz greeted them at the gate. Gajendra looked at the beagle and snorted. 'He looks like a bolster with a tail and two floppy ears,' he said. 'Now that Sheba is a real dog.'

Ratna thought of Gajendra's pet spitz. 'Who is Sheba? Your dog?'

'Madam, my doggie's name is Soumya. I am talking about the sniffer dog. She is the one who found the weapons before the gadgets did.'

'There he comes, Buqhari's right hand,' Ratna said, wondering at the almost gorilla-like lope that men with bulging muscles seemed to have.

Deva gave them a contrived smile as he came to the gate. 'Mr Buqhari isn't here.'

'We are here to see Mrs Buqhari,' Gajendra said.

'Oh, I see,' Deva said. He opened the gate with much reluctance, not even calling the dog away, Gowda noticed.

'Are any of you scared of dogs?' Gowda asked under his breath.

'That sorekai?' Gajendra snorted. Gowda grinned. Gajendra had a point. The beagle did look like a bottle gourd.

They followed Deva in while Bootz leapt up to lick Gowda's hand. Deva opened the main door and took them into the library. 'Madam will be here in a few minutes,' he said, waiting at the door as if he expected them to stow a few leather-bound volumes into their uniforms.

This library was a full-scale version of the cottage library. Floor-to-ceiling bookshelves. A rolltop desk. Two wing chairs. A pot-bellied lamp between the two. There was also a black leather couch and a goose-necked lamp arching over one side of it. An expensive rug was laid out on the gleaming wooden floor.

A maid came in bearing a tray with three glasses of water. Gowda took a glass and strolled towards the bookshelves. He felt a tremendous sense of satisfaction when he pulled out a volume and saw it was a replica of the school textbook bound in leather that they had found in the cottage.

Deva stepped forward. 'Buqhari Sir doesn't like anyone touching his books. Unless he gives them permission to do so.'

Gowda shoved the book back none too gently. 'I am not surprised,' he said. 'Such valuable books.'

\*

Janaki Buqhari walked in with a hesitant smile. She looked pointedly at Deva. He moved away from the library door to the vestibule.

'There is a package I need you to courier right away,' she said.

'Now?' Deva asked.

He didn't sound pleased, Gowda thought.

'Yes, now,' Janaki said firmly. 'It's on the table in the lobby,' she added and shut the door in his face.

Gowda and Gajendra looked at the rug as if it held the secrets of the universe. Ratna went to Janaki. 'Is everything all right, madam?' she asked gently.

Janaki didn't speak. She had a line of sweat beads on her upper lip. But she nodded and took a cough lozenge from her handbag. She sucked on it as if to calm herself.

Ratna took an untouched glass of water and offered it to Janaki. The woman gave her a small smile as she took the glass with both hands. 'Deva has been with my husband for a while,' she said as if to explain his territorial stance. 'And is sometimes overprotective.'

Ratna took the empty glass from her and placed it back on the tray. Gowda came towards Janaki with the blandest expression he could muster. He still hadn't been able to assimilate the fact that the woman before him had intended to kill her father in a fit of rage. He had debated with himself all night if he should tell anyone else about it. But he knew that would be a piece of pie everyone would want a share of. The police department to the media, everyone would hasten to make a production of it. While Janaki would be in the eye of the storm, the real criminal would be standing on the sidelines laughing his head off.

'Mrs Buqhari, you said you needed to speak to me.'

Janaki nodded. She opened her handbag and took out a plastic takeaway container.

'This afternoon I called DCP Sagayaraj to ask if I could enter my father's house. I thought I would sort out his clothes. There is an old people's home I help support. We need clothes for the elderly residents there. The DCP said I could go in as long as I didn't enter the kitchen area, the crime scene. I went to the house and was pulling out my father's sweaters and waistcoats from his cupboard. He has about half a dozen waistcoats depending on what he was doing, including one he wore when he was writing. I thought I would take that one with me as a keepsake. In its pocket, I found this.'

She placed the container on the table. Gowda opened it and realized he was staring at a set of upper dentures. Its edge was stained brown in a couple of places. Gowda took a swizzle stick, placed quite conveniently, he thought, in a cut-glass bowl on the table. He hoisted the dentures up.

'The Professor's?' Gowda asked and then remembered the corpse had most of its teeth intact.

'My father had all his teeth. In fact, he would tell everyone that he was old but he hadn't lost his bite,' Janaki said with a catch in her voice. 'They're my mother's. After she died and I was cleaning out her things, I noticed the upper dentures were missing. But my mother had died in hospital after three weeks in the ICU. So I assumed they were misplaced there.' She paused. 'Now I think my father kept them. Most people would keep photographs of a loved one to remember them by. But my father wasn't most people.'

'I get it.' Gowda nodded. 'But what does it have to do with his death?'

'I really don't know but there is something strange about the stains on the teeth, sir. My mother didn't chew betel leaves or smoke. I remember her smile as sparkling ivory. This isn't what her teeth were like. And I also remembered that my father was wearing this waistcoat on the night I saw him last. I thought you should know...' Janaki said, watching her mother's smile being packed away by the Head Constable.

Gowda nodded. 'Thank you, Mrs Buqhari. Now that you have had some days to think, do you have any suspicions you want to share?' Gowda's voice was gently coaxing.

'Suspicions about what, ACP Gowda?' Iqbal Buqhari asked from the door. 'I didn't realize you were dropping by.'

Gowda turned to him. The door to the library was now open. Deva stood a few feet behind him with the triumph of an athlete dashing past the finish line before anyone else.

'Hello, Iqbal,' Gowda said, appearing unfazed by the man's arrival, Ratna thought, though she felt her own heart slam in her rib cage. She waited for Janaki to say something about why they were there.

When she didn't, Ratna piped up, 'We wanted to check with madam on Mary Susheela, to verify if there was any suspicious behaviour on her part.'

'You don't have to worry about Mary. Her husband has been working for me for a long time.' Iqbal's tone was firm, as if he would brook no questioning. He turned to Gowda, holding out his hand for a shake. Gowda obliged and looked at his bandaged arm. He asked, 'How is the dog bite now?'

Iqbal shrugged. 'It will take a few days to heal. It was a deep bite.'

'Well, we have what we need so we will be on our way,' Gowda said. 'Thank you, Mrs and Mr Buqhari, for your cooperation.'

None of them spoke until they were in the vehicle. Deva and Bootz had flanked them as they walked down the driveway.

'What do you think about this new evidence, sir?' Gajendra asked.

Gowda said, 'Let's go to the Professor's house once again.'

## 4

Evening turned into a fiery dusk as they drove towards the house. The sun was a perfect orb as it began its descent into the horizon. Bangalore sunsets, Gowda thought, with a sense of pleasure as they drove up to the Professor's property.

Now that the ground search was complete, the two constables had been relieved of the duty of guarding the property. The gates were open, as if someone was expecting them. Once they were inside, Gowda saw Santosh was already there. He stood leaning against Aqthar's bike while Aqthar contemplated the wheelbarrow.

'I texted Santosh, sir,' Gajendra said, almost as if he had read Gowda's mind.

'Good,' Gowda said. Then he narrowed his eyes. 'What about Byrappa?'

'He must already be here, sir. I sent him here as soon as we left from the Buqhari residence.'

Byrappa emerged from somewhere behind the house as Gowda stepped out of the vehicle. Gajendra opened the main door and switched a light on. He put on the lights around the house too and came back to the porch where everyone else was.

A few insects began circling the porch light.

'When we are done here, I want the dentures sent to Simon so he can take a sample of the stain on them, ASAP,' Gowda said, staring thoughtfully at them. 'Keep the CCB in the loop as well.'

'What are we looking for, sir?' Santosh asked.

'Good question,' Gowda said, grinning at him. 'I suddenly had a thought or a series of thoughts and I wanted to run them by you all while standing at the crime scene.'

All of them drew closer to Gowda.

Gowda pulled at the bridge of his nose. Then he spoke slowly, as if attempting to bring a semblance of order to his thoughts that spun on their heels, whirling, dervish-like.

'What if the Professor used the dentures to bite Mary Susheela?'

They stared at him as if he were mad. Santosh and Ratna looked at each other. Santosh's eyes gleamed as the words spluttered out, 'The duty doctor who examined Mary Susheela said that the bite mark seemed more human than animal.'

'Why would he do that, sir?' Gajendra asked in a feeble voice.

'Maybe he was annoyed with her,' Byrappa said.

'Maybe this was some kind of experiment,' Aqthar said, after a pause.

Gowda gave him a grateful look.

Aqthar held up his phone to show Gowda what he had found. It was an announcement about the seminar that the Professor had been scheduled to attend: 'Why I Am Not a Hindu: My Experiments with Hinduism.'

'Why would he need to bite someone to experiment with Hinduism?' Ratna's query didn't hold a trace of condescension, Gowda decided, and so he shrugged. 'Maybe the experiment was for something else.'

'His laptop is with the CCB,' Aqthar said. 'It might hold the answers.'

Gowda went up the few steps to the verandah. He walked to the corner of the room with the huge table stacked with books and papers. The empty space once occupied by the laptop was covered with a fine patina of dust. He pulled open the line of drawers one by one and rifled through the papers. If the Professor was anything like his father, he knew what he was looking for. He found diaries from the years 2008, 2009 and 2010, all covered in navy-blue Rexene and bearing the logo of a bank.

He opened them one by one, and found within each notes in a cursive hand. The 2010 diary had several blank pages. 'We may find a clue to what he was thinking in this one here,' he said, spotting an entry for June 2012. Several pages later was the last entry marked November 28th.

*'No amount of experimentation can ever prove me right; a single experiment can prove me wrong.'—Albert Einstein.*

Beneath the quote was the Professor's notes for his talk:
*Start with the experiment on the Chinese whispers nature of rumour. Rumours that led to riots.*

*How can a religion that is practised as a ritual to mythology be anything more than a celebration of rumour?*

He looked up from the diary and said, 'Let's try and retrace what could have been the Professor's movements that evening before nightfall.'

Gajendra fished out the key for the lock he had used to shut off the kitchen area, from where a stench like that of a clogged drain rushed out to greet them. All of them trooped in, careful not to touch anything.

Gowda walked through the kitchen to the work area where he saw a sink with a draining tray and a grinding platform with its stone missing. A door with a now-sturdy latch opened into the yard beyond. He found a switchboard near the door and turned all the switches on. A light came on in the backyard.

Gowda opened the door and stepped out. A wall light cast a pool of brightness. There was another light on a post near the edge of the terrace, but it wasn't working.

Gowda turned to Gajendra. 'Check if this light was working on the night of the homicide.'

From the cemented yard, the cottage wasn't visible as trees blocked the view. Gowda walked to the end of the yard. Steps with a metal handrail led down to the next level but they were barely visible in the darkness. A low wall skirted the yard. He went down the steps littered with leaves, shining his torch. A greyish discoloured spot in the ground seemed like the place where kitchen waste was thrown. A big hibiscus bush grew nearby and Gowda made out a few broken branches still attached to the plant. He remembered Simon mentioning the soil in the finger-nail findings. Things were finally falling into place.

Gowda turned and looked up at the yard above. He hollered, 'Gajendra...' Gajendra's head popped up over the parapet wall.

'Stand at the top of the steps,' Gowda told him. Gajendra came to the gap in the parapet wall where the steps began.

Gowda crouched at the third step. He stood up and asked, 'How tall was the Professor?'

'About 5 feet 7 inches, sir.'

'Byrappa, come here,' Gowda said, making way for the constable. He looked at Gowda curiously as Gowda asked him to crouch on the step.

Gowda turned to Aqthar and Santosh. 'I want you to go to the cottage and look from there. Tell me what you see.'

They did as asked, jogging down the steps and heading towards the cottage. From where Gowda stood, he saw the trees swallow them up.

'What do I do, sir?' Ratna asked.

'Take your shoes off and stand in your socked feet where Gajendra is,' Gowda said.

'Call the boys and ask them to find a place from where they can spot Byrappa,' Gowda told Gajendra.

Gajendra called on Santosh's phone. 'I am holding on,' he spoke into the phone and then looked at Gowda. 'They are looking for a point from where they can see the house. Do you realize, sir, that it's like we are on top of a small hill and the cottage is in a valley?'

Gowda nodded. 'Because the slope is to the rear side of the property, we don't realize it from the front of the property. It was when I checked the perimeter of the property that I realized how much the dip is.'

Gajendra's face lit up after Santosh came back on the line. 'Stay on the call,' he said and turned to Gowda. 'Sir, they have found a spot.'

'Byrappa,' Gowda said, turning to the constable. 'Position yourself on a step from where you can reach Ratna's foot. Draw a circle there. But she mustn't be able to see you.'

Byrappa moved down one step. 'Do you see him, Ratna?' Gowda asked.

'No, sir, not in the darkness.'

Gowda stood contemplating the two of them. Then he turned to Gajendra. 'Ask the boys if they can see Ratna.'

Gajendra held a thumbs-up sign to Gowda after a few moments.

'Now, Byrappa, do you have a ballpoint pen with you? If you were to reach out with it and touch ASI Ratna's feet, see where it lands and draw a circle there. Do it with some force but not too hard.'

Ratna gave Gowda a grateful smile. By now all of them had realized what Gowda was intending to prove. Gowda took his phone and started taking a video. On the screen he saw Byrappa, almost crouched on the steps, reach out and position the tip of the pen above Ratna's foot. He pressed it down a bit. Ratna jumped in the air even though she knew it was Byrappa and no one else. It was creepy as well as frightening. She tried to compose herself.

Gowda turned off the video and said, 'Byrappa, now get up and climb the steps and walk alone around the house so you can access it from the front.'

Then he turned to Gajendra. 'Ask them to tell you what they see.'

Byrappa followed the instructions, adding his own contribution to it by pretending to be an eighty-two-year-old man with a stoop and shuffling gait.

In the distance, Aqthar and Santosh could see him at the parapet. He cast his gaze all around and then shuffled as quickly as he could along the house.

'I think Gowda Sir's sakkath sense just came into play,' Santosh said.

'What sense?' asked Aqthar.

'Sakkath sense.' Santosh grinned. 'You can see it in action soon enough. Let's mark this spot and join the others.'

Ratna thought it surreal that her entire team should be crouching to look at her foot. She stood with her foot up on a bench while all of them studied her ankle carefully. 'Give or take a few millimetres. That's all,' she said, stating what was on everyone's mind.

Gowda nodded. 'Take a look at this as well.' He played the video he had shot so everyone could see it. 'I suppose it's clear who bit Mary Susheela.' He tried to hide his grin. It was funny in a grim sort of way.

'Why did he do that?' Santosh asked.

'Where's the diary I gave you, Gajendra?' Gowda asked.

Gajendra pulled it out of his shirt front. Gowda held it up and said, 'The last note in it is his thoughts on how hearsay goes on to become accepted truth. Maybe this was an experiment of sorts, as Aqthar said. But more significantly, I think someone from the cottage saw the Professor and thought they were being spied on,' Gowda said.

Santosh gave a high-five to Aqthar and Byrappa and was heading to give one to Ratna, who was tying her shoelaces when Gowda snapped, 'Cut the drama. This isn't some bloody film!'

'Sir, it is a moment to celebrate. We have the motive,' Gajendra said.

'Indeed,' Gowda said, rifling through the diary again. 'We have the motive but we don't know what spooked the perpetrator or who he...' taking a long look at Ratna he rephrased his words, 'or who she is. Or what it is they were afraid would be discovered.'

The celebratory triumph deflated.

'No need to look so dejected,' Gowda said, wondering why he felt like the coach of a volatile basketball team. 'That's what we need to find out. Get a good night's sleep. We start at daybreak tomorrow. Meanwhile, find out from Paul Selvam who John Yaangba is and what is their connection.'

# 5

The good night's sleep he had advocated was easier said than done, Gowda thought as he tossed and turned in bed. It was a quarter to eleven. In the normal course of his sleep cycle, he would have been in the REM stage where dreams occurred of him punching DCP Vidyaprasad and sending various escaped criminals to jail. But tonight, all he felt was a growing restlessness.

Gowda got up and washed his face. He slathered on some cologne and wore a pair of jeans and a thick T-shirt. He took his bike keys—which he now kept in his room since Roshan was at home—and slipped on his heavy-duty biking jacket. Even within the house it felt chilly, and he didn't dare think of what a bike ride would be like without a jacket.

Gowda crept out of his room as quietly as he could. There was a light on in Roshan's room and he could hear muffled conversation in an American accent, interspersed by firing sounds. The boy was obviously lost in a show or a game.

He let himself out of the house and rolled the bike out of the gate, latching it quietly. Even at that hour, he saw the curtain upstairs part. He realized Mrs Tenant was watching him again. He frowned as hard as he could and stared back at the parting in the curtain. He stood his ground, continuing to stare so she could clearly see she had been caught out. Crazy woman, he mumbled under his breath as he started his bike.

The night air was colder than he had thought it would be, almost knife-like. Gowda was glad he had his jacket and riding gloves. At twenty past eleven he rang Urmila's doorbell. She opened the door almost immediately. 'Is this your version of a booty call?'

Gowda blinked. 'What? What booty?'

Mr Right jumped at his knee and leapt into his arms, covering his face with long, purple-tongued licks.

'Looking for a fuck?' she said through clenched teeth.

Gowda put Mr Right down and went to Urmila. 'Is that what you think of me?'

'You ignore me for days and land up at my door without even checking if I'm home. It's wrong on so many counts,' Urmila snapped. 'It's disrespectful, ACP Gowda.'

Gowda sighed. 'Guilty as charged.'

He slumped into a sofa. 'I haven't slept for two nights, U. And I cannot think straight. I need to rest and I know I can only if I'm with you. Will you let me sleep here tonight?'

Urmila didn't say anything for a long moment. Then she took his hand and led him into the bedroom. 'Get in,' she said. He took his shoes and clothes off and crawled in between the covers. She slid out of her robe and got in too, wrapping her arms around him.

Gowda closed his eyes. Then he opened them briefly to ask, 'How does one go about making a booty call?'

'Shut up and go to sleep.'

In a few minutes he had slipped into a deep sleep where he and DCP Vidyaprasad were in a bar and he had just splashed a drink with ice, lemon and a slit green chilli on the baboon's face.

# 7 DECEMBER 2012, FRIDAY

## 1

Gowda woke up to someone licking his face. 'U,' he mumbled, still half asleep, reaching for her.

'I wouldn't lick you awake. Seriously, Borei?' Urmila giggled.

Gowda opened his eyes to see the Maltese terrier looming over him. Urmila hoisted herself on her elbow and said, 'Mr Right is obsessed with you.'

'I wish it was his mistress who was obsessed with me.' Gowda offered his most cheesy grin. He was rewarded with a poke in the ribs.

It was almost 5 a.m. 'I should be going, U,' he said. 'But there's something I wanted to speak to you about.' He kept his eyes averted.

'What about?' She sat up.

'Your security men... they see me come and go... won't they wonder?' Gowda's voice was hesitant.

'They probably do but they know better than to ask questions or gossip.' Urmila's reply was dismissive of any consequences such speculation could cause.

When she saw he wasn't convinced, she laughed. 'I can always claim you are my cousin.'

'Cousin?'

'Why not?' Urmila said, turning to look at him. 'Remember how I would pass you off as my cousin in college?'

When Urmila came back from the bathroom, Gowda got up. He ran a hand through his hair as he looked at himself in the mirror.

'What did Janaki want to talk to you about? She was so agitated when she called me. I was surprised that she wanted to meet you with such haste. Especially as the funeral had taken place just a few days ago?' Urmila asked as she poured them both two cups of tea. Gowda sipped the fragrant first flush Darjeeling brew and wanted to spit it out. But he swallowed it and willed himself to not gag.

'Didn't she say anything to you?' Gowda asked, holding up the cup without taking another sip.

'No, she wouldn't tell me... Is it Iqbal? I can't stop thinking about how uncomfortable she is when he's around,' Urmila said, pouring herself some more tea.

When Gowda didn't respond, Urmila persisted. 'Something to do with the case?'

'Something like that,' Gowda said, staring into the teacup and wondering how this tepid coloured water did anything for anyone.

'You haven't taken more than a sip from your tea. I suppose you don't like it.'

'I should get going, U. Thank you for sleeping with me,' Gowda said with a wicked smile. 'And the morning licks.'

Gowda was still grinning when he stopped at a tea vendor's cart. He had had to go towards Cantonment Station, where a tea-seller could be found even at the crack of dawn. He had a sip and was relieved that it was strong, as he liked it. He lit a cigarette and smoked it as he drank his tea. When Gowda started his bike again, he felt ready to take on the world with all its troubles, chief among them being DCP Vidyaprasad, who was going to burst an artery when he discovered the Professor Mudgood case was still open and alive.

The thump of the four-stroke engine echoed through the city roads and filled him with a growing certainty that the facts of the case were finally emerging from the haziness that it had been shrouded in. His grip on the handle tightened and Gowda accelerated a fraction just to feel the power course through the body of his bike and into him. It felt good. It felt right.

It was half past six when he rode into the lane leading to Professor Mudgood's residence. The police vehicle was parked there and within it sat David. The others emerged from around the vehicle as his bike headlight blazed at the gate.

From the vehicle, Gajendra drew out a flask. 'Some coffee, sir?'

Gowda nodded. Between Gajendra and Shanthi, he didn't know who was attuned to his needs better. Gowda gulped down the hot coffee and felt the heat trickle down into his bones. The others watched as he took his gloves off and rubbed his palms briskly. He lit a cigarette, took a deep draw and said, 'Let's go.'

Byrappa was asked to stand at the top of the stairs like Ratna had the previous night while Aqthar and Santosh led the way, followed by Gowda and Gajendra.

'Where's Ratna?' Gowda asked. He had been surprised not to see her there.

'She is at the station, sir,' Gajendra said.

Gowda raised his eyebrows.

'Control room reported a 100 call. Domestic abuse. She's gone with the SI. She was quite annoyed, sir, that she couldn't be here,' Gajendra said. 'But she didn't want to wait for the lady constables to get to the station. She said this was a repeat incident and the man was a violent sort.'

'Hmm,' Gowda grunted. The day was breaking and bird sounds filled the air. A crow pheasant's low, thrumming note echoed through the air. Babblers whickered and a gang of rowdy parakeets screeched from a tall mango tree. In the distance they could hear the crackling pistons of a new tractor.

Aqthar and Santosh led them to the side of the cottage that overlooked the main house. They found the twig they had staked into the ground as a marker. Gowda stood there and stared at Byrappa, who was at least 500 metres away. He looked at Gajendra. 'Can you see Byrappa from here?'

Gajendra peered but the trees and shrubs blocked his view. 'No, sir,' he said. 'I can't.'

'How tall are you?' Gowda asked.

'5 feet 7, sir,' Gajendra said. 'Well, 5 feet and 6.89 inches to be precise.'

'And the two of you?' Gowda asked, turning to Aqthar and Santosh.

'I am 5 feet 10 inches, sir,' Aqthar said.

'And I am 5 feet 10.5 inches,' Santosh said, secretly delighted at being half an inch taller than his friend who seemed to be the flavour of the week.

'We know that the person who stood here must have been at least 5 feet 10. Anyone shorter wouldn't have been able to see the Professor from here.'

'And someone with good eyesight. It was late,' Santosh added.

Gowda said, 'It was a full-moon night.'

'How do you know that, sir?' Santosh asked.

Because Urmila and I were drifting in a boat under the moon-lit sky and drinking and not saying much. We were holding hands and gazing at the moon.'

'It was the micro moon, sir,' Aqthar said, looking up from his phone. 'The smallest full moon of this year.'

'So we have a man with good eyesight who is about 5 feet 10 inches tall. What else?' Gajendra asked.

'He is someone who recognized the Professor from this distance. Hence someone familiar,' Gowda said. And then he added, 'There isn't a window here or on this side of the house. Just ventilators. It wasn't a chance spotting. Someone was checking out the perimeter of the cottage. That brings me back to my original query: what on earth was going on at the cottage that shouldn't be seen?'

'It could be anything, sir,' Gajendra said, chewing on his lip thoughtfully.

'Money laundering, murder, rape, cockfight, drug deal, gambling, prostitution, terrorist activity, meth lab...' Santosh said.

Gowda looked past the trunk of a tree. 'Let's look around the place. I don't think we'll find much but we can't rule out any possibility.'

Gajendra called Byrappa to join them. 'He's got the best pair of eyes I know. He'll find what we could miss.'

# 2

There was something of a sniffer-dog alertness to Byrappa's countenance, Gowda thought as he watched him scour the land around the cottage. The others did as well but Byrappa seemed to have a grim determination about him. He found the butt of a mosquito coil a little away from the vantage spot.

Santosh laughed out loud. 'So we know that our man doesn't like mosquitoes.'

Gowda glared at him. 'No need to be snarky. What we know is he is probably a smoker. Do you see matchsticks? If he used a lighter, he isn't going to carry one just for the joy of it. So he's a smoker for sure.'

Santosh flushed and Aqthar made a mental note to park all his snarky comments while in Gowda's presence.

Byrappa continued examining the ground. 'There is nothing at all here. Like someone took care to ensure that he left nothing behind,' Byrappa said. 'The mosquito coil was an oversight. The person must have thought it'll burn to nothing. And maybe the heavy dew that night doused it.'

Gowda nodded.

Gajendra spoke up. 'Sir, do you think the murderer had already plotted the homicide? If so, maybe there wasn't anything actually happening at the cottage. And he was merely biding his time.'

All of them looked at Gajendra. He did have a point, Aqthar thought. Santosh shook his head. 'No, no... something was definitely going on at the cottage. First they ensure we find blood, then we find the blood cleaned up and then we discover it is animal blood. It is all very strange,' Santosh said. 'And remember the debris we found in a pit in the ground... the blood on the cotton wool. Mr Simon said it matched the smear on the steel almirah.'

Gowda nodded. 'Exactly what I was thinking.'

'So, what do we do now, sir?' Byrappa asked. 'I mean where do we start?'

Gowda began walking to the front of the cottage. Gajendra followed, twirling a key on a ring.

Aqthar watched them go with a curious expression. 'How long have they worked together, Santosh?'

'Seven years now. And I have been with them for four,' Byrappa answered.

Gowda was looking at the cottage. What had he missed? He was certain there was something that would start them off on this new line of investigation.

He opened the liquor cabinet and looked at each bottle carefully. 'There is a new bottle here,' Gowda said suddenly. He pulled out his phone and looked at the photos he had shot four days ago. 'Who has had access to the cottage?'

Gajendra shrugged. 'Apart from us, only the family.'

'We need to check with the constables who were on duty,' Gowda said. 'The new bottle is rum. Iqbal doesn't drink rum. He told me that himself.' Gowda opened the rolltop desk. He checked the photos again. Everything was intact.

The rest of the ground floor seemed untouched too. He walked into the storeroom. He folded his hands across his chest and stared at the mop and bucket stored in the corner.

'Sir,' Aqthar said. 'The mop and bucket look new.'

Gowda nodded. 'They do. They weren't here when we found the bloodstains in the basement bathroom.'

'Whoever cleaned up the blood must have replaced them with new ones. Should we fingerprint them, sir?' Gajendra asked.

'They will be wiped clean.' Santosh sounded tired. This case was beginning to feel like being trapped in a labyrinth.

'And that makes it suspicious,' Gowda spoke softly. 'Who wipes a mop handle clean unless they don't want to be identified. Let's check the basement.' Gowda began moving the wooden panels at the end of the passage. It had been boarded up again.

Gajendra and Byrappa joined in. Gajendra stopped abruptly and said, 'Sir, we didn't put the panels back. So who did it?'

Gowda went down the steps without responding. The others followed, their footsteps clattering down the wooden steps with a resounding thump.

Gowda paused in the middle of the basement, which felt enormous. Something about the architecture, he thought. 'What do we know about Deva?' He turned to Gajendra.

'We did a routine check on him, sir,' Santosh said. 'He's been with Iqbal Buqhari for about four years now.'

'What does he actually do?' Gajendra asked. 'Apart from being Iqbal's sidekick.' Gajendra didn't know why but something about the man got his back up.

Santosh shrugged. 'He has a criminal record. But nothing that requires us to probe deeper. He is from Bombay. Moved to Bangalore in 2004. Has been with Iqbal since 2008. Driver, bodyguard, muscle man, etc. The CCB team said that Iqbal had vouched for him.'

Gowda narrowed his eyes. 'Deva's details need to be probed further and verified. Iqbal vouching for him means nothing. And though he was supposed to be out of town on 28 November, check that security gate footage again. And find out where he was supposed to be and if there is any evidence to corroborate it. Tickets, bills, CCTV footage, photos, anything at all. This was a huge bloody oversight.'

Byrappa, who had been examining the basement inch by inch, came towards them with a grin that said: look what I found.

'You found the bottle, sir, I found the side dish.' Byrappa was holding up two halves of an orange with the rinds turned inside out. 'This was in the waste bin in the bathroom.'

Santosh frowned. 'That's a side dish?'

Byrappa nodded vigorously. 'You take the half, push the skin inwards a bit and pop the orange segments into your mouth whole. And you swallow them. It chases the fiery alcohol with a nice touch of sourness. And it's free.'

'You sound like a regular,' Santosh remarked, trying to wrap his head around how to suck the flesh off an orange skin in one slurp and gulp.

Byrappa shrugged, as if to say what he didn't know wouldn't hurt him.

Aqthar stared at the orange peel. 'Do they serve this at every bar?'

Byrappa held up a couple of empty plastic packets, each small enough to hold no more than 10 grams. 'See this...' He offered one to Aqthar. 'Sniff it.'

The packet smelt faintly of boiled peanuts. The other one had the pronounced smell of deep-fried dried prawns.

'So each bar has its own set of sides...' Byrappa began, wondering if it was time to shut up. Gowda was looking at him with a quizzical expression. He didn't think that Gowda was a temperance advocate, but perhaps he didn't approve of policemen haunting dodgy bars. 'Very few offer all three as snacks.'

Gowda came back to life and asked, 'What time do these bars open?'

Byrappa stretched his mouth into a sheepish grin. 'Legal or illegal time, sir?'

Gowda's eyebrows rose a fraction. Santosh's eyes were little saucers when he asked, 'Byrappa, what are you saying?'

Gajendra exchanged a glance with Gowda. How could any man, especially a policeman, be so untouched by life?

Byrappa was relishing being the resident expert on chappar bars. 'If you crave a drink at 4 a.m. and you are a regular, there is a back entrance of the bar you knock at. You'll get your quarter even though you'll have to pay a little more. But if you go at ten in the morning, the bar door will be open. The owner or the senior man there will have broken a coconut, adorned the photos of gods and goddesses with flowers, lit a lamp and an incense stick. He will look at your face and clothes and if he likes what he sees he'll welcome you with open arms. A man with money to spend is who the bar wants as its opening customer. No business wants to start the day by offering credit.'

Gowda gave Byrappa a piercing look. 'That was a very long answer for a very short question.'

Byrappa, undeterred, continued, 'Sir, if we don't know the system, we'll give ourselves away as policemen. And there won't be a punter or a regular 50 feet near you.'

'Agreed,' Gowda said. 'Lead the way, Mr Expert.'

'Too early, sir,' Byrappa said. 'It would be best if we go around 2 or 3 p.m. The casual customers would have come and gone and the regulars will start trickling in by then.'

Gajendra cleared his throat. 'Sir, I understand the need to go to the bars but what are we looking for there?'

Gowda frowned. 'Think of it as a field trip,' he said. He jabbed at the punching bag and hit it hard. It swung back and forth.

# 3

'There is something very unfair about this,' Ratna said, not bothering to hide her annoyance and fury.

'It is unfair,' Gowda agreed. 'But what do we do, ASI Ratna?' he added, stressing her designation so she would remember where she was and with whom. 'This is an undercover operation and taking you along would bring unnecessary attention and possibly put us in danger,' Gowda said.

'Besides, it isn't safe,' Santosh added, shuddering at the thought of Ratna walking into a chappar bar.

Ratna hissed and drew herself up to her full height of 5 feet 7. 'Not safe... let any of those loafers try anything...'

'Well, that's exactly what we are afraid of,' Gowda murmured.

'ASI Ratna, if it's any consolation, I won't be going,' Aqthar said.

'You are most certainly going. I am not asking you to drink but we need you to be there as well.' Gowda frowned. 'We form three teams.' He detailed the plan. 'Gajendra and Byrappa. You and Santosh. And I will scout on my own. How many bars did you say there were, Byrappa?'

Byrappa listed them in his head, counting on his fingers. 'Give or take about seven bars. All of them serve these three sides.'

Ratna turned to Byrappa. 'How do you know it isn't a bar anywhere else in the ten-kilometre radius, and why Oil Mill Road?'

'I know,' Byrappa said. 'In the month of December, when those small Nagpur oranges are heaped by the roadside, the Oil Mill Road bars serve them. Not many others do. Not around here, for instance, or on Ashoka Road or even in Lingarajapuram. It's like a speciality of that road and area.'

Ratna gazed at Byrappa, more than a little surprised. She had never smelt a whiff of alcohol on his breath or ever seen him look anything but fresh and perky. And yet he seemed to know all about the bars down to their sides.

It was a quarter past eleven. Gowda turned to Ratna and said, 'DCP Vidyaprasad is sending a bunch of school kids from one of the international schools to see what an Indian police station looks like. They will be here by noon.'

Gowda saw the protest form in her eyes. He added, 'Santosh and Aqthar will join you to talk to the children. It is part of the DCP's new PR programme.'

Not one of the three responded as they walked away.

Gajendra and Byrappa sat across from Gowda and wondered what was going on in his mind.

'Santosh and Aqthar are excellent police officers,' Gowda began. 'They haven't been in the field enough so I am not entirely sure what they will be able to find. But to tell them that will demotivate them so you have to be twice as sharp to catch whatever they miss out on.'

Byrappa looked like he was about to speak but decided against it. 'What is it, Byrappa?' Gowda asked. His regard for the constable had grown twofold.

'Sir, it would be best to send them to a slightly better class of bar on that road. They will give themselves away otherwise. Gajendra and I will go to the chappar ones.'

Gowda nodded. 'That's a sound idea.'

He stood up and collected his phone and keys. Gajendra and Byrappa jumped to their feet as well. 'I don't need to tell you this but perhaps you could tell the two young officers that at the bar they are not policemen but men looking for a quiet drink. Play the part.'

Gajendra and Byrappa nodded. Just as policemen could sniff out an ex-convict or a rowdy-sheeter in a crowded room, regular drunks could spot an out-of-place policeman in a bar with just a glance.

Gowda was on his way home when the call came. He had set a special ringtone for his father and so he stopped the bike. 'Appa?' Gowda asked. 'Is everything all right?'

'Borei.' His father's voice was shaking. 'It's Roshan. He had a fall. We are at the hospital. Providence Hospital.'

'I am on my way.'

# 4

Roshan was seated on a bed in the outpatient department. A bandage covered most of his forehead. A nurse was daubing antiseptic-soaked cotton on the bruises on his arm and knee. He greeted Gowda with a weak smile. Chidananda was seated on a chair nearby.

'What happened?' Gowda asked, relieved to see that Roshan was conscious.

'He slipped and fell down the staircase,' a woman's voice said from behind him. Gowda turned abruptly and saw Mrs Tenant. He preferred to think of her as that rather than Bhuvana.

'If it wasn't for Bhuvana, he would have bled to death,' Chidananda said and buried his head in his arms.

'Uncle, please... Roshan is fine,' Mrs Tenant said, rushing to take the old man's hands in hers. She rubbed them briskly.

'Ajja, I am all right,' Roshan said to his grandfather, who seemed more traumatized than him, Gowda thought.

'Appa, Roshan is fine. Can't you see that?' Gowda tried to comfort his father.

'Ajja, look at me,' Roshan added. 'I am fine.'

Gowda looked away and found himself studying Mrs Tenant. She wasn't a beauty but her even features and trim, petite frame gave her a charm which was enhanced by the clothes she wore—a pretty cotton top and blue jeans—and loads of silver jewellery. She looked like the trendy young women he would see at malls and restaurants. But that wasn't all. He was certain he had seen her somewhere before.

Roshan, Gowda was told, had gone upstairs to give Mrs Tenant an anatomy textbook. Roshan must have caught his father's astounded look for he hastened to elaborate, 'I had told her that understanding human anatomy would help her with sketching human figures. So when Bhuvana called me and asked me to drop it off before she went out, I ran up the stairs. I didn't even go inside, Appa. I handed over the book to her from the top of the staircase and when I turned, my foot slipped and I slammed my head on the step as I fell.'

'Bhuvana put a makeshift bandage on his head. Why do you choose to live in the middle of nowhere? Except for Bhuvana and her husband, is there another neighbour to call for help?' Chidananda growled. 'Or an autorickshaw stand nearby? Nothing. If this young woman hadn't run to the main road to flag down a vehicle, this child...' The old man shuddered again.

Gowda didn't speak for a moment. Then he said softly, 'Thank you, Bhuvana.'

'No, no, sir... I didn't do anything extraordinary for such praise. If my husband was home, he would have helped as well. That's what good neighbours are for.'

Gowda smiled at her gratefully.

Chidananda, feeling left out, said loudly, 'It helped that Roshan is a medical student, Borei. And then I told them he is your son and the doctors swung into action.'

Gowda ran his hand over his chin and turned to Mrs Tenant. 'Would you come to the lobby in about forty minutes? I'll go home and get the car to drop you back.'

'Oh, I am happy to be dropped off on your bike.' She shot him a look that Gowda couldn't fathom. Was the woman hitting on him?

Gowda shook his head. 'I don't have a spare helmet with me. And I can't let you ride pillion without one.'

'Yes, yes.' Bhuvana displayed her dimples. 'The police can't break rules.'

Gowda ignored that, his uneasiness with the woman rearing its head up again, and said, 'It would be best for my father to return home as well. I will wait here with Roshan once I drop you two back. Let me settle the bill, and I will be back soon. They will need a deposit for sure.'

\*

Gowda walked to the billing counter, which was alongside the main reception. The waiting area was bustling with people; about three attendants for every patient, Gowda thought, taking into account his own example. To many people a hospital visit appeared to be as much of an outing as going to a mall, perhaps. While the patient was poked and probed, the others would retreat to the canteen to stuff their faces with oily snacks and drink deeply of the coffee that always had a faint smell of antiseptic, and gossip about the patient and the people in adjacent beds.

Gowda was handing over his credit card to the billing clerk when from the corner of his eye he saw someone he recognized. The person was leaning on a stick, and his right arm was in a sling. Gowda turned to look at the man to confirm his identity.

It was Jagannath. Or Oil Mill Jaggi, as he was known. What the fuck was he doing here, so far away from his area? Or had he moved to this side of town?

'Sir, your pin,' the clerk said, turning the card machine towards him.

Gowda tapped in the pin as his mind raced. He grabbed the card and bill and went looking for Oil Mill Jaggi. But the man had disappeared into a room.

Gowda walked down the corridor and saw a horde of patients outside the door the rowdy-sheeter had emerged from. Gowda read the name plate. Dr Kedar Shetty, MBBS, MS, Orthopaedics.

Gowda went back to the lobby; he could wait no longer. He hummed under his breath as he rode his bike home. There were too many loose ends, all fraying from a single string. And that was the crux of the problem. Where did that string lead to?

Later, Gowda would tell himself that was why he didn't wonder about the faint whiff of engine oil that clung to the wall near the staircase. He had heard movement from above and wondered who was there. Bhuvana had said her husband was away. Must be the brother, he thought.

He had looked up at the staircase, thinking he ought to go and inform the brother that Bhuvana would be home soon. But the bloodstains on the staircase unnerved him. He felt the pulse at his temples throb. Gowda leaned against the banister, feeling almost legless at the thought that Roshan could have died or been disabled for life.

Gowda called up Gajendra on his way to Providence Hospital. 'You should go ahead as planned,' he said. 'I am not sure when I can get away. Roshan is being kept under observation, and I have to be with him until he is discharged.'

'What about your father, sir?'

'Bhuvana will take care of him,' Gowda said, honking at an enormous Jersey cow standing right in the middle of the road contemplating a banner of MLA Papanna.

'Bhuvana, sir?' Gajendra's voice was a strangled cry.

'I know. I had the same reaction when I heard the name. My tenant. Seems like a nice woman.'

Gowda parked the car and went into the hospital. A temporary driver he had called was waiting at the lobby. Gowda watched Chidananda leave with Mrs Tenant, who had a solicitous arm around him. When they reached home, he was sure Mrs Tenant would serve him lunch and tuck him into bed. Gowda didn't even have to ask. 'Don't worry, sir. I will take good care of Uncle. Right now we just need to ensure Roshan is fine.'

He knew he should be grateful. But the woman's niceness only raised his antennae.

# 5

Roshan's face was drawn even in sleep. The bandage around his forehead gave his face a waxen tinge. Gowda stroked his cheek with the tip of his forefinger. There was a huge lump in his throat. He cleared his throat, more to compose himself than anything, and went to meet the doctor who had examined Roshan. The young man gave Gowda a curious look. 'Aren't you ACP Gowda, sir?'

Gowda smiled self-consciously. 'I am,' he said, wondering how the man had recognized him.

'I am Arif Ali, sir. I have heard a great deal about you from my uncle Dr Khan, the police surgeon. I am hoping to specialize in forensics too, sir,' he added. 'How can I help you, sir?' He led Gowda to his tiny cubicle.

'My son Roshan was brought in with a head injury.'

Dr Arif Ali nodded. 'The medical student, yes... it could have been a nasty fall but he was fortunate or agile or both and he managed to break the fall to some extent. But we must keep him under observation, sir.'

'Of course,' Gowda said.

'Unless the patient is unconscious, the family tend to insist that they take the patient home.'

'DAMA.'

Dr Arif Ali's eyebrows rose at the abbreviation for Discharged Against Medical Advice. 'You know our jargon?'

'I have been married to a doctor for over two decades. And as an SI, the medico-legal doctors explained a few terms to me.' Gowda's eyes swept the surroundings to see if there was any sign of Oil Mill Jaggi.

'I don't think Roshan has any internal injury, sir. The X-rays are clear. Nevertheless, I would prefer to keep him under observation.'

'Doctor.' Gowda suddenly sounded businesslike. 'I just saw a man I recognize. He came with his leg in a cast and had a sling and several cuts and bruises. This is for a homicide investigation,' he added for effect.

Dr Arif Ali looked at him blankly for a moment.

'His name is Jagannath,' Gowda said. 'About thirty-five years old. Well-built. He should be about 5 feet 8 inches with hair streaked a dirty gold.'

Dr Arif Ali's fingers slid over the keyboard. 'I know it's against the rules to give out such information but...'

Gowda was left speculating.

'Ah, here it is. Jagannath. He came in with a broken femur and a hairline fracture of the elbow. And severe bruising. Reported as an accidental fall from a two-wheeler. Highly unlikely, though,' Dr Arif Ali said. 'The injuries are more suggestive of a brawl.' He gave Gowda a questioning look.

'Very possible. He is a well-known rowdy but not in this area so I'm curious as to why he is here,' Gowda said, moving to peer at the screen.

'Probably because the "accident" happened in the vicinity. See the time, sir.'

It was 2 a.m. Gowda felt his heart skip a beat. 'What day was this?'

'30 November, sir,' Dr Arif Ali said.

Gowda pulled at the bridge of his nose. 'I'll need a printout.'

Dr Arif Ali hesitated and said, 'I have to inform the hospital authorities, sir.'

'I need his case notes,' Gowda insisted. 'I could get a court order but that will take a while and the file might just disappear.'

Dr Arif Ali said, looking distinctly uncomfortable, 'Every mail, printout or download is registered in the system.'

Gowda raised an eyebrow. 'Is there a rule about taking photographs?'

The doctor stepped out of his cubicle, and Gowda used his phone to click pictures of the case notes. For good measure, he also took pictures of the cubicle with the computer screen displaying the case notes.

As Gowda stepped out, Dr Arif Ali told him, 'Sir, there was something that bothered me. When I was examining your son, there was an overheated engine-like smell on his ankle and arm, as if he had slid down a surface that had engine oil on it. That's rather odd, don't you think?'

Gowda stared at his phone blankly. Why had he been looking at it? The doctor's parting words had rattled him more than he cared to admit. For a moment, he thought about calling Urmila and asking her to go over. He would feel happier knowing that his father wasn't alone at home with just the tenants around. But something stopped him from doing so. His father would read meanings into it, and he didn't want to add further turbulence to the chaos raging in his head. Gowda called Shanthi on his way to Roshan's room. He felt more at ease once she said she would sit with his father until Gowda came home.

Roshan was awake and sitting up. 'How are you, Ro?' Gowda asked, using the nickname he had stopped using when Roshan became a teenager.

'My head hurts, and I think every bone in my body aches but otherwise I am fine, Appa.' Roshan tried to give him a big smile.

'What happened?' Gowda asked.

'I really don't know. I slipped.'

Gowda nodded. 'Try and sleep,' he said. 'We'll go home in the evening. You are fine, the doctor says. But it is best that you are here.'

'Yes, I know,' Roshan said, lying back on the pillow. Gowda covered him with a sheet.

He sat on a chair in the room and looked at Oil Mill Jaggi's case notes on his phone. After Roshan had fallen asleep, Gowda walked down the corridor to the nurses' station. 'I will be back soon,' he told a nurse. 'I am going to the canteen.'

The nurse nodded fervently. She knew the patient was the ACP's son.

Across the road from the hospital was a tea shop. Gowda walked there and got himself a tea and an egg puff. He ate the puff slowly as he drank his tea, flicking crumbs off his fingers. The tea stall man offered him a piece of newspaper to wipe his fingers with. Gowda asked for a pack of cigarettes and lit one. There wasn't anyone else at the stall. The owner asked Gowda, 'Sir, is it a family member at the hospital?'

Gowda nodded. He exhaled and said, 'My son.'

'Accident?'

'Well, it was a fall. They wanted to keep him under observation,' Gowda said. 'Are you open all day and night?'

The man nodded. 'Almost. From 6 a.m. to 11 p.m. If I could find someone reliable, I would keep it open twenty-four hours.'

Gowda looked at him and said, 'Let me ask around. Maybe there is someone looking for a job like this.'

'If you were to recommend someone then I will receive him as a long-lost brother.'

'So you know who I am?'

'I do,' the man said. 'I have seen you on your Bullet, Commissioner Sir.' Gowda was about to correct him when two African men stopped by. They bought a pack of cigarettes and asked for two cups of tea.

Gowda watched curiously as the man stirred drinking chocolate into a cup of milk and gave it to them.

'Didn't they ask for tea?' Gowda asked.

'They are Nigerian, sir. They call hot chocolate tea. Now if it's people from Senegal, they prefer mint tea. The students from Tanzania like masala tea. That way I know where in Africa they are from.'

'And you know this how?' Gowda asked, suitably impressed.

'By observation. I have a good memory.'

Gowda stubbed out his cigarette. 'In which case, keep an eye out for me. I can't do my job without the help of people like you. What's your name?'

'Charlie, sir,' the man said.

'I am ACP Gowda and not commissioner. I don't think I will ever be one,' Gowda said, with a movement of his lips meant to be a smile. He felt a small curl of satisfaction at having recruited yet another informer. 'This is my number.'

'What do I keep my eyes open for?'

'Anything unusual,' Gowda said. 'Anything that makes you think something isn't right.'

Charlie nodded.

'Is this your shop?' Gowda asked, seeing another bunch of students walking towards them. 'You seem to be doing well.'

'It is my shop and the business is decent but...'

'But what?'

Charlie's expression turned to annoyance. 'There is this fellow, Military. He helped me get the tea stall going.'

'Military, that's a strange name.' Gowda laughed aloud at how the man had said it: Mill Tree.

'That's what everyone calls him. I met him through a cousin.'

Gowda frowned. 'Does he take protection money?'

Charlie didn't answer but his silence was a tacit yes.

'What is his hold over this area?' Gowda persisted.

Charlie shrugged. 'The first time we met he was surrounded by a group of thugs. My cousin said that the men drove the garbage trucks MLA Papanna owns. But one look at them turned my blood into paper ganjee.'

Gowda let it rest for now. He didn't want to spook the man.

Charlie watched Gowda leave and decided to find out more about Military. Week after week, the man ate a portion of his earnings without moving a finger and it would be good to have him off his back. The tea shop was at a good vantage point and business had been good from day one. Military had come by the day after Charlie had signed the lease agreement and made known his expectations. As much as the weekly commission, it was his air of entitlement that made Charlie want to throw a few punches at him, and add a kick too.

# 6

The giant tree at the Kannur–Bagalur junction road had a couple of goats resting under it. Two autorickshaws were parked a little distance away. It was late afternoon and a chill had already set in. Aqthar was glad he had borrowed the faux leather jacket to wear over his T-shirt and jeans. He adjusted his aviators. They were uncomfortable, chafing his skin and pinching the bridge on his nose. He wished he could toss them into the nearest dustbin. Santosh frowned. 'I thought you hated sunglasses.'

Aqthar sighed. 'It goes with the leather jacket. But it's like having a clothespin fixed to the nose.'

Santosh grinned. 'Where did you get them from?'

'My uncle's driver. He told me to keep them.'

'Suits you,' Santosh said. 'How do I look? We need to blend in.' He bent down to retie his shoelaces.

Aqthar looked at Santosh. 'I was afraid you would end up wearing your uniform shoes,' he said, taking in the T-shirt, jeans and trainers Santosh wore. 'Tell me, why do you keep your hair so short?'

Santosh shrugged. 'A policeman has to look like a policeman.'

'You look like an NCC cadet,' Aqthar said. With a grin, he added, 'Don't you know that women like to muss up men's hair?'

Santosh flushed. He wondered if his attraction towards Ratna was so obvious.

'Our story is we drove down to Bangalore from Dharwad. You deal in timber. I am your friend. Don't forget to slip into our Dharwad lingo.'

Santosh nodded.

'And I have a friend joining us,' Aqthar added as an autorick-shaw stopped and a man got off the seat he had been sharing with the driver. He walked towards them, beaming.

Santosh frowned. 'Who is that? And why do we need him?'

'Neither you nor I drink. But we are going to pretend we do. And we need someone to keep drinking for us to stay in the bar for a while,' Aqthar said. 'And that by the way is the borewell operator. Raja Reddy. Get on the bike.' He started the Bullet.

'What about your man?' Santosh asked.

'He will as well,' Aqthar said, adjusting his helmet strap.

'You want us to ride triples? Are you out of your mind?' Santosh exploded. 'It's against the law. We are from the police...'

'Precisely why. Sometimes, Santosh, you are a ghughu...' Aqthar sighed. Santosh glared at him. Stupid owl was not how he saw himself.

'What about helmets?' Santosh mumbled as he climbed on.

'You might as well get hanged for a cow if you are going to be hanged for a sheep,' Aqthar said. 'Now make some space for Raja,' he said over his shoulder.

Santosh grimaced as Raja, who had tried to camouflage his sweat with a generous slathering of talcum, sandwiched him. On his way back, he would take an autorickshaw, Santosh decided.

The traffic on Oil Mill Road hummed with a steady drone. Aqthar pulled up outside a small eatery. Raja and Santosh hopped off the bike. A man standing by the eatery watched them.

Aqthar parked his bike along with a few others that stood on the road. He walked towards Santosh and Raja, slinging his helmet from his hand with a casual charm. Two girls walking along the road glanced at Aqthar, who seemed totally impervious to the looks that came his way. Their voices carried as they commented, 'Look at him! Isn't he cute?'

Aqthar frowned as he drew closer. 'Those girls! I wanted to turn around and ask them, "Don't you have a father and brothers at home?"'

Raja grinned at the absurdity of the situation. Santosh bit his lip, thinking it was bloody unfair that the man was so good-looking. On anyone else the combination of gold-rimmed sunglasses, fake leather jacket and sneakers would brand him as a street Romeo but Aqthar looked even more like a bloody movie star.

'This is my friend Santosh from Dharwad,' Aqthar told Raja.

'What's the occasion?' Raja asked. 'I was surprised when you called and said you wanted me to join the party.'

He looked up at the signboard: Kalyani Bar. Raja beamed. 'This is a top-class bar. I've never been here before. It will be expensive, Mams,' he said.

Aqthar tried to hide his smile at the 'Mams'. The suggestion of free alcohol had turned him into a beloved uncle, it seemed. He shrugged while Santosh wondered at the nature of bars Raja frequented if he thought this hole in the wall was top-class.

'Raja, it is his engagement next week.' Aqthar grinned as he pulled out a little plastic comb and gave his hair a quick flick. Santosh looked at his feet bashfully. Aqthar strode towards a doorway with a grimy curtain.

Santosh's eyes widened as the curtain that was heavy with grease and dirt opened to reveal a bar.

'Raja, I can't drink. I am on antibiotics. I thought Santosh shouldn't drink alone. I wanted you to join us because Santosh's to-be father-in-law rears fighter birds. Our Santosh knows nothing at all about them and he is afraid his father-in-law will think he is a clueless idiot. I've told him everything I know but he said he wanted to talk to someone who has actually attended cockfights so he can pretend to be knowledgeable. Bewarsi fellow that he is! And that's how I remembered you... Ashte!' Aqthar said as they walked towards a table. The bar wasn't exactly full but it wasn't empty either.

A group of what seemed like college students sat around a table. Their merriment and loud voices indicated a celebration of some sort.

'If your eyes widen any more, they'll pop out of your head.' Raja laughed at Santosh's expression as he took in the dingy bar.

'I've never seen anything like this,' Santosh said most truthfully.

'What are the bars like in Dharwad?' Raja asked, drumming his fingers on the table.

'I wouldn't know. I have never been,' Santosh said, more annoyed with himself than the rascal he was with. What kind of a policeman was he if he didn't know anything about the places criminals frequented?

'Are you serious?' Raja laughed aloud. 'Have you met your bride at least, darling?' he teased.

Santosh sighed. 'I have but I haven't got to spend any time with her. Not yet,' he said.

'Mams, your friend needs to be taught a few things,' Raja called out to Aqthar. 'Or he's going to be playing rummy with his bride on his wedding night.' Raja chortled.

'I will talk to him. I will,' Aqthar said, throwing a mischievous glance at Santosh. 'What about you, Raja? What shall I get you?'

'Old Tavern whisky,' Raja said, watching Aqthar go towards the bar counter. 'What line of business are you in?' he asked Santosh.

'Timber and real estate with Mams in Dharwad,' Santosh said.

When Aqthar came back holding a 60 ml for Raja, the man looked at the drink happily. 'Sit down, Mams. I'll be back in two minutes,' he said. 'Allow me to buy your friend his first drink.'

'Aqthar, what the hell, man!' Santosh exploded when Raja had stepped away from the table. 'I can't drink on duty!'

'Pretend to drink... you don't have to. Look like you are enjoying this,' Aqthar said sternly. Santosh twisted his mouth into a grimace.

Raja came back bearing a grin and a cutting of rum in a glass.

'I thought the boy must start with Hercules rum.' Raja placed the drink on the table and curled his biceps in the parody of a bodybuilder.

Aqthar clapped his hands. 'Super idea!'

Santosh glared at him but smiled at Raja. He raised his glass and clinked it against Raja's. 'Cheers,' he said, and took a long draw. 'I only said I haven't been to the bars. I didn't say I don't drink,' he said, taking in Aqthar's shocked expression.

Raja clapped him on his back. 'You are a sneaky one, aren't you? Pretending to be a schoolboy!'

'Raja Sir,' Santosh said, taking another sip and wiping his mouth. 'Tell me about cockfights. I have been invited to one in South Kanara during Sankranthi... My father-in-law's uncle is setting it up.' He beamed, enjoying the ease with which the lies flowed. He couldn't resist sneaking a glance at Aqthar, whose jaw would touch the table if it dropped any further. 'Mams, got you, didn't I?' he muttered.

'The thing is, all of you treat me like I am the village idiot who can't tell a string from a snake and I am sick and tired of it.' Santosh took another deep swig of his drink. Aqthar shook his head, telling himself he would never again be deceived by men appearing to be wet behind the ears. Was there such a creature as a truly naive man? He didn't think so. Not after this.

Raja looked at Aqthar as if to say that Santosh was a belligerent drunk, then touched Santosh's elbow. 'Santhu, do you know how to pick a bird to bet on? The bird that comes to the ring will be a handsome fellow like Mams here but what you have to do is find out what it has been reared on,' Raja started. 'Or it will be out of the fight in the first two minutes.'

'Like what?' Santosh asked.

'Like lizard meat, or cashews. It's serious business. So it needs to be taken seriously,' Raja said in his firmest voice, much to Santosh's amusement. 'Ask Mams here if you don't believe me.'

Aqthar was content not being part of the conversation. Ultimately, all zealots sounded the same. Whether the subject was religion or a cockfight, the zealot always thought he knew best, no matter how warped his view was.

'There are other things I have picked up over the years. Look for a powerful chest.' Raja drew an arc from his chest, shaping a curve with his palms. 'Shiny feathers and bright eyes. Like you, Santhu,' Raja guffawed. 'My drink is over. I want a cutting Darling and some side dishes too. Order it all, will you? And I will tell you more.'

Santosh threw him a baleful glare and went to bring a fresh round of drinks. To his surprise, he saw that the cashier sat within the cage, as did the booze. Aqthar went to the counter as well. 'Go easy, Santosh,' he said discreetly.

Santosh ignored him and asked the man in the cage, 'No oranges today? I was told it's a big delicacy at this bar.' The bartender ignored him and turned to another customer. Santosh muttered under his breath at the rudeness of the Bangalore lot and then acknowledged Aqthar's presence by pointing to the nylon string dangling from the ceiling. 'What's that for?'

Aqthar shrugged. 'How would I know?'

Another customer, a tall man with a pronounced forehead, said, 'It's to slice hard-boiled eggs.'

'Get a couple for your new best friend, Santhu,' Aqthar said, gesturing to a waiter.

'Do you think they ever replace it? It's probably home to a million bacteria,' Santosh mumbled.

A man standing behind him growled, 'I have been watching you since you lot landed here. Who the fuck are you to come to Kalyani and find fault with her?'

'Who the fuck is Kalyani?' Santosh growled back, his shoulders squared, his jaw clenched.

'The name of the bar,' Aqthar muttered helpfully. Santosh raised his palm to his forehead and flung it towards the man to suggest he should go get a life.

'Who the fuck are you?' the man glowered.

'Thikka muchkond hogo le,' Santosh snarled and walked away. The man stared at Santosh's retreating back, unable to believe that a total stranger, a loafer fellow, had come to his bar and told him to shut his ass up.

He plonked his glass on the counter and rushed to headbutt Santosh from the back. Aqthar stepped in and with his outstretched hand shoved him aside. The man went flying, landing in a heap on the floor.

The others lunged towards Aqthar, who dodged their flailing hands while throwing punches. Santosh joined in, suddenly sober from the adrenalin pumping in his veins. Aqthar didn't seem to need his help but Santosh wasn't going to stand there watching his friend fight a battle he had probably instigated in the first place. A nasty jab sent one man reeling and a knee in another's abdomen had him falling on his back.

One of the men flashed a knife at them. He thrust it towards Aqthar with a menacing growl. Aqthar reached forward, as if to take the man's hand in his. All it took was one swift move, the right palm tapping the radial pulse while the left palm slapped the phalanges. The knife went flying back towards the man and landed with a metallic clatter on the floor. The bar went silent. Aqthar stood his ground with clenched fists and a boxer's stance. Santosh stood at his side with a bottle in his raised hand. Where had the bottle come from? He didn't have much recollection of what he had done. But he seemed to have hurt a few of the men. When Aqthar dropped his hands to his side, Santosh bent his knee to lower himself and put the bottle on its side. It went rolling across the floor. The sound of glass against the cement floor filled the quiet. The fight was over.

'I am here to celebrate with my friends. Leave us alone or I will wipe the floor with each one of you,' Aqthar said and walked to the table where Raja stood in stunned silence. 'Your cooling glass is broken.' Raja pointed to the aviators that had fallen on the ground during the scuffle. Aqthar shrugged.

'Where did you learn to fight like that?' Santosh asked Aqthar. His bravado had flattened into docility. This was a side of Aqthar he hadn't seen before.

'At the gym. On the streets. Life is a great teacher,' Aqthar said. 'And you were not bad either,' he added.

Santosh swallowed hard. He didn't know what had come over him. He shuddered. He had been in a bar brawl like a luchha bugger.

Raja grinned. He clapped Santosh on his back. 'I knew it, Santhu, even when I saw you first, that you are a fighter! Street-fighter. Dirty fighter. I wish I had videoed the fight. And Mams,' he began, turning to Aqthar.

Aqthar interrupted him, 'Calm down, Raja... I forgot your side dish. Let me get it.' He walked back to the counter.

Santosh took a sip of his rum. This must be what horse blood tastes like, he decided. 'Do you have videos of the cockfights?' he asked Raja.

Raja unlocked his phone and held it out, 'Look, Santhu.'

Santosh wanted to kick him hard for calling him everything but his actual name. But he said nothing. 'Let me see.' He returned the phone after a bit. 'Boss, this is too good to watch in a hurry. Will you send it to me?'

'What's your number?' Raja asked.

Santosh gave him his alternate number. His notifications went a little crazy for the next few minutes. He decided it was time to leave. They were supposed to go to two other places but Santosh decided there was no further need to do so. Aqthar might need some convincing but he knew he could handle that. No matter what was claimed, the cockfights had happened, and he was quite certain they had taken place at the cottage. As Gowda said, some-one—probably one of the organizers—had thought the Professor had seen the gathering of people. The threat of him blowing the whistle on them had led them to silence him for good. That was all there was to the Professor Mudgood homicide. And he was beginning to think that maybe it would be him who took this case across the finish line.

Aqthar came to the table holding two glasses. 'Santosh, we need to leave,' he said and then turned towards the other man. 'Raja, the bill is settled and you'll find your way home, right.' He thrust a five-hundred-rupee note into his hand.

Raja nodded as he took the money. But he couldn't stop thinking about that strange expression on Mams's face.

# 7

It was a little past six and the day had turned into night. The streetlights had come on and the chill in the air made Gajendra pull the hoodie over his head.

'Where did you get this?' Byrappa asked about the neon-coloured sweatshirt Gajendra seemed to have disappeared into.

Gajendra offered him a sheepish smile. 'My daughter's.' His jacket was a dead giveaway for 'here comes the policeman, loud and strong'. So he had decided to borrow hers.

Byrappa frowned. 'Why does she need a fluorescent jacket?'

'I made her buy it. She goes jogging, college athletics team. I said she should wear something fluorescent. I don't want her getting run over.'

Byrappa laughed aloud. 'Hopefully you won't glow in the bar.'

'I'll take it off once we get there.' Gajendra bristled. 'Shall we go?' He walked towards an autorickshaw.

Neither of them spoke much as the auto leapt and dived through the potholes on Hennur Road. 'I hope this road will be repaired before the day I die,' Gajendra said as he felt the top of his head bang against the roof of the autorickshaw.

'I doubt it.' Byrappa sighed. 'If you want to know the nature of life, all you need to do is travel on this road. Ditches and pot-holes, roadworks and traffic jams, and in between a silken stretch.'

'Save your poetry for the bar,' Gajendra said.

'I don't think the auto fellow knew we were policeman,' Byrappa said after he had paid for the ride. 'He glared at me when I asked for the change.'

He suddenly struck a pose. 'How do you like my costume?'

Gajendra looked at Byrappa. He was a sight to behold in a multicoloured shirt that seemed to be mostly layers and pockets, all defined in white cloth. With it he wore tight jeans and white patent leather shoes. 'Where did you find the shirt and shoes?'

Byrappa shrugged. 'Didn't I tell you that my brother is now acting in TV serials. Prathish, that's his new name, used to play bit roles in the movies. He is always the roadside Romeo, the man in the crowd, the wedding guest or the dead man's son. He has a whole box of clothes. That way he gets more roles than the other extras.'

'Does he have a policeman's costume?' Gajendra asked.

Byrappa grinned. 'Of course. This one is the rich-village-boy-comes-to-the-city look.'

Gajendra was about to respond but Byrappa was already walking towards Pose Bar.

'What a strange name!' Gajendra said, looking at the signboard.

'It was Rose. ROSE bar, if you get the drift... but I think R's tail fell off and it's been Pose Bar for some time now,' Byrappa said. 'Let's go in. We need to go to three other places as well.'

# 8

Gowda kept stealing looks at Roshan. The headlights of oncoming vehicles threw streaks of light on his face. The boy still looked shaken.

'Are you all right, Roshan?' Gowda asked.

Roshan stared at the road. 'I could have broken my neck, Appa,' he said after a moment. 'I don't know how I slipped.'

'It's those Crocs you wear. They have no grip,' Gowda said, trying to comfort Roshan. He remembered his mother rushing to pick Roshan up when he kept falling down as a toddler. She consoled the bawling child by giving the ground a hard slap. 'How dare you make my Roshan fall?' And Roshan's cries would transform into enormous chortles of glee. But he wasn't a two-year-old anymore. He couldn't be easily distracted.

'The Crocs are fine, Appa. I'm not wearing them for the first time. I just don't get it.'

Gowda reached sideways and squeezed Roshan's shoulder. 'Put it out of your mind. Accidents happen. You are fine now. That's what is important.'

They drove in through the open gate to a house ablaze with lights. The gate lights, the garden light, the porch lights and light streaming from the open windows.

'What the hell?' Gowda muttered under his breath.

'I think Amma has turned up,' Roshan said, with an excited bark of laughter. 'She does this at home too. Lights up the place like it's the Mysore Palace at Dussehra time.'

'What?'

The main door opened as the car stopped. Mamtha stood framed in the doorway, the light behind her. She hurried to the passenger side. 'Roshan baby, are you all right?'

Gowda shut the car door gently. 'Hello, Mamtha,' he said.

'Why didn't you call me?' She sounded upset. 'Your father did.'

Roshan seemed to slump in his mother's arms. She held him tight and took his arm to help him up the two steps to the verandah.

Gowda watched, astounded, as Roshan hobbled. The boy had been perfectly fine when he walked from the hospital to the car. Drama queen. Gowda took a deep breath and followed mother and son in.

Chidananda was examining Roshan's eyes. 'You are fine,' he said, clasping the boy in a hug.

Gowda sat in a chair and watched his wife and his father fuss over Roshan.

'When did you get here, Mamtha?' he asked, wondering when his father had called her.

'Bhuvana called as soon as she brought Appa home. She said that I was not to worry and she would handle everything,'

Mamtha said, looking at the hospital discharge papers. 'I hired a cab immediately and arrived an hour ago.'

'I need to lie down,' Roshan said and got up from the sofa. Mamtha dropped the file and went with him. Chidananda followed them.

'The boy can find his way to bed,' Gowda remarked. Roshan probably wanted to be left alone.

Mamtha threw him a dirty look, and his father paused mid-step to snap, 'For heaven's sake, he is your son. Have a heart.'

Gowda sat in mutinous silence for a few minutes. Then he walked to his room to shower and change. It was a little past 7 p.m. He stood under the shower. His house suddenly seemed like K.R. Market with all the comings and goings.

As he dressed, Gowda was beset with restlessness. He wondered how his officers had fared. Just then, his phone rang. It was Gajendra.

'Nothing, sir. We didn't discover anything much.'

Gowda chewed on his lip. 'Let's meet first thing tomorrow. And you can tell me about it. What about Santosh and Aqthar?'

Gajendra snorted. 'Nothing much, except they got into a fight. Apparently, they made quite an impression.'

Gowda didn't hear the rest of what Gajendra said as he finished the call. He kept his track pants on and pulled on a full-sleeved T-shirt and a well-worn biking jacket. From the back of the wardrobe, he pulled out a pair of scuffed sneakers.

Mamtha stood at the door, watching him. 'And where are you going now?' she asked in a low but furious voice.

'Work,' Gowda said.

'And you expect me to believe that?' Mamtha frowned.

'I do,' Gowda said as he looked at himself in the mirror. 'You can come along if you want to but it's a third-rate bar so...'

'What about dinner? What do I tell your father and Roshan?' Mamtha persisted.

'Tell them the truth. I had to go out on work. I'll grab a bite somewhere,' Gowda said, forcing a smile on his face. 'You should eat and go to bed early. You must be tired.'

Mamtha tucked a strand of hair behind her ear. 'Yes, once I settle in Roshan and Appa, I will.'

'Don't worry about opening the door for me. I have my keys,' Gowda said.

She nodded and watched him leave from the doorway. As Gowda wheeled his Bullet out of the gate, he saw the curtains flutter slightly in the window upstairs and felt the now-familiar surge of irritation. He looked up and was surprised to see that the silhouette was that of a man. That must be the brother. Keeping tabs on the neighbour was probably a congenital ailment in the family. Gowda latched the gate after him and started his bike.

The rhythmic thump of the bike filled the night air. He rode through the streets of Green Park Layout and turned into the main road. The traffic had eased a bit even though airport taxis whizzed past every few minutes. Gowda turned into the service road at the Ring Road and continued towards Horamavu junction. He rode past it and went down another service road towards a haunt where he knew he would find one of his informers.

It had been a while since he had met Oblesh, or OB, as everyone including Gowda called him. Gowda wasn't too worried. Most serious drinkers seldom varied their routine. And on a cold December night, he was certain OB would be in the bar with no name. There, he was safe and didn't have to look over his shoulder.

Gowda parked his bike near a shop selling flooring tiles. It was only a quarter past eight but the shutters were down. He knew that his Bullet would be safe there. More importantly, no one would notice it. He stuck his hands into his jacket pockets and walked briskly down the road that abutted the tile shop. On one of the tiny lanes that housed a medley of shops was the bar with no name.

OB was holding court when Gowda walked in.

'The element of surprise—that's everything,' he was saying. 'The attacker expects you to use your fists and knees. But he isn't looking at your mouth. And that's when you send it flying into his face with a spitting motion. This bastard thought he had me. He was taller and bigger and it was a dark alley. But...'

The others hadn't said a word as OB revealed how he had ended up slashing his attacker's cheek. He opened his mouth to show them his tongue, where the razor blade was perched, ready to be turned into a weapon. But their attention was no longer only on him.

OB turned his head to look at what had distracted his audience. He closed his mouth. Gowda tried not to flinch. He knew OB lived with a razor blade in his mouth, but he still couldn't reconcile himself to the thought of how the man didn't cut his mouth open.

OB rose to his feet. 'Sir, what are you doing here? This isn't your kind of place.'

Gowda unzipped his jacket and pulled the least stained of the plastic chairs towards a table. He sat in it and said, 'That is why I am here.'

OB's coterie melted away into the shadows to other tables. He dragged his red-coloured chair to Gowda's table. Gowda raised his eyebrows.

'It's my chair. I don't like anyone else sitting in it.' OB waved to the man in the bar cage. On one side of it was a corrugated metal sheet wall with a door that customers kept leaving through and coming back in. And each time the door closed, there was a hard jangle of metal on metal.

'What's there?' Gowda asked, feigning nonchalance.

'Just an open place with a toilet. We use it to pee and vomit.' OB grinned. 'In the morning, one of the boys will sprinkle sand over the mess and clean it up... but for now, don't even think of going there, sir.'

A beefy man walked to their table. 'Who is this, OB? Is he troubling you?'

OB threw him a dirty look. 'Do I look like I'm being troubled? Fuck off from here. I am busy.'

He looked at Gowda. 'Sir, what will you drink?' OB asked. 'It's best we order.'

Gowda pondered his choices. He knew exactly what he would find in holes such as this one.

The drinks came to their table with two plates heaped with what looked like Chicken 65. The almost-neon orange colour of the meat made Gowda's eyes smart.

'Try these, they are delicious,' OB said, gnawing on a drumstick.

Gowda held the glass in his hand but didn't drink.

'What do you want to know?' OB asked, leaving the bone on the table. He licked his fingers and reached for another piece of chicken, picking one that was charred at the edges. Gowda wondered if OB even ate food with the blade in his mouth.

'I saw Oil Mill Jaggi at a hospital near Kothanur. He seemed to have multiple fractures. What do you know about that?' Gowda asked.

OB's eyes widened. He dropped the piece back on the plate and licked his fingers thoughtfully, then said, 'If you are not drinking...'

Gowda moved the glass towards him.

OB met his eyes for a fleeting second and asked, 'You don't mind.'

Gowda shrugged. 'Have it.'

OB took a big sip from the glass. 'Sir, last week I was at Kalyani Bar on Oil Mill Road. That's Oil Mill Jaggi's haunt. He was drinking on his own.'

'When was this?' Gowda leaned forward.

'About ten days ago. 27 November. I remember very well as I made a killing on a card game and I decided to celebrate. That's why I went to Kalyani Bar,' OB said.

Behind him, from beyond the open door to the yard, he could hear retching. The man throwing up seemed intent on flushing his kidneys out through his mouth, Gowda thought, trying to focus on OB's words.

OB got up to slam the door shut. 'Shut the fuck up,' he told the hapless drunk.

'You were saying,' Gowda prodded OB before he began telling him about men who couldn't hold their alcohol.

OB nodded and took one more swallow of the brandy, as if to calm his nerves. 'Then Military turned up there.'

Gowda looked up, startled. The tea seller outside the hospital, Charlie, had referred to someone called Military too, except he too had said—like OB—Mill Tree, and this Mill Tree seemed to be omnipresent.

'I made it a point to move away, sir. He is a mental fellow,' OB continued.

'As in...'

'Who dresses up like a military fellow when you are not in the military? Crew cut, camouflage pants, khaki T-shirt and boots. He even carries a satchel and wears a steel bangle. But I think he is mental mostly because there is no telling what he will do if he is pissed off,' OB said as his fingers hovered over the plate. 'Sir, don't you want the Chicken 65?'

Gowda shook his head. 'I just had dinner.'

'So early? I eat at midnight,' OB said as he tore a piece with his surprisingly shiny white teeth.

'Did you hear what Military and Jaggi spoke about?'

OB frowned. 'Not every word but some of it. He didn't seem pleased to see Jaggi there. He told Jaggi that it was a big day and a lot was at stake. And Jaggi told him to relax and that he knew what he was doing.' OB paused and grinned. 'Obviously, he didn't. But who could have beaten Jaggi up? He is good, sir. Very good with his fists and knees.'

Gowda grunted. 'This Military. Who is he?'

'Who knows?'

OB's shrug sent Gowda's antennae up. He noticed a man sitting some distance away turn his head away from them. Gowda stood up. 'I am leaving,' he said.

OB looked pointedly at the food and drink that had just been replenished.

'You ate the food. You drank the whisky. Why the fuck should I pay?' Gowda said, striding out.

OB watched him leave. He took up a chewed-up chicken leg and hurled it in Gowda's direction. The man who had been observing them came to OB's table. 'Your information was of no use to him. Don't trust a cop ever. Haven't you heard this before?'

'What information can I give him anyway?' OB shrugged. 'What do I know? I thought I was getting a sponsor for the evening. Bastard, he fucked my mood. I am going home.'

He pushed the plate away. OB stood up and went to the bar counter, still holding his chair. 'Put it on my account,' he said. He placed his chair to the side of the counter for safekeeping.

Then he walked out of the bar with a slow stride. Gowda was waiting for him by his bike. He slipped a crisp note into OB's pocket.

'Stephen, the man who came to our table, sir. He was watching us.'

'I know,' Gowda said. 'I'm going to call you tomorrow. I want you to describe this Military fellow to my police artist.'

# 8 DECEMBER 2012, SATURDAY

## 1

Gowda sat at his table, looking at his desktop screen. Santosh had checked the Professor's call records. There was nothing suspicious. A few calls. Hardly any text messages. Tech support had sifted through the emails as well. But Gowda had the notion that they had all missed out on something. He opened the attachments tech support had sent him at his request.

Gowda started reading the emails Professor Mudgood had received and sent. Associates, colleagues, former pupils, writers, historians. Most of them were meant to be gems of philosophy though it seemed more like gibberish. There were a few personal bits of information in them but nothing of consequence.

He clicked on another folder titled 'Drafts'. The box opened to reveal a dozen unsent mails. Gowda read through them one by one.

Nothing there either. What was the missing piece? He thumped the table in frustration. There was one more folder titled Lectures. In it, he found the document he had been looking for. It had a title: 'Notes for Lecture'.

Gowda opened it. It was dated two days before the Professor's death. This must be the file the tech support constable had told him about. 'Nothing there, sir, except one file of random jottings and family complaints,' Saira said. She was the sharpest of the lot and Gowda knew nothing would escape her eyes. So he had run only a cursory eye through it.

But he needed to read through all the mails carefully again, he had decided after a night of tossing and turning and wondering where he had run into the moniker 'Mill Tree' before Charlie had mentioned it. Was he clutching at straws? That was how most people in India said the word: Mill Tree. But at this point, he was willing to clutch at anything that resembled a straw.

He found the word in a few minutes.

Everything about India as it is today shows the emergence of a fascist regime. As in Hitler's Germany, it isn't the intellectual or the farmer who holds the reins of this country's future. It is the soldier who is the regime's instrument. Soldiers wearing uniforms and those who don't are but a mindless army trained to wound.

Last evening I heard Mary Susheela and her country brute of a husband arguing in the kitchen. The loud voices took me there. They shut up when they saw me.

But I had heard Paul say, 'Mill Tree will kill me.'

For a moment, I wondered at what he said. Mill Tree. Then it occurred to me that he meant the Military, of course. Not just you but the entire country will be destroyed by fascism's foot soldiers, I wanted to tell him. Though why anyone would kill that miserable worm defeats me. His being alive and dead is of no consequence to anyone. Not even his wife, I believe.

Gowda read it again. He tapped the end of his nose with a pen. There it was. Mill Tree. Military.

Charlie. OB. Paul Selvam. All of whom had referred to 'Mill Tree', which was merely their way of saying 'military'.

*

He heard the sounds of someone cleaning the yard. The broom-strokes were loud and brisk as dust and leaves were swept aside. Suddenly, the door to his room opened and a woman appeared with a bucket and mop.

'I didn't know you were here, sir,' she said, flustered to see Gowda in his room at half past six in the morning.

'It's fine. Go ahead.' Gowda walked to the door.

He paused at the sight of the bucket which had a milky pink liquid in it. 'What do you use to mop the floor?'

She stared at him, surprised. 'Phenyl, sir, why?'

'Do you use engine oil ever?'

She shook her head. 'No, no. If there are ants or those woolly caterpillars we trickle a few drops of kerosene on the ant path and sometimes I use it to control termites. But not to wipe the floor. Who would use anything like engine oil for cleaning the floor. People would slip and fall.'

Gowda nodded and walked to the mango tree. He lit a cigarette to brace himself from the cold. It was all beginning to make sense. He inhaled deeply and looked around impatiently. Where was everyone?

He pulled his phone out and called Gajendra. 'I am here, sir,' a voice said from behind.

Gowda turned around.

'You came in very early, sir,' Gajendra said, saluting him.

'I couldn't sleep and I wanted to check a file on my desktop.' Gowda stubbed his half-smoked cigarette in the cement pan.

A pained expression flitted across Gajendra's face.

'What?' Gowda asked.

'You wasted half a cigarette.'

'Better that than my lungs, no? When will the others get here? Don't they have any sense of time?'

'Already in the SIT room,' Gajendra said as he walked with Gowda towards the station house. Gowda was in one of his moods, he could see.

\*

Santosh was describing the fight to Byrappa and Ratna while Aqthar sat in a chair with his arms folded and an amused look on his face. All of them straightened as soon as they saw Gowda.

'Don't let me stop you,' Gowda said.

Santosh flushed. 'It's just that, sir, that...' he began. Gowda waved his hand.

'Did you discover something of interest to the case?' He lowered himself into a chair.

'Actually, we did, sir,' Aqthar said softly.

Gowda turned to him.

'I was asked if I would like to be part of a fight,' Aqthar said.

'To join a gang, you mean?' Gowda asked.

'No, sir, to fight for money.' There was silence in the room.

'You didn't tell me this,' Santosh said, leaning forward.

Aqthar nodded. 'I didn't because I thought I heard wrong.'

'You didn't,' Gajendra said, unable to hide his excitement. 'The word seems to have got around. Last evening, Byrappa and I were told at one of the bars we went to about a Dharwad fellow whose punch was like a gunny bag full of cannonballs being thrown at you. Like Muhammad Ali's.'

'Who's Muhammad Ali?' Ratna asked.

'The heavyweight boxer,' Byrappa said.

'Is that true?' Gowda asked, turning to Aqthar.

'Not really, sir. That is an exaggeration. But I do have some kick-boxing experience and can throw a punch if needed,' Aqthar said, trying not to look too pleased with himself, Santosh thought with a flash of irritation.

'Like I said, I didn't take it seriously. But last night, the man, I think he is called Babu, messaged asking if we could meet. He wanted to tell me more, he said,' Aqthar said.

Gowda felt one more piece of the jigsaw fall into place.

'Babu?' Gajendra asked no one in particular.

Byrappa frowned. 'Was he tall as a lamppost and did he have a forehead like a lorry's nose? Sticking out?'

Aqthar stared at Byrappa's accurate description. 'Do you know him?'

'Ditchie Babu.' Byrappa turned to Gajendra. Gowda looked at them, puzzled. He too had once known all the thugs in the area and their various monikers. But for some years now, he hadn't had the time for street murmurs. He was going to have to rectify that, he told himself. Intuition came from observation, for which a man had to lose some shoe leather.

'Who is this Ditchie Babu?' Gowda asked. 'And why ditchie?'

'Don't you know the word "ditchie"? Everybody—Kannadigas, Tamilians, Telugus—everyone uses it. To attack someone with the forehead. He uses that forehead of his as a weapon to give a ditchie, sir,' Byrappa said, miming the action. He brought his forehead down to crack an imaginary opponent's nose. 'When you hit the bridge of the nose with targeted force, it breaks almost instantly and spills a lot of blood.'

Gowda winced.

'He is also a full-time rowdy. Most times I don't think he knows or cares who he's threatening or assaulting. He is usually with Taaka Ravi,' Gajendra added.

'And who is Taaka Ravi?' Ratna asked in a bemused voice. For once, Gowda was grateful for Ratna's queries.

Byrappa slashed the air. 'When Taaka takes out his blade, you will need at least a few stitches,' he said. 'And he has two scars on his cheeks from a fight. That was how he decided to start using the blade as his weapon of choice.'

Santosh stared at Byrappa in admiration. The constable was a walking goondapedia when it came to antisocial elements.

'What did Ditchie Babu actually tell you?' Gowda said, interrupting Byrappa who had started to tell them about Deal Danny.

Aqthar pulled out his notebook. 'I was at the bar counter, sir. This was after the fight. Ditchie Babu sidled up to me. He gave me a sharp look. I thought he was going to pick a fight. So I moved away a little. He looked at me and said, "Mams, you are good. An intuitive fighter." I gave him a little nod. Then he said, "Do you want to fight for money?" I said I wasn't a thug to be hired.

'He laughed aloud and replied, "I wasn't asking you to beat up people. I am talking about a proper fight. You could win a lot of money—50,000 to 75,000 rupees and more for half an hour of your time. You don't even have to knock the other guy out. Just stay on your feet. Think about it." He said if I was willing, he would tell his boss.' Aqthar paused. 'I thought it was best Santosh and I leave then. Ditchie took my number and texted me again late at night. What do you think is going on, sir?'

Gowda didn't speak. He stared at a lizard on the wall. 'What did you hear about the fight at Kalyani Bar, Gajendra?'

'Nothing much. That it was a good fight. A hot-headed fellow who threw punches and kicks without making too much contact.'

Santosh clenched his jaw at what he realized was a reference to him. He had been feeling rather pleased at the thought he had wrapped the case up and now all he had for his trouble was a bruised rib and a sprained little finger.

'They also mentioned a calm fellow who knocked people down with ease. He was six feet tall and as wide. And he left one man with a smashed lip. If he had hit him really hard he could have broken a jaw. Seemed an out-of-towner, I was told, from his accent.' Gajendra looked at Gowda and added, 'I think they were talking about Aqthar Sir.'

'Are you thinking what I'm thinking, Gajendra?' Gowda asked slowly.

Gajendra nodded.

The door to the room opened. DCP Sagayaraj, wearing a grey jacket over a cream shirt and navy-blue trousers, stood in the doorway. 'Good... I am glad to find you all here.'

Gowda stood up to greet the DCP while the others stood to attention.

Gowda put on his most affable expression and asked, 'Any developments, sir? Has Gurunath confessed?'

Sagayaraj snorted in response. 'He confessed to every misdemeanour since he was born. From cheating in a maths exam in primary school to watching porn as a teenager to siphoning money from the Professor's account. But not to the murder. He insists he knows nothing about it.'

'What about his friend?' Gowda was quite certain there would be nothing there as well.

Sagayaraj shook his head. 'He is a tough one. But my men will prise the truth out of him—if there is any truth to be found.'

Gowda gestured to the others to leave the room. When they did, he asked the DCP, 'Are you having doubts about Gurunath being the perpetrator? We did notice—that is, Constable Byrappa did—that the ground where the weapons were found buried was hard as a rock. It wouldn't have been the case if they had been buried recently.'

The DCP looked at a point beyond Gowda's ear and then slowly met his gaze. 'That occurred to me as well. You know that feeling when everything points one way but deep within you know that there is something amiss...'

Gowda nodded. He wondered if he should tell Stanley about his suspicions. He knew he would have to do that eventually but at this point he wanted to pursue his leads without interference.

Gowda cleared his throat. 'Stanley, we have been looking into illegal cockfights. Apparently, they are happening fairly regularly in this area,' he began.

'Yes. I know... we have had some tipoffs. But we haven't been able to nab the bastards yet.'

Gowda doodled on a piece of paper as Stanley held forth. 'Are there other kinds of illegal fights that take place?' he asked casually.

'What other kinds are there?'

'Dog fights?'

The DCP frowned. 'Not in Bangalore. There are reports of those happening in Delhi. The dogs come from Pakistan and Afghanistan, I hear.'

'What about an illegal fighting ring involving men?'

Sagayaraj looked at Gowda. 'What have you heard?'

Gowda shrugged.

'You do know that the CCB has to be kept in the loop,' Sagayaraj persisted.

'Of course,' Gowda said, meeting the senior officer's gaze steadily. 'I was just curious. That's all.'

Sagayaraj exhaled. 'I know you are keeping things from me, Gowda. But you don't know what you are going to rake up if you pursue such cases on your own. You need us to handle them,' he said.

Gowda felt his hackles rise. 'You think we are not up to the job?' Then he remembered to add, 'Hypothetically speaking, that is.'

Sagayaraj cocked an eyebrow. 'Hypothetically speaking, I see... and my answer is your people are not trained for such cases. It's as basic as that.'

Gowda shifted in his chair, trying to contain his anger. He knew that Stanley was right but he didn't have to like what he heard. He would talk to his team and take a call, he told himself.

'It is too early to tell, sir. The moment I have something concrete, I will let the CCB know,' Gowda said, stalling for time.

Sagayaraj offered him a strained smile. He knew a delaying tactic when he saw one. A few minutes later, he left. And Gowda retreated to his room to collect his thoughts and to speculate on why the DCP had come to Neelgubbi station.

Strangely, now that he had spoken it aloud, his theory seemed more plausible than ever. He felt his heart thump in his chest. It wasn't possible, he told himself. And yet, everything seemed to point towards it. Illegal fights involving men instead of roosters, men who fought while bets were laid and money was won and lost.

But even if it turned out to be true, what did such a set-up have to do with Professor Mudgood's homicide? Were the two related, or had he merely stumbled upon something that at best would be a parallel case? That would necessitate mounting a full-scale investigation.

Gowda groaned. He didn't have the manpower or resources. It would be best to palm this off to the CCB. That was what DCP Vidyaprasad would demand he do. So would Stanley.

He stood up and went to the window. You have to pursue this, a voice muttered in his head. If illegal fights are taking place right under your nose, are you going to look away? How different are you from the policemen who are bribed?

Gowda paced the room as the voice persisted. When Gajendra knocked and entered, he glared at the Head Constable as if he was the owner of that hectoring voice in his head.

'Sir,' Gajendra said, almost taking a step back at the ferocity of Gowda's glare. 'Is everything okay?' he asked in an uncertain voice.

'I think there are illegal fights happening right under our nose...'

Gajendra nodded furiously. 'I think so too. But where do you think they are happening, sir?'

'I am going to have to ask Aqthar to say yes to the invitation to fight.'

Gajendra swallowed. He had hoped it wouldn't come to this. 'Aqthar Sir is a capable officer. But the risks...' An anxious note stippling every syllable.

'I have this strong hunch that if he does we'll find many answers.' Gowda ignored the trepidation in Gajendra's words.

'But what does it have to do with the Professor's homicide? Isn't that the case we are investigating?' Gajendra tried to protest. All their jobs would be on the line if this went awry.

'I can't tell you why but I think there is a connection,' Gowda said. 'Call in the others. Or better still, let's go into the SIT room. And I'll tell you what I am thinking.' He paused, seeing the discomfiture on Gajendra's face. He was clearly unsure of what came next and what the consequences would be. 'The burden of providing the proof is ours, Gajendra. You understand that, don't you? But hear me out first. This is Aqthar's decision. He can take it to the next level. But only if he wants to.'

DCP Sagayaraj had looked worried as he walked out of the station.

'What do you think is the problem?' Aqthar asked Santosh under his breath.

'Gowda Sir must have said something to both annoy and worry him,' Santosh said. 'They go back a long way. DCP Sir understands Gowda Sir very well. How his mind works,' Santosh said and quickly pulled his face into a study of seriousness as he heard footsteps approaching. Santosh looked at Gowda expectantly as he walked into the SIT room.

Gowda cleared his throat. 'Last evening the two of you stumbled upon something,' he began.

He looked at their faces one by one and paused when he came to Aqthar. He also caught Ratna's aggrieved expression. She was still smarting from suddenly finding herself out of the investigation.

'Tell me what you think, Ratna. You can look at this with some perspective since you haven't been so closely involved.'

Ratna's face brightened. 'Yes, sir,' she said.

Gowda took them through his thought process, detailing every little thing he could remember: the reference to 'Mill Tree' in the unsent mail; Charlie's connection with Military; OB's recounting of what he had seen at Kalyani Bar; and the sight of Oil Mill Jaggi with a broken limb. 'I think we are looking at an illegal fighting ring,' Gowda finished.

There was a stunned silence.

'Are you sure, sir?' Aqthar asked.

Gowda nodded.

Santosh asked, 'But what does it have to do with the homicide?'

Gajendra looked at Gowda. Santosh was reiterating his own words from earlier.

'What if the cottage on the Professor's property is where these illegal fights happen? It is secluded enough, and no one has access to it,' Ratna said. 'And who would even suspect a Padma Shri awardee to have such activities going on in his grounds?'

Gowda answered, 'You would be surprised at what Padma Shri awardees get up to. But in this case, the Professor probably didn't have any idea. And that's exactly what I am leading up to.'

Byrappa, who had been quiet until then, said, 'I think that's it, sir. Perhaps they thought that the Professor had seen them and so he had to be silenced.'

'Precisely,' Gowda said, studying each of their faces. 'But we have no way of proving it unless we can stack up evidence. We will need to conduct a raid while a fight is going on.'

'What do we do next?' Ratna asked.

'The CCB would like us to hand over the case to them. We are apparently only good to deal with illegal fights among poultry.' Gowda's expression made clear what he thought of that.

'We can't give up our case,' Santosh said.

Aqthar took a deep breath. 'Sir, what if I say yes to Ditchie Babu? That's the only way we'll know where and when a fight will take place and who is involved. And that should help us piece it together.'

Santosh stared at Aqthar, appalled. 'Are you out of your mind?'

He turned to Gowda. 'Sir, Aqthar has no idea what he would be getting into. You can't allow it.'

'I need to think about this,' Gowda said without giving away anything in tone and expression. 'Meanwhile, Gajendra, I want you to get Shenoy to do a composite sketch of this Military. You will need to take OB to Shenoy. He won't go to the kind of places OB frequents.' Gowda pulled out his phone to call Shenoy.

He turned to Aqthar. 'While I decide if you should say yes to the fight, I want you to keep as low a profile as possible. Don't wear your uniform and go out and about and don't come to the station. And if you do, don't walk in as if you belong here.'

Aqthar nodded. When Gowda left the room, Ratna exhaled loudly.

Santosh touched Aqthar's shoulder. 'You need to tell Gowda Sir you can't do it. This is dangerous.'

'I know.' Aqthar gave him a smile. 'But I won't say no. That's not who I am.'

# 2

Ratna and Byrappa sat across from Gowda at his desk. Ratna didn't bother to hide her annoyance. The boys' club was going to handle the whole fighting ring situation while she was being asked to investigate Gowda's tenants.

'I know exactly what you are thinking, ASI Ratna, so wipe that expression off your face,' Gowda said, his eyes on the computer screen.

'Something about this woman bothers me. For starters, her name is Bhuvana,' Gowda said, looking at Byrappa. 'Does that ring a bell?'

'How can I forget, sir?' He whistled through his teeth. 'I get it now, sir.'

Ratna looked at the two of them as they fell into a silence, remembering the horrific nature of the Bhuvana case.

Gowda found the case file he was looking for in a digital folder Santosh had created. Its contents kept growing even though they were yet to make any marked progress.

Gowda forwarded the folder to Ratna. 'Talk to Santosh and Gajendra. They will answer your queries, if you have any after Byrappa briefs you. I want you to find out everything you can about her.'

As they left the room, Gowda said, 'ASI Ratna. This needs to be done with utmost discretion. I have no reason to suspect her, and she must not come to know she is under scrutiny.'

'I understand, sir,' Ratna said, though she wasn't entirely sure she did. It all seemed very peculiar. What did a case from the past have to do with Gowda's tenants?

Gajendra came to speak to Gowda a few minutes later. 'I just finished talking to Paul Selvam, sir. He claims he doesn't know who the African man Yaangba is. Apparently, he found him bleeding and unconscious on the side of the road, and being a good Christian he hailed a passing auto and took him to hospital. When the man regained consciousness, he asked Paul to make some calls, and soon some of his friends came to be with him. Paul left. That is his story.'

'What was he doing at that hour away from his bed and home?'

'I asked him that, sir. He said he was walking his dog.' Gajendra looked sceptical. 'I asked him if he took the dog to the hospital too. And he said no. He took the dog back to his house and then ran to the unconscious man on the road.'

'What about the numbers he called? Check his call history.'

Gajendra shook his head. 'He used the African man's phone, he claims. He has an answer for everything, sir. He needs to be brought in for questioning if we are to find out what really happened.'

'Not yet,' Gowda said. He stood up. It was a quarter to noon already. Where had the day gone? He called for David. He would go home first, he decided. With Mamtha there, Bhuvana wouldn't have a free rein. Mamtha would keep her in her place and be polite but firm about not needing any assistance. Or so he hoped.

*

When Gowda turned into the lane that led to his house, he told David, 'Come back in an hour's time. And have lunch in the meantime.'

David didn't speak. Gowda clearly had something on his mind, and it was best to not ask him where they were going after lunch. He would bite David's head off. But he realized that it had to be some official matter. Gowda was scrupulous about using the police vehicle only for official reasons.

The door to his house wasn't latched shut. Gowda pushed it open. He could hear voices from Roshan's room. Laughter too.

Gowda headed straight there and felt an irrational rage at what he saw. Roshan was sitting up in bed, propped up by pillows. Mamtha and Mrs Tenant sat at the foot of the bed on either side. Mrs Tenant had her back to Gowda. His father was in a chair next to the bed, describing one of Gowda's youthful escapades with great gusto. 'And he ate the entire biriyani and left nothing for us or the guests we had invited!'

Gowda stood in the doorway, and it took a few seconds for them to realize he was there. The laughter died down abruptly, except for Roshan who continued to splutter in amusement.

Gowda walked to the verandah and took his shoes off, placing them on the shoe rack that seemed to appear each time Mamtha was home. She frowned at him wearing his shoes within the house and kept the shoe rack where Gowda would see it. Was this an example of the passive-aggressive behaviour everyone talked about these days?

He went to the bedroom and took his watch off for good measure. He heard the main door shut as he washed his face.

Mamtha came into their room, seemingly in a pleasant mood. Signs of the jolly conversation lingered on her smiling face. 'We lucked out with our new tenants,' she said, placing a set of ironed clothes in the wardrobe.

'And why is that?'

'Bhuvana is nice. And she works from home. So there is someone around to keep an eye on Shanthi.'

Gowda grunted. 'And why does she need to keep an eye on Shanthi?'

Mamtha frowned. 'I know you think Shanthi is god's gift to mankind but she isn't all that straight as you think. Half the groceries you buy end up in her kitchen. Bhuvana says that Shanthi never leaves without a bag full of things.'

Gowda didn't bother responding.

'By the way, Bhuvana was telling me she has applied for a tatkal passport. Would you make sure the police verification happens as soon as you hear from the passport office?'

Gowda looked at Mamtha and said, 'Police verification isn't done for tatkal passports. It happens after the passport is issued. But this is still highly irregular. You know that the applicant ought to give their permanent address or at least have stayed for a year at the present address, and she's been here for not even ten days.'

'Considering how helpful she has been, it's the least you can do to help the poor girl so she can accompany her husband to Malaysia.'

Gowda changed the subject. 'How is Roshan? As a doctor what's your assessment?'

Mamtha's forehead crinkled. 'He'll be fine after a couple of days of bed rest. All he needs is peace and quiet. I'll take him home with me when I leave,' she added, almost defiantly.

'In which case I suggest you don't hold a party in his room. Peace and quiet indeed. The ruckus from there was like in a fairground,' Gowda snapped.

'Why do you dislike Bhuvana? What did that poor thing do? They are such a lovely family. She is an artist. Her husband sings. Her brother is a mathematical whiz. You should be happy that we have them as tenants.' Mamtha glowered at him.

It occurred to Gowda that everyone had met Bhuvana's brother except him. 'When did you meet the brother?'

'He came down to say hello to Roshan. He is gay, by the way.'
Mamtha looked at Gowda's expression and persisted. 'Don't tell
me you didn't know...'

'I haven't even met him,' Gowda protested.

'I'm not surprised that he didn't drop in to say hello to you.
The police are not exactly known for empathy, are they? You
lot have turned being gay into a criminal offence,' Mamtha said
as she slammed the wardrobe door shut. 'Bhuvana told me how
many times he's been harassed. Uff!'

'What about my father and Roshan? Do they know?'

'Roshan isn't a child. Do you think he won't have figured it
out? I don't think your father realizes. Roshan and I thought it
best to let it be; his generation won't understand,' Mamtha said.
'By the way, what are you doing here?'

'I live here, if you remember.'

Mamtha threw him a dirty look and closed the door behind
her.

Gowda lay on top of the bedcover. Urmila had introduced
such niceties—bedspreads, porcelain and crystal ashtrays—into
his home. He wondered what Mamtha made of them. He folded
his arms over his forehead and closed his eyes. A deep fatigue
coursed through him even as his mind whirled around in circles.
For a moment, he wished he was in his hotel room on Kerala's
backwaters on their holiday. He remembered how at a certain
time of day the light on the water reflected on the ceiling. Urmila
and he had held hands and watched the light dance. The stillness
of the moment was what he missed. He needed stillness to focus.
And it seemed to him that everywhere he went there were people
and their incessant chatter.

He tried to fit the pieces of the jigsaw puzzle together:
Professor Mudgood's homicide. Iqbal Buqhari. The cottage.
Oil Mill Jaggi. And the mysterious Military.

The more he thought about it, the more convinced he was
about the illegal fighting racket. Who else was involved? Some

big names for sure. The betting stakes were high. Besides, to
the men who congregated there, it wouldn't just be the draw of
money but the smell of blood, the sharpness of sweat and the
white heat of violence that wasn't matched by anything else. If
it was happening right here, Papanna had to be involved, along
with his coterie. The nexus, Gowda realized, definitely extended
to those in power.

He sat up, adrenalin pumping through his blood. There was
something very satisfactory about the thought that this case would
rock several boats. But as he knew, everyone from Additional
Commissioner Mirza to DCP Sagayaraj to the lizard on the wall
in his office would demand to know how this was connected to
Professor Mudgood's homicide. What did the illegal fights have
to do with his murder? Gowda knew for certain, illogical as it
may seem, that one would lead to the other. But there was no case
without evidence and it was up to him to provide it. And now more
than ever he needed to have the headspace to think it through.

He called up David and told him to stay back at the station.

Gowda dressed briskly and went to the living room. His
father was there with the newspaper spread out in front of him.
The pages were opened to his favourite section: the obituaries.
Chidananda was checking photographs and reading the names
and messages beneath each notice.

'Anyone you know, Appa?' Gowda asked.

Chidananda grunted. 'The brother of a man I know. What
a tragedy!'

'Did you know him well?' Gowda asked, more to make conversation than anything else.

'I never met him.' Chidananda's finger scrolled down to a
photograph.

'Why did you say it's a tragedy then?' Gowda asked, sitting down.

'All death is a tragedy,' Chidananda said in a subdued tone.
'One day I too will be a photograph here.' He stole a look at his
son to see if his words had had the necessary impact.

Gowda's smile disappeared. He wondered if he should say what was expected of him. 'Please, Appa, don't talk about death, etc. etc.' But the words wouldn't form and instead he muttered, 'Everyone has to die one day or the other, Appa.'

Chidananda's brow furrowed. He hated it when Borei refused to take his fears seriously and talked down to him.

'Are you having lunch here?' Mamtha asked from the kitchen. Gowda had seen his father's face fall and felt a deep twinge of guilt. Why couldn't he say what his father wanted to hear? More to make up for his tone than because of hunger, Gowda called out, 'I'll have lunch with Appa. Is that all right?'

Mamtha had laid out a feast of dishes. Gowda didn't have time for an elaborate meal but he knew she would be offended if he didn't sample everything. Gowda forced a smile on his face and asked, 'What's the occasion?'

'Appa is here. Isn't that occasion enough?' Mamtha said.

Chidananda beamed in delight. 'You know you are my favourite daughter-in-law, don't you?'

Gowda looked at his plate, examining its contents with great interest. He had heard his father say the same thing to his sister-in-law numerous times. Like babies, the elderly had the ability to own the moment. And like babies, they knew instinctively how to manipulate emotions, he thought, as he saw Mamtha heap another spoon of pulao onto his father's plate.

'Don't you like what I have made?' Mamtha's query broke his reverie.

Gowda saw all of them staring at him staring at his plate. 'It's this case I'm working on.' He smiled apologetically.

'I might as well have served you rice and rasam for all the enthusiasm you are showing,' Mamtha said in a huff.

'This is delicious,' Gowda said, reaching for another akki roti. And because it would please her, he added, 'Your akki rotis are so soft. Shanthi's are like plastic. Brittle and tasteless.'

To restore peace, Gowda ate more than he should have. After the meal, he called Gajendra. 'I'll meet you at Shenoy's house. What time will you be there?' He knew he needed to have some idea of what Military looked like. That would give him one more piece of the puzzle to finish the picture that was beginning to form in his head.

Gajendra took a deep breath. 'I was just about to call you, sir. There is a problem. OB isn't here. And no one seems to know anything about him. Someone said he has gone to his village.'

Gowda groaned. 'I'll handle it.'

Gowda took off his uniform. He found the most faded of his T-shirts and a frayed pair of track pants. Mamtha walked into the room as Gowda was slipping his feet into chappals.

'Why are you dressed like this?' She laughed.

'Like what?' Gowda asked with such earnestness that Mamtha did a double take.

'Chappar class,' Mamtha snorted.

Gowda grinned. 'That's exactly what I wanted. Thanks.' He touched the stubble on his chin. He had been in too much of a hurry in the morning. And it added to the louche look.

Mamtha stared at him. Gowda wondered if at times she thought he was a little mad. He wouldn't be surprised. When she left the room, Gowda sat on the bed and called up OB. 'Where are you?' he asked.

OB hesitated and said, 'I am in my village, sir.'

'Where is that?' Gowda demanded, ensuring OB heard the annoyance in his tone. He stood up. If he stayed here any longer, he would get into bed and sleep for the whole week.

'Malur,' OB muttered.

'We will come there. And don't worry... we will be in my own car. The story is we are property developers. So that's what you tell anyone who asks.'

'Thanks, sir,' OB whispered.

Gowda called Shenoy next. 'Change of plan,' he said. Shenoy responded with a sigh. 'What's new?'

## 3

The verandah caught very little sun in the afternoon. Gowda sat on a cane chair. From within the house, he could hear various sounds. Mamtha was watching something on her laptop and Roshan was—for once—seated with his books though he also had loud thumping music playing in the background. His father was in his room. Gowda smoked his cigarette, tapping ash into a potted jasmine plant. When he was done, he folded his arms across his chest and closed his eyes. Exactly ninety minutes later, the police vehicle drove up outside the gate. David gave the horn a little pat and Gowda awoke with a start. He stood up and stretched. By the time he had splashed water on his face and rid himself of the sleep that still clung to his eyes, David had parked the vehicle and opened the gates wide. Gowda started his car. Shenoy had stepped out of the Bolero and was waiting. Gowda drove outside the gate and paused for Shenoy to step in. He got into the front seat and pulled the seat belt over his sizable paunch.

'What do you have in there? Triplets?' Gowda said, trying to keep a straight face.

'Tell me again why I'm doing this.' Shenoy sighed. How had he let Gowda persuade him.

'Because you want to do it. Because you miss the excitement. Because you are a good man and a conscientious citizen,' Gowda said. 'Because you seem to be doing nothing much these days but sit on your backside.'

Gowda drove towards Doddagubbi and then took the road that led to Avalahalli, and from there entered Old Madras Road. 'Once this road is built you can reach Chennai in less than five hours,' Gowda said.

'Is that where we are going?' Shenoy sounded wary. 'I don't even have a change of underwear.'

Gowda laughed. 'No, no... just till Malur.'

'And your man won't come into the city?'

'He can't. He's been shunted away,' Gowda said as he tried to avoid one more pothole.

An hour and a half later, they were at Malur bus stop though there was nothing there to indicate it was one. Just a clump of trees and a row of shops. OB was waiting for them there. He peeled himself off a tree stump and stood up as Gowda pulled up in front of him. Gowda parked the car and pulled out a cap from the glove compartment, one of Roshan's discards from his cricket academy days. He put on sunglasses as Shenoy watched in amusement.

'We need to pretend that we are real estate developers here to look at a parcel of land,' Gowda said.

'You forgot the gold dog chain around your neck,' Shenoy snickered.

Gowda got out of the car. 'You look more like someone who works in real estate than me. Come along. We have work to do,' he mumbled.

The portrait artist stepped out reluctantly. 'And now you want me to do undercover work,' he muttered under his breath.

Gowda took in OB's worried expression. The man was genuinely scared.

'One of the men at the bar mentioned to Deal Danny that I was talking to a stranger. Two of his men were outside my door first thing in the morning. They wanted to know who you were. I told them the truth. That you are from the police and trying to get some information from me,' OB said, looking nervously at Shenoy.

'And?'

'I had helped Deal Danny sell a stolen vehicle. That's what he thought it was about. So they told me to stay away for a few days.'

Gowda ignored the mention of the stolen vehicle. The three of them were walking through vacant tracts of land that belonged to OB's family. 'Once the highway is built, the price of this land will shoot up,' Shenoy remarked.

OB looked at him, pleased. 'Once that happens, I will start a bar, sir. OB Bar, All Kinds of Tasty Dishes.' He drew an imaginary signboard in the air.

Gowda threw him a look. 'You don't want to start a grocery store?'

'A man must do what he knows best,' OB said with a sage expression.

'I think we have seen enough. Let's go back to my car,' Gowda said. OB trailed after them. Gowda sat in the driver's seat while OB and Shenoy sat in the back.

OB described the man he called Mill Tree as per the cards Shenoy showed him. Face shape. Eyes. Nose. Forehead. Hairline. Chin.

Then it was Gowda's turn. 'How tall is he? Would you call him thin, fat, normal?'

'A little shorter than you.'

Gowda sighed. 'His voice? Anything specific you remember? Cuts, scars, tattoos, anything at all?'

OB shook his head. 'I don't remember.' Then suddenly his face lit up. 'He is very muscular. And, sir, I think he is from Mangalore. The accent slips out once in a while.'

'Well, that's something,' Gowda said.

OB looked outside. 'It's best I go, sir,' he said abruptly. In the rearview mirror, Gowda saw two men watching the car from a distance.

Gowda nodded. 'I'll send you the sketch and you can tell me if it is your man.'

OB stepped out, followed by Shenoy. Gowda passed him a 500-rupee note. 'Give it to him so the men can see it,' he muttered to Shenoy, who shoved the note into OB's shirt pocket.

'Do you want to tell me about that, sir?' Shenoy asked Gowda once he was in the car.

'I wish I could. But I am still figuring it out myself.' Gowda started the car. 'Thanks, Shenoy. I could not have done this officially, which is why I needed you to come here.'

'I got that the moment you called me,' Shenoy said.

As they neared the station, Gowda asked, 'How much time will you need?'

'I could stay on here and do it right away,' Shenoy said, knowing it would be better to do that. Gowda was quite capable of calling him every few minutes to check how far he had got.

When Shenoy had been seated in the SIT room and given everything he needed, Gowda retreated to his room. A few minutes later, he went to check on the portrait's progress.

Shenoy was studying his boards. He looked up and saw Gowda at the door but didn't say anything.

Gowda skulked back to his room and files. There was enough administrative work pending to keep him there for the next six months. He gritted his teeth and got down to it.

When he glanced at his watch next, he realized that an hour was nearly up. Surely Shenoy would have something to show him now, he told himself as he rose.

And he did. Gowda stared at the almost-complete portrait. He didn't need OB to corroborate the image, though he would to be doubly sure. But he had to talk to DCP Sagayaraj right away.

'Do you recognize the man?' Shenoy asked.

Gowda nodded. 'Once you are done, I'll have OB look at it as well. But I know this man. And it makes the case twice as complicated.'

'When did you ever have one that wasn't, sir?' Shenoy said from the corner of his mouth as his pencil moved briskly on the sheet.

*

Gowda called Aqthar into his room. 'What have you decided?'

Aqthar looked at him and said, 'I will say yes to the fight, sir.'

'Have you spoken to Ditchie Babu?'

'Not yet, sir,' Aqthar said.

'Leave for Dharwad right away. En route, call Ditchie Babu and tell him you are ready to fight,' Gowda said. 'Keep in touch with Ditchie Babu. Tell him you need to know at least two days in advance so you can return to Bangalore in time. Meanwhile, find out whatever you can from him on how these fights are organized. Be as discreet as possible and see if you can figure out who else is involved.'

Aqthar sat down, suddenly overwhelmed by what was expected of him. He swallowed. 'Would I need to fight? I'm not really in form.'

'No, we will move in before that. But you need to be prepared for any eventuality.'

Gowda watched the play of emotions in Aqthar's eyes. He could see the young man wanted to do it and back out at the same time.

Gowda knew he was putting Aqthar in grave danger but he couldn't bring himself to hand over the case to the CCB and relinquish control. He was about to tell Aqthar that it would be better to drop the idea when Aqthar stood up and said, 'I will leave for Dharwad right away, sir.'

Gowda smiled in relief. 'Don't worry. You are not going to have to fight. We'll ensure that the raid happens before that. But I still want you to prepare as if you are going to. Share details of how you are working out and preparing with Ditchie Babu. Stay away from your station at Dharwad. Do you understand?'

Aqthar nodded.

'One of the commandments of undercover work is to become the person you are pretending to be,' Gowda added, holding Aqthar's gaze. 'If you lose your nerve, the undercover operation will fall apart.'

*

His mobile rang.

'Sir, that's him.' OB's voice at the other end jangled through the room. Aqthar looked at Gowda curiously. Gowda cut the call after a few seconds and turned to Aqthar. 'Bring in the others. Once we are done, leave for Dharwad right away.'

When everyone was seated, he placed the sketch on the table.

'But this is Deva Shetty, Iqbal Buqhari's man,' Gajendra said, unable to hide his shock at Shenoy's portrait. 'It's fortunate that Aqthar and Deva have never met.'

'Why don't we just haul him in?' Santosh asked.

'Yes, sir. Why don't we? Then Aqthar Sir doesn't have to get into this fighting business,' Gajendra said.

Gowda looked at them for a moment. 'You know as well as I do that if we do, he'll be out in twenty-four hours, if not earlier. And, what do we charge him with?'

'And,' he said, waiting for what he had said to sink in, 'we need to get to the bottom of the fighting ring. Deva Shetty is just one person. Who are the others? Aqthar has to be at the fight for us to raid the place. Only he can lead us to Deva and everyone else involved.'

He could see from their faces that they weren't really persuaded but would do whatever he had asked of them. Aqthar alone seemed excited at the prospect of what lay ahead. For a moment, Gowda wondered if it was an act. What if he lost his nerve and opted out once he reached Dharwad?

There was still one more thing to be done to set the plan in action. He picked up his phone and called Sagayaraj. 'I need to see you, sir, it is important. And urgent.'

'Can't you just tell me over the phone?' Sagayaraj asked. 'I am just getting into a meeting with the Anti-Terrorism Squad. Between you and me, Borei, the ATS is a paper tiger. They haven't made a single arrest yet. But you can't really blame them because their powers are also limited. A review meeting is a review meeting in any case and God knows when it will end.'

'I think it would be best if we meet in person,' Gowda said. 'And not at the station.'

# 4

The Coorg Room was empty. In a sofa by the window, an elderly man with rheumy eyes sat staring into the depths of a glass. The evening light shadowed most of the room except where lamps cast their muted pools of light.

'And you are sure Iqbal Buqhari won't walk in on us?' Gowda asked, looking over his shoulder.

'No. He won't. And even if he does, there isn't anything to worry about. We are colleagues and college mates. He knows that,' Sagayaraj said, taking in Gowda's full-sleeved shirt, formal trousers and polished shoes. 'What's the occasion?'

'This,' Gowda said, gesturing at his surroundings. 'I didn't want to be restricted to the lawns where we would be completely exposed. Who knows who would see us together. Or overhear us.'

Sagayaraj grinned at Gowda. 'If I didn't know better, I'd think you were paranoid.'

'In all honesty, I wish it was just paranoia.'

The steward came with their drinks and plates of peanut masala and mini samosas. Sagayaraj signed the chit and waited for the steward to leave. He raised his glass of rum and Coke to Gowda, who peered gloomily at his glass of fresh lime soda and said, 'Enjoy your Old Monk while I have my schoolgirl drink.'

Sagayaraj guffawed. 'You can't drink and drive, Gowda. You are a policeman.' Then he spoke in a low voice with a swift change of expression. 'So, tell me...'

Gowda took a deep breath. 'Janaki Buqhari asked to see me.'

'The whole denture business...' the DCP said impatiently.

'No,' Gowda hesitated. 'This was before that. We met at Urmila's apartment. The previous evening.'

When Gowda finished narrating what she had told him, Sagayaraj demanded in a furious whisper, 'And you decided to tell me about this now?'

'As you very well know, Mrs Buqhari didn't kill her father. All she did was incapacitate him with the blow. But someone else did. Someone who found him slumped over. And that someone decided to finish what Janaki Buqhari began. I don't know if that someone knew that Janaki had struck her father on his head. So we come to the fundamental question of why the perpetrator wanted the Professor dead. The answer will clear up who it was as well.'

'You might as well tell me, Borei,' Sagayaraj said. 'Though it feels like you are running with conjecture rather than actual facts.'

Gowda finished his lime soda in one gulp and said, 'I knew you would say that. Which is why I want you to hear me out.'

When Gowda was done, he showed the DCP some photos on his phone. 'I want you to look at this. My informer, referred to a man named Military. I had Shenoy—you remember our sketch artist?—prepare a portrait based on his description.'

Sagayaraj studied the portrait. 'He looks familiar. But I can't place him.'

Gowda took a deep breath and said, 'That's Deva. Iqbal Buqhari's right-hand man.'

Gowda had the satisfaction of seeing Sagayaraj's jaw drop before he made a quick recovery. 'Are you certain?'

'Yes. OB identified him as "Military or his twin brother if it isn't Military". That's the name he goes by on the streets.' Gowda grinned at the DCP. It wasn't often that he had the opportunity to throw DCP Sagayaraj off kilter.

'Let's bring him in,' Sagayaraj said.

'Not yet.' Gowda lowered his voice. 'He will clam up. And we'll lose out on the chance to catch everyone involved. I think we need SI Aqthar to lead us to the fight.'

When Gowda had finished recounting the happenings at Kalyani Bar, Sagayaraj stared at his empty glass for a long moment. 'You realize that we are opening a can of worms.'

Gowda didn't speak for a few seconds. 'There may be political repercussions too.'

It was Stanley's turn to go silent. When he spoke, all he said was, 'Let's take this to Additional Commissioner Mirza. We need him to be on board. But Aqthar cannot be on his own there. And like I said before, the CCB will need to be part of the operation.'

Gowda didn't particularly like the idea of the CCB muscling in on his turf. But Sagayaraj was right. He couldn't sacrifice Aqthar on the altar of his ego.

'Yes, I get it,' he acceded.

'And you think this is why the Professor was murdered?'

'I am quite certain, Stanley, that he was merely collateral damage.'

'And you don't want another fresh lime soda?' Sagayaraj asked as he waved to the steward.

'Nope,' Gowda said, standing up. He reached towards the plate of mini samosas and popped one into his mouth. End of conversation.

# 5

Urmila opened the door on the third chime of the doorbell.

'Surprise!' he said, trying to muster up an apologetic expression for not having called or texted for two days.

Urmila didn't smile. 'How come?' she asked, evading his embrace.

Mr Right, however, had no such compunctions and greeted Gowda with little barks and whines. Gowda reached down to lift the dog into his arms.

When Gowda sat on the couch, she made it a point to sit in the wing chair on the other side of the coffee table, well away from him.

'Yaake Amma, no love only?' Gowda whined in his most rustic accent and drooped his mouth into a sad clown face.

Urmila burst into laughter. 'Where did that come from?'

Gowda grinned back. 'Roshan. The youth have their uses after all.'

Urmila stood up and walked towards Gowda. He took her hand in his and kissed it with elaborate muah sounds.

'Cut the drama, Borei, and tell me what you want,' she said with an exasperated smile.

'What I want is for the next few days to go away so my team is safe and the Professor's murderer is in custody. I want my tenant to vacate the premises. I want ACP—no—DCP Vidyaprasad to be sacked. I want all rapists and child-traffickers to be castrated. I want the end of poverty and I want world peace. But I'll settle for a drink. A stiff drink. I just met Stanley and he sat across me sipping rum and Coke while I was given a bloody fresh lime soda that wasn't even sweet enough.' Gowda's disgust was apparent.

'I just needed to see you, U. There is so much going on in my head that I feel I am going to explode and splinter in a thousand directions.'

She held him tight. 'I won't let that happen. Talk to me about it.'

Gowda sighed. 'I wish I could. But I can't, U. You know the deal, don't you?'

Urmila stiffened against his shoulder. 'Let's get you a drink first,' she said, slipping out of Gowda's embrace.

He watched her walk to the bar counter. He knew she was peeved that he couldn't discuss the case with her. But there wasn't much he could do about that. But there was something he could tell Urmila about.

'Urmila, come sit down,' Gowda said, patting the couch.

She came towards him with two glasses, one brimming with rum and Coke and the other containing a tiny peg of single malt. 'Are you planning to get me drunk and seduce me?' Gowda leered.

Urmila threw him a stern look and plopped down next to him. She curled her legs beneath her and leaned against a cushion. 'Someone is in a good mood, I see,' she said as he took her hand in his.

'You always put me in a good mood, baby,' Gowda murmured.

'From anyone else I would think these words are just words. But you, Borei.' Urmila glanced at him, not bothering to hide her feelings. 'I think you actually mean it. So what's been the trouble?'

Gowda took a sip. 'Old Monk?' he asked with surprise.

'You left a bottle here, remember, and I thought I would give you what you like. It's painful to see you splash soda and ice into a single malt, Borei.' Urmila grinned.

'Good idea.' Gowda grinned back. 'So, I was going to tell you something. Roshan was hospitalized yesterday...' Gowda paused. Was it only the previous morning?

'And?' Urmila sat up, whisky sloshing against the side of her glass. 'You're telling me now.'

Gowda swallowed. 'Like I said, it's been chaotic, U.'

'I don't like that you shut me out, Borei,' she said. 'You make me feel like a crumpet.' Gowda decided it wasn't an opportune moment to ask her what a crumpet was.

Almost as if she had read his mind, she said, 'Your bit on the side.'

Gowda looked at her. It was as if she had crumpled from within. 'I'm sorry, U,' he said, guilt seeping through his veins. 'I just didn't know what to do with Appa at home and Roshan in hospital.'

'Your wife?'

'She came in last night. By which time Roshan was discharged too,' Gowda said, leaning back and pulling Urmila into the crook of his arm.

'You could have called me to come over. I would have sat with your father while you were at the hospital,' Urmila said, torn between wanting to give Gowda an earful and wanting to nuzzle into him.

'I would have. I really would have, but the tenant upstairs played good Samaritan.'

Urmila frowned. 'Meaning?'

'Yes, this young couple, remember I told you? They moved in early this month. Something about the woman bothers me.' He stared at an arrangement of lilium in a vase. 'It's the feeling I get when I see those flowers. They look so fresh and alive that you wonder if they're plastic.'

Urmila raised an eyebrow. 'Borei, I can assure you those flowers are real.'

'I know... but you get what I am saying,' Gowda persisted. 'In less than ten days, she's become my father's companion, my son's best buddy and my wife's younger sister. I don't like these friendships that burgeon and bear fruit overnight. I don't like people who ingratiate themselves into your life. I am downright suspicious of that.'

Urmila watched the play of emotion on Gowda's face. 'What about her husband?'

'I have barely seen him. It's always the wife who is cosying up with my family, even Shanthi. I notice how she keeps track of my comings and goings. I found that very odd, creepy even. And when I tell you her name, you won't believe it. Bhuvana.'

Gowda saw Urmila's eyes widen in shock. She knew the name well enough. Then he saw her expression change. 'Are you sure you aren't being a wee bit paranoid? It's not a common name but it isn't rare either.'

He shrugged. 'That's what I told myself too. That I was over-thinking it. But when I went home from the hospital yesterday to pick up the car, I got a strong smell of engine oil on the staircase. What if she had left it there to make Roshan slip and fall? She's the one who summoned him upstairs. Roshan is an agile boy and he managed to break the fall. Nonetheless, he has a head injury, U. And before that, she takes my father for a movie and the next day he was ill.'

'Why would she do that? I do think it's a coincidence that her name is Bhuvana.'

'That's what I tell myself too but what about the engine oil?' Gowda demanded, almost angrily.

'In which case, you should evict them. Why would you keep them there?'

'I can't do that.' Gowda pressed his fingers to his temples. He felt the beginning of a headache behind his eyes.

'It's your house, Borei.'

'What do I say to evict them? And my wife seems very taken by her.' Gowda paused as he saw Urmila stiffen at his tone. He wanted to kick himself. He was venting his frustration on her because she was in front of him. 'I'm sorry, U,' he said. 'I didn't mean to snap at you.'

'But you did anyway,' Urmila said in a cold voice.

Gowda felt both a fool and a heel. He stared down at his hands. When he looked up, he saw Urmila's mouth tighten. She had thought he was looking at his watch.

She stood up. 'I think you are seeing patterns where none exist, ACP Gowda. And yes, I also think you need to go home. It's a quarter to ten and your wife must be wondering where you are.'

An uneasy silence slipped into the room. As long as Mamtha was away in distant Hassan, it was easy to make-believe that he and Urmila were two single people whose relationship would never wear the sordid garb of a fling. But Mamtha's presence in the city tore through the pretence.

Gowda rose to his feet and said, 'Don't do this, U. We both knew what we were getting into...' He lifted her chin to meet his gaze. 'Look at me.'

She did so.

'We are good, aren't we?'

'Yes, Borei, that we are,' Urmila said, forcing a smile on her face.

He kissed her hard, hoping it would tell her everything words never could or at least sufficiently enough. She clung to him for a moment and then pushed him gently.

'Go, Gowda, go...'

And, so Gowda went.

But as he rode home, he couldn't erase the image of her forlorn face from his mind. And that she had chosen to put distance between them by addressing him as Gowda. Here he was, heading home to his family unit complete with creepy tenant. And she had the cold comfort of silk cushions, whisky in a glass and a dog called Mr Right. Something tore at him. Gowda took a deep breath and turned his thoughts to the meeting scheduled for the next day.

Mamtha was asleep when Gowda got into their bed. He glanced at her for a moment. What was he to her, he wondered?

A few months ago he had gone to Hassan to spend a weekend with Mamtha and Roshan. Late one night, he had finished his last smoke and gone into their bedroom, certain that Mamtha would be fast asleep. Instead, he had been surprised to see her sitting up waiting for him. She made small talk for a while about her work and her siblings and Gowda wondered what she was leading up to. Eventually, she said, 'Borei, there's something I have to talk to you about. Since menopause, I am not inclined towards the physical part of marriage. I hope you understand.'

She had said this as if talking about an instalment plan loan drawing to an end. A burden that had to be borne but now was finally over. She had waited for him to respond; react even. But Gowda had only felt relief. It had always been a bloodless relationship and now they no longer needed to pretend otherwise. 'If that's what you want,' he had said.

And so here they were. Man and wife and no more. At least, neither of them needed to feign desire or pretend connubial bliss at the end of the sexual rite, he told himself, turning onto his side of the bed.

# 9 DECEMBER 2012, SUNDAY

## 1

'I did a preliminary check on the tenants, sir,' Ratna began even as she walked into Gowda's room. Gajendra drew out a chair for her and gestured for her to sit.

'And?'

'It's just as the real estate agent indicated. The husband, Shashank, works with an IT firm at Manyata Tech Park. Mid-level job. He graduated from an engineering college in Tamil Nadu and was based in Chennai before this. But I couldn't find out anything about the wife,' Ratna said.

Gowda frowned.

'It is strange, sir. I asked the agent and he said they came to him through a relative of his. And...' Ratna paused.

'And?' Gowda prodded.

'And he said that a woman's credibility is drawn from her husband. If she wears a mangalsutra that's all the guarantee he needs.' Ratna didn't bother to hide her disgust. She was relieved to see that Gowda's annoyance matched hers.

'I am going to meet her today,' Ratna said.

'And what's your story going to be?'

'Can't we just haul her in for questioning, sir?' Gajendra asked.

'That's not even an option, and on what basis anyway? But

Ratna was just going to tell me what she had in mind.' Gowda gestured for Ratna to resume.

'As part of Jana-Maitri, the police and community interface programme, an art camp is being organized.'

'What is this art camp? I didn't receive a briefing.'

Ratna grinned. 'That's my story, sir. I am going to meet her and ask her to be part of it. I will tell her that you recommended I ask her since she is an artist.'

Gowda ran the idea through his mind. 'Do it tomorrow when I'm not home.'

'All right, sir,' Ratna said, getting up. If there was nothing to be done today, she would go home and do her laundry, she decided. A whole week's clothes waited in a basket.

Gajendra looked at Gowda, hesitated and then decided to speak anyway. 'Sir, I think Byrappa should accompany Ratna Madam.'

'I don't need protection,' Ratna said, sitting down again.

Gajendra shook his head. 'Byrappa is not there for protection. He will just be an extra pair of eyes and ears. The sight of a uniformed constable might force her hand into doing something which will hopefully be a lead.'

'He has a point, Ratna. Take Byrappa along. He is the best human lie detector we have,' Gowda added, not acknowledging Ratna's indignation.

When Ratna left the room, Gowda took a deep breath.

'Should we put a couple of constables on duty at your home?' Gajendra sounded worried.

'No,' Gowda said. 'She won't try much at this point. She is not a fool.'

Gajendra nodded reluctantly. He wasn't happy about it. But Gowda knew best. 'There is something I wanted to tell you before you left for the meeting, sir. Byrappa and I went back to Kalyani Bar last evening. We thought they'll see us as regulars if we go there two days in a row. I was hoping we'd find some information.'

'Are you sure that's a good idea? What if someone identifies either of you, Gajendra?' Gowda asked.

'I thought about that. So we took along Byrappa's brother.'

'How would that make a difference?'

Gajendra grinned. 'He is a minor TV star. And since it was a Saturday, the place was filled with people. So everyone wanted to meet him and take selfies with him. And amidst all the commotion, we remained unnoticed.'

'And?'

'We discovered that Papanna's men come there once in a while. And probably have something to do with the fights too.'

Gowda thought of the MLA's aides. Scrawny men whose one job was to form an entourage and little else. 'Chowrappa and the rest of them?' Gowda's voice rose in incredulity.

'No, sir... not those goobes, sir,' Gajendra responded.

Gowda smiled at the word. But he added, 'Don't dismiss the owl as a foolish bird. They are predators at night.'

'Not them, sir. What can those losers do except be Papanna's tail? The men I am referring to are those who handle the garbage trucks. They are thugs, brutes who have tossed their human side into the garbage trucks. Papanna uses them to intimidate, threaten and beat up anyone he thinks needs a dose of his treatment. Apparently, there is this Sumo Mani whose speciality is to pummel a man to death with his bare hands. Like he's been put into a sack and beaten to death. I heard that he was in a bar fight with Deal Danny and that in another fight elsewhere, he left Oil Mill Jaggi with multiple fractures,' Gajendra finished.

Something clicked in Gowda's head. The body found in the eucalyptus grove near Doddagubbi Lake. The other body extricated from an abandoned quarry three months ago. The body at Tumkur that Dr Khan had referred to. What if these men had died because of internal injuries from a fight? What was it Dr Khan had said? Bundled into a sack and beaten. Cause of death: brain haemorrhage.

He looked at his computer screen and clicked on his mailbox. There it was, the file that Dr Khan had forwarded to him. He read through it quickly and turned the desktop towards Gajendra. 'I am sending this to you. Tell me what you think.'

When Gajendra left the room, Gowda read through the report again.

How much murkier was this going to get? Gowda wondered. And to think that he had thought that this happened everywhere but Bangalore. He hoped this new piece of information would convince Additional Commissioner Mirza to give him the nod.

Gowda called in Zahir, the Station Writer, another of DCP Vidyaprasad's stooges. He could be counted on to faithfully recount everything back to his lord and master. Zahir came in bustling.

'Zahir, I want a list of missing men cases registered here in the last six months. Missing men aged between twenty to forty years,' he said.

Zahir peered at him curiously. 'That is very specific, sir,' he said after a moment.

'I am usually very specific,' Gowda snapped.

'I'll put it together,' Zahir said, wondering what was afoot. 'What is it for?'

'The CCB wants it,' Gowda replied. 'Meanwhile, send out an alert to stations in the outskirts of Bangalore to find out if there are more such cases.'

Gowda got into the police vehicle and muttered, 'Commissioner's office.' David nodded and started the vehicle. He could see something was most definitely on Gowda's mind. Once upon a time, he would have thought it was Gowda wondering when he could escape to the nearest alcohol shop to buy himself a full bottle. But that Gowda no longer existed. The man had cut down on his drinking and seemed to think of nothing else but the case on hand.

# 2

Additional Commissioner Mirza was on the phone when Gowda and Stanley entered the room. They saluted the senior officer, who gestured for them to sit. 'It's Additional Commissioner of Police and not Assistant Commissioner. Do you understand? Good. Then make sure you do not make the mistake next time you quote me in an article.'

Mirza put the receiver back in its cradle. 'Journalists! So quick to report and so lazy to fact-check,' he said in irritation. 'I've been getting flak from the department for this. Can you imagine? As if this is the most important thing on our hands...' He stopped abruptly and wiped his brow with a sparkling white handkerchief.

ACP Mirza was a handsome man who seemed to become more elegant as he aged. DCP Sagayaraj and ACP Gowda were his boys and they knew they had his ear. 'Well, so what's it you wanted to discuss with me?' Mirza asked.

Sagayaraj looked at Gowda. 'I think you should tell him.'

Gowda nodded and began. He took Mirza through his findings as well as the corroborative evidence. 'I cannot believe these illegal fights have been taking place, sir,' Gowda finished.

Mirza moved a few papers on his table as if buying time to process his thoughts. 'We could bring in Deva for questioning but that would send everyone else underground. I have heard about them but never managed to find any leads.'

Gowda snorted and quickly turned it into a little cough.

'I know, Gowda.' Mirza's tone was dry. 'Our men themselves have a hand in it. And the rich and powerful of the city are probably involved. This could have greater ramifications than you realize.'

'Are you suggesting we look away as well?' Gowda blurted out.

'Hold your horses, Gowda. Mirza Sir just asked if you know what this could lead to,' Sagayaraj stalled Gowda before he offended the senior man.

'Like what?' Gowda demanded.

'Like toppling the government,' Mirza said softly.

'In all honesty, sir, if the government is involved then it ought to be toppled,' Gowda said, refusing to back down.

'Indeed.' Mirza smiled. 'Still the same old Gowda, extreme reactions, extreme responses. I wish I lived in your world where everything is black and white and nothing in between. So what is it you want to do?'

This time, Sagayaraj answered. Mirza listened carefully and replied, 'This is going to be a very sensitive and dangerous operation. This SI Aqthar, you vouch for his ability to pull it off?'

'I do, sir,' Gowda said, trying to ignore the image of the young officer who suddenly appeared in his head wearing the wreath of the sacrificial ram.

'And my men will be there to keep an eye out for trouble,' Sagayaraj added.

'Keep me informed at every point,' Mirza said. 'And make sure that the SI is protected.'

Gajendra was waiting for Gowda when he reached the station. 'The CCB team is here, sir,' he said.

Gowda nodded. He had known Sagayaraj would waste no time. This was a whole new bunch. Natraj was the only officer from the earlier lot. Gowda saw that the team consisted solely of Stanley's trusted inner circle. Peter—or Mr India, as he was called, because of his India-shaped birthmark—Ullas and Ismail. Anytime Sagayaraj thought a case was a particularly tough one, he brought them in. Their success rate as a team was legendary, and Gowda wondered how his own officers would fare compared to them. It suddenly seemed like a race.

'We are calling it Operation King Cobra,' Gowda announced to the team after the briefing. Ratna had not been included in the team as they had not seen a role for her. Santosh had some thoughts about this but decided against voicing them when Gajendra looked at him with an imperceptible shake of his head.

'At this point, all we can do is prepare ourselves for the time that Aqthar is called for the fight. Once he knows its whereabouts for certain, everything has to work in a synchronized fashion. There cannot be a mistake. The operation is a dangerous one,' Gowda said. He paused, seeing Mr India's smug smile. 'Peter, do you find something amusing?'

'Sir, both Ullas and I are trained shooters. Danger doesn't worry us,' he said.

'Well, it should. You are up against more than revolvers,' Gowda growled. 'The battle is against real estate barons, politicians, bookies and compulsive gamblers. To many of them an illegal fight is not just about making money. There is something about the reek of blood and the cries of pain that excites them. At that point, they cease to be men and become predators on the scent of a kill. I have one of my boys putting his life up there and I don't want a cocky officer fucking it up. Trust me, Peter, you don't want that on your conscience. And nor do you want to reckon with me if something goes wrong.'

Mr India flushed. 'I understand, sir,' he said meekly.

'We'll go over each aspect of what needs to be done, so when Aqthar lets us know we can move in without missing a step,' Gowda said, rising.

Gowda tried to bring a semblance of calm within himself as he looked through his case notes. He had tried calling Urmila but she had cut his call. He didn't know if she was busy or miffed with him. He decided he didn't want to find out. Perhaps he should go home and be the family man everyone expected him to be. It was a Sunday, after all.

Gajendra cleared his throat. 'So, we are going ahead with it.' Gowda nodded.

'I have a bad feeling about this, sir,' Gajendra said.

Gowda sighed. He was apprehensive too but he wouldn't admit to it. Instead, he sought to reassure the Head Constable that everything was covered and Aqthar would be in no danger.

'If you say so, sir.' Gajendra sounded even more unconvinced.

'Do you know why I've called it Operation King Cobra and not just cobra?' Gowda asked, trying to bolster Gajendra's enthusiasm. 'The king cobra kills and eats other cobras. It's a cannibal, in human terms. And that's what an illegal fight is, Gajendra. Men using men for sport, for money... do you know that the king cobra's venom can kill a grown man in less than forty-five minutes? So what do we do if a king cobra enters our home? Do we let it live there? Are we going to offer it cobras to kill and devour? We need to coax it out. We need someone who is both capable and fearless. A mongoose. The only creature that can kill it. The mongoose is immune to the venom, you see.'

'So Aqthar Sir is to be a mongoose?' Gajendra muttered. 'And we think he will be immune to a king cobra's venom.'

Gowda didn't respond. Gajendra made both the operation name and the operation itself sound ridiculous. But he wasn't going to let the apprehensions of the Head Constable deter him.

'Tell Santosh to keep a low profile and not call Aqthar. And he shouldn't try anything on his own. That goes for all of you too,' Gowda said. Then, seeing that Gajendra needed to take his mind off the impending fight, he told him to dig up as much as he could about Papanna's garbage truckers, especially Sumo Mani.

'They are transients and keep disappearing while new ones take their place.' Gajendra shrugged.

'That's what you need to find out. Why do they disappear?' Gowda said. 'Where do they go? Are they even reported missing? Take a look at all the unidentified corpses in the last six months all over Bangalore Urban and Rural. Set aside the photographs of any whose postmortem findings match the two we already have. I have asked Zahir to pull out a list of missing men aged twenty to forty registered in our station, and to send an alert to other stations. Ask around. See if anyone remembers them and if they had anything to do with Papanna's garbage empire. You don't need me to tell you how to do it. And go to Providence Hospital and see if you can get any details, address or phone number for the African man. It's imperative we find him. Bring me something, Gajendra. It's all conjecture until then.'

# 10 DECEMBER 2012, MONDAY

## 1

Ratna looked at Byrappa. 'I'll get my bike; it's best we don't use the department vehicle.'

Byrappa nodded, looking apprehensive at the thought of riding pillion with a lady driver.

'Cheer up.' Gajendra read his mind. 'She has great road sense.'

'What will people say if they see me on a bike behind a woman?'

'Nothing at all,' Gajendra said. 'Men who let the world's opinions bother them aren't men at all. Haven't you seen me ride pillion with my daughter?'

Ratna and Byrappa climbed the staircase. It wasn't steep, nor were the steps uneven. Roshan's fall was puzzling. He was an athletic young man and could have found his balance even if he missed a step.

Ratna looked at Byrappa. 'ACP Sir was right to think there's something fishy,' she said. He nodded.

The door opened before they rang the bell. Ratna held her breath. Fortunately, she hadn't mentioned a name. Gowda had warned them that Bhuvana would be watching from the window and they ought to be careful what they speak or do. She had probably heard them. But she didn't let it show.

Ratna put on her most beatific smile. 'Hello, madam,' she chirped.

The woman gave her the hint of a smile. 'What's the problem?' she asked. She took Byrappa dressed in a white shirt over regulation khaki trousers and the brown polished shoes. 'Are you here for the passport verification? I thought it happens only after the passport is sent.'

'No, no, madam,' Ratna said. 'Gowda Sir asked us to meet you.' Ratna kept smiling.

Bhuvana opened the door wide. 'Come in,' she said.

The apartment was a replica of the house below. Except that this one was sparsely furnished with only a few pieces of brand-new furniture. 'Please sit down.' She gestured to them to take the sofa.

'I am ASI Ratna and this is Senior Constable Byrappa. We are with Neelgubbi police station,' Ratna said, sitting down. Byrappa sat on the other sofa with his hands folded on his knees.

'Yes, what can I do for you? But first, what would you like to have? Tea or coffee? Or hot badaam milk?' the woman said, about to get up.

'No, no, madam. We don't want to trouble you,' Byrappa said.

The woman threw him a smile. 'Absolutely no trouble at all. Do tell me what you prefer.'

Byrappa shook his head. 'No, madam. Gowda Sir will give us an earful if he discovers that we made you enter the kitchen. He said Bhuvana Madam is like my little sister. Don't trouble her unless it is really necessary.'

The woman blushed. 'Gowda Sir is very protective of me. We are like a family.'

Byrappa beamed. 'We heard.'

'Madam,' Ratna began again as she saw Bhuvana had let her guard down. 'As a part of our Jana-Maitri scheme, we are planning to run an art camp where artists from the neighbourhood, the people of the area and members from the police force will participate.'

Bhuvana flicked a strand of hair from her face and gazed at Ratna. 'Who would have thought that police officers can paint?'

Byrappa said, 'Precisely why ACP Gowda wants to hold this camp. We want the public to know that we are like them. And not monsters as they tell you in the movies. Ratna Madam here is an accomplished artist. You should see her work.'

Ratna swallowed hard. On a good day, her drawing of a cat looked like a bus with whiskers and a tail attached.

'Is that so?' Bhuvana smiled at her. 'I would love to see your work.'

'Ratna Madam should have gone to Chitra Kala Parishad. That's the art college in Bangalore,' Byrappa added.

'I know,' Bhuvana said.

'Where did you study art, madam? In Bangalore or...' Ratna asked.

Bhuvana shook her head. 'I am self-taught. I grew up in a small town in Tamil Nadu. There are no art schools there.'

'Is that so? But your Kannada is so good,' Byrappa said with a surprised look. Gowda had said that she didn't speak Kannada.

Bhuvana shrugged. 'I had relatives here, so I spent a lot of time here once I turned sixteen. And never really left.'

Ratna nodded as she made rapid calculations in her head.

'Is this yours, madam?' Byrappa asked, gesturing at a painting on the wall that seemed eerily familiar. 'May I take a picture?'

Bhuvana nodded. 'It's a replica of a Raja Ravi Varma painting. Sure, please do.'

Byrappa shot a picture and noticed that Bhuvana was getting restive. 'How long does it take to do a painting like this?' he asked, trying to prolong their stay.

'Days, weeks, months. Depends,' Bhuvana said, glancing at the clock on the wall pointedly. She stood up as if to end the visit and said, 'When is the art camp to be held?'

'In about ten days, madam. At the police station grounds,' Ratna said.

Bhuvana touched her middle finger to her mouth and drew her lower lip down a fraction. 'Oh, oh,' she said. 'My husband and I are planning a holiday. We will be gone for at least a couple of weeks.'

'Oh, I see,' Ratna said, her disappointment a tad exaggerated. 'Let me talk to ACP Gowda. Maybe we can reschedule it for when you return...'

'No, no, don't do that on my account,' Bhuvana said, walking to the main door.

Ratna had no option but to follow. 'We can't have the art camp without you, madam. Gowda Sir won't like it.'

'He thinks you are a great artist,' Byrappa chirped. 'By the way, madam, you mentioned a passport verification. Is it for you?'

Bhuvana nodded. 'Yes, my husband's sister lives in Malaysia. She wants us to visit them. That was the holiday I mentioned.'

'We'll make sure the verification happens as soon as we receive the intimation from the passport office,' Byrappa said. 'When you are ACP Gowda's tenant, what more do we need?'

'That's exactly what Chi...' Bhuvana began and then stopped abruptly, as though afraid that she had almost blurted something she shouldn't have. 'I told my husband that he should go on his own but my brother said not to worry and that my passport verification will come through.'

'We'll be in touch, madam,' Ratna said with a cheery wave while Bhuvana watched them leave, looking decidedly unhappy.

'If she is an artist, I am the Mysore Maharaja,' Byrappa said once they were out of the gate.

Ratna grinned. 'That was my thought too. That she is pretending to be an artist.'

'Not a trace of paint or a single brush around the house. And the house itself was like a stage set for a play,' Byrappa said. He pulled out a piece of tape. 'This was attached to the underside of the chair. I don't think the furniture is older than a couple of weeks. You can still smell the varnish on it.'

Gowda was reading a report when the two of them walked into his room. He peered at them through his reading glasses. 'How did it go?' He put the file down and gestured for them to sit.

'Something isn't kosher, sir,' Byrappa said.

'And what did you think, ASI Ratna?' Gowda noticed she looked graver than usual.

'She seemed nice, sir. Too nice, in fact. And that made me suspicious,' Ratna began. 'Like PC Byrappa said, everything seems staged, sir. She was lurking behind the curtain as you said. She was very welcoming and prattled on about how you were all like family.'

Byrappa snorted. 'With family like that you don't need enemies.'

'Have you or anyone in your family seen her paint?' Ratna asked.

Gowda thought for a moment. He hadn't, and he didn't think anyone at home had either, despite running in and out of the flat upstairs. 'No, I don't think so,' Gowda said.

'She is hiding something, sir,' Ratna said.

'One other thing, sir. She thought we were there for a passport verification. She has apparently applied for a tatkal passport and has received it,' Byrappa said.

'She mentioned it to my wife, who mentioned it to me saying that we shouldn't delay the verification,' Gowda said, crinkling his forehead. 'Do you think this is what the extra friendliness was for?'

As Byrappa and Ratna left the room, Gowda said, 'Send Zahir in.'

'I am still working on the list, sir,' Zahir said when he answered Gowda's summons.

'Make sure it reaches me by the end of the day,' Gowda said. Then he added, 'Also, a police verification request will be coming in from the passport office. A woman called Bhuvana. It's for a tatkal passport. Let me know as soon as it does.'

Zahir frowned. ACPs didn't actually check on passport verification unless... 'Relative, sir?' he asked with a barely disguised
sneer to suggest that even Gowda wasn't immune to nepotism.

Gowda met Zahir's gaze with a steely glint. 'Tenant,' he said
with a bland smile.


Mamtha was in a foul mood. All through dinner she maintained
a silence that was rife with unspoken recriminations.

Gowda wondered why it felt like the morning of board exam
results—trepidation about the unknown and if the results didn't
go well, the fear of what next?

Had Mamtha sensed Urmila's presence in his life? Had his
father or Mrs Tenant dropped hints?

Gowda chewed his mouthful of food. Urmila had suggested
he chew every mouthful thirty-two times. Apparently, it aided
digestion. At their dinner table, it was easier to chew than to
speak. Mealtimes had always been a field of landmines and this
evening seemed no different. He darted a look at Mamtha. She
was moving rice grains on her plate this way and that without
actually eating.

His father and Roshan were subdued too. What on earth
had happened, Gowda wondered as he tried to break the static
in the air by praising the food. 'Very nice mutton curry. Where
did this come from?'

Mamtha looked up from her plate. 'What do you mean by
where did this come from? It was made here in this kitchen by me.'

Gowda swallowed the retort and said in a soothing voice,
'It's excellent.'

Mamtha, to Gowda's relief, seemed mollified by the comment.

However, the beginning of a smile turned into a scowl when
Roshan said, 'Did Bhuvana give you the recipe?'

And Gowda knew exactly what the problem was. For now he
was off Mamtha's radar. But Roshan wasn't. He decided to test
out his theory. 'How are you feeling, Roshan?'

'Well enough to gad about,' Mamtha snapped. Roshan flushed and his grandfather looked up from his plate to say, 'Leave the boy alone.'

Mamtha glared at her father-in-law but didn't respond beyond clanging the ladle loudly against the steel basin of soppu saaru.

As Gowda helped Mamtha clear up, she gave him a strange look. 'Are you all right?'

'Why?' Gowda asked as he stacked up plates and glasses.

'You don't usually do this...' Mamtha said as she loaded the dishes on a steel tray.

'I do this every day.'

'You never used to. You thought it was beneath you,' Mamtha persisted.

'I was a patriarchal misogynist once,' Gowda said, parroting some of Urmila's favourite words. 'I treated women like they were subaltern creatures. I am not that man anymore.'

He swept the top of the table with a hand brush into a pail and with a flourish emptied the crumbs into the kitchen bin.

Mamtha stared at him. 'Sometimes I feel like I don't know you at all.'

'At times, I don't know myself.' Gowda sighed. And then with his customary frown, he asked, 'Is there any dessert? Or are we going to stand here discussing me?' He wanted to shut himself in a room and plan the course of action.

Anyone who tells you to leave work in the office hasn't ever done any work for real, he thought. Speaking of which, he wondered with a deep sense of dread what was happening to Aqthar. He knew he had instructed Aqthar to not call him or anyone from the team. The silence was unnerving.

Mamtha came back with a box of sweets and laid some out on a plate. Gowda stared at the Dharwad peda. 'Where did that come from?'

For a moment he wondered if it was a message, like the mafia sending fish wrapped in a newspaper—a box of peda to indicate that Aqthar was done for. Or was it a message from Aqthar? The Dharwad connection wasn't easy to ignore.

Mamtha stared at him. 'Are you okay?' she asked again, frowning at his frown.

'Where did this come from?' His voice rose as he reached for the box. 'Who gave this to you?'

'For heaven's sake, Borei, what's got into you?' Mamtha demanded in a low voice. 'If you want to know, a colleague of mine gave it to me on the morning Roshan fell. It was in my bag and I brought it with me. Do you want details of the colleague now?'

Gowda held up his hands in a gesture of apology. 'Sorry... I didn't mean to interrogate you... It's just this new case and...'

'And?' Mamtha asked.

'And one of my undercover boys is from Dharwad. So a box of Dharwad peda suddenly seemed like more than a box of sweets.' Gowda flushed.

Gowda took the plate with sweets to the living room where his father was watching a cookery show with great interest. Roshan looked tired but he was still immersed in the delights offered up by his phone. Mamtha walked in with a file and her reading glasses.

Gowda looked at the tableaux in front of him. He wondered if this was how every middle-class home in Bangalore played out their after-dinner hour. The thought was comforting and crippling.

'I am stepping out for a walk,' he said, popping a peda into his mouth. He put his cigarettes into his pocket and took his phone with him.

Mamtha grunted. The chef on screen was hacking away at a piece of meat that was most definitely beef. Gowda wondered if his father knew that. There was a beef ban in Karnataka and cow slaughter was now a punishable crime. For a moment he paused at the door, tempted to tell his father, and then realized he would be pulled into a discussion on beef-eating which to Chidananda was akin to eating one's neighbour.

Gowda had been walking for twenty minutes when his phone rang. It was Zahir. 'Sir, your tenant's passport has come for verification.'

Gowda stopped in his tracks. 'One or two?'

'Just one, sir. For the lady, Mrs Bhuvana Shashank,' Zahir mumbled as he wondered if DCP Vidyaprasad would like to know of Gowda's peculiar interest in his tenant.

'Keep it on hold until I tell you to act on it,' Gowda said.

As he continued walking, Gowda's thoughts found their way back to Aqthar and the case. Had things started moving?

# 2

Aqthar was playing cricket with his son in the living room of his house when Ditchie Babu called. The man hadn't answered his messages except to dutifully send him a 'Good Morning' GIF every day complete with kittens, butterflies and flowers in bloom. He dropped the bat to answer the phone as his son gave him an aggrieved look. Two minutes, Aqthar mimed as he walked into the bedroom to speak with the caller.

'Where are you, Mams?' Ditchie Babu's voice rang loud and clear as if he were in the next room and not 500 km away.

'Dharwad, guru, where else?' Aqthar inserted a breeziness into his tone even though his heart had begun hammering.

'We need you back in Bangalore.'

'When?'

'Right away. It's going to take place soon.'

Aqthar sensed that he was being guarded on the phone.

'Are you sure? And how soon? I can't abandon my business and come sit in Bangalore indefinitely,' Aqthar tossed back.

'It will happen very soon. Get here. The boss said that your stay and food and... anything else you need will be taken care of,' Ditchie Babu mumbled.

'All right. I'll leave early from here and call you as soon as I am at Tumkur. Then you can tell me where to go,' Aqthar said, cutting the call without waiting for a reply.

He sat on the bed, going over the conversation. He looked around his bedroom with its old wooden furniture and heavy drapes. A toy car sat on the dressing table. His son had been playing with it earlier in the day. He wondered where his wife was. She was four months pregnant. She and their son were his entire life. Nothing else mattered. What had made him say yes to Gowda's dangerous plan?

Now that it was becoming real, Aqthar felt a curious mixture of dread, apprehension and, above anything else, a deep tingle of excitement. He pulled out a backpack and began putting his things in. He wished he could take his service revolver. But it would be too dangerous. It would give away precisely who he really was.

# 3

Papanna was cavorting with two young women in a swimming pool. They were giggling and splashing water on him. The sight of their fit bodies in tiny bikinis, the perfect bow shape of their lips and the softness of their fingers made him harden. When he reached for one of them, the other woman pulled her away, laughing.

'You can't have just one; you must have the two of us or no one,' one of them whispered in his ear before splashing more water on him.

Their shrieks of laughter gave way to the incessant ringing of his mobile phone. Papanna roused himself reluctantly from his dream. It wasn't a number he recognized, but very few people had his private number so he knew it must be one of them.

'It's me,' the low, husky voice said.

'What is it now? I told you it's set up,' Papanna growled at the Peanut, who was becoming a nuisance.

'There is a passport verification I need done,' the voice said. 'Your ACP Gowda is refusing to let it move forward despite the passport reaching us.'

Papanna reached for a glass of water. His mouth was dry and he could feel a headache starting.

'What's the name on the passport?' Papanna asked.

'Bhuvana Shashank. I want it cleared first thing in the morning,' Chikka said, cutting the call.

Papanna groaned and lay back on the pillow. It wasn't even 11 p.m. He had dozed off while watching TV and there was no way he could go back to sleep now. He decided to wake up DCP Vidyaprasad and ask him to get that fucking passport verification done at daybreak if necessary and send it on its way.

Gowda's phone rang in the middle of the night. He dragged himself out of the uneasy sleep he had fallen into. He looked at the time and the caller ID and frowned. Which idiot called Rameez Mobile Services wanted to speak to him at a quarter to midnight? Suddenly, he sat up straight. 'Yes, ACP Gowda here,' he said.

'Leaving for Bangalore now,' Aqthar said and cut the call.

Gowda felt his mouth go dry. He reached for the bottle of water at his bedside and gulped some down. Then he lay back, staring at the darkened bedroom, trying to compose himself. Mamtha was fast asleep. Every third breath, she snored. A snore that hovered between a honk and a growl. She tugged at the quilt and turned on her side, taking all of it.

Gowda got up and went out of the room, taking care to make as little noise as possible.

He opened the main door and stepped onto the verandah. He shivered a little in the cold, glad he was wearing a long-sleeved T-shirt and track pants.

He lit a cigarette and watched the night.

# 11 DECEMBER 2012, TUESDAY

## 1

They had a room ready for him in Davis Lodge, attached to Davis Bar, which was a stone's throw from Kalyani Bar. It was a little past noon. Ditchie Babu would be here anytime now. Aqthar went over a mental checklist once again to see if he had taken every precaution to protect his identity. Then he remembered the most obvious thing. He took out one SIM card from his official phone and left the other SIM card in. He snapped the official SIM card in two and threw it into the wastepaper basket after wrapping it up in the bathing soap packet. He knew he was being paranoid but instinct told him to be extra careful.

His room overlooked Oil Mill Road and was diagonally across a paan shop. A tin box that had enough room for several brands of cigarettes, betel leaves arranged in a plastic tub of water and a man to sit within it. A couple of plastic stools were stacked to one side. Aqthar saw a man approach the paan shop. He loitered for a while, smoking a cigarette. Then he moved a little farther away to talk to an autorickshaw driver.

Aqthar turned around at the knock on the door. He peered out through the peephole and saw a face with a forehead like an overhanging cliff. He opened the door.

Ditchie Babu's forehead entered the room, followed by Ditchie Babu.

'You got here all right, Mams?' Ditchie Babu asked.

Aqthar tried not to flinch at the 'Mams'. No matter how often he heard it, the word jangled. He nodded.

'Is everything to your satisfaction?' Ditchie Babu gestured at the room, which had a bed, a TV, one window and a painting of a virulent sunset complete with three black squiggles flying across the sky.

Aqthar shrugged. 'It's fine. Who is that watching the place?' he asked, walking towards the window. The man in question was now eating a banana. Ditchie Babu joined him at the window. 'Are you referring to that HMT?'

Aqthar frowned. 'What?'

'Half-motte-thale, Mams,' Ditchie Babu grinned, gesturing to the man's perfect arc of a bald pate.

Aqthar thought of the HMT watch Gowda wore with such pride. He wondered how he would react to his beloved watch brand being reduced to an abbreviation for a man with a hairline that began at the back of his head. 'One of yours?'

Ditchie Babu grunted. 'You are very sharp, Mams. I didn't think you would notice him. Most of the fighters are known. You are our wild-card entry. It's best that no one sees you or knows about you. So Military posted a man to keep an eye on you.'

'Isn't this just a fight? This isn't a gang war, is it?'

Ditchie Babu ignored his questions and sat down on the metal chair that was placed next to a table with a plastic jug and a glass.

Aqthar chewed on his lip for a moment. Was Ditchie Babu making himself comfortable? Was he also here to watch him?

'It's way past noon,' he said, looking at Ditchie Babu pointedly.

'Are you hungry?' Ditchie Babu asked.

'I am and I am stepping out to get lunch,' Aqthar said, taking his wallet and bike keys.

'There's absolutely no need. Just call for food from the restaurant. So convenient, Mams. What would you like? Anything you want—chicken, mutton, beef, fish, prawn. Anything but alcohol.

The boss has said strictly no alcohol,' Ditchie Babu said, looking at a printed sheet that was the menu.

'I am beginning to think this is a mistake,' Aqthar said, his voice rising a bit.

'Why, Mams? What's the problem?'

'There is your HMT watching the lodge. There is you watching me. What's the big deal?' Aqthar demanded in a strident voice. 'And stop calling me Mams.'

Ditchie Babu poured a glass of water. 'Calm down, Mams. Here, drink some water.'

Aqthar glared at him, ignoring the glass.

'Sit down, Mams. I'll explain.' Ditchie Babu sighed.

Aqthar leaned against the window jamb. Ditchie Babu placed the glass on the table.

'A few days ago there was a big fight. Military, that's the boss, had a lot riding on a fighter called Oil Mill Jaggi. The day before the fight Military found him at the bar where we met—Kalyani Bar—drinking away. Military let it be because he thought Jaggi knew what was at stake. During the fight he started off by knocking down a well-known fighter. That was brutal. The stakes went up. Next, Oil Mill Jaggi had to fight an African man who was said to be unbeatable. And Military raised the stakes even higher. But the next opponent was Sumo Mani, who beat the shit out of him. And the fucker didn't even last two rounds. They had to take him to the hospital. Oil Mill Jaggi fucked up badly. Military lost 50 lakh rupees that night.

'So he is trying to make good on his losses with you. No one knows you or what you are capable of. The surprise element is what Military is banking on.'

Aqthar walked to the table and drank from the glass. He looked at Ditchie Babu, who was looking at him anxiously. Aqthar could see he was wondering if he had said too much. So he gave him a smile and said, 'I get it now. By the way, when do I get to meet Military?'

'He'll come by and talk to you soon,' Ditchie Babu said. 'Have you decided what you want to eat?'

Aqthar nodded as he pondered on how to open a line of communication with Gowda or someone from the team. Gowda had been very specific that he shouldn't reach out to anyone. But Ditchie Babu had just stated for a fact what had until then just been Gowda's hypothesis.

## 2

'Military will be here in an hour's time. He will talk to you, Mams,' Ditchie Babu said when lunch was done. He wanted to smoke but Aqthar refused to let him do so in the room.

'I am going to nap till he does,' Aqthar said.

Ditchie Babu looked lost at the thought of having nothing to do. 'Take a walk until Military gets here,' Aqthar suggested.

'No hanky-panky, Mams.' Ditchie Babu wagged a finger in Aqthar's face.

Aqthar shut the door in his face with a gentle thud. He waited, looking through the peephole to see if Ditchie Babu had left. He saw him shuffle his feet, uncertain about what to do, and then walk away.

Aqthar opened a plastic bag that he had stuffed deep into his backpack and pulled out a digital spy camera. Aqthar examined the little wooden barrel with a key ring attached. No one would think of it as anything but a fancy keychain.

Aqthar slung his bike key onto the chain and wondered where to place it to capture the meeting with Military. Three hours video and three hours battery life, his cousin Jalil had said when he had given it to him a year ago.

When he heard a knock on the door, Aqthar was ready. He took a deep breath and walked towards it. He looked through the

peephole and gazed into an eye that was peering in. Aqthar kept
his eye fixed on the eye on the other side and opened the door
abruptly. Ditchie Babu hurled forward. Aqthar held him to break
his fall, and put an arm around him as he led him inside. 'Are you
all right?' Aqthar asked at his solicitous best.

'He will be fine,' someone said from behind.

Aqthar looked past Ditchie Babu. A burly, middle-aged man
with short hair, wearing a khaki T-shirt and military fatigues,
came towards Aqthar, his combat boots squeaking with every
step. 'You must be Aqthar,' he said in a deep voice.

'And you must be Military,' Aqthar retorted. He recognized
the man from Shenoy's sketch but didn't let it light up his eyes.
Instead, he gestured for him to sit.

Military turned to Ditchie Babu and gestured for him to
leave. When he heard the door slam shut, he turned to Aqthar.
'All comfortable here?' he asked.

Aqthar shrugged. 'I've seen better and I've seen worse.'
Military scanned the room as if checking for a potential threat.
His eyes took in the half-open backpack with clothes streaming
out of it, the balled-up socks on the floor, the empty bottle of
water lying on its side and the betel chew packet near a pillow.

Aqthar gazed at him blandly. He had mussed up the room so
nothing would stick out.

Satisfied, Military plonked himself on the lone chair by the
window. Outside, the skies had begun darkening and the traffic
sounds had grown with the peak hour fast approaching. Aqthar
turned on a couple more lights.

Military asked, 'Any apprehensions?'

Aqthar shrugged. 'I would be lying if I said no.'

Military allowed a smile on his face. 'Good. A man who isn't
afraid is an idiot, but one who is afraid and yet prepared to do
what is required of him is a courageous one.'

Aqthar recognized the tired line from a WhatsApp forward.
But he pretended to admire the sentiment as if hearing it for

the first time. 'True,' he said, sitting down on the bed. 'Tell me about the fight.'

Military looked at him. 'What do you want to know?'

'Everything,' Aqthar said. 'It helps with the mental preparation.'

Military made a dismissive gesture. 'There's nothing to it. You fight till you are knocked down or you knock out the other fellow. You get paid either way. This isn't a championship. So don't worry too much about winning and losing. But if you get past the first round you get a bonus. Make sure you survive the first round. That is where the game will change.'

Aqthar asked, 'So you can raise the stakes on me? Am I expected to win or lose the second round?'

'Let's see if you are on your feet after the first round. Better fighters have kissed the ground. So don't get too cocky. What kind of supplements are you taking?'

'I don't need to. I eat well and exercise well. That should suffice.'

Military frowned at him. 'This isn't a scuffle between two people. There is a lot of money on the table. You need some chemical support.'

'Like what?' Aqthar demanded.

'I'll give you a shot to boost your strength. When you are in the ring I want you to be a raging bull. It doesn't matter if you kick, punch, throw, laugh, cry or bleed but I want you on your feet.'

'For the first round?'

'Yes, that's critical.' Military opened his backpack. He pulled out a vial from a cooler bag and loaded a syringe.

'Lie down on the bed and pull down your pants. This shot has to be given on the buttocks.' Military dropped the vial into the dustbin.

'What is it?' Aqthar asked, suddenly petrified.

'Just steroids to increase your strength,' Military said, loading another syringe.

'Who is the second one for?' Aqthar asked as he lay on his stomach with his T-shirt pulled up and his track pants pulled down to expose the muscle.

'I'm giving you a double dose. Drink lots of water. Eat well. And Ditchie will take you to a gym where you can work out,' Military said as he pressed one needle down into the left buttock and then the other into the right. He gave the two spots a brisk rub. 'This is so the medicine doesn't coagulate there,' he said, walking to the bathroom to wash his hands. 'I'll be in tomorrow. Do as Ditchie asks. And remember, it's just the first round you need to survive.'

When Military left, Aqthar went to where his bike key was slung on the corner of the painting. He took it down and turned the spy camera off. Military hadn't even given it a second glance.

He was going to buy his cousin Jalil a big plate of mutton biriyani and kebabs when he saw him next. And then it occurred to him that he had failed to pack the camera's charger.

# 12 DECEMBER 2012, WEDNESDAY

## 1

Gowda got up and stared into a corner of the room. When his phone on the bedside table gave a muted ping, he looked at it and realized that was what had woken him up. It was half past one in the morning. He unlocked the phone and saw a WhatsApp message from a number he didn't recognize. Check mail, it said. The message also contained a photograph, a still shot from a video. It showed a man loading a syringe. The light was on his face and Gowda didn't need to look twice to identify him.

He got off the bed and picked up his laptop. He crept softly on the balls of his feet to the living room. After putting the table lamp on he sat in his armchair. His mailbox took a while to open. Gowda felt a frown gather on his brow. He had let Roshan use his laptop and the boy had probably crammed the hard disk with rubbish.

Aqthar had sent him a video. He had also sent him a requisition for a charger for the spycam. He had sent the specs of the spycam as well. He said he would be in touch on how it could be sent to him.

It was all falling into place now. Deva, aka Military, was organizing the illegal fights. And probably using the cottage basement on Professor Mudgood's property to stage it. He remembered the cement posts in the adjoining plot that seemed to have been moved. That could be the access point. Which meant Papanna was part of it too. The land belonged to him, after all.

Had he seen the Professor lurking in the backyard and worried about being found out? Was that why the murder had taken place? Was there nothing else to the homicide? A man murdered because someone thought he had witnessed something?

Gowda paced up and down. It all seemed so clear now, but on him lay the burden of providing the proof, for which he had to let Aqthar go ahead with the fight. There could arise an opportunity to nab all the culprits together. He realized that he was putting Aqthar in grave danger but what else could he do? It was what he would have done himself. He looked at his laptop and moved the cursor to reply. 'Call Ratna,' he typed quickly and sent it off. He went back to bed and lay down. The previous day had been spent at the courts for an eight-year-old extortion case hearing. He had been grateful that it occupied his mind as he waited for Aqthar to make contact.

Everyone on his team was on tenterhooks after the first midnight call. In fact, Gajendra had followed him to his smoking spot last evening. Gowda had told him, 'So it's happening soon.' Saying the words out loud made the situation seem real. Gajendra had nodded and looked away. For once, even he seemed lost for platitudes.

He wondered at how they would respond when he shared the video with them. Gowda turned to his side and tried to summon sleep. It was just a quarter past two in the morning. There was nothing for him to do at this point.

## 2

The SIT room was bursting at its seams, with the presence of four officers from the CCB as well as Gowda's team. Like two

PT masters corralling their individual school teams at a football match, Gowda and Sagayaraj sat at the head of the table.

None of them were saying much. The image that Gowda shared with them had left them stunned. It suddenly felt all too real. One of their own was on undercover duty and the number of variables involved meant they had little control over how the situation would turn out.

'What do you think? Should we just haul in Deva and start interrogating him?' Gowda asked, turning to his senior officer. 'We have just about enough grounds to do so...'

Sagayaraj didn't answer immediately. 'No, not yet. Let's see if Aqthar can reach ASI Ratna or one of us. If he doesn't by this evening, then we'll do just that.'

Mr India touched his India-shaped birthmark and ran his finger along its edge. He had been gazing thoughtfully at an enlarged image on his phone screen. 'I know this place,' he said. 'See this.' He pointed to a reflection on the TV screen in the photograph.

'Do you see that?' His impatience at their inability to see what was obvious to him made him rise from his seat.

Santosh saw it first. 'I can but I don't recognize it,' he said, cocking his head.

'That's because you don't know that road as I do,' Mr India said with a cocky grin.

Gajendra gritted his teeth but in his most affable voice asked, 'And that would be?'

'Oil Mill Road,' Mr India and Byrappa said in unison.

'The reflection is of the Vinayaka Temple. It has a very tall gopuram,' Mr India hastened to add. Just then, Ratna's phone rang. She looked at the unknown number. She was about to cut the call when Gowda bellowed, 'Take it.'

A voice said, 'Sahiba, this is your Aqthar. I am in Bangalore.'

Ratna felt her jaw drop. Why on earth was Aqthar talking to her as if they had a thing going on? She swallowed. Then it struck her that he was touching base with her, as Gowda had said he would. And that he was being watched. Maybe even being listened to. 'Put it on speaker,' Sagayaraj murmured.

Ratna did as asked, taking a deep breath and dredging up her thickest Tannery Road Urdu. 'When did you get here, jee?' She lapsed into a tirade about husbands who had no loyalty, about school fees and new shoes.

'That was Aqthar,' Ratna said when she hung up, even though everyone in the room had heard the conversation.

'He was pretending that I'm his wife...' Ratna continued, still bemused.

Gowda drummed his fingers on the table. 'That means someone was there in the room with him.'

'I thought as much, sir,' Ratna said.

Aqthar looked at Ditchie Babu, who had said that any call he made would have to be with the speaker on. Satisfied? Aqthar's gaze demanded. He had said that he had to call his second wife. Ditchie Babu had looked at him suspiciously. 'You have two wives?'

'Actually, I have three. And I keep all three of them happy,' Aqthar said with a breeziness that made Ditchie Babu envious. How did a man have the energy for three wives? Life with just one wife was a struggle.

'You heard her, right. Look, I forgot to tell her something. I am calling her again. Do you still want to listen in?' Aqthar asked, throwing Ditchie Babu a smile.

'No, Mams. You can do your kitchie-cooing on your own,' Ditchie Babu said, lying on the bed with his hands propping up his head.

Aqthar held the phone to his ear. 'Listen, my sahiba, about the money you asked for...' he began. 'Can you come meet me? No... I can't come home this time. Davis Lodge. Room 5. Oil Mill Road.

Do you know where that is? Why do you have to bring Sulaiman? Ah, all right... By five in the evening. I am busy after that.'

Ditchie Babu sat up, agitated by what he had heard. 'Mams, why have you invited your wife here? Military won't like it.'

'She needs money. And I need to see her. A man misses his wife.'

'Which one?' Ditchie Babu sniggered.

Aqthar ignored him and continued, 'Her brother will bring her here. Just fifteen minutes. Nothing for you to report to Military.'

Ditchie Babu's forehead crinkled. The sight was as alarming as it was magnificent. Aqthar paused.

'No ding-dong business,' Ditchie Babu muttered, his forehead going back to being a craggy cliff. 'No drinking or sex. I explained it to you, Mams.'

'I got it, guru. I just need to give her money. I don't want her landing up on my doorstep in Dharwad,' Aqthar said in his most earnest man-to-man voice. 'Also, can you advance me 10,000 rupees? I need to give it to her... it's not even half of what is due to me.'

Ditchie Babu scratched his chin. He wasn't sure if Military would agree. But he knew enough people to raise half of it in the next hour. He didn't want to upset Mams before a fight. Military had promised him a bonus as well if Mams survived the first round. After all, Ditchie Babu had found Mams. 'I can arrange 5,000 right away. You will have to wait for the rest. I'll be back soon,' he said, rising from the bed.

Ratna put her phone down and looked at Gowda. 'So I am to meet him at 5 p.m. and I am to be accompanied by my brother Sulaiman,' Ratna said. 'Who do you think is Sulaiman?'

It was Gajendra who replied, 'Byrappa's brother plays an auto driver called Sulaiman in some TV serial. Aqthar wanted you to take Byrappa along.'

*

When the meeting came to an end, Ratna followed Gowda into his room.

'What is it, Ratna?' Gowda asked, unable to hide his impatience. Ratna seemed tense. 'ASI Ratna, what's the problem?'

Ratna swallowed the angry retort and muttered, 'Sir, I think it's unfair that you haven't let me in on what's going on... I mean, I don't even know what Aqthar is up to or who I am meant to be. His wife, his mistress, his whatever...' Ratna was unable to contain her ire any longer.

Gowda flushed. He held up his palms in a gesture of contrition. 'The CCB has stepped in and they told us to share information only on a need-to-know basis. Since you couldn't be actively involved in this case, it just so happened that there are some developments that I was unable to share with you.'

Ratna frowned. 'And now I am part of it?'

Gowda smiled. 'Now you are, and working undercover too. And what you are going to do is as dangerous as it is important. Listen carefully.'

When Gowda finished explaining what had been decided by the CCB team and his own, he saw Ratna's face become a picture of worry. 'But, sir, this is really dangerous. SI Aqthar is putting his life on the line.'

'I know. We need to ensure he isn't harmed. Right now you are the conduit. And you are all we have,' Gowda said. 'And I know for a fact we can count on you.'

Ratna offered him a smile of gratitude. Gowda didn't often offer praise, and when he did it felt like New Year, Dussehra and a birthday rolled into one. 'What should I do?'

Gowda detailed what she and Byrappa would need to do. 'Don't worry. I'll have the CCB fellows in mufti at the street corner. If you have the slightest hint of danger, leave the place immediately. Don't go poking your nose into anything. I don't want them to have even a whisker of a doubt,' Gowda added. 'They won't spare Aqthar if they get suspicious.'

Ratna nodded. Then she cleared her throat. A knock made her look up. Gajendra stood in the doorway.

'Join us, Gajendra,' Gowda said, knowing what he was going to say would upset Gajendra even further.

'Oh,' Gajendra exclaimed.

'I'm going to ask the CCB to put two men there. That way Ratna and Byrappa will be covered. And Aqthar.'

'What about SI Santosh, sir?'

Gowda interrupted Gajendra. 'I need him to pull out whatever information he can on Deva. Though I have begun thinking of him as Military now.' Gowda shook his head. 'I need him to speed up the tracking in Mangalore. We need to know for sure if Deva was actually there on the days of the homicide as he claims. We should have checked on it long ago. The newspapers are not too wrong. We are a bunch of inept idiots. Eleven days since the homicide was discovered and we are still nowhere close to knowing who actually killed the Professor.'

Gowda spent yet another long and dull afternoon at Mayo Hall. The case went back five years. A land deal was used to trap a corrupt revenue inspector whose family had then attacked one of the witnesses. The man had died at the hospital.

Gowda had been the Investigating Officer but could barely remember the face of the deceased. But here he was, testifying to what had happened. Fortunately, the case files and the public prosecutor had helped him remember the details and Gowda hoped there wouldn't be another hearing. Sometimes the judiciary made justice seem like a tin of rasgullas long past its expiry date.

The courthouse clock said it was almost 4 p.m. He wasn't sure how long he would have to wait. There was nothing he could do at this point. The CCB officers were to come into the station at 3 p.m. They hadn't been able to source a charger as specified by Aqthar. Instead they intended to send with Ratna a better quality of spycam. They would show Ratna how to use it and in turn, she would have to instruct Aqthar. He knew the two of them were efficient police officers and didn't need handholding. Nevertheless, Gowda wished he was there as well.

# 3

The man at what passed for the reception desk was startled to see a woman in a burkha climb the few steps up to the lobby. Behind her was a young man in a kurta pyjama. He had a clean-shaven face and kohl in his eyes. A plastic shopping bag hung from his hand.

'Room 5,' the man said, walking towards the counter.

The clerk looked at him and said, 'Wait here.'

He picked up his phone and ran his finger over the touchscreen to make a call. 'There is a man and a woman here to see your guest.'

The clerk took the phone away from his ear to ask, 'What's your name?'

'Sulaiman,' Byrappa said. 'And that's Raiza.' He pointed to Ratna, who immediately dropped the flap of the burkha over her face as if intimidated by the clerk's scrutiny.

'You can go up. Climb to the second floor. It's the last room on the right.'

Byrappa and Ratna went up the staircase. At the top of the stairs on the second floor was Ditchie Babu lurking behind his impressive forehead. Byrappa thought of the Avalibetta clifftop. If they ever barred entry to that place, Ditchie Babu could rent out his forehead to the twenty-something idiots who perched on the cliff's edge for selfies.

'You can wait downstairs,' Ditchie Babu growled at Byrappa.

'I'm not going to leave my sister alone here,' Byrappa growled back. 'No way.'

'Uncover her face,' Ditchie Babu said, unfazed.

'Are you mad? Aqthar Bhai will separate you limb by limb if he knows you asked to see his wife's face,' Byrappa snarled, taking a step forward.

Ditchie Babu scratched his chin for a moment. 'Come along,' he said slowly.

They followed him down the corridor. He paused near the door before knocking. When Aqthar opened it, Ditchie Babu said, 'You can show your man your face, can't you?'

Ratna moved towards the door and raised the face flap of the burkha.

Aqthar's grin assuaged Ditchie Babu's suspicion. 'And this is her brother?'

Aqthar nodded. He let the two of them in and closed the door in Ditchie Babu's face. Byrappa walked towards the table where the TV remote was. He put the TV on. A Kannada soap was playing and it had enough dramatic music and shrieking to muffle their voices.

Ratna took off the burkha. 'Are you all right, sir?' she asked.

Aqthar quickly explained what was happening. Ratna opened her bag and pulled out the spy camera and a couple of memory cards. 'We couldn't find the charger so the CCB sent a new device with extra memory cards. You need to use it if Military comes in again,' she said, giving him a quick tutorial. 'Or anytime you think something can be presented as evidence. The CCB men are at the end of the road. Just so you know.'

Byrappa was watching the road from the window. He saw Ditchie Babu go down towards where he had parked the autorick-shaw and give it a quick dekko. 'We should go,' he said. 'Or at least I should.'

Byrappa left the room and ran downstairs. He sauntered towards where Ditchie Babu was examining the vehicle. 'If you like it so much, why don't you buy it?' Byrappa said with a loud laugh.

Ditchie Babu turned, surprised to see him. 'What are you doing here? Where is your sister?'

'A man and his woman need some privacy, don't you agree? She will be here soon,' Byrappa said, putting on an embarrassed expression.

As soon as he said that, a burkha-clad apparition descended the steps to the road. The woman's stride was quite unlike her mincing gait when she went up. Ditchie Babu frowned. Was someone else hiding under the burkha? Before Byrappa could get into the autorickshaw and start it, Ditchie Babu raced upstairs. He knocked on the door loudly.

Aqthar opened it with a puzzled expression. 'What's wrong?'

The eyes beneath the forehead suddenly turned placid. Aqthar thought of a charging rhino that abruptly stopped in its tracks and turned into a benign being raising its head to a cloud of yellow butterflies.

'Nothing, nothing,' Ditchie Babu said.

'Did you think I escaped wearing a burkha?' Aqthar teased.

'No, no... nothing like that, Mams,' Ditchie Babu said, sheepish at being caught out.

'I came here of my own free will. Why would I run away?' Aqthar said, walking towards the window. HMT had returned. He wore a shiny grey windcheater as if in preparation for the cold that would creep in as the sun disappeared.

# 13 DECEMBER 2012, THURSDAY

## 1

They were gathered in the SIT room once again. The memory card brought back by Ratna was inserted into the laptop. The video was a little grainy and the sound low but there it was—the conversation between Deva and Aqthar and the injecting of steroids. It was evidence enough. Both Gowda and Sagayaraj had the same thought at the same time. They could start building the case right away but that would mean they would stop only this fight, not the next one, or the one after that. Deva was the key but he wasn't the kingpin. Only a raid at an actual fight would reveal who was actually in attendance, and the stakes involved.

Gowda asked, 'How do we go about this?'

Sagayaraj said, 'We'll take it from here, Gowda. We'll run the surveillance and when Aqthar is taken to the site we'll be close behind. We'll move in as soon as the fight begins. Don't worry. We will take good care of him.'

Gowda nodded. 'I understand, sir.'

Santosh was shocked at his meek acceptance. Gajendra was staring at the wall opposite as if it held the secrets of the universe.

Chikka walked into the ladies' room, his heart beating faster than ever.

He wore a white A-line tunic and grey and white striped pants. His hair was a shoulder-length wig and his make-up was subtle. Over the years Chikka had learnt that over-the-top make-up was a dead giveaway. So none of that blue eyeshadow and mauve lipstick.

The attendant gave him a smile and ignored him thereafter. He went into a stall. For a moment he almost put the toilet seat up. Then he pulled down his pants and panties and sat down. He would pee like a woman. He would soon be one.

Soft, tinkly music played as he washed his hands. The attendant offered him a towel. He smiled at her as he took it. He opened his bag and pulled out a lipstick. He ran the almost-nude pink shade on his lips. He made a moue as he watched himself in the mirror. The attendant was tidying the toilet stall. Chikka looked into his bag again. The passport in there was his vehicle to freedom. Once he returned from Thailand, Chikka would cease to exist. And there would only be Bhuvana.

'You are looking very nice, madam,' the attendant said from behind him. Chikka smiled at her in the mirror. He gave her a 500-rupee note. She stared at him in disbelief. 'Today is my birthday.'

The woman beamed and said, 'Happy birthday, madam!'

Chikka tossed his hair over his shoulder, slung his Gucci bag from the curve of his elbow and walked towards the bar. Like most five-star hotel bars, this one too was shadowy and softly lit. It was exactly the kind of respite that Chikka needed after the bright lights of the ladies' room. He found a sofa that wasn't too far from the bar counter. A steward appeared almost instantly. Chikka threw him a smile, 'I am waiting for a friend. Would you in the meantime get me a watermelon juice?'

Chikka had been planning this for several months now. He needed a passport to leave the country. His family owed him a great deal and despite what was said about him, none of them believed it. So his cousin in Vellore, Anu, who resembled him distinctly and another second cousin who had a job in Bangalore had been summoned to play husband and wife and then he had looked for a house near Gowda's house. When the real estate agent had said Gowda was looking for a tenant, Chikka had said he would take the upstairs flat no matter what the rent was. Chikka had felt a grim sense of satisfaction. He would use the man who had ruined him to help him escape forever.

His cousins did what he had asked of them. 'Distract him, keep him busy with problems, even if it's a tatkal passport, he can stall the police verification from going through.' Once he left, they had to disappear too, he had said.

'Don't think about taking up a job for a while. As promised, I will have the money reach Vellore. All cash, so be careful with it,' he had added as he had packed his suitcase.

Gowda's bike had been parked outside. Chikka looked at it for a long while. Fuck you Gowda, he muttered and went towards the waiting cab.

Chikka watched Papanna saunter into the bar. He glanced at the slim ladies' watch he wore. It was just past three in the afternoon. The man was late by half an hour. But Chikka had known he would do exactly that. He took another sip of his watermelon juice. Then he raised his head. He saw Papanna's eyes pause at his face briefly and move on.

He raised his hand and held up two fingers to say, here I am. He saw Papanna look his way, puzzled. Chikka spoke in a loud whisper, 'Papanna...'

The woman seemed vaguely familiar to Papanna. But it was the voice that told him who she was. He hurried towards her, unable to hide his astonishment. The Peanut actually passed for a proper woman, and an attractive one at that. He wondered what it would be like to fuck a man dressed like a woman. He sat on the sofa. 'Chikka, you have some nerve appearing in public like this,' he said.

Chikka held his gaze. 'I've told you never to call me Chikka.'

Papanna flushed. To his relief, a steward appeared at his elbow. 'I'll have a Black Dog,' he barked at him in Kannada.

Chikka raised his eyes to the steward and said, 'A large Black Dog for the gentleman and another watermelon juice for me with 30 ml Smirnoff on the side. Thank you.'

The steward smiled gratefully, wondering at the strange duo. The beauty and the beast, he thought as he walked away.

'You speak English very well. Like my son Sagar. So why here?' Papanna asked. 'And what's so important that you demanded I come immediately?'

Chikka pushed a wing of hair away from his face. 'I am staying here.'

'Here. Like this?' The Cheeslings that Papanna had stuffed his mouth with erupted in small crumbs from his lips. He had heard that Chikka was a strange creature. Everything he had seen until now just confirmed it.

Chikka handed him a tissue and said, 'Clean up. You are disgusting. And what is so shocking about me staying at Windsor Manor. I have always wanted to, ever since we moved to Bangalore as children. I thought why wait any longer. My brother and I used to collect garbage from a block of flats on Palace Road. That was in the late eighties. I was six years old then. Where were you then, Papanna? Whose ass were you licking then?'

Papanna wanted to crush the Peanut under his feet. But he didn't know what it was Chikka had on him. Until then he would need to rein in his fury. He took a big gulp of his Black Dog, which had just appeared before him.

'I wanted to meet you here because there is a change of plan. I am catching a flight to Thailand on Saturday. I need the money latest by tomorrow. Not Sunday.'

Papanna looked at him in shock. 'It's a lot of money... Chik... Ram...' he blustered, not knowing how to address this creature who seemed oblivious to anything but himself.

'I know it's a lot of money, which is why I'm giving you twenty-four hours' notice.' Chikka delivered this line and rose to his feet. 'Pay the bill, Papanna.' He sashayed towards the door.

Papanna continued to sit there for a few minutes. Then he gestured for the bill. While he waited for it, he picked up his phone.

'We need to advance the fight, Deva. Everything stays the same except the date.'

# 14 DECEMBER 2012, FRIDAY

## 1

Gowda looked like he wanted to smash a few things. David wondered what had happened. Gowda had been in a good mood when they set out for DCP Vidyaprasad's office. He had even asked David about his children, which surprised the constable. He didn't know that Gowda was even aware he had children.

But something seemed to have upset him during his meeting with Vidyaprasad. The usual devilish glee he wore after raising the DCP's hackles was missing. In fact, he was furious. And David knew better than to speak to Gowda when he was upset.

Gowda gave everyone a curt nod as he walked into the station. David parked the vehicle and went to find Gajendra. He had just got around to telling Gajendra to be wary of Gowda when he saw Zahir go into his room. Gowda was in a rage, judging by what David could hear. It was something to do with a passport.

Zahir's reply was muted but David heard some of what he said. 'I am helpless, sir. What could I do when DCP Vidyaprasad demanded that the passport verification be done immediately?'

David wondered why Gajendra suddenly looked so worried. How could a passport verification cause such uneasiness?

*

It was a quarter to seven in the evening when someone knocked on the door. Ditchie Babu opened it. The person standing there was not who he had expected. 'I thought it was Saturday,' he said.

'Change of plan!' the man said loudly.

'Since when?' Ditchie Babu demanded. 'Military didn't tell me anything.'

The man offered his phone to Ditchie Babu. 'Here, call him and ask him yourself.' He gestured to someone standing a little further away to join him.

Ditchie Babu ignored the phone and went to sit on the chair by the window. From within the bathroom, he could hear sounds of water splashing on the floor. This was Aqthar's fourth bath since the morning. Was he a man or a frog?

'Mams, how long will you take?' Ditchie Babu hollered even though he had heard the tap being turned off.

A few minutes later, Aqthar opened the bathroom door and stepped out. He was in track pants and a T-shirt. He had shaved and his skin gleamed as if he had rubbed a pumice stone over it. The sandals he wore made him look like he was stepping out to pick up some milk rather than preparing to pulp an opponent in a fighting ring. He stared at the strangers in the room. 'Who are these people?'

'This is Satisha and his friend Swami,' Ditchie Babu said. 'Mams, there is a change of plan. The fight is tonight.'

Aqthar felt his heart sink. He hoped the CCB officers were keeping a close watch. He maintained an outward calm. 'All right,' he said. 'The sooner the better,' he added for effect. 'But I thought you said it was to be on Saturday. What happened?'

Satisha shrugged. 'Ask Military when you see him. His boss is the one who decides.'

'Military has a boss? I thought he is the boss,' Aqthar said, sitting on the bed and switching on the TV. He saw the two strangers exchange a glance. He ignored them and continued, 'When I saw him last afternoon, he didn't mention anything.

He talked as if it was to be on Saturday. Now you tell me that he is not the one who decides. Who is this boss?'

'What do we know? Military is our boss. We do as he says. We don't know who he reports to.' Satisha reached beneath the chair and brought out a plastic bag.

'Look,' he said, holding the bag out. Inside it was a full bottle of Hercules XXX rum. 'Ditchie, call for some side dishes,' he said with a grin. 'And four glasses and water. Mams, how do you want yours? With water or soda?'

'With Pepsi,' Aqthar said, keeping his gaze on the TV screen. He didn't drink, but he didn't want to cause even the slightest suspicion. 'Tell me something.' He cocked his head. 'Ditchie Babu forbade me from drinking. You two want me to drink. What's the deal?'

Satisha paused as he poured a drink. 'We thought you might need some courage.'

Swami lit a cigarette. Ditchie frowned. 'Open a window,' he said. 'Mams doesn't like cigarette smoke.'

Aqthar looked at Ditchie Babu, who kept pacing the room.

Ditchie Babu turned to Aqthar and said with a nervous smile, 'The fight is today, Mams. You heard that, didn't you?'

Aqthar smiled as if to say, I know, but how does it matter. He watched Satisha measuring out a mega pint of rum. Who was that for? 'Where is the fight going to take place?' he asked.

Swami blew out smoke and narrowed his eyes. But it was Satisha who spoke. 'How does it matter? We'll take you there.'

Aqthar held up his palms, a gesture of resignation to say, screw you too.

There was a knock on the door. Ditchie opened it and a steward in an ill-fitting uniform and scuffed shoes came in holding a tray of dishes covered with paper napkins. He placed it on the table and stood there expectantly.

'Are you serious?' Satisha growled. 'You expect me to tip you to do your job. Don't stand there like a scarecrow. Pour our drinks and serve the food.'

The steward, without a change of expression, measured out Pepsi into glasses. Aqthar held his hand up. 'Get me a fresh glass. I want just Pepsi.'

'You don't want a drink?' Swami, who hadn't spoken a word until then, burst out, astounded, as if he had been told that Aqthar had a pair of wings. The improbability of such an occurrence made his voice a loud whisper.

'No,' Aqthar said. If he had been a drinking man, he would have downed a few to bolster his courage—he feared it would desert him any moment as the hour of the fight drew closer.

Satisha clicked his fingers, gesturing for the steward to leave.

'When the fight is over, I'll have a full bottle,' Aqthar said, reaching for a kebab that glistened with spice, oil and food colouring.

'When the fight is over, you may not even be able to sit up,' Satisha guffawed. 'We'll have to fit a nipple on the bottle's mouth for you to drink from.'

Aqthar jumped to his feet and raised his fist.

'Mams, Mams, calm down.' Ditchie Babu burst in between the men. 'Don't take him seriously. He is just trying to rile you.'

Aqthar took his glass and drained it clean in one gulp. When Satisha opened his mouth to speak, Ditchie Babu nudged him. 'Don't irritate Mams. Military will flay the skin off your back. That is if there is anything left of you after Mams is done with you.'

Satisha cocked an eyebrow. 'Really?'

'He's been having the injections. Double dose for three days now. He is like an angry bull. You don't want to wave a red rag under his nose,' Ditchie added under his breath.

For a while there was silence as the men drank and ate. An hour later, they stood up. Aqthar began putting his phone, wallet and keys into various pockets of his trackpants.

'You don't need to carry those things,' Ditchie Babu said.

'I do,' Aqthar snapped. 'I'm not going to leave my bike keys or wallet here. Did you see that waiter? He looks like he will steal even your underwear.'

Satisha laughed and stood up. 'I will wait downstairs,' he said. His friend joined him.

'Where is this place?' Aqthar asked Ditchie Babu as he stuffed his things into his bag.

Ditchie shrugged. 'It's some distance from here.'

'Does it have a name?'

'I think it is somewhere beyond Devanahalli. All I know is it's the basement of a house,' he said.

Aqthar sensed his evasiveness and knew he wouldn't reveal anything. 'Give me a moment,' he said.

He walked into the bathroom and cross-checked the spy camera. He wasn't going to switch it on till he got there. He wouldn't waste the battery on the journey.

He squeezed toothpaste out of a tube and wrote on the rear of the door: COTTAG. There wasn't enough to write an E but he managed to smudge the toothpaste into a proximation of the letter.

Satisha was waiting by a bike. 'Let's go,' he said, handing over a helmet to Aqthar.

'All three of us on a bike?' Aqthar demanded.

'Ditchie and Swami will follow on his bike,' Satisha said, mounting his 100 cc Pulsar.

'That way if there is any trouble we have a second bike,' Ditchie said, putting his helmet on. Swami climbed on behind him. Aqthar hoped the surveillance team were doing what they were supposed to.

# 2

The police jeep was parked in a side lane. Gowda sat in a coffee shop on Nehru Road. Gajendra and Santosh sat across from him, watching Gowda light one cigarette after the other only to stub each one out. Gowda had said they needed to be near Oil Mill Road.

'But the fight's tomorrow.' Santosh hadn't understood the urgency.

'What if they decide to have it today or the day after? We just need to be prepared,' Gowda had said earlier. 'We can't afford to be complacent. So unless you have something more important to do...'

Santosh had followed Gowda quietly and joined Gajendra in the back seat.

Santosh looked around the coffee shop with interest. He was no longer the young man who had been intimidated by the sophistication of a posh coffee shop or shocked at its prices. He knew how to deal with condescending baristas and supercilious stewards. Once this case was filed, he was going to ask Ratna out for coffee.

Gowda took out yet another cigarette and tapped it on the tabletop. Nehru Road hummed with evening traffic. The coffee shop was filled with young men and women, armed with their laptops and notebooks. They sat huddled, drinking coffee and spitting out words with an American twang. When did coffee shops become work spaces? Where did boys and girls go on dates these days?

Soon, the table next to his in the smoking area emptied. Gowda called up Sagayaraj. 'Any updates?'

He heard the sharp intake of breath at the other end. 'How did you know the fight would probably happen tonight?'

Gowda merely grunted. He hadn't known for sure, but something had told him to be on high alert.

'They left about twenty minutes ago. My team is following them. You can relax, Gowda. We are handling this,' Sagayaraj said.

'I know that, sir. But Aqthar is my boy. It worries me.' Gowda stirred his spoon in the nearly empty cup of coffee. He had a distinctly bad feeling about this.

When he was done with the call, Gowda placed the phone alongside the coffee mug and gestured for Santosh to join him. 'Apparently they left twenty minutes ago. The CCB team is following them.'

'What do we do now?' Santosh asked, his annoyance at being relegated to the sidelines evident.

'Chill,' Gowda said. 'Where's Byrappa?'

'He's taking a stroll. Or that's what he claimed,' Gajendra said as he joined them.

Gowda picked up his phone to call Byrappa. 'I want you to go back to Davis Lodge. Tell the reception clerk you need to leave something important for your brother-in-law. And then see if he has left us a message.'

When an autorickshaw screeched to a halt outside the lodge, the receptionist looked up. He saw a man jump off the driver's seat and stride into the lobby. 'Room 5. Aqthar. Has he left already?' he demanded.

The clerk frowned. 'Who's asking?'

'I am Sulaiman. Don't you remember me? I came here two evenings ago. Aqthar Bhai's wife is my sister. She was wearing a burkha,' Byrappa said with an earnestness that was hard to ignore. The clerk stared at the spruced-up Byrappa, who looked nothing like the auto driver who had kohl-lined eyes and mawa in his mouth.

'Remember me?' Byrappa lapsed into Tannery Road speak.

The man nodded. 'They left some time ago. You can leave whatever it is you want here.'

Byrappa shook his head. 'I have to pick something up from him. It's a dress for my sister. Tomorrow is her birthday. I came here in the middle of an auto ride. Just let me into the room. I'll pick up the bag and leave.'

The receptionist looked at him, trying to gauge the truth of his words. Byrappa gave him an imploring smile. It seemed to work.

'I'll send the room boy with you,' he said eventually, summoning a man who looked like he was on the wrong side of fifty. 'Go with him. He needs to pick something up.'

Byrappa ran up the stairs with the elderly room boy tagging after him. The man opened the door. A fug of alcohol, cigarette smoke and deep-fried spicy kebabs greeted them. The bedsheets were wrinkled and the pillows stacked together. There was an oil stain on the bed. A glass on its side lolled on the floor. Poor Aqthar Sir, Byrappa thought with a shudder. He was so finicky about cleanliness.

The room boy wrinkled his nose. And as Byrappa looked around for a clue, he began tidying up, picking up the fallen glass and arranging the pillows. Next, he went into the bathroom. Byrappa followed him there, only to see him use a towel to wipe something written on the back of the door.

'Hold it,' he cried.

'Why?' he asked. 'Useless rascals... ruining a good door with toothpaste.'

'What did you do? That was Aqthar Bhai's love note,' Byrappa snarled at him.

'Who writes love notes with toothpaste?'

'Aqthar Bhai does, like he leaves gifts on the bathroom door, look...' Behind the bathroom door was a shopping bag. 'Here it is,' Byrappa said brightly. He took a picture of the bit of writing left on the door. Three letters had been wiped out. There was a smudged letter after that, but it could also be just a smudge.

'Thanks, guru,' he called as he slammed the door behind him and began running downstairs.

'Did you find it?' the receptionist called out as Byrappa passed him.

Byrappa gave him a thumbs-up.

At the Yeshwanthpur traffic light the CCB driver finally managed to get to three vehicles behind the fleeing bikes. There were 180 seconds before the light turned green. Mr India had kept his eye on the men on the bikes. As they turned right onto NH75, Mr India realized that one of the bikes had managed to lose them. 'Don't lose this one,' he said to the driver. At the next traffic light, they drew alongside the bike and suddenly Mr India hit the door handle in rage. 'Those tomato fuckers have played us. The fellow at the back wasn't Aqthar,' he snarled. 'We have been following the wrong bike.'

Natraj stared at him in shock. 'What? DCP Sagayaraj will kill us.'

'It's Gowda we have to be worried about,' Mr India mumbled as he called up the DCP.

Neither Natraj nor Mr India spoke for a few minutes even though they continued to follow the bike. They were still smarting from what Sagayaraj had told them. Natraj erupted, 'Those bewarsi bastards knew we were tailing them and took us on a sightseeing tour. Let's head back.'

As the driver took a U-turn, Mr India snarled at a woman on a Scooty riding alongside, an autorickshaw driver and a van filled with trays of eggs. Everyone was slowing them down. 'Just get there as quickly as you can,' he said, shoving his hand out of the window and banging on the side of the door.

A few minutes later, the driver said, 'Sir, the bike we were following is now following us.'

'What?' Mr India and Natraj hollered in unison.

'Lose them,' Mr India said.

'We can stop them and ask them what they are up to,' the driver said half-heartedly.

'Just do what I ask you to,' Mr India said, tracing the India-shaped birthmark almost frantically.

Byrappa walked into the cafe with a shopping bag. He placed it on the table and began unpacking its contents. Inside it was a shawl encrusted with sequins. Its folds contained two memory cards. Gowda checked the bag for a note of some sort.

Byrappa said, 'Sir, I don't know if this means anything but something was written on the back of the bathroom door. The room boy had wiped off most of it by the time I entered. But I took a photograph.'

Gowda enlarged the picture but apart from 'TAG', it was impossible to figure out the word.

The coffee shop stewards were looking at the posse of policemen staring into a phone. 'You think they are watching porn clips like those MLAs in the legislative assembly,' one of them sniggered.

Gowda looked towards them, as if he had heard. The stewards dispersed, getting back to wiping surfaces clean as they readied to shut shop.

Gowda looked around at his officers with a broad grin. Byrappa, Santosh and Gajendra stared at the smiling Gowda. Had all the stress got to him after all?

Gowda picked up his phone and walked out of the cafe. Gajendra, Santosh and Byrappa followed, waiting outside on the pavement and watching Gowda. 'Hey, U,' they heard him say. All of them pretended not to have heard. What was Gowda doing? They needed to keep track of Aqthar and instead Gowda was calling his lady friend for a chat?

Gowda had just remembered how he had woken up one morning during their holiday in Kochi to find Urmila missing. He had crept out of bed, only to see her seated in the balcony with a cup of tea. She had her reading glasses on and was scrawling something in the newspaper with a pencil. 'What are you doing?' he had grinned at her, bleary-eyed.

'Nothing at all, Borei. Just doing the crossword.'

'Oh,' he had said, stumped. Crossword puzzles made no sense to him at all. How could anyone deduce a five-letter word for 'awry' to be 'askew'. 'Since when?'

'Since forever,' she had said, taking off her glasses and putting the newspaper away.

As he waited in the coffee shop, Gowda had had a brainwave. He would pick Urmila's brain. If she could figure out that a four-letter word for 'picnic pests' was 'ants', she could find a six- or seven-letter word with the letters 'TAG' in it.

'I need help to figure out a word. Like you would in a crossword,' he said.

'Are you all right, Borei?' Urmila asked in an amused voice.

'It's serious, U. One of my boys left a message on a bathroom door before he was taken away and most of it was wiped off. All we have are three letters: T, A, G.

There was a pause at the other end.

'There are words,' Urmila said, and rolled out a few. 'Hashtag, retag, nametag.'

'It could be a place name...' Gowda said.

'If there is an e at the end, it could be stage, cottage. Let me send you a list.'

She listened to his silence and asked, 'What is it, Borei?'

'Repeat the words you just said,' Gowda asked.

'Stage. Cottage...'

She heard Gowda exhale. 'Did I ever tell you that you are a gem among gems, the flower among flowers, star among stars...'

'Shut up, Borei.' Urmila laughed. 'I suppose you got the word you were looking for. What is it?'

'Cottage,' Gowda said. 'I have to go now. I owe you.'

'Tread carefully,' Urmila whispered.

'I will. The staircase is made of wood,' Gowda stage-whispered back. He was still smiling when he walked back to join his team.

Gowda said, 'We were right all along. The fight's happening at the cottage.'

'But how is that possible, sir?' Gajendra asked.

'I'll explain as we go,' Gowda said. 'But let me check with the DCP on what the CCB team has found out.'

The others walked ahead to the jeep and Gowda followed with his phone held to his ear.

Sagayaraj answered on the second ring. 'I was just about to call you, Gowda,' he barked into the phone. 'We have lost him.'

'How is that even possible, sir?' Gowda asked, unable to hide his anger. David kept his eyes on the road but Gowda could see in the rearview mirror that the others were listening in.

'Trust me, Gowda. I have just finished telling Natraj and Peter what I think of them. But that's not going to help us now. I had a thought. If we check the hotel room, Aqthar may have left some indication of where he is headed. He's a smart young chap.'

Gowda smiled into the phone, unable to hide his glee. 'Already done, sir. And that's why I called. I think it's happening at the cottage on Professor Mudgood's property.'

David turned the police vehicle into 80 Feet Road at Banaswadi and headed towards the outer ring road. The road was packed with people and vehicles. They had to cross the Ring Road and take Horamavu Road, which would take them to the Professor's property quicker than Hennur Main Road.

'You think?'

The DCP's question smarted but Gowda bit back his retort. 'I had a hunch about this,' he began and then wished he hadn't. In a world where evidence was king, a hunch was a vaporous concept that very few could see sense in. 'Hear me out.'

As the Bolero trundled over potholes, Gowda finished his explanation and added quietly, 'We don't have much time to lose, sir. I cannot sacrifice my officer while waiting for your team to get there. We are headed there too. As you draw closer, please call PC David on the wireless. He will tell you how to approach the property from the back entrance.'

'Keep going and when you come to a dead end turn right,' he instructed David, gesturing to an alley.

About twenty minutes later, they turned into a narrow road that seemed to run forever. There were no streetlights on that stretch. Gowda finally spotted the arch between the eucalyptus grove and a coconut plantation.

A thin mist had settled around them.

## 3

Aqthar was sure that Satisha could hear his heart thudding loudly in his chest.

The two bikes had gone down the Outer Ring Road towards Nagawara leading to the Hebbal flyover. At first, Aqthar had been thrown. Had he got the venue of the fight wrong? He and Satisha seemed to be heading towards Nelamangala when the bike swerved into a parking space on the right while the other bike continued up the road towards NH75.

Satisha stopped at the parking lot for a few minutes and then started the vehicle again. As the bike wove its way through traffic and alleys with consummate ease, Aqthar wondered if Satisha had earned his badge as an expert chain-snatcher.

Aqthar realized that Satisha and Ditchie Babu had factored in the possibility of being followed and so had got in a decoy bike.

Satisha turned and gave him a wolfish smile. 'All okay?' he asked. The cold wind tore the words from his mouth.

Aqthar gave him a thumbs-up sign. He wondered if Gowda and team had discovered his message on the door. He was suddenly afraid of what lay ahead. All along he had told himself that Gowda was in control of the situation. But he wasn't sure anymore. A shove and a kick and a few self-defence tactics had brought him to this point. But at the real fight, he knew he wouldn't be able to stand his ground. If the CCB and Gowda and his team didn't get there on time, he would be done for.

Gowda had shown him the photographs of the two dead men. Cranial bleeding was the cause of their death. But they had also been pummelled like they were pathar-gosht. Aqthar felt his chest constrict. 'How much longer will it take?' Aqthar leaned forward to ask.

'Soon,' came the cryptic answer. The bike went through lanes and alleys and main roads. It wasn't till almost forty minutes later that Aqthar had a sense of where they were: Hegde Nagar. And he realized that they were heading back towards Kannur. It seemed that Gowda had been right all along.

The long and convoluted ride had been undertaken to throw anyone off their scent as well as befuddle him. He was also willing to bet his last rupee that it was Military's plan. Satisha was no more than a stooge, and only as sharp as a sickle left out in the rain.

Satisha turned into the road that ran behind Professor Mudgood's property. Soon they had entered the dirt track that led to the gate of the water tanker filling station. Satisha rode through the land. There were two visible tracks that led to the edge of the property abutting the Professor's land.

Aqthar saw the cottage as they entered a makeshift opening created by shifting the fence posts. 'But this is a house,' he said. 'Is it the venue?' he asked, trying to conjure up a sense of incredulousness in his tone.

'It looks like a house but it isn't,' Satisha said and turned towards the clearing. He parked alongside a car and a few bikes. 'Follow me. Don't take your helmet off. I don't want anyone seeing you,' he said. 'And don't wander away. You could get lost here. Who knows what wild animals lurk in the bushes. The reserve forest isn't too far from here.'

There were no lights around them except for the mobile phone torch that Satisha had switched on.

'Where exactly are we?' Aqthar asked again.

'Outskirts,' Satisha said as he led Aqthar down a side path. 'We were on the road for more than one and a half hours. Didn't you realize that?'

Aqthar grunted.

There was a side entrance that Aqthar remembered as leading to the kitchen. 'Where are the others?'

'They will get here soon. Military didn't want anyone seeing you. So he wanted you to get here early,' Satisha said. Around him two men bustled around with crates of beer and bottles of whisky and rum.

Aqthar wondered who the alcohol was for. From what he reckoned was the hall came the sound of laughter and voices. The voices of men silken with alcohol, loud with bestial roars. 'Who's there?' he asked, raising his eyebrows.

'The big people who come to see you fight. They need lubrication. The smell of sweat and blood is enjoyed better then,' Satisha said as he led him downstairs.

Aqthar barely recognized the basement from the last time he had seen it. In the middle of it was a circular fighting ring created out of sandbags and rope. Two sandbags, one atop the other, around which two lines of rope had been coiled and turned, leading to the next sandbag pile a few metres away. Within the ring rubber mats were laid out. Plastic chairs were placed all around it, a few feet away from the ring.

'Where are the other fighters?' Aqthar asked.

'They will get here when it is time. Don't worry about that.' Satisha led Aqthar towards the room in the basement. The almirah had been moved away from the door. 'This room here is set aside for you. Military wants you to wait there. I'll send Ditchie to you as soon as he gets here. Do you want a drink now?'

'No,' Aqthar said as he shut the door in Satisha's face. He quickly reached for his phone and called Gowda. The call wouldn't go through. He frowned and looked at the screen. The signal strength was strong. He tried again and again. The bastards had a jammer in place.

He didn't know if it was a time or frequency breaker but it would most certainly interfere with the police wireless too. And then it occurred to him that Satisha hadn't been careful enough to ask him to give up his phone for that very reason.

He was on his own here.

Aqthar sat down on one of the chairs abruptly as he felt his legs give way. He was no better than a rooster at a cockfight, and just as dispensable. He closed his eyes and tried to meditate. He wasn't a fighter. But he knew his moves. An illegal fight had no rules, though. Again, the images of the dead men flashed through his mind. Amidst the tussle of thoughts he would need to find a way to focus and do his job. Aqthar whispered under his breath a prayer: Yaa Ali Madad.

# 4

The SUV headlamps alternated between high and low beam. 'Where are we headed, sir?' Santosh asked in a low voice as the vehicle passed an El Dorado billboard.

'Go a little further, David. To the left is a eucalyptus grove. Stop there and turn the headlamps off,' Gowda said as they drove through what seemed like empty tracts of agricultural land.

'We are on a parallel road to the main road. The parallel road has two access points to the path that runs alongside the Professor's property. One leads to the water tanker filling station. The other one to the gate near the line of rooms. The water tanker road will be busy but no one uses this road,' Gowda explained, turning towards the men in the back seat.

'Santosh and I will head there by foot,' Gowda said, stepping out of the vehicle. 'Here is what I want you to do, Gajendra.'

The two men watched the jeep's tail lamps as it went back the way it had come. The cold crept in with fingertips of ice. Gowda shivered. It was probably 16 degrees Celsius but it felt more like 10. Gowda wished he had worn a thicker jacket.

'It's really cold, sir,' Santosh, who had a guileless knack of stating the obvious, said. He rubbed his palms briskly. 'I think it must be 5 degrees—the back of my head is freezing.'

'In which case tonight makes history. The lowest recorded temperature in Bangalore was 7.8 in January 1884,' Gowda said with such seriousness that Santosh knew he was being mocked. He grunted and began walking down the road.

'Don't go too far,' Gowda spoke softly. 'We can't be spotted.'

Gowda turned his back to the road and lit a cigarette. He took two deep drags and stubbed it out.' He retreated into silence while Santosh paced up and down. About twenty minutes later, they saw the headlamps of a vehicle approaching from the other side.

Gowda stood up. He touched the service pistol wedged into the waistband of his trousers. Santosh, he knew, was wearing a shoulder holster beneath his jacket. He hadn't been to the shooting range in months but the thought of the loaded revolver reassured him to some extent.

'Let's go closer,' he said in a low tone to Santosh. 'Try and note down as many vehicle numbers as you can.'

Santosh adjusted his phone camera in response. Sleuthing had become a lot easier with technology, and for that very reason, it seemed that the criminal elements had upped their game too. There was no option but to keep up, Gowda told himself as he heard the faint click of the camera.

'The cicadas are a great cover for the sound, sir,' Santosh said as if he had read his mind.

Gowda acknowledged the remark with a quiet hmm.

Soon, fifteen four-wheelers and half a dozen superbikes had driven into the dirt track that led to the water filling station. There would be more coming in, probably. Gowda felt his chest grow heavy with dread. Aqthar was on his own there. He ran the risk of being pulverized by a professional fighter. Or being killed if his cover fell apart.

Natraj and Mr India didn't talk to each other. Sagayaraj had called to tell them the fight was happening at the Professor's property. 'Get there ASAP,' the DCP had thundered. 'ACP Gowda and his team are almost there.'

As they drew closer to Byrathi Cross, the driver said, 'Those bike fellows are clinging to us like a flea on a dog, sir. I can't shake them off.'

Natraj waggled his finger in his ear. 'Go to Neelgubbi station. We'll figure out what to do there. They will retreat once they see us enter the station.'

A few minutes later, they turned into the station gates. Natraj and Mr India stepped out and walked towards the building. The bike waited for a few seconds and sped away.

When Natraj was certain that the bike had left, he demanded the keys to a Cheetah bike and grabbed two helmets.

# 5

The police vehicle cruised down the main road towards the Professor's property. Ratna was parked near the nunnery. She got into the Bolero. Santosh had insisted on that.

'Why, sir?' Gajendra had asked.

'What if there are women there? We will need a female police officer,' Santosh had retorted.

Gajendra nodded his head, though it was more a series of shakes as if to ask a rhetorical question to the world: Women at an illegal fight? What am I to do with this fellow?

They found a small cul-de-sac that backed on to a property with giant trees. David parked the SUV and turned the lights off.

Byrappa glanced at the dashboard clock. It was 10.08 p.m.

*

Gowda's phone vibrated in his pocket. He hoped it was Aqthar. It turned out to be Gajendra. 'We are in position, sir,' the Head Constable murmured.

'Anything from Aqthar?' Gowda asked quickly.

'No, sir,' Gajendra said, realizing that Aqthar hadn't reached out to Gowda either.

'Stay there till I ask you to come in.' Gowda cut the call as he saw a familiar-looking vehicle arriving. Not too many people owned a Porsche 911 in Bangalore. And there was just one in the neighbourhood. It belonged to Sagar Papanna, Papanna's son and his blind spot. Which is why for his twenty-fifth birthday, the MLA had bought his son a lemon-yellow Porsche 911 Convertible.

'Did you see that, sir?' Santosh's voice was low but furious. 'The garbage prince is here too.'

'And I'm sure the garbage king is there as well,' Gowda said. 'Gajendra hasn't heard from Aqthar yet.'

Santosh didn't respond.

'Maybe a network issue,' Gowda said.

'We have a strong signal,' Santosh said.

Gowda closed his eyes and exhaled. Either they had taken away his phone or they were using a signal jammer.

It was 10.40 p.m. 'Let's go towards the cottage,' he said, moving deeper into the shadows. Santosh followed. 'Thank God there are no dogs this side,' he said.

'I think that too is no coincidence. Dogs barking at strange vehicles this late in the night would raise suspicion. And they know how even a stray word said to the wrong person could reach us. These are people who won't stop at anything so don't underestimate them, Santosh.'

The ground was damp with dew which muffled their steps when they stumbled on the uneven surface. The moon was in its waning phase and barely visible. The mud path was lined with trees tightly packed together. Santosh, who had seen the area only in daylight, was struck by the ease with which Gowda negotiated the terrain. He remembered Gowda telling him that police work was legwork. And nothing could replicate that.

As they neared the end of the mud path, they could see the giant metal gates of the water tank station were wide open, but several garbage lorries were parked there, a makeshift 20 foot barrier to shield any signs of movement within the property and beyond.

Gowda and Santosh slipped into the tree cover and waited. A garbage lorry moved into the property making enough space for a car to go through.

Two men were huddled by the gate, waving in the cars which drove in. Gowda realized that they would head straight to the fence of the Professor's property. The barbed wire would have been moved, so they could go straight to the clearing by the cottage. Voices carried, the forked ends of laughter and the burnt-coal smell of beedi smoke.

Gowda wondered how to reach the cottage. He crept towards the mud path. Gowda gestured for Santosh to follow him.

They walked a few hundred metres. Santosh realized that they were heading towards the Professor's property. At a certain point, the granite fence again turned into a barbed-wire fence. Gowda peered around in the darkness for the broken cement post. He knew the gate would be locked and they had to find a way of getting in. He had remembered seeing a broken cement post where the barbed wire had sagged or been pushed down to allow it to be stepped over.

When he found it, he stepped over. As Santosh followed, he held the post. It began giving way. Gowda moved quickly to hold it in place.

Santosh shot him a grateful look. He opened his mouth to thank him but Gowda shook his head. In the quiet of the night, any sound was amplified. If they were discovered, the men at the gate would slit their throats without the slightest compunction that they were police officers.

Gowda led the way towards a line of rooms.

The building was wreathed in darkness. Two of the doors were locked. A third one had been latched from outside. Gowda opened the latch as quietly as he could. The room he stepped into was bare except for a TV and a gas cylinder. A couple of mats were propped up in the corner and there was a makeshift shelf containing some jars. Beneath it was a line of steel utensils and two plastic pots. Alongside a wall were two plastic chairs.

'Don't put on the light,' Gowda said.

Santosh wouldn't have anyway. But neither did he protest that he wasn't an idiot. Once a man has been kissed by death he is scarred for life. And Santosh was afraid.

# 6

The door opened abruptly. Military entered, looking at Aqthar, who sat on a chair staring at the blank wall opposite, as if it were the ocean and he couldn't drag his eyes away from it. He raised his head and met Military's gaze.

'All good, Aqthar?' Military asked, coming in.

Aqthar gave him a thumbs-up sign.

'There is this Manipuri fighter. Some days ago he took on some of my most brutal fighters and destroyed them. He is small but all muscle. And he is light on his feet. He is a tough opponent. Very vicious too. Like I said, you don't need to knock him out. Just ensure you are still standing. In the next round, whether you win or lose doesn't matter. At least not too much,' Military said.

Aqthar looked at Military and asked without a trace of emotion, 'What about my money?'

'You will be paid 50,000 rupees. And if you manage to get past the first round you'll get 50,000 more.'

Aqthar nodded, hiding his surprise. Ditchie Babu had told him his earnings would be 25,000 rupees. Everyone made money on a fight, it seemed.

Military saw Aqthar's phone on the chair near him. 'There is no signal here,' he said.

'I realized that... I wanted to call my wife.'

Military shrugged as if to say 'tough luck'. 'Give me your phone,' he said. Aqthar handed it over to him without protesting.

Aqthar stood up and paced the length of the room. He didn't think any of the other fighters were sitting in rooms before the fights. They were probably working themselves into a pumped-up state to unleash their brutality. He would conserve his energy, he decided.

The Manipuri fighter had a lot riding on him, and Aqthar was the wild-card entry to tip the betting pool. He felt a nerve throb near his right temple. How did you prepare when you didn't know what or who you were fighting?

'What about the people who live here?' Santosh asked.

'I'm quite certain that Muniraju who lives here is in on the action. So he sends his wife away,' Gowda mumbled as he searched the house.

'How do you know this, sir?' Santosh asked.

'I know,' Gowda said triumphantly. He had found what he was looking for—a steel tiffin box stuffed with a wad of 1,000-rupee notes.

'My mother does that too,' Santosh said.

'Does she keep 15,000 rupees in tiffin boxes?' Gowda asked. 'That's how much it is.'

Santosh retreated into silence. Gowda was on edge too, he could see. He wondered what the others were up to. He wished he had never suggested bringing Aqthar here from Dharwad. The man had a family. Why hadn't Aqthar backed out from the fight? He didn't know if the man was a hero or a fool. Meanwhile there was nothing to do but wait.

He was relieved when Gowda said, 'Let's go towards the cottage.'

Ditchie Babu pushed open the door of the room. 'Sorry, Mams, I took so long,' he said, from beneath his forehead.

'What happened?' Aqthar asked. He was in the middle of a set of push-ups.

'Khaki,' Ditchie Babu said, watching him.

'Khaki?' Aqthar asked, starting on squats.

'Cops. Don't you call them Khaki in Dharwad? They were following us. Satisha managed to lose them and get you here,' Ditchie said, sitting on a chair. Then he grinned. 'When they realized they were chasing the wrong bike, they turned back. And then we started following them. When they went into the police station I got away and came here. What ra, Mams? You don't look happy.'

Aqthar jumped to his feet. 'I was just imagining their faces.' He managed a big smile. 'So what happens now?'

'You get ready. Once the punters are here, the fight begins,' Ditchie Babu said, groping in his pocket. 'Mams, the Manipuri fighter is really tough. He is undefeated. Military lost a lot of money because of him. Let me give you something,' Ditchie said, taking something out of his pocket and coming forward. 'Put this on,' he said, opening his palm to reveal a gum guard. 'The Manipuri doesn't wear one. He thinks no one can come close to him. He is that quick on his feet.'

Aqthar picked up the gum guard gingerly.

'Mams, it's a new piece. I'm not going to bring you a used one,' Ditchie Babu said encouragingly.

Aqthar nodded and smiled at him gratefully.

'Mams, one other thing...' He held out two briefs. 'Put this on over yours. One can't be careful enough, no?'

Aqthar took them.

'There are no gloves used in these fights. Some of these fellows handle the city's waste with bare hands. So a glove to them is like a man wearing bangles—too girlie,' Ditchie Babu added.

'I need straps,' Aqthar said hurriedly.

Ditchie Babu went to the corner cupboard. 'There were a few rolls from last time... why didn't you ask me earlier, Mams?'

'You never told me the rules of the fight,' Aqthar said. 'Did you?'

'There are no rules, Mams. You fight till you fall or the other man does. That's it!' Ditchie Babu pulled out two rolls of crepe straps. 'You are lucky, Mams...'

'Do a lot of fights happen here?' Aqthar looked at the straps. They were brand new.

Ditchie Babu shrugged. 'Once every few months at least. But this time it's a bit different. It was set up very quickly and then the date of the fight was changed.' He dropped his voice. 'You are the surprise element. So the stakes are big...'

'Look, can you do me a favour?' Aqthar asked suddenly. Ditchie Babu looked at him. 'For you anything, Mams. I am like your manager now.'

'I need you to make a call. My phone isn't working,' Aqthar said.

Ditchie Babu made a face.

'What?' Aqthar demanded. 'I thought you were ready to do anything for me.'

'Tell me the number,' Ditchie said after a moment. He entered it in his phone and left the room.

When her phone vibrated in her pocket, Ratna knew it would be Aqthar. Instead, a strange male voice said, 'Hello, I have a message for you.'

Ratna put a finger up to signify silence in the vehicle. 'Hello, who is it?'

Gajendra's eyes widened at Ratna's change in tone. Byrappa, who by now was an ardent admirer of Ratna's multiple talents, grinned.

'Your nousho said to not latch the door. He will be late reaching home but he will come home,' the voice said hastily.

Ratna snorted. 'Leave the door unlatched. Is he mad? Just tell him I will be waiting for him. And he better get there if he doesn't want to make me angry.'

When the line went silent, Gajendra stared at her. 'What does that mean?'

'We had come up with a code. Leave the door unlatched means the fight will begin soon.'

'You will be waiting means everyone is in place. You'll be angry means we will be there,' Byrappa finished.

Gajendra suddenly felt very old in their presence.

'I wonder how he managed to get this man to call,' Gajendra asked. 'And from where.'

Ratna looked at the number. It was a landline, and a familiar one. 'It's the Professor's landline,' she said. And what had seemed like a brilliant ploy now seemed a rash risk that Aqthar had taken, she thought with a mounting sense of fear.

'Let's leave the vehicle here and go on foot,' Gajendra said. He paused and said, 'Ratna Madam, maybe you should stay back here. It will get rough there.'

Byrappa looked away, not wanting to be a part of the conversation. He knew Ratna was capable of holding her own. And she wouldn't like it if he spoke up for her.

'No way, Head Constable Gajendra,' Ratna asserted, using the designation to remind him that she was his superior. 'We are in this together.' She patted the revolver slung on her hip.

# 7

Ditchie Babu hummed under his breath as he wound the crepe bandage carefully, away from Aqthar's thumb towards his wrist. Military walked in, accompanied by a young woman. Aqthar acted oblivious to their presence. He had taken off his jacket and shirt. A white vest stretched across his pectorals and outlined his 'biscuits', as Ditchie Babu had called his four-pack muscles. He had come in wearing track pants, and now, with the bulk of the jacket and shirt gone, he realized Military would see him for who he was—a slimly built man.

Aqthar jabbed the air a couple of times as if to test the fit of the bandage. He saw Military's eyes gleam.

'So this is your surprise fighter?' The woman's voice was low and husky.

Military nodded.

'He is cute,' she said. 'But can he fight?'

Aqthar glared at the two of them.

Military suddenly stepped towards him with his palm outstretched to slap him. Aqthar sidestepped him, grabbing Military's wrist and twisting it hard. 'What the hell, man?' Aqthar snarled.

Military extricated his wrist and said from the corner of his mouth, 'I needed to know if you are as fast as Ditchie said...'

'Rather late in the day, no?' the woman asked.

Military shrugged. 'I've known fighters who lose their nerve. Looks like our hero here might surprise us...'

'In which case I will take a chance too,' the woman said, taking in Aqthar's physique once again.

Aqthar suddenly felt stripped naked and judged. He had never felt like this, an object of desire, and it was both disconcerting and humiliating. Was this how women felt when men's gazes lingered over their bodies?

'The Manipuri goes barefoot.' Military glanced at Aqthar's trainers.

'I don't.'

'It makes him quicker on his feet,' Military persisted.

'Good for him,' Aqthar said, stretching his palms to check the fit of the wrap. Then he turned towards Military and jabbed the air near his face with a series of lightning moves.

Military took a step back. 'Save that for the ring. Let's see how you fare there.'

'Cock-sucker,' Aqthar said under his breath as Military and the woman left the room.

Ditchie Babu looked away. Military had wanted to rile Mams, and he seemed to have succeeded. Now it was up to him to finish the job of getting Aqthar mad as an angry wasp. His heart rate had to go up before he entered the ring. 'The Manipuri is a tough bastard, Mams. But Military is a bigger one.'

'Once this is done, I'm going to beat the shit out of him,' Aqthar growled, wondering how long he could keep up the act. The adrenalin, nervousness and excitement was a heady cocktail but it wasn't easy to pretend raw aggression.

A Cheetah drew to a halt near them. Gajendra peered at the two faces within the helmet casings.

Mr India took his helmet off. 'It's me,' he whispered.

'About time,' Byrappa muttered under his breath.

Mr India ignored the barb and said, 'What's the POA?'

'We will go in there and surprise them,' Ratna said.

Natraj stuck his finger in his ear and waggled it fervently. 'No, no... there is a man at the gate. A man with a dog. We checked on our way here. Here's what I suggest we do,' he said. 'Madam, Gajendra Sir and you come in the police vehicle. When you reach the gate, please put the beacon and signal on; it is quite possible someone will come to talk to you. We'll find our way in then. Byrappa, please come with us. We need someone who knows the layout of the property,' Natraj continued.

Ratna pursed her mouth in annoyance but didn't argue. The CCB men did have a point.

Gowda and Santosh waited in the cover of a giant tree a little away from the line of rooms. The vehicles had stopped arriving. Through the stillness of the night, an echo rang out as the giant metal gates were dragged shut. The grating sound had an ominous subtext: the fight was about to begin.

# 8

The door opened. Military gestured with his chin for Aqthar to step out. Ditchie Babu gestured to his mouth. Aqthar popped the gum guard in.

And all the churning, the countless trains of speculation, the swarms of butterflies in his belly, the weightless feeling in his legs, all of it curled into a ball of uncertainty in the pit of his belly. But he had to keep standing no matter what. At least until his colleagues came in.

The Manipuri fighter was small, as Military had said. But he was all muscle and tattoos—a formidable sight. Both his arms and his chest were inked. Beneath his navy satin shorts, tattoos were visible, running down his thighs to his ankles. A loud cheer rose from the men standing behind the front-row seats. 'Jingz. Jingz. Jingz.'

The Manipuri was a showman. Instead of stepping over the rope, he executed a version of a Fosbury flop, falling on his back and bouncing on to his feet in the same momentum. His supporters cheered even louder.

The money placed on Jingz would fetch great returns tonight, Sagar Papanna smirked at Military, full of contempt for Military's fighter, who seemed clueless and dazed. Sagar didn't understand what his daddy saw in Military. Aqthar walked into the ring. Everything pressed in on him. The ropes, the cheering strangers and the Manipuri who seemed to know everyone including the sandbags.

A burly man in a white T-shirt and jeans stepped into the ring with the two of them. 'Three rounds of three minutes each,' he said. 'And ninety seconds' rest between each round.'

The Manipuri bounced on the balls of his feet. Mirroring him almost unconsciously, Aqthar began moving on his feet in a zigzag manner.

The referee continued, 'You have to stop when I blow the whistle or you will be disqualified. No biting; no eye-gouging; no strikes to the balls; no grabbing or hitting the throat; no head-butting or striking the back of the head.'

'What's left?' Jingz demanded in chaste Kannada. Aqthar looked at him with new respect.

'Yeah, what's left?' Sagar demanded loudly. The crowd sniggered.

From the corner of his eye, Aqthar saw the woman who had visited him with Military sit beside Papanna. She seemed completely unaware of the fact that she was the lone woman in the room. Was she the MLA's mistress? That would explain her nonchalance.

The referee blew his whistle.

Aqthar was a good five inches taller than his opponent. His sneakers added to his height. The Manipuri was an annoying and lethal wasp, darting this way and that. Aqthar felt like a lumbering sloth bear. It suddenly occurred to him that this was his opponent's secret—to unnerve his adversary with energy and speed.

The crowd roared: 'Knockout, Jingz... get the bastard.'

Ditchie Babu's lone voice called out, 'Careful, Mams.'

Aqthar, holding his fist close to his chin, let the Manipuri dart his way. Jingz was aggressive. Even as Aqthar tried to deflect a punch, he was caught by surprise. Jingz turned on his feet and threw a backwards kick at his belly. It was as lethal as it was beautiful.

Aqthar leapt back just in time. The crowd groaned. From where he sat, Military saw Sagar Papanna stare at him.

'Kill the bastard, Jingz,' Sagar Papanna hollered. His father looked at him with adoration and a tinge of wariness. The boy certainly wasn't a namby-pamby wuss but he hadn't known just how much he hated losing. He was the same.

'Hit the rib-bu,' he added his voice to Sagar's.

For a moment Aqthar was distracted. A punch flew through the air to land on the side of his head. Something exploded in his skull; the faces and the lights blurred, and deep within came a stillness, as if he was slipping away to another realm accompanied by hot air whistling in his ears. He wanted to crumple on to the ground and lie there curled into a ball.

'Stay on your feet, Mams,' Ditchie hollered. Aqthar gathered all his strength, shook himself alive and found his feet, only to see Jingz advancing towards him with a murderous gleam in his eye. Aqthar ducked and grabbed him by the waist, taking him down. As he raised his fists to thump the man to a pulp, the referee blew the whistle.

Ditchie Babu vaulted over the rope towards Aqthar, 'Mams, you are doing good... just keep at it.'

A punter walked around a rope collecting fresh bet amounts.

Aqthar barely had time to catch his breath before the whistle blew again.

A subterranean drone as they approached the cottage. Gowda exhaled softly. It wasn't a cheering audience but a buzzing one. Which meant Aqthar was fine as of now. 'Let's move faster,' Gowda murmured to Santosh.

# 9

The police vehicle slowed down as it approached the property. The gate lights were dimmed, as was the porch light of the house.

A man got off a bench on the verandah and ran towards the gate. It was Mary Susheela's husband, Paul Selvam. 'Good evening, sir,' he said, raising his hand in a half-salute. A black Mudhol hound stood by his side.

Gajendra asked, 'Why are you here?'

'Iqbal Sir asked me to sleep here for a few days till the security agency sends someone,' Paul said. He lowered his voice. 'The neighbours had said they had seen people coming here at night. So he thought it best that there's a guard.'

'Should I send someone?' Ratna asked, looking beyond Paul. She turned to Gajendra and said, 'Head Constable, let's take a look.'

Paul looked stricken. 'No, no, madam, it's fine.'

Ratna looked at the hound that was sniffing around the gate. 'Whose dog is this?' She was trying to stall for time as the two CCB officers and Byrappa jumped over the granite fence.

The dog growled. Paul tugged at the chain. 'Shut the fuck up,' he said. Then he smiled. 'It's mine, madam. Bhairava. That's his name.'

'Really? I thought you had a Rottweiler called Rocky,' Ratna persisted.

Gajendra hid his smile and added a frown to his brow. Paul shot them a coy glance. 'I have two dogs. Bhairava was at my friend's house. His bitch is in heat. And Bhairava was there to do his manly duty.'

The leer in his eye made Ratna want to slap him hard. Instead, she snorted. 'Manly duty, is it? This dog is just a pup.'

Paul's leer grew creepier as he mumbled, 'He just looks like a puppy. He isn't. Bhairava is fully grown where it counts.'

Gajendra, who had had enough of Paul's innuendoes, said, 'Watch your tongue, bewarsi. And who is this friend? Does he have a name?'

Paul threw up his hands. 'Next you will want the dog's horoscope, I suppose?'

'Yes, I would definitely like to see this one's. I can match it to the report of a missing dog. A Mudhol hound pup. Stolen dogs are big business,' Gajendra snapped.

'Sir, this is my dog, Bhairava. He'll listen to my commands, see...' Turning to the dog, Paul said, 'Sit.'

Bhairava sat.

'Shake hand.'

Bhairava stretched out a paw.

'See, see...' Paul's relief was palpable.

Ratna decided to step in. 'I'm sure the dog will sit and shake hands even if I ask it to. Want me to show you? Or you can just tell us who the friend is. Start with the name and mobile number.'

Paul reached into his shirt pocket. Then he patted his trouser pockets. 'Ayyo... I don't have my mobile with me...' he said, appearing genuinely bewildered.

Gajendra glared at him. 'I have my eye on you...'

'Let's go, we'll get this loafer another time,' Ratna said. The seven minutes the CCB men had asked for were up. Byrappa must be leading them towards the cottage.

She turned to look at Paul. 'You heard what the Head Constable said, didn't you?'

Paul nodded absently as he looked around the ground for his phone.

Gajendra and Ratna waited till Paul and the dog returned to the house. They watched him tie Bhairava to a tree.

'Radio in for assistance,' she told David. 'And send them to the cottage as soon as they are here.' Ratna slipped out of the vehicle. Gajendra followed.

They watched Paul go onto the verandah. The dog, sensing the presence of strangers around, began barking. After a couple of minutes he came back and took the dog in with him. Bhairava continued to bark and they could hear Paul admonish the dog. He slammed the door shut. Through the closed door, they could hear the dog's agitated barking. Then they heard a series of yelps.

Ratna and Gajendra quickly climbed over the locked gate before Paul returned to the verandah. As they crept away from the driveway into the darkness, Ratna's foot struck something. In the faint light from the porch, she could make out it was a small phone. She picked it up and showed it to Gajendra.

Byrappa was waiting at a short distance from the bottom of the steps. 'They said they would handle it from here,' he whispered.

Ratna rolled her eyes but didn't speak. She tilted her chin to say, let's go.

Papanna frowned at his phone. There seemed to be no signal and then he remembered that they used a jammer. He would have to go up and head towards the fencing to be able to make a call. The minister was an impatient man. And what needed to be said was confidential as well as urgent. He didn't particularly care about this evening's fight as he already knew how it would all end. Papanna jumped to his feet and went upstairs. He stepped out of the cottage, unaware that Gowda and Santosh were waiting in the shadows.

## 10

Aqthar spat out the water sprayed into his mouth. He took another sip. 'Mams, you are doing great. Let him get tired. That way his jabs and kicks won't have the effect they usually do,' Ditchie Babu said again.

Aqthar nodded and shoved the gum guard into his mouth as the referee blew the whistle. 'Mams, stay on your feet... No matter what... stay on your feet.'

The dim room hummed with a rare energy. The euphoria of one's triumph accompanied by a decimation of the other. In the end that's what separates us from animals and makes us lesser creatures, Aqthar thought. Animals don't kill for pleasure or derive pleasure from watching a fight. And then there was no more time or place to think or do anything. He had to stay on his feet.

Jingz didn't let anyone see how furious he was. The man opposite him was no real fighter. He just knew how to defend and stay out of reach of jabs or kicks. Which was a problem because defensive fighters just showed you up. He was going to need to make him turn offensive. And that was when he would go for the kill.

Aqthar saw the manic gleam in Jingz's eyes. He knew the man was coming for him. Jingz started throwing punches at him with lightning speed. Aqthar moved on his feet, around Jingz, away from his vicious jabs.

The crowd groaned. Sagar Papanna hollered, 'What the fuck are you doing, Jingz? Kill him!'

Ditchie Babu, not to be outdone, screamed, 'Mams, finish the round quickly. Your wife is waiting, don't forget!'

Military asked, 'How do you know that?'

Ditchie Babu grinned. 'I'm the one who called his wife to pass on a message.'

Military frowned. 'When?'

'Just before the fight,' Ditchie Babu said, his eyes on Aqthar. 'Mams, go for it.'

'Whom did you call?' Military snarled.

'His mistress. Chill, Military. I have met the woman. And her brother Sulaiman,' Ditchie Babu said, his eyes glued to the ring, where Jingz's jab had found its mark on the side of Aqthar's head. He was tottering.

'Show me the number,' Military demanded.

'Can't it wait?' Ditchie Babu said as he scrolled down his phone and showed him the number. Military frowned. The number had a familiar sequence. He opened his phone contacts.

Through the pain and the wasps buzzing in his head, Aqthar realized two things. Military was looking at his phone, and the Manipuri, using his short stature, was throwing himself at him trying to grab his waist. Aqthar, seeing the unguarded side of Jingz's face, raised his fist and landed a full-bodied punch. The Manipuri reeled.

Sagar Papanna screamed, 'Foul!' Some of his supporters jumped into the ring. From the other side, Ditchie Babu and three others joined the melee. In the ensuing scramble, no one noticed two burly men running down the stairs as police vehicles drove into the property, their sirens screaming.

Fists and feet flew. Kicks and shoves. Jabs and punches.

Military saw Sagar Papanna waving a revolver. There was only one thing to do. He ran to the circuit-breaker box at the corner of the basement and pulled the switch down. The basement sank into darkness. Each man for himself, he decided, as he crept into the bathroom and hid there.

As the room went dark, Aqthar felt a wrist clamp down on his and drag him away. He roused himself from the shock of having a gun pointed at him by the young man who seemed high on something. He pushed his way through arms and legs, sandbag and rope. 'It would be best to get near a wall,' a voice said in Hindi. Aqthar stared at the direction from which it had come. Jingz was his saviour.

'Thanks,' he muttered. And then, still overwhelmed by what had transpired, he asked, 'Why? You rescued me. Why?'

'We are not enemies. We are both just their pet animals. I can see this is your first time. This is my eighth fight and most of them end like this!'

They were both silent as the chaos around them continued. The sound of flesh slapping against flesh, grunts and cries of pain resonated.

'Dungeons of hell...' Jingz said softly.

# 11

Byrappa, who had followed Mr India and Natraj, was halfway down the stairs when the lights went off. He felt bodies jostling past him. He vaulted over the banister and landed on what could be two people rolling on the floor or just mattress rolls.

He stumbled over the pile to find the wall. Somewhere to the left was the circuit-breaker box. He remembered seeing it placed in an alcove beyond which was the bathroom. He was quite sure someone had turned the power off.

And then a gunshot rang through the commotion.

People running, shattering glass and upturning furniture in their haste to get away. Papanna had finished his call and was returning to the cottage when he heard the gunshot. He stumbled and fell, grabbing at whatever he could. The jagged end of a twig slit his palm open. But it was neither fear nor pain that he felt. Instead it was dread. He had warned Sagar to not take his revolver.

The cucumber farmer's son was still cooling his arse in Parapana jail after the Fits Club shooting.

But Sagar had done exactly that. Papanna turned back to run to his car in the clearing. He had to get away before he was found here. He would have to sort out the mess that Sagar had made. For which he needed to get to his home first. He heard the police siren and moved away from the car towards his property. He knew where he could stay hidden until it was safe for him to step out.

Chikka had followed Military into the bathroom.

'Madam, don't step out of here,' Deva said, surprised at how she had appeared at his side. He slammed the door shut. He saw the relief in the woman's eyes as she noticed the clothes hanging on the door. A pair of jeans, a T-shirt and a jacket. Aqthar had hung up what he would wear after the fight.

The woman began taking her clothes off.

'Turn the other way,' she said when she caught Deva looking at her.

The sari, blouse and skirt dropped at her feet. She tossed the padded bra off and in minutes had turned into a young man with a long ponytail wearing an oversized T-shirt and jeans with rolled-up bottoms. He took his jewellery off. 'Let's get the fuck out of here.'

\*

The bathroom ventilator rose 18 inches above the ground and was 28 inches wide. Deva removed the glass slats and placed them on the ground.

'I'll go first,' the woman who had turned into a man said as he hoisted himself and slid through the ventilator. Deva appeared at his side a few moments later. He crouched, watching the police officers circle the cottage. But Deva knew the lay of the land better than anyone else. And so he knew exactly how he could get to safety.

As the lights came on, the room froze in a tableau of shock and horror. Gowda and Santosh rushed towards a man lying prone on the ground. He had been shot through the head. Sagar Papanna looked as stunned as everyone else. Gowda and Santosh ascertained that the man who had been shot wasn't Aqthar. Mr India and Natraj had reached their side. One of them took Sagar Papanna's revolver away and the other led him outside. The rest of the constabulary began rounding up the people who hadn't managed to flee.

Aqthar looked at the dead man and felt something akin to remorse. Or was it sorrow? Ditchie Babu had been shot dead. He had joined the fracas in the ring and thrown himself in front of Aqthar. 'I'll take care of this, Mams,' he had shouted and aimed a ditchie at one of Sagar Papanna's stooges with his forehead.

And then the lights had gone off.

Santosh looked at Gowda and asked, 'Where's Deva, sir?'

Byrappa beckoned them towards the bathroom. He pointed out the ventilator slats kept neatly in a pile. The shower cubicle was littered with women's clothing. 'Was there a woman here?' Gowda asked, perplexed.

Aqthar said, 'There was one with Military, sir. But I don't think she is here.'

Byrappa pointed to the hanger. 'I think she left in men's clothes.' He paused as he took in the padded bra and the wig. 'Actually, I think it was a man dressed up as a woman.'

Gowda groaned so loudly that they turned in surprise. He suddenly remembered why Mrs Tenant had seemed eerily familiar. But he had been too distracted or plain dense not to have seen the resemblance. She was probably related to Chikka, who had known the best way to get an official passport in the name he wanted was to rent Gowda's house so passport verification wouldn't be an issue. It would appeal to that perverse streak of that twisted mind, to outsmart Gowda on his doorstep. But that still didn't explain what Chikka was doing at the cottage and what he had to do with the fight. 'Come on,' he said, turning to rush back to the top of the staircase, where Gajendra and Ratna met them. They had helped round up some of the 'escape artists', as Gajendra had referred to them. The bunch included a prominent philanthropist, a socialite who was a Page-Three fixture, the well-known CEO of a start-up, and a couple of local ward members. They always got away. Not this time, though, Gajendra had thought as they were led away in handcuffs.

'Have you seen Deva?' Santosh asked.

'We thought he was down there,' Ratna said.

'He was. He escaped,' Aqthar said.

'We have people covering every inch of the grounds,' Mr India said, coming up to them.

'You won't find him there,' Gowda said succinctly, putting his phone torch on. 'Bring in Paul too.' He strode towards the main house.

'What about the dog?' Santosh asked.

'Bring the dog too,' Gowda growled. 'Keep him at the station house for now.'

# 15 DECEMBER 2012, SATURDAY

## 1

They found Deva in his room at the Buqhari residence. DCP Sagayaraj had called up Iqbal even before his men reached the house. It was a little past two in the morning.

'Are you sure?' Iqbal Buqhari demanded, unable or unwilling to comprehend what he was being told.

'I wouldn't be calling if I wasn't,' DCP Sagayaraj snapped. 'It is best you cooperate.'

Deva was lying on his bed, his head cradled on his arms and his eyes wide open. He didn't even bother sitting up.

'We have a better room and bed waiting for you,' Mr India said.

'That's why I thought I'll get as much time as I can on this one,' Deva said, getting up slowly.

Natraj and Mr India went towards him and slapped on a pair of handcuffs.

He saw Aqthar standing with Byrappa as the CCB officers dragged him away. 'You had me almost fooled…'

'Ditchie Babu is dead,' Aqthar said quietly.

'Good,' Deva said over his shoulder. 'That fucker brought this on me. I would have shoved his face into the toilet bowl and killed him myself if he was alive.'

No one spoke. Had Deva just admitted to having killed the Professor? Or was it just the angry boast of a cornered man?

Gowda leaned against the table. On a chair sat Deva, who seemed curiously impassive about being in custody. The CCB had taken him to a safe house. They were worried that Deva would be murdered or bailed out if he was kept in custody or remanded to a sub jail. If he talked, a lot of people would be in trouble.

'Your politician friends might get you out of this case, though Papanna will probably pin Ditchie Babu's shooting on you. Do you think he'll give up his precious son?' Gowda snorted. 'You might as well tell me the truth about everything. The fighting ring and the Professor's murder.'

'I suppose it's convenient to pin that on me as well.'

Gowda's voice was steely as he said, 'You see, Deva, you made a mistake. You said you were in Mangalore. We have information that you were here in Bangalore on 28 November. There is CCTV footage as well as witnesses. The CCB is picking up Oil Mill Jaggi as we speak.'

'Janaki Buqhari had killed him. I was merely cleaning up what Janaki Buqhari had done. At best, I am only an accomplice.' His laugh was triumphant.

Gowda looked at him for a long moment. 'That isn't true and you know that very well.'

'What do you mean? I saw Janaki Buqhari strike him with his walking stick. I saw him fall.'

Gowda crossed his arms. 'And so you pushed his face into a cauldron of boiling water to make it seem that he had slumped into the water and died as if he had a heart attack?'

Deva nodded. 'That's all I did.'

'Tell me, why did you want to frighten him into leaving?'

'He was a nuisance, and I knew he was curious about what was happening at the cottage. I organized a few TV shoots there to convince him that that was all that was going on. But he was a wily old jackal. I had set up a big fight for the next night, and at about 9.30 p.m. I saw him snooping around and I knew it wasn't safe anymore. I went there to frighten him into moving in with his daughter. But when I saw that she had attacked him, I thought that plan wouldn't work. So I thought I would finish the job so he doesn't survive.' Deva gave a chilling smile.

'There were scratches on the table to indicate that he put up a fight to stay alive. He was conscious when you pushed his head into the vessel. Stop lying, Deva. You know his death wasn't caused by the blow. He was asphyxiated, scalded and drowned all at the same time, if that is even possible... and you did it. The evidence is strong. It's only a matter of time. Besides, you already admitted to finishing what you thought Janaki Buqhari had begun.'

Deva didn't speak. He continued to look at the floor even when Gowda left the room.

Gajendra and Ratna went to Gowda's house to bring in his tenants for questioning. The police machinery had swung into action to send forth a lookout circular to all immigration points for a female traveller named Bhuvana Shashank. But Gowda knew that Bhuvana—aka Ramesh, aka Chikka—would lie low again. It had been a clever plan. Brilliant in its simplicity. It would even have worked since biometric scanning hadn't yet reached Indian airports.

'Get whatever you can out of them, though I don't think it will be much,' Gowda had said. 'But every little scrap of information is valuable.'

Santosh was waiting for Gowda when he returned to the station.

'Where is Aqthar?'

'He is at his uncle's home. Resting,' Santosh said. 'What happens now, sir?'

Gowda smiled. 'The DNA results will need to come in before the prosecution starts building their case. The courts will take their time before the case goes to trial. Meanwhile, we get back to doing our job. Maintaining law and order.'

# 18 DECEMBER 2012, TUESDAY

## Epilogue

It was a little past eleven but Gowda felt he was drowning in a swamp of fatigue. Mamtha and Roshan had returned to Hassan and his father had gone back to his brother's house.

When Paul Selvam was taken into custody Mary Susheela refused to accept the dog. 'Let him loose if you can't keep him,' she had said.

'What do we do with it?' Gajendra asked, looking at the dog, which had an enormous appetite.

Gowda thought of the empty house that awaited him, the silence that had become oppressive. 'I will keep Bhairava,' he said on an impulse.

He looked at the dog seated by his side. For some reason Bhairava seemed to have attached itself to him and howled if he went away from its side.

A strong, gusty wind blew. Leaves rustled. The house was in darkness except for the verandah light. Gowda lit another cigarette. In the last two hours, he had smoked ten already, he thought, counting the stubs in the ashtray.

Urmila had asked him to meet her for lunch. Gowda had said he would come by after his meeting at the Commissioner's office. The CCB had taken over the case but Gowda had the satisfaction of knowing that he had done what he had intended to even if it hadn't ended exactly the way he wanted it. Chikka had escaped again and Papanna hadn't been taken into custody despite being found in the pump house. He was still pulling strings.

When Gowda reached her apartment, there was no dog to greet him. 'Where is Mr Right?' Gowda asked.

'At the groomer's,' Urmila said, shutting the door after him.

'I am so exhausted, U,' Gowda said.

'What will happen to Janaki?' Urmila asked.

Gowda shrugged. 'Depends on what the lawyers will make it out to be... it is best that she confessed though. The poor woman. Driven to murder as the only act of agency in her life.'

'Interesting that you should use the word "agency",' Urmila said, giving him a long, steady look. 'Do you want a drink?'

Gowda stared at her. Urmila didn't like daytime drinking unless she was on holiday. Something about the way she held herself and the timbre of her voice alerted him that there was more coming.

He stepped onto the balcony to smoke. Behind him he heard the clink of glasses and the hiss of a Coke bottle being unscrewed.

When he looked for the ashtray to stub the half-smoked cigarette, he couldn't find it. He realized the room looked different too. Everything was covered in dust sheets and all the pretty things had been put away. There were no flowers and the house plants were missing.

He closed the balcony doors and stepped back into the living room.

'Sit down, Borei,' Urmila said, gesturing to the chair opposite hers.

Gowda felt his heart hammering in his chest.

'Sit down, Borei,' she said again. 'We need to talk.'

He had always wondered how it would end. But now that it had happened, he didn't know how he felt. Furious with himself?

Devastated by a sense of loss? Crippled with loneliness? Or just numb until it sunk in that Urmila had said it was over.

He inhaled deeply. He didn't want to go back into the house. He was afraid of being alone with his thoughts. When the police vehicle pulled up outside his gate, he was immensely relieved. This he knew. This he could handle.

'You might as well come along for the ride,' he told the dog as he stood up and walked to the police vehicle.

The wireless crackled. 'BG 4 come in. BG 4 come in...'

# HOT STAGE

Over the last few decades, forensic science has played an increasingly important role in tracking down criminals and narrowing down the list of suspects that the police need to investigate. The ability to identify a suspect from a DNA sample has helped identify many suspects over the years, but DNA samples are not always left at a crime scene and with no DNA database, trace forensic evidence is often what will lead the police to a suspect. After any DNA samples are taken from evidence left at a crime scene, the search is continued with a hunt for any distinguishing hairs, fibres and particles that do not seem to belong at the scene.

Senior forensic scientist David Sugiyama, works in the trace evidence section of the Tulsa Police Department Forensic Laboratory where they analyse hairs, fibres, paint and particles of glass found on suspects, victims and at crime scenes.

One of the distinguishing features of glass is its refractive index and Mr Sugiyama has found the Becke Line method for assessing a particle's refractive index a fast and convenient way of telling if glass fragments found at a crime scene could be linked to a certain source. The key advantages of this technique are that it is non-destructive, relatively fast and inexpensive.

The thermal stage has enabled the users to be able to use just one refractive index liquid, rather than trying to find those that are the closest match, and made the technique into an excellent first screen to test for similarities between glass particles. Of course, real-life stories are never simple and even a match from one piece of evidence does not necessarily make a suspect guilty.

Read the full article at:

https://www.chromatographytoday.com/article/microscopy-and-microtechniques/4/company/thermal-microscopy-in-the-forensics-laboratory/649/download

# A CUT-LIKE WOUND

## ANITA NAIR

### *The first in the Inspector Gowda Series*

It's the first day of Ramadan in heat-soaked Bangalore. A young man begins to dress: make-up, a sari, and expensive pearl earrings. Before the mirror he is transformed into Bhuvana. She is a *hijra*, a transgender seeking love in the bazaars of the city. What Bhuvana wants, she nearly gets: a passing man is attracted to this elusive young woman—but someone points out that Bhuvana is no woman. For that, the interloper's throat is cut. A case for Inspector Borei Gowda, going to seed, and at odds with those around him including his wife, his colleagues, even the informers he must deal with. More corpses and Urmila, Gowda's ex-flame, are added to this spicy concoction of a mystery novel.

"Anita Nair is a feminist and highly regarded Indian novelist. *A Cut-Like Wound* is as startling a debut crime novel as you are likely to read this year" *Sunday Times*

"Nair captures the seedy side of shiny new India vividly, and Inspector Gowda—with his weary self-knowledge; his secret, wistfully aspirational biker tattoo; his stagnating marriage and his confusion when an old flame re-enters his life—is a welcome addition to the ranks of flawed-but-lovable fictional cops." *Guardian*

"Nair immerses her readers in Bangalore's alluring and sinister mélange of Hindu and Moslem cultures, revealing a people afflicted by the inability to allow unqualified praise for anything or anyone. Complex, psychologically deep characters are a plus." *Publishers Weekly*

£8.99/$14.95
Crime Paperback Original

ISBN 978 1908524 362
eBook USC ISBN 978 1908524 379
eBook ROW ISBN 978 1912242 863

www.bitterlemonpress.com

# CHAIN OF CUSTODY

## ANITA NAIR

### *The Return of Inspector Gowda*

What does thirteen-year-old Nandita's disappearance have to do with the murder of a well-known lawyer in a gated community? As Gowda investigates, he becomes embroiled in Bangalore's child-trafficking racket. Negotiating insensitive laws, indifferent officials and uncooperative witnesses, he finds himself in a race against time to rescue Nandita from one of the most depraved criminal rings he has ever encountered. Children often picked up by scouts on trains or abducted on the streets of villages are brought to the city. If lucky they are forced into slave-like domestic service or factory work—the boys mostly. The less lucky—the girls—end up in brothels, under heavy and brutal guard. Gowda's splendid detective skills are tested to their limit in this fast-paced story.

"Just finished this. Fine follow-up to Anita Nair's first Inspector Gowda book. Harrowing but compassionate tale of modern India."     *Ian Rankin*

"I love Inspector Gowda. He is a brilliant creation, loveable, flawed, smart and doggedly determined. A truly good man in a bad world."

Peter James, author of
*Dead Simple* and *Looking Good Dead*

FAVOURITE CRIME NOVELS OF THE YEAR: "Bangalore is India's Silicon Valley, the rich face of Indian success in modern technology and its commercial accompaniments. Such wealth attracts crime. Inspector Borei Gowda is an admirable three-dimensional creation, quick tempered and emotional. The search for a missing 13-year-old girl develops into the more serious discovery that Bangalore has become a hub for the sex-trafficking of young girls. It is Anita Nair's home town and it shows, in the lively portrait of a city in uncertain transition and in the passion with which she endows Gowda in his war against evil"     *The Times*

£8.99/$14.95
Crime Paperback Original

ISBN 978 1908524 744
eBook USC ISBN 978 1908524 751
eBook ROW ISBN 978 1912242 696

www.bitterlemonpress.com